Elena Moya Pereira grew up in the Mediterranean coastal town of Tarragona, south of Barcelona, in the last years of the Franco dictatorship. After attending University in Spain, she was awarded a Fulbright scholarship to do a Masters in Financial Journalism in the U.S.

Elena worked in newspapers in Barcelona and Reno, Nevada, and settled in London in 1998. She is currently a business reporter for the Guardian, having worked at Bloomberg and Reuters newswires previously. She lives with her partner in North London.

The Olive Groves
of Belchite

Elena Moya Pereira

The Olive Groves
Of Belchite

Vanguard Press

VANGUARD PAPERBACK

© Copyright 2009
Elena Moya Pereira

A CIP catalogue record for this title is
available from the British Library.

ISBN 978 1 84386 576 6

Vanguard Press is an imprint of
Pegasus Elliot MacKenzie Publishers Ltd.
www.pegasuspublishers.com

First Published in 2009

Vanguard Press
Sheraton House Castle Park
Cambridge England

Printed and bound in Great Britain

"A la abuela Martina"

Acknowledgements:

I would like to thank, first and foremost my partner Maria for her continuous support and belief in this project, for the love and stability she's brought to my life.

To my editors and friends, Nicola Godwin and Amanda Vinnicombe, for selfless hours of reading and editing.

To my mother, Carmen, for telling me the tales of her childhood under Franco, for opening up the family history, and for introducing me to Leandro Saun and Carmen Casas, two communists who fought Franco and had to seek exile to escape his ruthless repression.

And to my sisters, Susana and Sofia, for their unconditional support.

Thanks to the many Spanish and British Republican soldiers and volunteers whom I've talked to, and who still believe in the ideals that led them to risk their lives.

To my Danish family for their interest and for having taken me just as one more.

To my American family, the Lerudes, who followed the steps of US volunteers from Reno, NV, to Belchite and shared their passion for Spain with me.

To my lifelong friends in Tarragona, who have read, researched or believed in the Republican cause, Eva Marrugat, Sol Inglada, Albert Vives and Rafel Cabré.

To Roger Suárez and Esther Pujol, for being wonderful masters of ceremonies and for making the most beautiful cover – both only accepting roasted chickens as payment.

To my friends Dan Pierce, Kate Slotover and Julia Kollewe for their support, and for their proof-reading and design help.

And to everybody who believes in peace, democracy and freedom. Salut!

1

Maria usually felt uncontrollably sexual in airport business lounges. On her way back from meetings abroad, the twenty-six-year-old financier liked to sit back with a gin and tonic in one hand and a copy of MARIE CLAIRE in the other, flipping absently through its pages. After relaxing for a few minutes in the chairs of British Airways lounges across Europe, she usually started to feel horny; she opened her senses after a hard day's work, especially when she wore her £800 Armani suit, which made her feel powerful, the ultimate aphrodisiac to many. But they were all fantasies, as her satisfaction almost never materialised.

Maria, tall and svelte, walked discretely towards the large ladies' room at London Heathrow's lounge, gently putting her long, shiny, black hair behind her ear, shyly looking down. Inside, some women were putting make-up on, sitting on well-cushioned, wooden chairs, using the marble table that had plenty of little white towels within reach. The large, long mirror was well lit, reflecting the tired faces of the businesswomen who were now trying to hide their exhaustion. Maria looked at her well-toned body, imagining Jordi behind her, hugging her, caressing her. But Jordi, her boyfriend, hardly put his hands on Maria; and if he did, he went to confession afterwards.

Maria imagined Jordi's naked body – she'd never seen it completely – his muscled torso, his tight abdominals, his strong arms around her soft, olive skin. Her imagination couldn't stop. *It's human, it can't be that wrong. It's not my fault that my boyfriend is a radical Catholic, a member of Opus Dei. They are such extremists.*

Maria longed for a night with Jordi. Not that she hadn't tried it, but as an Opus member, he refused to use contraception and said that consummation should only come with marriage, not before. When the issue was raised during their University years, when they met, she initially refused to continue a relationship on these grounds, but the strong bond between the two and the peace and laughter that she found in him made her go back to Jordi. A person of few friends, it was him that Maria still felt most comfortable with. And, in truth, she didn't really know what she was missing; after twenty years of Catholic education, she was still a virgin.

Still staring at the mirror, Maria sighed.

She thought of the things that Jordi surely would be doing to contain temptation. He had told her about Opus self-flagellation practices, including the use of the celice, a spiked chain worn around the upper thigh, leaving small prick holes in the flesh. When he was younger, at about fifteen and thought that he would dedicate his life to God in celibacy, Jordi had also used a cord-like whip against his buttocks or back, he once told her. Maria had read somewhere that the Opus Dei founder was so zealous in using the whip that he splattered the bathroom walls with blood.

Maria felt a breeze of cold air as she remembered these confessions, although Jordi had tried to calm her by saying that the celice wasn't that bad and that there wasn't that much blood after all, only a few scratches. Maria had tried to ignore it and decided to wait for the wedding to stop all this nonsense. Now, in just six months, Jordi would become as 'normal' as her.

"Departure of British Airways flight 8567 to Barcelona. Passengers please proceed to gate fifty-four. Flight 8567 to Barcelona, please go to gate fifty-four," said the voice through the speakers, waking Maria up from her thoughts.

Standing in front of the mirror, Maria looked at herself in despair. *When am I going to have a normal sex life? Soon, very soon. Shit, the plane.*

Maria washed her hands and, on her way out of the door, she picked up a copy of *¡HELLO!* magazine that somebody had left behind. It was her favourite reading material, so distracting.

Maria ran to gate fifty-four.

"*HOLA carinyo!*" said Jordi with a big smile, as Maria walked through the arrivals gate at Barcelona's A Terminal. With one arm around her, he kissed her on each cheek. "How was

14

your trip? How was London?" Jordi presented one red rose that he had been holding behind his back.

Maria took it and smiled. *So predictable.*

Jordi, also twenty-six, had been waiting for her with flower and a smile, as usual. Ill or busy, he would always greet her at the airport – except when his football team played at home.

"*HOLA* darling!" Maria said, kissing him briefly on the lips, smiling, looking him over from head to toe. He was wearing his usual, well-ironed, blue Ralph Lauren polo shirt and his Levi's, with a navy blue cashmere jumper tied around his neck. His neat, short haircut highlighted his big green eyes and long nose.

"I've missed you," Jordi said. "You've been away a whole week. I couldn't wait for you to come back, sweetheart." Jordi gently touched Maria's back. He hugged her and the two stayed without moving for a while. Maria felt the warmth of his arms around her, the gentleness of his touch. She withdrew shortly afterwards.

"I am so tired," Maria said in a quiet voice. "There were so many meetings with that Council. they were so difficult! It was very, very, busy. They have very strict guidelines on what can be built and not. We'll see what happens."

"You poor thing," Jordi held her closer, started to massage her shoulders.

"That's lovely, thank you darling." She withdrew again.

"Anything for you." He stepped back and looked at her. "Are you hungry?"

"Yummy, yes please!" Maria now looked excited. "I'm desperate for some good food. I've had enough of butter and cream on everything. I want a decent piece of fish or meat, can't wait for a good *pà amb tomaca.*"

"Come on, let's go then."

They walked arm in arm, Jordi carrying her luggage through the car park to his old Volkswagen Golf, which he called Oscar. He also drove a Jeep Grand Cherokee, but with Maria, he preferred to use Oscar because of the memories it brought him. Oscar had a little Barça flag hanging from the rear-view mirror, accompanied by a silhouette of the Virgin of Montserrat, patron saint of Catalunya. Exactly the way it was when he met Maria, who still wondered, after four years together, how she would survive so much football.

"We won," Jordi said turning the radio on, tuned to the hysterical Catalan sports station that he listened to at every opportunity.

"Two-nil, Iniesta and Puyol scored. It was sensational!" the broadcaster shouted.

"It was a good game," Jordi said. "I spoke to Enric Folch at half-time, he has such a good seat, right next to the VIP box. Lucky him. I need to get a seat a few rows closer. Anyway, he said their two new hotels in Mallorca will be ready this summer, so he'll be doubling his cava order soon."

"Good, that'll be almost twenty thousand bottles, won't it?" Maria said, interested.

"Yes, yes, business is good at the moment. Tourism is really picking up," Jordi said, settling back in his seat. "Shame about the rest of the national market."

When Maria was about to ask about the sales, the Catalan radio broadcaster suddenly elevated his tone: "The second goal was further proof of Iniesta's genius," he said. "Stay with us."

Jordi didn't seem that keen on talking about business. "I can't believe Puyol scored from outside the box, what a shot!" Jordi said, enthusiastically, while paying the car-parking fee with his Visa Gold card. "When will you come to watch a match with me?"

"Oh, I am glad you enjoyed it. But you know I'd rather to go to the gym, with the very little time that I have," Maria said. She hated football. "Are we going to yours?"

"Oh yes. I'm sorry I didn't say. The maid is cooking some delicious rabbit for dinner. The smell was all over the house when I left. Fancy it?"

Maria's mouth was watering at the thought.

"Just what I need," she smiled, leaning back in her seat. Jordi could be predictable and boring, Maria thought, but he definitely made life comfortable.

The couple arrived at Jordi's parents' big *masia* near Vilafranca del Penedès, adjacent to one of the family cava production sites and surrounded by vineyards. It was almost dark now, but they could still see the trees, smell the earth, and feel the thinness of the air. Jordi drove Oscar through the cast-iron front gate, with its huge Mas Gratallops sign, with the family emblem in the middle. After driving past more vineyards and through groves of cypresses, Jordi parked next to his father's Mercedes and the collection of four-wheel drives and sports cars belonging to him and his three brothers. They were all employed at the family business, although it was Jordi, the smartest of the lot, along with his father, who pulled the strings.

Jordi turned off the car and remained still for a few seconds. Maria watched him carefully.

"It's six months until the wedding," Jordi said, looking at her, a bit shy, but with a smile. He was confident with many people, but in matters of the heart, he didn't seem at ease, a product of a lifetime of repressive, Opus education, Maria thought. He leaned over and kissed her dryly on the lips.

"Yes, six months to go," Maria said. She didn't know what else to add. Like him, she was also a bit scared. *God, only six months. It's taken us a while, but now it's almost here. Almost here...*

"I can't wait," Jordi said, embarrassed, looking away.

"Neither can I," Maria said, also without looking at him.

I know things will improve when we finally have some passion.

The two held hands and went to Mas Gratallops' front door.

***

Heir to the Gratallops cava empire, a business spanning three generations that now exported thousands of bottles of cava to Britain and California, Jordi spent twelve-hour-days running the plants in Sant Sadurní d'Anoia, in the Penedès wine region, just south of Barcelona, leaving little time for anything else. An exemplary son, a decent student, a dedicated boyfriend, Jordi represented every Spanish mother's ambition for their daughter.

Unlike his brothers, Jordi had not dared to bring a woman home until he knew that she would be the one to marry. He remembered it as if it were yesterday when he so proudly introduced Maria to his parents on their graduation day, three years ago. He still thought Maria was the most beautiful woman he'd ever seen. Sometimes, he blushed when looking at her.

Standing at his parents' front door, Jordi looked at Maria intensely, observing her short skirt, and her toned, beautiful, long legs, covered by the black, silk stockings he loved to caress.

I have to contain myself, still six months to go, he thought, and looked away.

Jordi took a deep breath and opened the immaculately polished double oak doors.

"Hello, hello," said Jordi's father, a few seconds later. The big man, wearing a business suit, had a cigarette in one hand and a mobile phone in the other. "I can't talk now, I am in the middle of a business call." He went into another room, closing the door behind him.

Oh father, always working.

Jordi left Maria's suitcase by the antique chest in the lobby. He knocked on the main living-room doors and opened them slightly after his mother shouted "I am on the phone."

Jordi's mother started having her own life years ago. After the children were raised, nothing seemed to bond her to the family, who centred their leisure time in the company, a world that Jordi's father had always closed to her. Jordi's parents never seemed to have much to tell each other, or anything at all. But divorce was not an option for their generation. Forbidden under Franco, only allowed from the 1980s after the restoration of democracy, divorce still had some of the heavy stigma associated with it during the four decades of dictatorship.

Jordi and Maria went upstairs to the terrace of the three-storey, nineteenth-century modernist *masia*. They sat on the white-cushioned straw chairs, overlooking the ash trees at the back of the garden, the cypresses, dozens of red and yellow roses and purple geraniums, all surrounded by acres and acres of vineyards. Jordi loved sitting silently with Maria, away from the noise of the adjacent plants, and the multiple business problems he had to resolve every day. Shy as he was of intimacy, he preferred to speak with his eyes and his smile, rather than words.

"How was the trip?" asked Jordi's father, arriving abruptly. "Are we going to have a site soon? Ah, a warehouse in London, that will make our sales rocket. Can you imagine? A warehouse in London! In the biggest market!"

"The English are such pissheads, aren't they?" Jordi said, trying to be funny to his father, who ignored the comment and called the maid to order some drinks and *tapas*.

From the arched, terracotta-tiled terrace, the three could see a typical red Mediterranean sunset, and noticed the last workers leaving the fields, looking tired after handpicking grapes all day. Jordi loved the red colour of the land, he felt it was as much a part of him as his own bones. God, Maria and his Catalan land, that's all he needed.

"It was good," said Maria. "Patrick, the agent, showed a promising area, Islington, which is trendy, full of bars and restaurants." She took one of the cava glasses the maid offered her from a silver tray. She also helped herself to a *chorizo*, perfectly arranged on the little table next to the chair, along with tortilla and toasted almonds. "From there we could also reach the restaurants in the West End easily."

"Do you think we'll keep it under budget?" Mr Gratallops asked aggressively, tapping the top of his glass with a finger, impatiently.

"I don't know yet," Maria said. "The local council may be tricky. In principle, they want to create jobs, but they are very picky about building guidelines. Plus, rentals have gone through the roof in London."

"A site like this will create at least fifty jobs, remember," Jordi's father, President of Caves Gratallops, said patronisingly. "We can't spend any more euros on this project. England is already very expensive."

"Yes, yes, I know." Maria said, leaning back on her chair, defensively. "But the Council won't let us build more than three floors because the neighbourhood is a conservation area. We may have to look for other, flatter, wider sites."

"Not one euro more!" Mr Gratallops almost shouted, making Maria open her eyes in surprise. "Two million euros is already stretching it very far." Mr Gratallops looked Maria straight in the eye.

Oh Father, be gentle for once, Jordi thought, crossing his legs nervously.

"Patrick said he's looking at several sites," Maria said, looking down. "I will go back to London in a couple of weeks to see what he's found."

"I am sure there are other options," Jordi said, trying to calm things down.

Caves Gratallops had mandated Banca Catalana, where Maria worked, to find and finance a warehouse in London. Jordi, his father and Maria's boss, Andreu, met at Barça's stadium every other Sunday, for the home game. Jordi had been going to the Nou Camp with his father since he was a child. At half-time, a group of about twenty men, not a single woman among them, chatted about football, smoked cigars and drank coffee and cognac. Most of them had white hair and wore expensive leather jackets and Burberry scarves. The Barça bar that served the most exclusive part of the stadium was where most of the Catalan business decisions took place.

After securing the Caves Gratallops' mandate, Andreu hadn't hesitated to assign the project to Maria, assuming she'd do a better job than her colleagues as she would belong to the family in a few months' time. Jordi was not sure family and business would work well together, he had seen the combination crumble at home too often.

I hope this all ends up well, he thought anxiously.

"I am sure it'll all work out well." He held Maria's hands, warming them up. She smiled at him.

"Let's hope so, but remember our limit," Jordi's father said. He lit a cigarette and stared at his vineyards for a few seconds, creating a tense silence.

Maria finally said: "I am feeling rather tired, it's been a long week. I think I'll just go and get a good rest if you don't mind," and she stood up.

Jordi was surprised. *Already?* "Oh darling, are you sure? Are you not staying for the rabbit?"

"No, sorry, thank you," Maria said. "I think I just need to go home."

Jordi could feel his father had upset her, always pushing business, never letting in anything else.

Jordi glanced at his father. *See what you've done? Now she doesn't want to stay here. You're a brute, father. My own family will be so different from this.*

"I am just sick of this boycott of Catalan products," Jordi's father said when the couple was about to walk away. He sighed with his glance fixed on the vineyards. "I heard on the radio this morning about this village in Castille where they smashed the windows of a winery selling cava bottles, can you imagine?"

Maria looked at her future father-in-law, now looking at her. "This will pass, after the Catalans negotiate the new statute of autonomy, people won't remember," she said. "There's some of that attitude at home, in Belchite, unfortunately, but I am sure it will go away soon." Maria smiled at him.

Jordi and his father nodded at the same time.

The couple walked away.

"Are you all right sweetheart?" Jordi delicately touched Maria's long hair as they reached the front door.

"Yes, don't worry, I'll feel better tomorrow."

"As you wish." Jordi was disappointed, but tried to be understanding. He had been waiting for Maria all week, with no time for fun or friends. He had only worked, slept little and just endured tense family meals with his parents and brothers. He had been dreaming all week of holding hands with Maria, going to the cinema with her. Just feeling her next to him made him content.

"As you wish, I will drive you home." He managed to give a genuine smile.

He was a gentleman.

Jordi waited in his car after dropping Maria at her flat in central Barcelona. He saw her closing the door, waving at him with her lips drawing the smile he had fallen for so many times.

You are so beautiful. God please help me contain myself until we marry.

As young as seven, the wealthy, clever, non-troublesome boy had become a target of the teachers at La Farga, the Opus-owned school near Barcelona, who succeeded in making him believe that God had chosen him to reach sainthood through Opus Dei. Without the knowledge of his parents, who were too busy running the business and fighting, Jordi was invited on horseback rides, ski trips, spiritual retreats at country homes in the mountains, or study and sport camps, all as a hook to attract teenagers into the organisation. Like his peers, Jordi found it hard to refuse the opportunity of leaving the parental home to spend a weekend or a week away – and Opus had always mastered the making of those camps as an attractive destination.

His parents thought he was safe spending most weekends away at school-organised activities. He was also a shy boy, so nobody was too surprised that he didn't bring female friends home, unlike his three brothers, whose regular trouble involving fast cars and women consumed Jordi's parents' attention. Little did they know their second son had been poached one summer afternoon, when he was thirteen, during a week-long study camp in an Opus-owned mansion just outside Barcelona. His mentor, Father Juan Antonio, took him into a room, shut the blinds, reducing daylight to almost nothing, and in a deep voice talked to him about Opus, insisting that God had called him to join the group because of his intelligence and human superiority.

He would become, at age eighteen, during his first year in Pamplona, a numerary – one of the most distinguished members who live in celibacy in Opus' luxurious apartments and houses, giving their entire salaries and lives to the cause.

These plans changed after he met Maria. He had also been slightly tempted by other women, but Maria was the one who caught his heart. The two had watched each other for weeks during their cigarette breaks outside the library, in the middle of the freezing cold Pamplona winter. They had also glanced at each other inside the reading room, from their customary seats. Maria always sat by herself by the window.

Jordi had a suspicion there was something more behind those dark, deep eyes. Sometimes he caught a look of unmistakable sadness on her face as she sat watching the world go by through the window. Struck by her beauty, intrigued by her mystery, he couldn't get Maria out of his mind.

He finally plucked up the courage to ask her for a cigarette, which ignited a friendly conversation about the University and the horrible weather. The same night, he and a friend bumped into her at the cinema. She was sitting by herself, in the last row, as was her habit. They asked her to join them for a drink afterwards and, surprisingly to Jordi, she said yes.

Day after day his efforts to look away and avoid temptation were in vain. The help of his spiritual director was also futile. His temptation became unbearable. He felt a hypocrite at the daily compulsory mass when he had to tell a confessor that he was elated about giving his life to God, in celibacy.

After an exhausting process, but always keeping his serenity, Jordi decided to become a supernumerary, or the Opus members who marry, although they are still committed to God and to a spiritual director, going to daily mass and sometimes contributing more than half of their salaries to the organisation.

Jordi knew that abandoning his commitment to celibacy didn't mean leaving Opus Dei. He didn't want to end up like all the people he had heard or read about, who abandoned the group and faced emotional disturbances for the rest of their lives. Some even killed themselves, he had heard. Jordi had grown up with Opus. It was his life. He would never abandon his safety net.

A few weeks later, sparked by the spring sun and his new freedom, Jordi tried to have and provoke as many light chats and cigarette breaks with Maria as he could. One day, very directly, he finally asked her if she wanted to go to the cinema.

After seeing GREEN CARD, where they shared the popcorn he had had ready for almost an hour before she arrived, Jordi drove her to her college and kissed her on the lips, briefly, in the car.

During the following weeks, Jordi couldn't hide his infinite happiness. The days went by full of cinema trips, coffees and hours in the library, with more flirting than study. Time passed as quickly as he'd ever experienced, with the almond tree in front of the University's main building flourishing before they knew it. The saying went among students that if one hadn't started studying by the time the first flowers of the tree blossomed, better not bother. Jordi and Maria were the exception, that year.

Jordi caressed the steering wheel in central Barcelona, by Maria's flat, remembering the good old Pamplona days. He gently touched his hands, almost unconsciously, after his girlfriend closed the door behind her, with her suggestive short skirt.

Maria... Jordi thought with desire, still feeling the lingering kiss before she got out of the car. He circled his lips with his tongue.

God please help me get to the wedding like a true Christian, showing full respect for my Fiancée. He had to repeat these words to himself over and over.

In Pamplona, sex before marriage was a rarity among students, only practised by a hugely segregated, radical, local Basque minority, to which neither Jordi, Maria nor any of their friends belonged. The time the couple spent was mostly on common ground, as men weren't allowed in Maria's college and Maria could only visit Jordi's flat during certain hours in the afternoon. The arrangement, with Jordi's flatmates, was that women weren't allowed to stay overnight. Not that any of them would have considered it, as they all belonged to Opus.

Most of Maria and Jordi's friends at University had eight or nine siblings. They followed the guidelines of Opus' founder, José María Escrivá de Balaguer, a Spanish priest who in the late

1920s started the group with a clique of elite Spaniards. The group flourished in the 1950s, at the peak of the Franco dictatorship, attracting those wealthy enough to be able to feed as many children as God gave them – contraception was seen as an unnatural intruder. Four decades afterwards, Opus had grown to control some of the most influential media, businesses, banks, factories and, of course, nurtured their children at their own schools with the best moving to the University in Pamplona, the conservative capital of Navarre.

Hordes of now successful businessmen had begun their networking careers in Pamplona bars, mostly at the University's cafeteria, Faustino, where the waiters, all of them male, wore white jackets with golden buttons and black trousers. They didn't serve alcohol, only coffee and soda drinks to the brand-clad students who, after chatting with each other, walked to class along the highly polished, black and white marble floors, where they could almost see themselves reflected. At Jordi's flat, a maid cooked them lunch and dinner and ironed their shirts, as well as cleaning the place – something not unusual among male students. Women were expected to be responsible for their own domestic duties.

In Pamplona, a kiss was practically an engagement, but Jordi's kisses increased in length and passion as the months passed. When filled with desire, after arriving in his room after a long kiss and a few drinks, Jordi would use the celice or, if unable to control himself, he would fall into temptation, although he would confess with unbearable guilt the following day.

He loved talking with Maria, even if it was to hear her rage about the University's right-wing ideology. She would often complain about the censorship at the library, which classified books from one to six, with the latter being the least recommended and therefore unavailable. This group included Lorca, Orwell or Marx; even Hemingway's stories about the Spanish Civil War were hard to find. *EL PAÍS* newspaper, the country's best-selling daily, wasn't readily available in Pamplona because of its left-wing tendency. Not even to the journalism students.

Jordi didn't care much whether those books were available at all, and hadn't even noticed EL PAÍS wasn't on the shelves, as he read the more conservative LA VANGUARDIA of Barcelona. He just loved seeing Maria's personality and passion coming out, her eyes gleaming with ideas. Even if he didn't agree. He just loved looking at her.

As the weeks went by, Jordi found it hard to cope with temptation. One night, while watching the sea waves in San Sebastián, the two started kissing passionately inside the car. Maria's breath became louder and louder and closing her eyes she suggested moving to the rear seat, a moment that Jordi had feared since the beginning. Aware she was not an Opus member, how could he persuade her to wait until marriage?

As he told her, as carefully as he could, that he belonged to Opus, Maria leaned back. He had avoided telling her anything about this during the few months they had been together for fear she would run away. He tried to cuddle her and explain what God and Opus meant to him, how they had made him the person he was, but she wouldn't let him touch her anymore.

The night ended in tears, with Maria not being able to understand what Jordi said, or what religion meant to him. He was also on the verge of tears as it was such a gargantuan effort for him to hold onto his desires for her. Still, he was more used to containing himself than her.

Maria broke off the relationship for a few weeks, saying that she felt rejected. She had suspected him of being close to Opus, but she had hoped common sense would impose itself and the two would fall into their passions naturally. She had told him that she didn't expect anybody would ever think she could have as many children as God gave her, ten, twelve, perhaps more. She would never be that kind of woman, not even to him, as much as she loved him.

Jordi was heart-broken and spent days and days writing her letters full of warmth, respect and love. He wanted her more than anything in life, and never lost hope that they could work things out, one way or another.

Maria finally came back one day, saying she missed their time together too much and that she loved him enough to wait. They both agreed to put on hold the decision of how many children they would have if they ever married.

That was probably Jordi's happiest day ever.

Jordi would love her for this spirit and generosity even more. He would do little things for her, continuously, always guessing what she needed: when she had exams, he would bring her groceries; he would know when to fix the punctures on her bike, or when to book cinema tickets for movies she was longing to see, even if she hadn't mentioned them to him. He always guessed right.

A loud beep woke Jordi up from these thoughts. He took a deep breath and started the car, driving home along the Diagonal, now dark and silent.

What a woman. She's been so patient with me. I will make her happy. I promise I will. She's my entire life.

***

That night, at her Barcelona flat, Maria listened to her favourite Cuban music. She wandered outside onto the terrace, the October air still warm, and looked in at her apartment; all the candles were lit, just the way she liked it.

Her high salary allowed her to rent a double-bedroom top flat in a Modernist building in Aribau Street, in the centre of the city. From her terracotta-tiled roof terrace, she could see the Rambla Catalunya and the spires of *Sagrada Família*. She loved the summer nights here, with her geraniums and cooking herbs. It was her own little world, where she could watch the stars, look at her plants, think of nothing, smoke cigarettes and enjoy a glass of Raimat Abadia, her favourite red wine. As a matter of fact, she preferred wine to cava, although she'd never mentioned this to Jordi, let alone to his father.

Bombillo wondered out from the flat and looked up at Maria, purring, making her smile. He climbed up and settled down on her tummy.

Oh, you're so needy when I've been away, aren't you? Maria cuddled her much-loved cat. He swished his tail from side to side.

Old Bombillo, the cat she'd had since she was seven, had moved to grandma Basilisa's when she went to University; Mama didn't want him. He died of old age while Maria was in Pamplona. After days of not speaking a word immediately following the death, and years without being able to talk about or caress cats, Maria had finally got another one, Bombillo II, a present from Jordi, who knew her well.

She looked up at the sky.

Six months until the wedding.

She sipped more wine, relaxing her shoulders. She took a deep breath and imagined Jordi's warm hands caressing her, a fantasy she'd had since her Pamplona days. For hours, she had day-dreamt about Jordi in her women-only college, where every student occupied a small, individual room furnished with a single bed, a desk and a little sink to wash in. A crucifix was the only decoration permitted. Posters and photographs weren't allowed, they said, to avoid distraction, or perhaps they meant temptation – something that Maria sometimes couldn't avoid. But she would never admit it in confession, which she took every day at the 'voluntary' mass at seven in the morning, before breakfast. In theory, attendance wasn't required for members of the college, which had its own chapel, although the reality was that absence was not well regarded and all the students and the staff felt obliged to go. On her knees, on the wooden confession cabinet, and through a purple velvet curtain, Maria never confessed her nocturnal thoughts to Father Domingo, the priest in charge of the college and also a professor at the University. Father Domingo, covered head to toe in a black cassock, used to walk always by himself, limping, along the University corridors, showing his cynical smile. His penetrating look as he walked by, in sinister silence, always gazing around, made him one of the most feared figures among Pamplona students.

Maria didn't miss her University days. She loved the activity in Barcelona and thought of herself as independent and mostly happy. Her life was so full, she didn't have much time to think. This was a good thing, she always told herself.

She only hated the numerous bank holidays in Spain when life came to a standstill and she lost the thrill of her daily routine, of work, gym and the Blackberry.

It was those days she found empty and difficult, or on Sundays, which she usually spent with Jordi and his friends, although those gatherings made her feel less isolated, part of a group or a family that loved and cared for her. Opus were good at making people feel cared for. Walks in picturesque villages north of Barcelona, hikes in the Pyrenees, laughs over coffee and shared tortillas and other *tapas*, Jordi and his friends would fill the emptiness she felt in the quiet hours. Sometimes she would default to the loner figure of the early University days, until Jordi would rescue her and bring her back to the happy, unquestioned Opus world where, as if in a Disney film, everybody is wealthy and happy.

Still, her favourite pastime was to sit by herself on her terrace, under the warm Mediterranean air, at nights, and live in her own world, without really seeing people or, more so, without letting people really see through her. She spent long lapses of time day-dreaming, about all and nothing, building passionate love stories that were real only in her mind. Sometimes she would not be part of them, sometimes she would, but worlds full of love, care and passion were always alive in her imagination.

Six months until the wedding.

Her heart sank.

It has taken me so long to say 'yes'.

Jordi proposed to her a year after they graduated, when both were well established in their jobs in Barcelona. She had asked for more time and spent a year deciding whether to go along with a future that offered her safety, gentleness and comfort, or

29

break up and wait for a movie-type adventure. The kind that she always fantasised about.

Movies only happen in movies. Be real. He will love me forever. He's the right choice, she had told herself many times. She didn't want to end up like her grandma. Her mother had always told her that Gran Basilisa fell for a worker who left her on her own, pregnant, and stole most of the family's coffers. She had never discussed this with her gran, whom she adored.

Those passionate stories never end well, Mama had always warned.

But Maria didn't want to end up like her mother either, caught in a marriage where she had never, ever spotted the slightest hint of passion or true love, whatever that was.

This contradiction always left her exhausted, and that's when she craved for Jordi and for his secure and gentle love. A year after he proposed, Maria had finally said 'yes'. She looked at her diamond ring.

What do stones know about love?

Bombillo sniffed her face all over, then sat on her tummy again and closed his eyes, rubbing his head up against Maria's breasts.

So small and vulnerable, Maria thought.

Suddenly, she remembered when she was small and vulnerable in her room, in Belchite, when she was a little girl. Tears immediately filled her eyes.

2

Inmaculada Concepción de la Vega, or Conchita as she was known, was looking at the ancient, twisted trees through the kitchen window. The olives were almost ready to be picked and hopefully this year would be better than last when the drought cut the olive oil production to a level she had only seen once or twice in about thirty years. This winter it had already rained enough for a good harvest.

Conchita, a tall woman with big, strong arms and a long eagle nose, spread some thyme on the lamb and put the clay pan on the stove. Today it was Pilar's day, saint and birthday of her eldest daughter, and there would be a family meal; all would be there except Maria, her youngest daughter, who had given a silly excuse, she thought.

She always does what she wants. No respect for other people's traditions. So selfish that girl. And yet she'll want us all to be there for her wedding.

Conchita, in a black skirt and a gray blouse buttoned up to her neck, took her apron off and left the big family house in the outskirts of Belchite, a village in the dry, flat land half way between Barcelona and Madrid. She loved walking around the hundreds of olive trees that the de la Vegas had owned for at least four centuries. They smelled of earth and nature. Some were more than a thousand years old. All she knew about them, and about the family, was what her mother had told her. Conchita's grandparents on her mother's side had been killed during the Civil War, although she didn't know many details. On the other side of the family, she didn't even know who her father was. Her mother had told her, many years ago, that he was a Red who escaped with most of the family's money. Conchita, and nobody else in the village, had ever dared ask much else.

Raised by the nuns while her mother worked dawn to dusk to regenerate the olive trees and the land right after the War ended in 1939, now, at sixty-seven, Conchita still took solitary walks through the fields just as she had as a child. She used to climb the twisted trunks to build little houses on the branches; little did she know then that sixty years later a Japanese businessman would offer her twenty-five thousand euros for the oldest tree – believed to be one thousand and five hundred years old – which they called *El Abuelo* or 'The Grandfather'.

Over my dead body would I sell that marvel, Conchita thought as she touched one of the ancient branches. She stared at the tree, walking around it, taking deep breaths. The symbol of peace, its branches and dark colour, the majesty of its presence brought tranquillity to Conchita's heart. *El Abuelo* imposed its age and solemnity upon her moods every time she walked around the perfectly aligned fields.

Conchita walked on, stopping to touch some of the olives coming out of a younger tree.

Five weeks more and this will be ready to be picked. This year will be much better; I can feel it, at least five hundred thousand kilos. She looked at the sky, now covered with clouds. *God, please give us just a bit more rain.*

Conchita went into the production building, almost next door to the family's house, just to check everything was in place. Her daughter Pilar was now running the business but Conchita still felt responsible for it. Maria had never bothered much about the company for reasons Conchita still couldn't understand.

I hope Jordi will bring her back to her feet after the wedding. If she could only realise she has a first-class business to run at home.

Conchita turned the lights on and saw the German machinery she bought years ago with a bank loan – *that* was taking responsibility for things, taking risks to feed the family, she thought.

Pilar was now planning to buy new equipment from France, a far cry from the old machine that Gran Basilisa had bought in the late 1940s, when electricity finally arrived in Belchite. On the corner, she could see the heavy stones that her grandparents used, pulled by mules, to smash the olives. She still remembered seeing her mother push them with her arms, after the War, when the country was so devastated that not even the mules survived. Now, the new machine could even pick the olives mechanically.

Conchita stared at the stones.

My mother also sweated for this. I wish my daughters, especially Pilar, had the same spirit, but they've never had to fight for anything. Maria is different; she has the drive, but that girl doesn't care about this at all.

Conchita had a last look around the room. Proud of her business and with her usual firm and confident manner, she walked back to the family house, picking up the local newspaper, just delivered to the porch. She gave a quick look at the front page:

"New socialist mayor to open Old Village to tourism."

Conchita stopped and read more:

"Pablo García, the newly elected first socialist mayor that Belchite has had in sixty-five years, wants to open up the Old Village for tourism and build a Civil War museum inside the old church, which was destroyed in 1938."

Leave the dead alone. Still to this day they won't shut up. She read on:

"The Old Village of Belchite, which Franco wanted to keep intact after it was destroyed during the Civil War to show the barbarities that the Reds were capable of, may be regenerated and opened up to tourism. The mayor will lobby in Madrid and Brussels to raise funds to rebuild the church, where a planned museum will show through photographs, texts and maps how Belchite fell to the Red army in 1938, and how it was regained by the Nationals a year later."

33

Conchita gave a sigh and walked into the house. From the window by the dining table she looked at the church or the remains of it, as only the arches had survived. The ceiling, some columns and walls, like all the buildings in the Old Town, had been bombed and destroyed in 1938. In the Old Town, every street, every house, remained exactly as it was when the War ended in 1939; only some grass had grown around some streets and stones. Belchite's inhabitants moved to a new village, adjacent to the old one, which was built with the labour of the famished political prisoners. The last families to move to the new town did so as late as in the sixties.

The Old Town had been walled up about ten years ago because it had become dangerous for people to walk around; anyone could have been hit by a falling brick or metal from the crumbling buildings. Not that it attracted any tourists anyway, only the odd foreigner and some young Spanish historians every now and again. Only the birds and the wind could be heard within the walls of Old Belchite. Last time Conchita went there, more than ten years ago, for a memorial to National soldiers shot in the War, she ran away quickly, as the wind had pushed the frame of a window, making a cracking noise that made Conchita think of ghosts living among the ruins. She was happy the place had been sealed off. The past belongs to the past.

Conchita looked at the newspaper again and put it in the bin, thinking that if her mother and Soledad, her housekeeper and also her mother's closest friend, saw it, that might spark a family discussion, which she didn't want today. It was *Santa Pilar* and she didn't want any upset.

At sixty-seven, I want peace. Maria's absence will definitely help.

Not that Conchita didn't love Maria. She loved her daughter dearly, but Maria's controversial character made it difficult to feel relaxed around her. Maria's political differences with her father didn't help either, even if Conchita had, many years ago, forbidden any talk about religion, money or politics at the dinner table. She admired her daughter for sticking to her guns, though. Unlike Pilar, Maria had left Belchite and made a career of her own, even if it was among bankers that Conchita always referred to as 'sharks', to Maria's annoyance.

That was not too different from what herself and her mother had done, fighting against the world to become solid, strong, independent women. But there was that point of insolence in Maria that Conchita couldn't stand.

Why can't she just have some respect for her family and come today? Her sister's birthday, for God's sake, and she says she has to work. I have never missed any commitments, and if I had to work more, I would do so at night, even if I was exhausted. This generation doesn't know what suffering is or means. They just think it's all easy. They'll find out the hard way.

Conchita nodded with her head in silence; she stirred the stew.

They should have lived through a War.

The wall clock said two o'clock when she heard her mother and Soledad open the front door.

"Hello, we may have just escaped the rain," said her mother, a little woman, who once had been very strong, with curly white hair and big blue eyes. Soledad, ninety, took her coat off and came straight into the kitchen.

"That smells wonderful," she said. A former schoolteacher during the Republic just before the War, Soledad hid in the mountains after Franco's victory because she had belonged to the Socialist Party. A few years later, she finally moved into the de la Vega's home, helping Gran Basilisa raise Conchita. She taught her how to read and write while her mother was working day and night in the fields, sometimes pressing the olives with her own feet. The War had only left dust and hunger behind.

Soledad was finally safe after Gran Basilisa secured a document signed by a general saying that the former 'Red' wasn't a threat to the state any more. Soledad never worked as a teacher again, never under the new regime, and as far as Conchita could remember, she'd always been her mother's housekeeper and friend.

Decades later, when Maria was born, Gran Basilisa moved out to a new home of her own. Almost sixty, Gran Basilisa said

35

she had worked enough and wanted some peace, after a life of battling. Conchita managed to convince Soledad to stay at the family house, helping her with Pilar and Maria. At sixty-five, Soledad still wanted to feel useful, and helping Conchita raise the children made her feel better than staying with Gran Basilisa in her new home, doing nothing.

Despite their political differences, Conchita loved Soledad to her bones. She had spent most of her childhood and youth with the *Esclavas de Dios,* or Slaves of God nuns, and the little warmth she had came from Soledad, more than her own mother. Conchita hadn't actually seen much of her mother during her childhood and teen years as Gran Basilisa had worked her life through.

"Look, I've received a postcard from Maria, from London!" Basilisa exclaimed in triumph, proud of her granddaughter. She showed the picture of Buckingham Palace and the guardsmen to Conchita, although Soledad also glanced over her shoulder.

"*Viva la República!*" Soledad immediately said. "Down with the monarchy! *Viva la República!*"

"Ninety, and still a political activist, God keep your spirit," Conchita smiled, although the postcard had made her feel a bit envious, she hadn't received one. Conchita knew she had been extremely busy while raising Maria; maybe she hadn't given her all the time she'd needed.

"Maria is so intelligent," the proud grandmother said aloud. "She is such a sweet girl."

I am not sure if 'Sweet' is the word, Conchita thought, trying to remember the last time Maria had given her a kiss and a hug.

The three women looked at the lamb, now fully cooked. Tying their aprons on, they cooked a tortilla and a salad, using the best home-made extra virgin olive oil. Basilisa examined the golden colour of the oil through the glass container.

"It was a bad harvest last year, but the colour still glows," she said, spreading some on a hunk of bread, which she ate in one go. At eighty-five, she had kept her appetite.

Still the War. This generation doesn't have any moderation when it comes to eating. They must have been so hungry; I did well to hide that newspaper.

"Hello everybody!" Pilar, a tall, slim woman with the same long nose as her mother, entered the house with her noisy children.

"Happy birthday!" Soledad said, while Conchita and her mother almost said at once: "Happy *Santo*!" Unlike Soledad, they preferred to celebrate the saint day rather than the birthday. Pilar never showed any preference, while Maria, much to Conchita's despair, ignored her *Santo*.

Pilar unwrapped a lovely bunch of flowers that her grandmother had prepared for her, and when she opened the bin to throw the wrapping away, she saw the newspaper.

"Oh, I have already seen this at the hairdresser," she said taking the paper out of the bin. "They want to open up the Old Town!"

Conchita tried to secretly warn Pilar to drop the conversation, but her daughter couldn't read the signs, and said, aloud: "What are you saying Mama?"

Conchita rolled her eyes and let it go. She missed Maria, despite all the tension she brought. Unlike Pilar, Conchita and Maria understood each other well, at least, business-wise. They could communicate with the blink of an eye. Maria was quick and sharp, whereas Pilar took a long time to do anything – she had been planning to buy that French machine for years, it would be obsolete by the time she made a decision, Conchita thought.

"I also saw some television cameras in the *Plaza Mayor*," Pilar continued. "I heard at the hairdresser that they are from the BBC, from England. They are doing a documentary about the Old Village."

Damn it, damn it Pilar, Conchita thought.

Conchita hadn't told her daughters the little she knew about the family history. She preferred not to mess around with the past as it always made her mother and Soledad angry and sad, and at eighty-five and ninety, neither could handle emotional jars well any more. *It is best to hide these things. Let's not open a can of worms; whatever happened, happened.*

"They can go back to their country and dig up their own dead if they want, not here," Conchita quickly interrupted Pilar, who looked a bit surprised.

"I'll talk to them if they're from the BBC," Soledad sounded excited. "I don't want to talk to the silly reporters from Spain, the television here is controlled by fascists who don't want to dig in the past because they are too embarrassed by their own atrocities. I'll talk to the English, they're more informed and they came to help the Republic. I'll go." She stood up. Conchita quickly put a hand on her shoulder.

"Wait, wait, wait, Soledad," Conchita tried to stop her, although the ninety-year-old was already reaching for her jacket. "Leave them alone, they'll find other people. You have to take care of yourself and this always upsets you…"

"I want to talk! I want to speak up!" Soledad said, now with her coat and hat on. She raised her left arm and said: "*Viva la República!*"

Conchita sighed in resignation. "And what have the English lost in Belchite?" She angrily stirred the lamb with a wooden spoon.

"Soledad, what about the lamb? It will get cold!" she shouted, but Soledad, a little deaf, didn't answer.

"Mama, somebody should go with her," Pilar said, surprised at the scene.

"I won't," Basilisa said, abruptly. She looked upset.

I knew this Civil War business can only bring trouble, Conchita thought.

Pilar's children, Inma and Ignacio, were shouting and playing with a ball by the kitchen, disobeying Conchita's strict orders about balls in the house; they weren't allowed at all. All of a sudden, the children, who were seven and five, hit a jar, breaking it to pieces. It was a wedding present to Conchita from her mother.

"You little devils, the china jar!" Conchita shouted, dropping the wooden spoon on the counter, furiously. She ran towards

Inma and Ignacio and slapped them on the face, one each, quickly, strongly.

"Discipline! That's what you need," she shouted as they covered their now, red faces with their arms, as if expecting more.

Conchita stopped for a second, still red in anger, still with her arm raised, but she let it go.

"I have told you many times you can't play with the ball inside, don't you understand?" she shouted

"Yes," they replied, almost at once, with their delicate voices. Sobbing, they walked away towards their mother.

"Mama, please leave them," Pilar begged, cuddling her children, and looking scared herself. "They are only children…"

Conchita and Pilar heard the front door close, and realised Soledad was out. They saw her through the window, walking towards the BBC crew, easily visible as they were carrying cameras and they were all quite white, skinny and tall. In her excitement, Soledad tripped on a stone, almost falling.

"Somebody has to go with her," Pilar insisted, still cuddling the children, still in tears.

At the end of the day, it's always me. I always have to do everything.

"I will go," Conchita said in a dictatorial tone, taking her apron off and throwing it onto a chair. "Pilar, you can clear the mess your children have created. Mother, you watch the lamb. And you children, stay quiet!" she shouted again, making them hide behind their mother.

Pilar sighed and turned to her children. "Don't worry, she just has a bad temper, don't worry, Mummy is here…" She was gently caressing their heads.

Bad temper? What bad temper? They should thank me for still feeding them after that behaviour. The nuns would have locked me in my room for one or two days without food if I had broken anything in the convent. Children now have no discipline.

"She's also getting a bit old," Pilar whispered to the children.

Conchita, who had acute hearing, felt like turning to slap Pilar for her lack of respect, but she just remembered Soledad almost tripping outside and walked out to the front door. At the same time, her husband was walking in.

Honorato had well-combed white hair and always wore a jacket and a tie, even if he was just playing dominoes with his friends at the local casino. He had deep Spanish eyes and thick eyebrows, almost joined in the middle. A low-ranking officer in the Spanish army during the Franco dictatorship, Honorato had met Conchita in his mid-twenties during a local trip to Rome to see the Pope.

"Hello, is the lamb ready? I am so hungry," Honorato said leaving his hat in the entrance. He hadn't cooked anything since they married almost four decades ago.

"Yes, but I have to go with Soledad who's now into entertaining foreigners in the Old Village," Conchita said abruptly.

"I heard in the casino that the BBC are sniffing around. What did they lose here?" Honorato snorted with contempt.

"For once, I agree with you." Conchita left, slamming the door behind her.

"The Republic was very good. It was the best thing in the world, Spain would today be like France or England had they let it live," Soledad was telling the very interested BBC crew. "Education was at the top of their agenda, they hired eight thousand teachers, like me. Come here boys, I'll show you where my school was."

Conchita caught up with the group in a derelict building that could have been anything, but apparently, and according to Soledad, had been the primary school. She didn't know. She'd never been in the Old Town with her, or with her mother.

"It was so different then. We had boys and girls together in the class, we had some lessons outside, surrounded by trees and plants. We taught music, gardening, theatre; we rode bicycles and read poems in the forest... I even took a class to a Lorca reading, by Lorca himself in Zaragoza once."

Really? Conchita didn't know much about Lorca. His writing had been forbidden in schools after the War. Not even Maria or Pilar had studied much of Lorca at school, only a brief reference. Conchita, like many other Spaniards, only knew that he was a Red and, even worse, a homosexual.

"Along with another teacher, we stayed at nights to teach reading and writing to the many adults who couldn't even spell their names," Soledad sounded sad.

"Illiteracy was around sixty per cent at the time, right?" asked the reporter holding the microphone.

"Yes, well done boy, you've obviously done your research," Soledad said. She had often expressed her liking for the English. The word around Belchite was that she had had an affair with a Brigadista from Cambridge University, until he was tragically shot dead in the Battle of the Ebro. She had never spoken about it, as far as Conchita knew.

"Until then it was only the rich who were educated, and that's what the Republic tried to change," Soledad continued. "The educated rich against the illiterate poor. They were a world apart."

"And that's what triggered the War...?" the reporter said.

"It was the rich against the poor, the Catholics against the agnostics, the Catalans and Basques against the Madrid centralists: all against all," Soledad turned towards the derelict building. "We tried to educate everybody, but five years of Republic couldn't repair four centuries of distress."

"You mean it all started with the Inquisition?" asked the reporter, looking at Soledad full of interest.

"Since then, Spaniards have felt it was a sin just to be themselves, it was a sin just to *be*. Our fate would be negative, ever since. We tried to change that through education, but we couldn't. We didn't have enough time."

Soledad looked down.

"Everything changed dramatically after the War," she carried on. "Then, the girls went with the girls and the boys with the boys. Nuns and priests replaced the teachers and hung crucifixes in place of maps and posters. The classrooms became dark and children couldn't even hold hands together when playing outside, the very limited time of leisure they were allowed. They spent almost half the day in church, and the other half memorising names of conquerors who destroyed cultures in South America."

She took a deep breath. "Words are easier to learn with some blood – that was the philosophy."

That sounds just like my school. Conchita had heard Soledad talk about the Republic many times before, but never as clearly as this.

"It was a tragedy," Soledad said, now with watery eyes. "The Franco soldiers, when arriving in town, shot all the left-wingers, including the teachers. So many teachers were assassinated by the walls of cemeteries, and their bodies are still buried in common graves that nobody has opened yet. They don't even know where Lorca is." The words were now difficult to speak.

"How did you survive?" the reporter asked.

"I wanted to go to France, like the thousands who filled the roads with their mules, cars, mattresses, whatever they had, but it was very dangerous from here as I had to cross territory controlled by the Nationals." She then looked at Conchita.

"I also had to help my friend, Basilisa, who was alone and pregnant with her," she pointed at Conchita and carried on. "My friend's parents died during the War and she was alone and pregnant. I stayed with her."

Conchita shivered and swallowed twice in a row. She took a deep breath. Although she had already heard this from her mother, that was many years ago. Not a word since, like many people of that generation. Trauma and fear of Franco's brutal repression silenced an entire generation for decades. Conchita remembered that her mother had had to show a permit just to travel to Zaragoza, only thirty-five miles away. Control over people was absolute. Women needed written permission from their husbands to find a job. Associations or group meetings were prohibited, or needed a Civil Guard to be present if the group had the permission to meet at all.

"It's time to go, Soledad, you're getting tired," Conchita said, trying to stay cool.

"It was a tragedy," Soledad carried on in tears. "The country fell into the hands of a dictator who still after the War killed fifty thousand people, sometimes just for being family or friends of Reds. Anybody with a brain was either killed or left for exile. You can imagine the type that was left, and they ran the country for forty years."

"But you stayed..." the reporter said.

"I hid in the mountains, with others, they called us the *maquis,* and sometimes my friend would let me stay with her, helping her at the house. She finally bribed a general with litres of olive oil, until he signed a document saying I was attached to *the cause.* I was safe afterwards, as long as I kept my mouth shut. So I shut up. I've been shutting up for seventy years."

Silence followed. The reporter looked as if he was waiting for more.

"In this country, nobody talks, too many shameful secrets to hide." Soledad looked down, exhausted now.

Conchita was listening with big open eyes.

I wondered what happened to my mother. And my father, where was he? Is it true that the Reds *killed my mother's parents for being the rich olive-tree owners of the village, the employers who refused to increase the wages of five pesetas a day for the men, and two and a half for the women, for the same job? Was this why they killed them? Who saw it?*

Now is not the time to ask.

"Come on Soledad, time to go home," Conchita took Soledad by the arm. "The lamb must be cold by now."

"You don't know how lucky you are for being English," Soledad told the reporter and left, without saying goodbye, arm in arm with Conchita.

The two, still in the Old Town, stopped at what might have been the village's main Plaza. Soledad took a deep breath and said: "It all happened here, Conchita, right here."

Soledad almost fainted when Conchita had summoned enough courage to start asking questions. But she refrained herself.

This is not the time.

"Come on, let's go home," Conchita said.

"I hope you told the BBC that the Reds killed your grandparents just because they owned a factory," Honorato said as Conchita finished the washing up, after everybody had left. He was watching Real Madrid play on television.

Conchita didn't answer.

I could have also told them how you married me just because I had that factory. Who are you to blame others? What have you done? I do everything, I run the house, I run the business. What do you do? You brought in your mules, you do the accounts, and that's it.

"And now that young idiot socialist mayor wants to rebuild the Old Village, what a thought!" he said, fixing his tie's knot. "They should just leave it like it is to show what the Red brutes brought with them: rivers of blood and death."

"Let's leave it, Honorato," said Conchita. "It's a long time ago and neither you nor I were there." She'd had enough of a day and wanted to end up in peace.

"My father had all his life the marks of a couple of bullets on his leg, he was shot during a procession, during the Republic, when those idiots forbade religious acts. But my father was brave and came out with the Virgin on his shoulders, only to be shot by those animals. Was that a democratic government? Stones and pots and pans, and even a *jamón*, those pirates threw anything they could get hold of at people in the processions."

Honorato loosened his tie now as sweat started appearing on his forehead. Real Madrid had scored a goal and he hadn't noticed.

"And they also shot my grandfather, just because he had a pig farm with five workers," Honorato had his gaze fixed on the wall. "The poor man."

I knew this idea of rebuilding the village would bring nothing but trouble.

Conchita had heard many times at the market how the communists in Belchite had let pigs and mules loose in religious processions during the Republic. Even if public religious acts were not allowed, the local Catholics insisted on continuing the Easter and Corpus Christi observances, causing dramatic tension. Locals said that a month before the start of the War, a group of Barcelona anarchists arrived in town, went into the church, blasphemed against the sacred symbols on the altar, burned the building and shot the priest. They cut him in half and stuck him on a post outside Belchite's main Plaza, with a sign saying: "Pig's meat sold here."

Conchita took her knitting basket.

"Let's just have a quiet evening, please, it's been enough already today," she said. She didn't want her husband to talk about the War. The only time she had let him talk at the table, he and Soledad almost ended up fighting with arms and fists.

Silence is best.

Reclining in her armchair, Conchita started a little jumper for Maria's first child, who, she hoped, would arrive nine months after the wedding.

"Anyway, the champagne that I bought for Pilar's birthday was good, wasn't it?" Honorato said, as the football seemed to get a bit boring.

Conchita looked up at her husband. "Yes, not bad. How come you didn't buy any of Jordi's cava?"

"I just wanted a bit of a change," Honorato said, his glance fixed on the football.

Conchita looked at him in suspicion. "Are you sure?"

Honorato turned his head towards her. "What do you mean?"

"Are you sure you're not falling for this stupid boycott of Catalan products?" she said. "I don't like many of the things they do, but our own daughter is going to be part of a cava family soon, we should not boycott."

Honorato looked back to his football. "It was just for a change."

Who are you fooling?

The two stayed in silence for a long time, until the phone rang on the little table by Conchita's armchair.

"Ah, Maria, hello, how are you? Are you already back from London?" Conchita said, without excitement.

"Yes, I am well," Maria said. She always said the same. "How was Pilar's birthday?"

"It was good," Conchita said. "You missed it; but listen, you have to come here because I have bought many things for the wedding: I got the paper and envelopes for the invitation, the cigars for the men, I have already ordered the flowers for the church..."

Maria interrupted:

"What?" she shouted. "Mama, I've told you many times I want to see everything. What flowers have you ordered? What invites? What if I don't like them? I've told you many times and you keep acting as if it was *your* wedding, and not *mine*."

All the things that I do, and nobody appreciates anything. Anything!

"But can you not wait and let me explain?" Conchita was becoming angry.

"No, Mama, I've told you many times and you keep doing it," Maria didn't sound very patient, either.

"It's a lovely pink and green envelope..." Conchita started saying.

"Pink and g-r-e-e-n?" Maria sounded horrified. "I won't use them, and leave me alone, it's *my* wedding and *I* will make the decisions." Maria sounded dictatorial.

A tense silence followed.

"But it's *my* money," Conchita finally said.

"You can put that money wherever you want – *I* will pay for it."

Maria hung up.

A 'Sweet Girl'? Conchita remembered her mother's words. *She can be sweet with her, but not with me.*

46

Maria's irreverence irritated Conchita enormously. Hanging up the phone to your own mother! Had she been in front of her, she would have slapped her face, as the nuns did with her when was disrespectful. Conchita had hit Maria many times as a child as she used to break things and answer back all the time. She was almost expelled from school twice, but managed to stay, thanks to her mother's intervention with the nuns, the same ones she had known thirty years ago. A few litres of free olive oil for the convent also helped the nuns feel more positively disposed towards their most rebellious student.

When is this daughter of mine going to learn some discipline? She has to learn that life is not a rose garden; it is suffering, we're only here to suffer. That's what I've done, that's what my mother's done, and what my grandparents surely did. She has to accept it and stop acting like a revolutionary. She thinks life is a game. Somebody has to bring her back to her senses, and if that's not her own mother, who will that be? The higher she climbs, the further she'll fall. She has to do as we all have done: put her head down and accept things. Why does she think she is special?

Why does she think she can neglect and ignore her family, and the family business? If I had left like that, like she's leaving now, who would have taken care of the land? Of the family trees? My mother also stuck to them. And here comes the child and ignores it all. I could have gone as well, to study in Madrid and marry somebody decent, instead of this parasite that I got. But I stayed to help my mother, my land. Why can't she do the same?

Conchita continued knitting, her hands now trembling. She remembered how she used to hit Maria with her high-heel shoes when she was a child. Today she had hit her grandchildren; she didn't like doing that, but sometimes they deserved it, like today. Maria was far worse as a child, though, and she got a lot more, she remembered. She could have killed her the day she caused a power cut at home by putting food on the wires, attracting the birds to chew them, cutting them off. She would do that repeatedly, until Conchita understood what caused the power

47

cuts, which ruined her food in the fridge in the days of scarcity. That day she hit her so hard, with her shoe and her belt, that the little girl bled. That wasn't the only time.

And she hasn't learned yet.

Conchita carried on knitting, now praying silently.

I don't even know why I am doing this little jumper; nobody appreciates anything I do.

3

Maria landed at Stansted Airport before two p.m on a cold Friday afternoon in November. She'd chosen this smaller airport, to the northeast of London, to be closer to King's Cross, near an industrial area that Islington Council had suggested for the warehouse.

She was scheduled to meet Nell Easton, the new planning officer assigned to the case after the first proposal was rejected by the Council. The two women had spoken a few times over the phone during the past couple of weeks. They had agreed that the Council and Patrick, Maria's agent in London, would seek a two-storey site that met the Council's height restrictions. Patrick had selected one and had sent Maria some photos, maps and measures. The banker was now here to check the site, which was, like the first one, in an industrial area between Islington and King's Cross.

Impeccably dressed in her black Armani suit and a Burberry coat, and holding the big rolled warehouse plans and documents that Patrick had sent her, Maria stepped out of a black cab at Brewery Road at three thirty on the dot. She didn't have any luggage as the plan was to see the site in a few hours and go back to Barcelona on the last flight.

Standing in the cold and drizzle just before the darkness fell, Maria scanned the area, crammed with empty land and derelict buildings. She spotted a slim, dark figure walking towards her in the distance. She was sure this was the Council officer – there was nobody else around.

What a weird place to meet. Maria looked down the street and she could only see one commercial sign: Dalston Pipelines.

"Hello, I'm Maria de la Vega, are you Ms Easton?" Maria asked with a smile, offering her hand.

The woman, dressed in black trousers, a thick black anorak, winter boots and a woolly hat, looked surprised to be offered a handshake, but reacted quickly and caught hold of Maria's hand.

God, she's freezing, Maria thought.

"Hello, I'm Nell Easton, nice to meet you in person," Nell said with a slight smile. "Thanks for your interest in Islington. Patrick, your agent, was very keen on this site, and of course, we are very pleased at the Council."

Yeah, I hope this time it's a bit easier, Maria thought, remembering the week she spent the previous month, battling against the Council for the project that was finally rejected for being too tall.

This Council officer seems a bit better than the other one. Maria observed Nell's big, round eyes; they were the colour of the Mediterranean, shiny, a sparkling light blue.

"Should we see the site?" Nell started walking along the dirty pavement, full of muddy holes. "I hope you found the photos and the maps useful."

"Yes, thank you very much," Maria replied. "They were very high quality, thank you."

It was getting darker. Two big, black clouds met on the horizon, reducing daylight to a minimum. Nell began to talk.

"How long do you think it would take to build the warehouse?" Nell asked without looking up at Maria. She walked slowly, with her hands in her pockets, eventually coming to a halt.

"It depends on the state of the site, but from what you told me on the phone, maybe about six or seven months, I guess," Maria said. "But we would start looking for employees quite early in the process. As I said in the emails, we only want the best treatment for our bottles; we want people who can handle them with care and learn the business. In the plan that I sent you, you could see that we'd create fifty jobs, maybe more if our expansion goes well."

It started to rain.

"Well," Maria said, pulling a small umbrella from her handbag. She opened it and took Nell's arm. She started to walk, drawing Nell under the umbrella as she was getting wet.

Nell immediately removed her arm.

"I am all right, thanks." She pulled her hood up.

How cold, Maria thought.

The two continued walking as the rain intensified. They finally stopped in front of a site, about one hundred meters long, with a ramp leading to a gate and two industrial doors for the loading and unloading of trucks.

"I see." Maria recognised the building from the photographs, but she was disillusioned by its state of abandonment. The site was shut and it seemed as if nothing had been produced there for more than a century.

"Large and empty, ready for business," Nell said proudly. "We're only a mile away from the King's Cross Railway Link and the international freight terminal – that would be convenient for you, wouldn't it?"

"It certainly would, but this looks so kaput," Maria said looking at the site, which had some broken windows on the second floor. "Are these the only loading points? What's on the sides and at the back?"

"There's only one emergency exit at the back; you saw on the one side there's the road and on the other one there's a school ground."

"We would definitely need more loading gates than those two," Maria sounded firm. "Could more entry points be built on the school side? Can I see it?"

"We can have a look, but nothing can be built because the school's football pitch is next door." Nell started walking.

They arrived at the school gate, from where Maria could see the football pitch adjacent to the building.

"We need more gates, we need loading space." Maria looked away for a few seconds. "I wonder why Patrick didn't specify this in his report."

"I don't know," Nell said. "But I am afraid the football pitch is unmovable."

51

"We could never build a twenty-first century site in a nineteenth-century building. We need more access," Maria replied in a business-like tone.

Nell looked at Maria, raising an eyebrow.

"We can't leave a school without a ground, it's the only green space that hundreds of people in the surrounding estates have nearby. I am sure you understand."

Maria looked around, searching for those estates, but she couldn't see much because the rain was heavy and the wind was beginning to blow hard. Maria had to hold tight to her umbrella. Somewhere away towards the horizon, there was thunder. Nell didn't seem to notice.

"We could make an offer for that space and you could use the funds for your policies," Maria almost shouted as the wind threatened to blow her umbrella out of her hands.

Let's see what her price is.

Nell stepped forward, standing very close to Maria.

"I am afraid that pitch can't be removed," Nell said, sounding distant. "People here can barely pay their bills. Most don't have jobs, and those who do, for the most part, hate them. For lots of them, Sunday football is all they have, and they play in this ground. My job is to help them but not at any cost."

We'll see about that; wait until I put the right amount on the table. Everybody has a price.

Thunder clapped across the darkening sky, the rain drilled down, heavier than ever. Both women stood, stuck on the road, completely soaked.

Nell started to walk away. "Maybe we could talk over a cup of tea? It's getting pretty nasty out here."

"That sounds good," said Maria, now desperate for some shelter.

The two women walked in silence for about a minute, hunched against the wind and rain. Maria had to walk fast to keep pace with Nell, who was able to walk much more easily with her strong boots. Nell looked back and saw Maria's effort to catch up; she was literally trying to run with the rolled plans and documents, as well as the umbrella, now flipped completely backwards by the wind. Nell smiled and when she caught up, helped Maria with the umbrella; the two stood under it.

They found refuge at a café on the corner of York Way.

"Phew, what a tragedy this weather, is this normal?" Maria asked, taking her coat off, putting the umbrella in the corner, water dripping behind.

Nell was at the counter, also taking her anorak off. "This is bad, even by British standards," she said. "Would you like a cup of tea?" She smiled.

"I'd love some coffee, if possible," Maria said, sitting at a table in the corner of the little café, which only had one other customer inside, a middle-aged man reading the DAILY MIRROR.

Nell came back with Maria's coffee and a cup of tea for herself and looked through the window. "It's terrible, indeed." She looked at Maria and sat down. "I am rather surprised that Patrick didn't let you know about the gates. I thought he would have noticed it."

Maria felt better with the first sip of coffee. She relaxed her shoulders, although her jacket was still wet.

"Well, these agents aren't bankers or wine growers, are they?" Maria said with a bit of superiority. "I guess they seek sites for many clients and they can't know all industries well enough to be aware of their specific needs."

"Why are those gates so important?" Nell asked. "Why aren't two sufficient?"

Maria put her coffee on the table and sat back on her chair. "It's crucial to have order when loading and unloading," she said in a business tone. "I've seen it too often in the small shops that they have chaos during the day because some drivers have to wait, queue, and that causes delays, and you know what happens, especially in London: if you hit the West End after eleven in the morning, no restaurant is going to take your wine because they're already preparing lunch and they don't want to be bringing products in."

Nell looked at Maria attentively. "If you parked the vans outside, they wouldn't mess around in front of the gates."

"Mmmm," Maria mumbled. "I don't think I would leave ten vans parked in the street here. It seems there's not that many people around at night."

"That is true," Nell admitted. "But can't you organise it in a way that the drivers know the exact times to come and go?"

"That'd be my dream," Maria smiled. "Unfortunately, in distribution, things don't always work to the clock and blockages occur more often than not. We need flexibility and agility. Loading a van takes about fifteen minutes, and any delay can break an order."

"I would have never guessed," Nell said, resigned. "I wonder why they didn't build more gates if that's always been the case."

"It's an old building," Maria said. "Now you've got to serve the client to perfection. There's too much competition to replace you if you don't."

Nell looked a bit incredulous. "How long have you been in the wine or distribution businesses?"

"I am a banker, I am not a specialist in wine or logistics, but I've already worked on a few similar cases," Maria responded, without showing off.

"How long have you been a banker?" Nell seemed curious.

"About three years, since I left uni," Maria smiled.

"Did you go to University in Barcelona? Is that where you come from?" Nell asked. "I love that city."

Maria smiled and looked at Nell; she felt more relaxed now.

At least this Council officer is warm and polite. This will be easier.

"No, I went somewhere else," Maria responded. She didn't want to give many details about Pamplona, she preferred to talk about Barcelona. "I am not from Barcelona, but I love living there, close to the sea."

Nell opened her eyes wide. "I am so envious," she said. "Where are you from then?"

"I am from Belchite, a small village near Zaragoza, between Barcelona and Madrid."

Nell looked surprised. "I know Belchite, the village destroyed during the Civil War, isn't it?"

Now, Maria looked surprised. "Yes, how do you know?"

"It was on the BBC the other night, there was a programme about it," Nell sounded excited. "Also, my very good friend's grandfather was killed there, he was a BRIGADISTA who went to fight against Franco, and unfortunately he was killed. My friend's family talks very proudly of him."

Maria stayed silent. *Ah the War, there's no escape, even in England I find traces of it.*

"I've seen photos, it looks very spooky, it's all in ruins." Nell seemed to want to talk more about the subject.

Maria felt the assertion was more like a question. "I know, Franco built the new town next to the old one, so everybody moved there. Luckily my family didn't have to as they have a big house on the outskirts; it was a miracle that it wasn't bombed."

"How interesting, was your family able to escape from the bombs then?" Nell asked.

"No, I am afraid my grandparents died," Maria said. "Although I don't know much about it, you know, Spanish families don't talk about it. It's very taboo."

"Still?" Nell seemed surprised.

"Still." Maria let a few seconds go by. "You may have seen my grandmother's friend on the telly, if you watched the BBC programme. My mother told me they were filming there, a few weeks ago, and Soledad, who's always lived with us, talked to them."

"Oh really?" Nell seemed to be having a great time. "What does she look like?"

"I wasn't there when they were filming, but my mom told me she showed them the old school in the Old Town, where she used to teach…"

Nell interrupted. "The teacher! I remember the teacher! What a wonderful lady!" She exclaimed.

Maria was happy, and shocked, about the coincidence. *Who would have told me that good old Soledad would be known in a café in the middle of nowhere in London?* But her heart felt a bit smaller, she didn't like talking about the War too much. She only knew that nobody had answered her questions, and that any talk about the issue always brought a family upset, between her father, her grandmother and Soledad. She put her coffee on the table and looked down at it.

Nell seemed to notice Maria's discomfort.

"What took you from Belchite to Barcelona's banking world then?" She asked kindly.

"Well, Belchite isn't exactly a hub of opportunity." Maria smiled without adding anything else.

A strong, long rumble of thunder could be heard from outside. The branches of the trees opposite were thrashing in the wind, plastic bags bobbed and wheeled down the street.

"Are you flying back tonight?" Nell asked.

"Yes, I hope so; though with this weather..." Maria looked outside.

"If I were you, I'd call to check if they're flying," Nell said.

"That's a good idea," Maria said. She took her Blackberry from her handbag, pressed a button, and briefly spoke in Spanish for a few seconds.

Maria left her Blackberry on the table.

"What did they say?" Nell asked.

"Oh, I just asked my secretary to check it out."

"You have a secretary?"

"Yes, it helps with all this travelling, I can't do it all myself."

A couple of minutes later, the Blackberry beeped.

"Oh shit, yes, my flight has been cancelled, and it was the last one and all the others are full, damn it!" Maria said. "It always happens on Fridays, it's impossible to fly to Barcelona from London, all the planes are packed. Damn. My boyfriend was going to come and pick me up."

Maria clasped her hands and thought for a couple of seconds. "Let me give my boyfriend a quick call and ask my assistant to book me into a hotel here. Damn."

Fifteen minutes later, Maria hadn't heard from her secretary and Nell kept looking at her watch.

"I am so sorry, but I am afraid I have a party to go to, I have to get going," she said. "I wish I could stay and help you."

Maria looked at Nell. "Not a problem, I am sure that my assistant will find a hotel soon. Don't worry, please go ahead, I'll just wait here," Maria said with a forced smile, as she looked at the now empty little café. The lady on the counter looked at her, at the same time, and said, "We're about to close, ladies."

"Oh shame, it's one of those nine-to-five places," Nell explained. "You're very welcome to come to my party if you want to, you can stay as long as you want, at least you'll be warm in there."

Maria thought for a couple of seconds, looking through the window.

A drink is what I need with this weather, and this could help the deal. "Why not?" Maria smiled.

"It's a friend's birthday and they're delivering a cake, I have to be there to pay for it, that's why I need to get there so early," Nell explained. "It's not too far – in Chancery Lane – it won't take us long on the bus."

"Yes, not a problem, let's go then," Maria said. She started to stand up but sat down again when she noticed Nell wanted to add something more.

"By the way, it's a gay pub, just so you know," Nell said.

"Sorry?" Maria wasn't expecting anything like this.

"It's a gay bar," Nell said louder. "Just in case you have any problem with it."

"Oh, no, no, I'm alright," Maria said, somewhat surprised. "Well, I don't think I've ever been to a gay bar, but that's fine, I can go." Maria laughed nervously. She felt curious. She took a deep breath and made an effort to relax. *This is interesting. Is this woman a lesbian? Or maybe her friend is gay – this being London, that's quite possible.*

Maria observed Nell's cropped hair and short, unpolished nails.

Lesbian.

Despite the rain, Maria enjoyed the afternoon bus ride through London. She looked down from the upper deck, asking what things were. Nell pointed out some buildings, such as St Pancras and the BT Tower, as they approached Chancery Lane.

About twenty minutes later, they reached a dark pub on a corner, in the little streets behind Holborn, which had a rainbow flag hanging limply outside. Men with tattoos and shaved heads were seated at the bar. They all turned to Maria and Nell as they walked in. What Maria thought must be a transvestite was playing at the noisy fruit machine. The ragged sofas were empty.

Behind the bar, a woman with short, chemically-blond hair, vivid red lipstick and artificially voluptuous breasts, smiled.

"Hello Nelly, welcome back," she said, surveying Maria from head to toe.

"This way," Nell said to Maria, walking towards a staircase. Maria followed her throwing glances left and right as she went.

The room upstairs had light, orange paint and candles everywhere, creating a warm atmosphere. Plates of sandwiches were laid out on tables covered with white paper tablecloths. Balloons and colourful paper banners decorated the walls.

"It's my football teammate's birthday today, they'll be here soon," Nell said, walking into the little bar in the corner. "Tea or coffee?" she said, switching the kettle on.

"Coffee please," Maria smiled, relieved to avoid tea.

Maria walked around the room, looking at the photos on the walls. They were all of women, mostly playing football or hugging each other after a goal. Other photos showed them camping or sailing. They seemed so full of life.

Maria stopped and stared at one of them. Two women were kissing each other on the mouth. She'd never seen anything like it before, not even in a picture. She couldn't stop looking at it. She felt a knot on her throat. A few moments later, she walked towards the window, in silence, and lit a cigarette.

Nell came with the coffee. "You aren't supposed to smoke in bars any more," she immediately said.

"Oh sorry," Maria apologised, looking around in search of an ashtray to put down her cigarette.

"Well, if it's too hard, I've seen them making an exception here, when they have parties upstairs," Nell said. "As a matter of fact, many of my friends smoke, and I am sure they'll do so tonight, so feel free."

"Are you sure?" Maria asked, wondering if Nell was just trying to be polite.

"Yes, go ahead," Nell said. "But smoking isn't going to win you any favours."

Oh no, I hope she's not one of those fussy, green, vegetarian, anti-smoking carrots, Maria thought.

"I know it's not good, I don't smoke a lot," she said. Maria still loved smoking every now and again.

"Anyway, this looks like a lovely surprise for somebody." Maria didn't want to start the endless smoking-non-smoking debate. "I am sure your friend will have a lovely birthday."

"Thank you. It didn't take me long to arrange it," Nell said.

"Oh, did you arrange all this?" Maria sounded surprised.

"Yeah, but it didn't take long, believe me. I had to meet you not far from here, anyway, so I was happy to drop by at lunch time," Nell looked down, modestly. "Plus all the others work too far or they can't take the time."

What a lovely thing to do. The English are so thoughtful. Maria remembered Soledad's comments about the English, she always said they were the most polite of all. She made a mental note to send her a postcard from the airport, she knew her and Gran loved receiving them.

The two women could still hear the thunder outside the windows. They looked at each other in complicity.

Nell took off the smart black polo neck jumper she was wearing, under which she had a Manchester United shirt.

Nooooo. I can't believe she's wearing that. What lack of taste.

More thunder could be heard just outside the windows.

"How can you survive this weather? Don't you get depressed?" Maria asked, puzzled, looking outside.

59

"You get used to it," Nell said a bit defensively. "In the summer it's very nice, though. And in the winter, you'll see – good parties indoors."

"I can see," Maria looked around the room. "Therefore a cava warehouse would be ideal, if you spend your winter drinking."

"We don't drink champagne around here, we like beer and wine," Nell replied quickly.

"It's cava, not champagne," Maria corrected. "Champagne is from France, only. We make a much better product and far cheaper."

"Yes, I know, I like cava, I think there're a couple of bottles in the fridge, for later," Nell said. She looked at Maria, who was taking her coat and jacket off.

"Feel free to stay in for the cava if you want," Nell said, looking away. "I'd love to hear more about Belchite, I'd love to visit some of the Civil War trails, it's been here in the papers, recently. I find the subject fascinating."

Maria looked at Nell with scepticism. *This could be a good opportunity to smooth out the relationship with the Council. We're going to be working on this for a while, so it'd better start well.*

"The Civil War is a long story," Maria finally said with a raised eyebrow, followed by a sigh.

"I am patient," Nell smiled. "We should wait for the birthday girl to open the cava, but I think there's some wine as well. Fancy some?"

"Sounds good." Maria lit another cigarette and looked around.

Half a bottle of wine later, about ten people, and the cake, had arrived and Maria was wearing the Manchester United shirt. She had put her white top in a plastic bag to stop herself catching a cold. She felt masculine, but at least she was warm. Nell had a tight, black, sleeveless top under the football shirt, showing a tattoo of a snake on her shoulder. Maria eyed the tattoo nervously; she felt a bit scared. As far as she knew, in Spain, only truants and truck drivers had tattoos.

Nell also had a lovely necklace, with an emerald, matching her eyes, which gave her an air of femininity, Maria noticed.

Nell introduced Maria to the guests, all women. Despite her shyness, Maria managed to keep up with conversations, helped by the number of glasses of red wine she was consuming. Nell's friends were also open and easy to talk to – the fact that some smoked helped Maria as they could light cigarettes for each other, talk about the smoking ban, and its absence in Spain. Those who didn't smoke talked mostly about sport – they all played football in Hackney at the weekends, Maria found out.

I'ts fine, I can stay here for a bit more. The Council Officer seems fairly decent. But I must solve this football pitch issue tonight. I need to uninhibit myself. I need more wine.

Two hours and two bottles of wine later, Maria's Blackberry was inside her bag, in the cloakroom, full of messages and missed calls, including one from her secretary, telling her which hotel she'd been booked into. But Maria, more than merry and clearly enjoying herself, was standing in the middle of the party. Then she noticed two women kissing on the sofa.

Like in the photo, Maria couldn't take her eyes off them. Her heart started to beat faster when all of a sudden the delicate face of an old schoolfriend came to her mind. She hadn't thought about her in years, despite how close they'd become in their early teens. They spent days and sometimes nights together, often staying at each other's homes. They read stories together, combed each other's hair and sometimes, in bed, they whispered secrets while holding hands under the blanket. She could still remember her friend's pure wool blanket. Nobody had duvets in those days. Maria felt warmed by the memories. It was a shame they lost contact after her friend moved away from Belchite.

Maria was still looking at the two women kissing. She had certainly kissed Jordi many times, but nothing like this. The two women seemed to be seriously enjoying themselves.

God, I've never seen a kiss like that. But this is completely different to what we did. We were teenagers, at that age we were just exploring, discovering intimacy and affection. We didn't do anything or touch each other like that, at all. These are proper lesbians.

"Having a good time?" Nell suddenly said, waking Maria up from her dreams. She was now standing next to her, holding a bottle of wine. "You look good in that United shirt."

"Ugh," Maria mumbled, not convinced about her outfit. "Your friends are great," she added, remembering her old group of friends, Jordi's friends, in Pamplona. She missed belonging to a group, like Jordi had and Nell seemed to have.

Nell topped up her glass.

"I don't know if I should drink more wine, though, I think I may have had enough, thank you," Maria said, aware of the slight headache that was beginning. "Maybe I should go to my hotel."

"It won't do you any harm, it's a good Rioja," Nell said, also looking quite merry.

"Rrio-j-a," Maria corrected; by now she had forgotten about the hotel.

"Rioja!" Nell shouted, as if a louder voice improved her accent. But at that point, not even Maria's Spanish was that clear.

The two women, now drunk, laughed and drank some more.

"Now, seriously Ms Easton,"

"Oh come on, call me Nelly, Nell, whatever you want."

"Okay, Nell, now, seriously, why is a football pitch more important than my loading gates? Is it because you also play football with your girlfriend?" Maria said purposefully.

"Well Ms De la Vega,"

"Maria," she said shyly.

"Okay Maria," Nell smiled. "Why do you want that site so much?"

She's not saying whether she has a girlfriend. Maybe she didn't hear.

Maria tried to explain, although her drunkenness didn't help. "We need the vans to get to the restaurants; they don't sell cava anymore because they say it's very downmarket, it's on special offer in every Tesco or Sainbury's. It's not classy. Idiots. We need to change that."

Maria took her time, as if she was thinking hard, and continued, even if she could barely stand up. "Plus, as you say, many people can't really afford champagne." Maria smiled, raised her glass, ready for a toast. Then she said triumphantly: "Cava is the answer."

"You don't give a shit about the people who can't afford champagne, come on," Nell said, trying to tease Maria, who turned serious after the comment.

"You know nothing about me," Maria said defensively. Mama had told her countless times how poor she had been and how hard she worked from a very young age, until the business became profitable. She made Maria and Pilar live an austere life, while they were at home, despite the family's wealth. Unlike her University colleagues, Maria's parents never gave her a car and she just had enough clothes, never too many or too fancy. She used to work throughout the summers, instead of travelling abroad or just being on holiday, as most Pamplona students did.

A tall, black woman with an extremely tight top stepped between the two of them, pushing Maria out of the way and kissing Nell on the mouth, holding the kiss for several seconds.

She's kissing with her tongue. Maria stared. *Is that her girlfriend? She's not very pretty.*

Nell finally pulled back from the kiss. She looked at Maria's wide eyes.

"You look surprised. Haven't you seen two women kiss before?" Nell asked.

"Never." Maria didn't know what else to say as the other woman was still standing between the two. She lit a cigarette and said: "I am getting married in six months." Then she blew the smoke away.

The black woman moved away, slapping Nell on her bottom. "Don't get into trouble!" she told Nell in a sarcastic tone.

Both Nell and Maria smiled. Maria was now feeling more relaxed, or probably just drunk.

"She's the birthday girl," Nell said after her friend left. "But congratulations to you on your wedding! We must celebrate. Drink more wine."

"Is she your girlfriend?" Maria enquired with small eyes, slightly turning her head away.

"Nope, just a friend," Nell answered.

Ah. "But you're a lesbian, right?" Maria was still partially looking away, trying to hide her interest.

"Yes," Nell answered, bemused.

Maria felt proud of her discovery. *If Jordi saw me, or my mother, they would have a heart attack. Ha ha.*

"*Más vino?*" Maria was clearly enjoying her little, off-track adventure.

"*Sí,*" Nell said.

Maria noticed Nell's intense look, straight into her eyes, which were now shining. She also felt Nell glance at her body, head to toe. Suddenly, Nell looked away.

Becoming friends will facilitate negotiations. Hic!

"Are you happy being a lesbian?" Maria asked.

"Sure, or are you referring to the sex?" Nell replied.

"Yeah," Maria said, embarrassed, looking away.

"It's good. You've never slept with a woman?"

"God, no."

"Ah, it's a lot nicer, softer, bit more intense," Nell said, putting her hand on Maria's lower arm, gently. Maria felt a slight current from the touch and, scared, backed off a little bit.

"I had a girlfriend who was fantastic, just perfect," Nell said.

Nervously, Maria continued drinking. She had to make a real effort to keep her balance.

"Why was she perfect?" Maria was intrigued. *I am missing my life because of this Opus boyfriend. Damn. Everybody is enjoying themselves while I am living like a nun, even the lesbians are having more fun. Brrr.*

Nell came closer, so close that their hair touched slightly. "She would kiss me at the bottom of the spine and continue very softly, gently, all the way up, to the neck. Sometimes it took an age to reach the top, on my back; I don't know how she managed to do it so slowly. I'd have goose-pimples everywhere, the tension was unbearable; sometimes I had to ask her to stop because it was too much. I've never experienced anything like that. I miss that."

Maria closed her eyes. Nell's words made it hard for her not to imagine a woman kissing her own back. Maria felt her temperature rise, slowly; she moistened her lips and swallowed. She sighed and looked at Nell full of attention, with such intensity that for a second she felt an impulse towards her. Standing now very close to her, Nell moved her head towards Maria who stayed immobile, surprised at Nell's move, her heart beating fast. Maria closed her eyes before she could feel Nell's lips on her, for a few seconds that seemed an eternity. Despite all the alcohol in her body, the kiss seemed very different to Jordi's, it wasn't the same taste, it was sweeter, gentler, it felt as if it was coming from the heart.

What am I doing? Maria froze and took a step back. *I am drunk, I need to get to the hotel. I am losing it.* "Nell, sorry, but I am getting a bit tired, I think I am going to the hotel, I am sure my assistant has found it by now." She could barely walk. Her face was white, her eyes red, and random.

Nell looked chilled.

"I'll go with you. I brought you to this party, I can't leave you to find your way alone in this state," Nell said, calmly.

"No, no, I am all right," Maria insisted, almost falling over.

Nell helped her stand still, held her arm. "Come on, let's go, I'm tired too. I'll grab your coat and the documents," she said. "You wait here." She moved towards the cloakroom.

Maria said nothing. A couple of seconds later, she collapsed on the ground.

4

Jordi parked Oscar outside Belagua, an Opus Dei church at the corner of Avinguda Pedralbes and Avinguda Diagonal, one of the most expensive locations in Barcelona. The modern building was hidden away behind some trees and neat bushes, grass and flowers, out of the sight and knowledge of most Barcelonians.

After his usual, daily, twelve hours at the Caves, Jordi took a deep breath and rushed into mass, the start of his all-male club weekly meeting. About ten other young men, also in their late twenties, were already on their knees, holding their heads with hands together, praying, just a couple of minutes into the ceremony. Father Juan Antonio nodded as he saw Jordi walk in. Like the others, Jordi sat on one of the old wooden benches by himself, in absolute silence. They reflected, until the priest, a short, round, middle-aged man dressed in an immaculate black cassock, carried on with the mass:

"O God, through the mediation of Mary our Mother, you granted your priest St Josemaría countless graces, choosing him as a most faithful instrument to found Opus Dei, a way of sanctification in daily work and in the fulfilment of the Christian's duties. Grant that I too may learn to turn all the events of my life into occasions of loving You. Our Father, Hail Mary, Glory be to the Father."

"*Amen*," the boys replied at once.

They stood up in silence, in the cold church. Opus usually turned the heating off to keep its members fresh and alert; they were also advised to have cold showers in the morning and to avoid baths, all to reduce temptation.

Today's topic was purity, Father Juan Antonio announced.

Again, Jordi thought. Rare was the meeting when Opus didn't bring up, almost obsessively, the importance of chastity. *This comes in handy, though. The months ahead of the wedding are getting too long. I wish it was next week.*

Father Juan Antonio went on:

"Don't forget that purity strengthens and invigorates the character. Remove, Jesus, that filthy crust of sensual corruption which covers my heart, so that I can feel and readily follow the touches of the Paraclete on my soul. Without holy purity one cannot persevere in the apostolate."

Jordi had been hearing this since he joined Opus at age thirteen, when Father Juan Antonio had lured him into the organisation. A way of escaping the regular domestic upsets, a guarantee to focus on his studies and sport in a luxurious and elitist environment, Jordi didn't hesitate and committed to Opus at the age of eighteen, as soon as he was officially allowed to.

At home, he spent time in his own room or, mostly, working at the Caves. Jordi took the responsibilities that his brothers never wanted to accept, their lives being about women and fast cars. In the old days, Mr Gratallops spent most of his time on export trips abroad, leaving Jordi, still in his teens, managing a small group of workers and handling some of the company accounts. Jordi took those assignments diligently, without a single complaint; he preferred running the business to going out with his brothers dancing and flirting with girls. Instead, he stayed locked in his room, trying to avoid temptation with the celice that Father Juan Antonio had given him.

To Jordi, these were perfectly normal activities, common among his peers. He had been told not to share these experiences with anybody outside Opus, as *they* wouldn't understand. That wasn't different from the group's other routines, mostly kept to themselves. Self-flagellation was just one more thing, there was nothing especial about it, in Jordi's mind.

His family never knew about his practices. When one of his siblings suggested that Jordi could be gay, his parents said he was just different. They thought of him as a good Catholic who went to mass every day.

Jordi made an effort to keep his eyes open, after the week he'd had. He listened to his mentor:

"Procreation is a necessity for the species only, not for the individual. When you have sought the company of a sensual satisfaction, what loneliness afterwards! To defend his purity, St Francis of Assisi rolled in the snow, St Benedict threw himself into a thorn bush, St Bernard plunged into an icy pond... you..., what have you done? No ideal becomes a reality without sacrifice. Deny yourself. It's so beautiful to be a victim!"

Jordi still believed in these words, although he knew he could still reach sainthood by marrying Maria, as long as he followed Opus' guidelines. He had never regretted abandoning, in Pamplona, his dream of becoming a celibate numerary as his passion for Maria rose each day. Neither did he miss having to recruit new members. At University, his spiritual directors asked him to make lists of 'targetable' friends whom he had to try to draw into the organisation. Friendships based on honest appreciation of another's personality, without wanting or expecting anything back, became a thing of the past. His old, non-Opus friends, the ones he knew from playing football in the streets of Vilafranca as a little boy, started to be neglected as he saw them as sinners, removed from the Opus values. Those old friends didn't enjoy getting telephone calls only to be invited to Opus gatherings, either. Eventually, they didn't return the calls, or pick up the phone at all.

He had become a 'smurf' – this is what non-Opus students in Pamplona called the Opus members, as they all shared the same values and ideas and dressed practically the same: navy-blue trousers, smart shoes, a classic striped shirt and a round-neck cashmere jumper. They were perfectly shaven and all had short, well-cut hair.

Opus was Jordi's family, where he felt appreciated and valued, where his worries and concerns were addressed and dealt with. At home, everybody saw him as a sort of monk who was better left alone, and so they did, creating a void that Opus quickly saw, and filled, more than ten years ago.

In the sepulchral silence of the church, Jordi prayed for his mother and father, whom he loved dearly, although more because it was Christian to do so, rather than for the things they shared or the time they spent together. Football and work was all he talked about with his father, while his mother seemed to spend her life with her friends.

Immediately after the mass, coffee was served in a room next door, where the supernumeraries chatted about work, football and fiancées, before the Father arrived. They knew each other well as most went to the same school, La Farga, probably the only Barcelona school where children wore jackets and ties, looking *too* English for the locals, who accused them of snobbery. It was indeed odd that in the middle of the May and June Mediterranean heat, children had to wear shirts, jackets and ties, making them sweat throughout the day. After school, some students, usually the brightest, gathered at a club for a weekly meeting, also called Circle because of the way they arranged the chairs. Mediocre students were never invited.

Father Juan Antonio walked into the room, serious as always, holding a cup of coffee, still dressed in his cassock. He sat in his comfortable armchair, the others on simple, wooden chairs. With his big, hairy hands on his knees, showing his thick, gold ring – symbol of his marriage to God and to Opus – Father Juan Antonio opened his copy of 'The Way,' the Opus Bible, and started reading. He made pauses for people to reflect in silence. Nobody was expected to speak up and least of all challenge any of the readings. This was doctrine, not discussion.

"At the time of temptation think of the Love that awaits you in heaven: foster the virtue of hope – this is not a lack of generosity. Domine!

...

69

Lord, SI VIS, POTES ME MUNDARE, if thou wilt, thou canst make me clean.

...

Suffering overwhelms you because you take it like a coward. Meet it bravely, with a Christian spirit: and you will regard it as a treasure."

Jordi was struggling more and more to contain temptation. Just before Maria left for London, the couple had gone to the cinema where Jordi caressed her legs; he found her irresistible when she wore black silk stockings and a short skirt. He had to stop to avoid an arousal, which he actually didn't manage. Back at home, and despite taking a cold shower, he sinned, for which he went to confession the following morning.

Jordi woke up from his thoughts about him and Maria, naked in bed, on their wedding night. He was almost counting the seconds to it. He raised his head and realised the group had been quiet for a while.

Father Juan Antonio stood up and asked if anybody had any comments or questions; nobody did. He made a couple of announcements about a theatre trip and other activities coming up and invited the group to go home. Releasing tension but still looking rather sombre and serious, the young men, one by one, took their jackets and started to leave.

"Jordi, can I have a word with you?" Father Juan Antonio tapped Jordi's shoulder as he was walking out.

"Of course," Jordi said, waving to his club colleagues.

"Come on, boy, sit here with me." Father Juan Antonio took his black cassock off, under which he had grey trousers and a navy blue jumper. He folded it and carefully placed it inside a shiny oak wardrobe. Every piece of furniture at Opus venues was always spotless.

The two sat in the comfortable and expensive black leather armchairs, under a soft light. Opus had the habit of turning things dark, by switching some lights off or putting the blinds down, when they discussed serious matters, including any talk about Opus itself, which they did as little as possible, especially to outsiders, strengthening their reputation for mystery and secretiveness.

"How are you? Are you doing well?" the Father asked, showing the one golden tooth in his denture.

"Yes, yes, Father, all going well, working hard as usual." Jordi looked down, a symbol of respect.

Like all Opus members, Jordi saw professional activity as a way to reach sainthood. Even cleaners were told off for not sufficiently polishing Opus' residences and apartments; if they didn't, they were told they would never reach the apostolate with so much dust on the shelves. The cleaners, of course, laughed, just to increase the Opus members' sense of superiority and difference.

"Well done, boy, well done, keep working hard," Father Juan Antonio said. He was looking into Jordi's tired eyes. "I hope you're still making time for Maria and to prepare for the wedding." He smiled.

"Oh yes, Father," Jordi smiled as soon as he heard his girlfriend's name. "She's wonderful as usual, and we'll soon begin to choose all the little details, the flowers, the dresses, you know. I am very happy, and lucky." Jordi, although pale and exhausted after a long day, was still smiling. "She's so smart as well, she's doing so well at the bank," he added, proudly.

Father Juan Antonio didn't look impressed. He never showed any interest in Maria's career or that of any other woman. Opus' founder had spelled it out clearly in 'the Way': men were expected to climb to their professional heights to reach sainthood, whereas women just had to be feminine.

"Good, good, I hope the two of you are, of course, living a Christian engagement, JF you know what I mean," Father Juan Antonio was now looking intently at Jordi. "I know at this age

71

the impetus can be strong." he said, embarrassing Jordi. He then recited two quotes from 'The Way.'

"If you only knew what you are worth! It is St Paul who tells you: you have been bought 'at a great price'. And he adds: 'That is why you should use your body for the glory of God'.

Father Juan Antonio looked Jordi straight in the eye and continued:

"Longing for children? Children, many children, and a lasting trail of light we shall leave behind us if we sacrifice the selfishness of the flesh."

Jordi looked down again and said: "Of course Father, of course we are acting under the principles and values."

"Good to hear, boy," the Father said. "I am sure you know what you can do when you have temptations, it's human, we all have them, just don't forget what I taught you."

Jordi understood. Of course he used the celice.

"Yes," Jordi said, still looking down.

"I am happy to hear that, I just wanted to make sure, since, you know, Maria doesn't belong to our group, you never know; and as the wedding approaches, some people think they can relax. But that would be a gigantic mistake, you would throw all those years of chastity away."

"We are all right, Father," is all that Jordi said. A tense silence followed.

All right Father, I am hungry and tired, it's Friday, I just want to go home. I am already making a huge effort to stick to the rules.

"There's one more thing," Father Juan Antonio said in a low tone.

"Yes Father?" Jordi was surprised now. The Father usually checked on whether he was masturbating or not, but apart from that, he didn't seem to have much more interest in his life.

"I have noticed that your voluntary contribution to the club has fallen over the past couple of months," the Father said, again with an intense look in his big, brown eyes. "I was just wondering if everything's all right."

Jordi took a deep breath and sat back. "Yes, it is." He let a couple of seconds go by. Jordi had given, since he graduated, about half of his salary to the club, in line with the other members. The money helped Opus keep its luxury locations in Barcelona and its elite image around the world. It also helped to pay for programmes and activities designed to poach the young and clever, including horse riding, trips to the Vatican or weekends at the many country houses that Opus owned around Spain. To the members, giving money to Opus was like giving it to God and who would dare decline to understand such a charitable act?

"You know you can trust me and tell me anything that's bothering you, boy," Father Juan Antonio said to break the silence.

Jordi looked up, he seemed concerned. "It's a bit tight at the company now, there's lots of competition, and we're also feeling this boycott against Catalan products," he finally said, trying to tone the problem down.

"That must be hurting you," Father Juan Antonio said.

"Yes, indeed," Jordi said, feeling a bit more relaxed. He took a deep breath and spoke with honesty. "And you know, I am also building a flat for Maria and me."

"Ah," Father Juan Antonio nodded. He looked at him with a raised eyebrow. "None of my business, and I hope you don't mind me asking this, you know this is all between you and me, but usually fathers help their children when they buy a house. Sorry, I know it's none of my business, but I imagined this would be your case as well."

Jordi looked nervously around. He felt the pressure of the big figure of his spiritual director, who was still looking at him. As much as Jordi knew that Father Juan Antonio loved him as a son, he was also aware that Opus didn't want any losers, and a cut in his contributions wasn't a good sign. Also, he had always been Father Juan Antonio's protégé, always used as an example to others, always spotless and obedient, and he didn't want to disappoint the man who had guided him along the right path for more than ten years. Jordi could decline to comment, but that would be seen as odd, and as a lack of trust, a Christian value.

"Well, my father has already had to put some extra money in the business, and we may need to take a loan as well," Jordi said, feeling he was speaking in absolute confidence. "You know he is seventy-five now and had some heart problems last year. He'll retire next June and I think the best I can do for him is to give him a peaceful last few months."

Father Juan Antonio nodded, although he didn't look convinced.

"You know he's been working non-stop for the business since he was fourteen. The Caves are his whole life, we can't have problems this year." Jordi now sounded convincing.

"Well done, boy, well done, you are a good son," the priest said, looking at him with scepticism. "You must be tired now, let me know if you need anything, and you know you can come to me if anything's bothering you, I am here for you." Father Juan Antonio showed his fake smile.

He doesn't mean any harm. He's just doing his job. Jordi took a deep breath, releasing tension and fatigue.

"Thank you, Father," Jordi said. "I don't know what I would do without you. You're always there and you don't know how much I appreciate that. Thank you," he said with humility.

"It's God who's always there for you," the Father said. "I am just his servant."

Jordi smiled: "And don't worry, I will keep sending you the bottles of the year's best vintage, as always." Jordi stood up, putting his jacket on.

"Aha! Now you're talking!" The Father smiled, as he and the community of numeraries where he lived loved to drink free bottles of Caves Gratallops' vintage cava on Sundays.

"Go with God, Jordi."

Oh damn, Jordi thought as he switched his mobile on once inside the car and heard Maria's voice message.

I just wanted to see her today so much. Damn English weather. He reclined his head on the seat and took a deep breath. He looked at the dozens of cars along the Diagonal, full of people going home, to their families, he thought.

I can't wait to have my home with Maria. Jordi thought about the flat he was building for the two of them, a loft on top of an old house in Barcelona's upscale Sarrià neighborhood. He hadn't told Maria many details about the three-bedroom apartment and its ceiling-to-floor windows overlooking the city; it was a surprise, a wedding present from him to her. But Maria had opposed the idea ferociously, saying she made good money and he didn't have to bear the financial responsibility, accusing him of being old-fashioned. Jordi felt it was his responsibility to provide for his future family. He was also sure that Maria would love the flat, as she had pointed at newspaper ads showing similar penthouses, always like an unreachable dream.

Jordi tried to relax, he wanted to see Maria, to feel her closeness. The latest sales figures and the Spanish boycott against Catalan products had given him an awful week, he just wanted to forget about it all.

Oh well. I'll see her tomorrow, he thought with resignation. *Although I so wish I was in her arms.*

He listened to another message, this one from his brother, Bernat, saying he couldn't pick up their father at the airport tonight, asking him to go.

Bernat, I always have to rescue you, don't I?

Bernat, his older brother, also worked at the Caves since dropping out of University in his first year. He lived in central Barcelona with his wife, and drove his fast cars to the Caves every day, where he was in charge of marketing – at least that's what his business card said.

After the initial disappointment, Jordi thought it would not be very Christian to tell his father he was too tired to pick him up from the airport. Still sitting inside the car, outside the church, he texted Bernat saying he would go. He drove in silence towards the airport.

5

"You can come to mine if you're not feeling too well," Nell told Maria as they left the pub and walked towards Chancery Lane tube station. Maria was feeling slightly better, after Nell rescued her from the floor, helped her lie on a bench in the pub and brought her some water and a camomile tea.

"I am so sorry, I don't know how I got into this state," Maria mumbled, feeling very embarrassed about her collapse, and even more about the kiss. *How did I end up like that?* The fresh, cold air was doing her good. "I'll just go to my hotel."

"Pub wine is dangerous," Nell said, with a smile.

"I am telling you, England needs that cava warehouse," Maria said, still having hiccups.

Nell smiled and held Maria's arm, giving her some support. She also took the plan rolls, which Maria was holding with some trouble.

Maria removed her arm. *Don't touch me. It's already been enough.*

"I feel bad," Nell said. "I induced you into all this, sorry."

"Don't worry," Maria said, lying. Wishing to get back to her own world as soon as possible, Maria opened her bag in search of her Blackberry.

"Oh shit! No battery!" Maria looked at the device, disbelieving. "I can't believe it, now I don't know where my secretary booked me. Damn. Damn!"

Maria stopped walking and looked down. *I guess I can't call her in the middle of the night.* "What time is it?"

"Almost midnight," Nell responded.

"God, at this time in Spain people haven't even started going out," Maria was surprised about leaving a party that early in the night. "But of course, if you hit the bar at five, then I guess that's the same as starting at midnight and going home at five or six."

But I still can't call my assistant this late. "You don't have a battery charger, do you?" Maria asked.

"At home, sorry."

Maria's shoulders dropped; she looked down at the ground. "Why's everything going so wrong today?"

Nell put her hand on Maria's arm.

"Come on, it's not that bad, it's only a battery," she said, calmly. "All I can offer is a sofa, but I can make it comfortable for you. Or better, I will sleep on the sofa and you can use my bed. How about that?"

Maria felt scared. *I am exhausted. Where am I going to go now, looking for a hotel, in this state, in the middle of the night? After what happened, that kiss, damn it. But what else can I do?*

Maria looked at Nell again, as if she was checking her. *Are you reliable?*

As if reading her thoughts, Nell replied. "Don't worry, it's just spending a night on a sofa, I am the council officer on your project, I am not going to eat you or assault you, you'll be all right." She smiled.

Maria felt relieved. A few seconds later, she agreed. "Okay, let's go then. Where?"

"It won't take us long." Nell started walking in the cold night.

***

It was just past eleven at night when Jordi tried to call Maria several times from Barcelona's Airport arrivals gate, but he only found her voicemail.

I hope she will find a good hotel, my poor little baby, stuck in London tonight. I'll make sure she gets a grand reception tomorrow. Perhaps I could get her a little necklace instead of flowers? Maybe flowers aren't a surprise anymore.

77

Pere Gratallops came out through the national arrivals' gate with a small suitcase, looking tired and angry.

As usual, Jordi thought. *God help me be the opposite from him.*

"Hum," Jordi's father grunted as he met his son. "Where's Bernat? He can't do anything right, that boy. I have to talk to him."

"I don't know Father, he just said he couldn't make it," Jordi always tried to avoid conflict. "I am sure he had a valid excuse. Come on, let me take your luggage."

They walked to the parking lot in silence, until Jordi spoke.

"How come you arrived so late? These are strange hours for business on a Friday night," Jordi said. He had always suspected his father had love affairs outside his unhappy marriage. In fact, he would arrive late quite often, when Jordi knew nothing really pressing was happening at the Caves. His father was everything he wanted not to be. For years now, Jordi had longed for a happy, stable family with Maria.

"You know in Madrid, they take a three-hour lunchbreak so it all gets postponed," his father replied. "They are really a bunch of bureaucrats."

He raised his glance towards Oscar. "Why did I buy you that lovely Grand Cherokee with all leather inside if all you use is this little shitty Golf that's almost older than me?" the man said, entering into the car.

"I use the Cherokee all the time, Father," Jordi said. "I was meant to pick Maria from here as well tonight, you know we love this car."

"Where is Maria then, has she already arrived?"

"No, she got stuck in London, the last flight was cancelled because of the weather, she has to stay overnight, she'll be back tomorrow." Jordi sounded sad.

"Bah, what's a night?" his father said. "She'd better get used to nights apart." He sighed. "Son, we'd better speed up that London warehouse, we're going to need more sales from England soon, this boycott may get even worse."

And you haven't seen the latest numbers, thank God.

"What's going on?" Jordi asked. No need to give the poor old man more bad news. His father rarely was this pessimistic about business affairs.

"There's talk that the central government may now persuade the Basque minority to pass the national budget; they may not need the support of the Catalan party, and therefore we may not have as much help to stop the boycott as we think," he said. "But we have to be positive, the Basque minority are quite hard to deal with. Let's be positive."

He opened the window slightly and stretched his neck a bit to see the sky.

"How many stars today, how rare." He seemed to be in his own world.

Jordi knew that his father was a farmer at heart. In his youth, he cultivated the land himself and turned it into a big business. He admired his father's sense of work – the only thing he appreciated in the agnostic old man.

Pere Gratallops leaned back on his seat and looked at the icon of the Montserrat Virgin that Jordi had hanging from the rear mirror. "We may even need the help of the Virgin of Montserrat!" he joked.

"She can help us, Father, you know I believe she can," Jordi said.

His father sighed.

"Little I knew you would turn into such a Catholic when I brought you to that Opus school," he said, not sounding very happy. "Well, at least I should be happy they didn't catch you, that would be such a tragedy; you would end up giving the Caves to them. They suck everything one has." The old man laughed.

Jordi remained silent.

Father, please. Oh God, help me with this. And please bring me Maria back soon. I feel I am going to need her now more than ever.

***

Maria followed Nell out of the tube at Bethnal Green. They waited in silence outside the station until a 388 bus arrived, bound for Hackney. They completed the seven-minute journey in total silence. Maria's headache made her feel the pot-holes of the road more accutely.

After getting off at Cassland Road, Nell and Maria walked down a series of poorly lit streets and alleyways. Maria struggled to avoid tripping over the old mattresses, bins and bits of an abandoned car that littered their path.

Jesus, how did I end up here? Jordi…

Maria missed Jordi's warm hands and deep respect for her. The security that he always gave her. Maria looked from side to side then, back, over her shoulder, fearful that somebody might jump out and attack them.

"We're just round the corner," Nell said.

"Okay," Maria replied in a low tone, without meeting her eyes. She stopped for a second to light a cigarette. She then continued to walk with her head down, but came again to a halt when a rat darted across her path through a pool of lamplight. Maria closed her eyes, took a quick deep breath and continued walking at a faster pace.

This is too much. This is dangerous. How did I end up doing this? Was I that drunk? The warehouse isn't worth this. Is it really business I am here for? Have I just kissed a woman? How did that happen? A woman who lives in a place like this. Jesus. How am I going to get out of this one?

Her eyes became watery. Her feet barely cleared the ground as she walked. Maria had never been anywhere as grim as this, let alone been confronted by the repulsive rodents.

Maria shivered; the night was getting colder. "Are we nearly there?"

"It's just round the corner," Nell replied.

She stopped a few seconds later in front of a dark brick building, about four or five stories high. The front façade had graffiti all over and a bicycle on the rack nearby was missing its back wheel. The street was deserted; there was complete silence. Maria shrugged her shoulders, looked around.

"Welcome home," Nell smiled.

Ugh.

Maria followed Nell up four floors; the smell of urine got stronger the higher they got. Maria felt as if she was going to be sick.

"Sorry about the smell," Nell said embarrassed, even without seeing the look of repugnance on Maria's face. "Some people here are disgusting, but most are all right."

"Not a problem," Maria said, trying to keep her nerve.

Nell looked at her with a raised eyebrow. "You are such a bad liar."

The two laughed, finally releasing some tension, though Maria's laugh was still a little nervous. Maria felt sad and lonely, cold, tired and lost. *I want my bed, my goose-feather duvet, Bombillo.* She tried to be rational. *This is only for one night.*

"Well, this is it," Nell said as they arrived on the fifth and final floor.

She opened the door and was immediately greeted by a shiny, short-haired black cat, which reminded Maria of Bombillo, of home.

"Pepa! Hello Pepa, how are you?" Nell gave the little cat a cuddle, then turned to Maria, noticing her sad face. She stood up and touched Maria's shoulder.

"Are you all right?"

"Yes, yes, I am really tired, maybe I should just go to bed." She took a deep breath. "Why do you call your cat 'Pepa'?" she said, making an effort.

Nell looked at Maria for a few seconds.

"Please make yourself at home. I'll hang your coat up if you'd like," Nell said. She opened a nearby cupboard to take out a pair of fluffy slippers, which she placed by Maria's feet. "I am sure you'll feel more comfortable now."

Maria looked at the pair of brown, winter, bushy slippers on the wooden floor. *This feels good.* The slippers reminded her of Gran's, she would always have a pair ready for her at the entrance of her little cottage in Belchite.

Maria started to feel more relaxed and looked at the photos in the entrance hall, all of young people, smiling, dancing, playing guitars, football. She could recognise some faces from the party.

She has so many friends.

"Why do you call your cat Pepa?" she asked again. "That's a Spanish name."

"I know," Nell said. "My dad won the lottery one year – only a few hundred pounds – and we went on holiday in Spain, it was quite an extraordinary thing to do, back then." Nell smiled, she continued. "I was five or six and the lady who rented the apartment to us, somewhere near Málaga, had a cat called Pepa. We loved her, her food and her cat so much that when I got a cat in London a few years ago, I just wanted to give her the same name."

Aw. Maria gave her a genuine smile.

"Come on in," Nell said, walking into the living room, switching the lights on. "Please have a seat. I'm just going to get comfy. Can I get you something to wear, a jumper or something like that?"

"If it's not too much trouble."

"I have some tracksuit bottoms that will fit you." Nell walked into her bedroom.

Maria looked around. She liked the dark wooden floors, matching the cream walls and the hall's Japanese-style lamp. *The flat feels definitely better than I expected, but God, I wouldn't live in this neighbourhood for a second.*

"Have you lived here for a long time?" Maria asked in a loud voice so Nell could hear from the bedroom.

"Yeah, about three years, I love this place."

The main room felt cosy. It had a big brown sofa with black and white cushions on each side, with an L-shaped corner unit that looked inviting. Nell had some plants by the window and, on the oak table, a vase with tall white lilies that filled the room with their scent. Maria perched on the sofa.

I like the colours, they are warm. This woman is cold outside but warm inside – at least her flat. Maria sat back. She turned and surveyed the books on the shelves. She saw a few by someone called Sarah Waters and Germaine Greer – *who?* Simone de Beauvoir, Sartre, Camus, The Communist Manifesto, New Labour, The Anarchists, Che Guevara: A Life.

What a radical! I'd better keep the Margaret Thatcher memoirs that I am reading inside my handbag.

"Are you hungry?" Nell shouted, still from the bedroom.

"Not really, thanks."

"I am, I'm going to make myself some soup, would you mind?"

The English are so polite. "Of course I don't mind." *You don't have to ask me permission to cook in your own home.*

"Well, I'll make it; anyway, you are more than welcome to have some if you change your mind," Nell came out of the bedroom in some red pajamas and a navy blue, tight, jumper that, Maria noticed, set off the blue of her eyes.

"You've discovered my favourite spot in the world," she said. "I love that corner on the sofa. I paid a fortune, but it's worth every penny of it."

"Very comfortable, indeed." Maria didn't know where to look, up to the ceiling, to the lilies, to the floor. She scratched the back of her ear. *And now, what do we do?*

"Oh, your clothes, sorry, I forgot, let me go and get them," Nell walked back into her bedroom. She came back with some old jogging trousers and a green top. "I hope they're OK. The bathroom is just there if you want to use it," she pointed towards a door at the back of the room.

What a small bathroom, Maria thought as she changed. *And these clothes, so baggy. She has no re-hydration creams, and she uses cheap shampoo and bath gel. The towels are hard and small. But the living-room is stylish and the cat is lovely. I shall just go to bed.* Maria's body shook a bit as she pulled on the trousers. *Keep calm.* She put the slippers back on and looked at herself at the mirror.

How awful.

Feeling ridiculous in the ill-fitting, borrowed clothes, Maria made an effort and, thinking she would be back in Barcelona in just a few hours, she walked back into the living-room. The lovely smell of fried tomatoes and garlic helped her feel better.

"Mmm, that smells good, what is it?" She walked into the small kitchen.

"I'm just cooking one of Jamie Oliver's soups."

"Whose soup?"

"Jamie Oliver."

"Who?"

"Jamie Oliver?" Nell looked at Maria, stirring the food at the same time. "He is a TV chef. I thought they showed his programmes all over the world."

"Well, not in Spain, but anyway, how do you see him, if you don't have a television?"

"Yes, well spotted, I don't have one, but he's everywhere, he has written books, he's on ads in the street, everywhere." Nell looked at Maria in her baggy trousers.

She's too polite to say how horrible I look, Maria thought.

Nell quickly washed the herb masher and put it back into one of the cupboards. "Anyway, he does really simple and quick recipes. See, I just mashed tomatoes, basil, garlic, some spinach, chickpeas and VOILÀ! Pesto. Try some," she offered a teaspoon to Maria, who didn't think twice and tested it.

"Lovely, maybe you could add some *jamón*? It would give it more taste."

"*Jamón*? I'm a vegetarian, I'm afraid."

"Really? Don't you eat meat at all? Wow."

Maria, who grew up on lamb, cow and pig steaks, found it hard to believe in the benefits of being a vegetarian. *That's why she's so white. Look at her, she's lovely, but so pale. If Mama, Gran and Soledad saw her, they wouldn't leave her in peace until she'd eaten a cow.*

"Yes, I haven't eaten meat in years and I'm quite all right, I think." Nell smiled.

"Good Lord. You wouldn't be able to live in the little village where I come from, it's all meat."

"I know, things in Spain are quite different, I remember from my holidays there. I feel sick when I remember the pigs' heads hanging in the butchers' shops. Ugh."

Jesus, if she saw my family's fiesta of the matanza – or the pig's slaughter – she'd die.

Maria didn't like that day herself, held every first Saturday in December, although it was her mother's favourite. The family got together to slaughter a pig to make *morcillas* and *chorizos* for the winter. Maria had never enjoyed the ambiance of her mother's kitchen; she was always moving around fast and shouting. She preferred her grandmother's, quiet and full of character. And, mainly, warm. Maria loved, and missed, the domestic intimacy of a peaceful kitchen, like Gran's, like Nell's, she thought.

I will go to see Gran as soon as I can, she resolved.

Maria, Nell and Pepa sat on the sofa. Nell stood up to put on some of her favourite world music, some African 'chill'.

"Are you OK?" Nell sat down and briefly rubbed Maria's lower back.

"Yes." Maria sounded short, although she welcomed the gesture. *Her hand is warm; it feels wonderful in my back, so gentle.* Maria thought of her schoolfriend, the one she used to spend her days with, and shared her teenage secrets at night, often in the same bed, where they caressed each other, innocently.

Maria's eyes were half closed; she was reliving those moments. She cried for days when her friend's father got a job in Madrid and the family left, when the two girls were about fifteen. Unfortunately, they hadn't stayed in touch.

"Are you sure you don't want any soup?" Nell said.

"No thank you, I am not very hungry, just tired."

"Okay, let's go to bed in a minute, as soon as I finish this. I'm also very tired, it's been a long day."

Very long.

They sat in silence. Maria felt her face blush as she remembered the kiss at the pub until the ceussonal.

The dark, square figure of her mother suddenly came in to her mind, with her angular features, her tight lips and penetrating glance. Mama wanted, more than anything, for her to be strong and independent. Unlike Pilar, Maria felt her mother never allowed her a break. Some of the words that her mother used to tell her off as a child still resounded inside her head: "You are going to get all dirty if you play 'Moors against Christians' with the boys and will embarrass all the family in church. After all the time I spend hand-washing and ironing your beautiful dresses and look, this is what you go and do to me, after such hard work." Or: "Go to England to study? Don't you know the crops haven't been much good at all? Would you stay abroad, having fun, while the rest of the family stays here, working hard for you, while you're God-knows-where doing God-knows-what?" Or: "If you aren't good God will punish you, as he did with your grandmother. You're old enough to be responsible."

Mothers are such powerful figures.

"All done," Nell dropped the spoon and returned the bowl to the kitchen. "You can sleep in my bed, I'll stay in the sofa."

"No way, this is your home, you sleep in your room. I'll be fine here," Maria said.

Nell reached up, opened a cupboard and took down some clean sheets.

She pulled the sofa a bit and the two women prepared the bed in silence.

"All ready, *señorita*," Nell smiled and looked down, she seemed embarrassed. "I know what happened in the party is a bit awkward."

"We must forget immediately about what happened in the party," Maria said quickly, without looking at Nell.

"All right," Nell said.

"Good night."

Nell left the room and shut her bedroom door behind her. Maria took a big, deep breath, got into the sofa-bed and hugged the pillow.

A few seconds later, Nell came back.

"If you are worried about the warehouse and the fact that I am a lesbian, please don't, you're really not my type." Nell spoke with conviction from the bedroom door.

Maria stared at Nell, surprised. "Why is that?"

Nell turned the living-room light on and looked at Maria for a few seconds: "You're too conservative and a bit dodgy," Nell said with a sarcastic smile.

"What?" Maria opened her eyes. Her appreciation of British humour, as yet, lacking.

"I prefer them blond and a bit more trendy," Nell smiled. "No offence, though, I think you're wonderful. Good night." Nell turned towards her room.

"Am I not trendy?" Maria asked, still wondering what was going on.

"That bag, did you borrow it from your grandmother?" Nell joked, until she noticed Maria's frown.

"Don't you ever dare make fun of my grandmother, or I'll…"

Nell walked towards Maria and gently put her hand on her shoulder. "I am only joking," she said calmly.

Maria relaxed and tucked herself under the blanket.

"Have a nice rest," Nell said, slowly moving back towards her bedroom, switching the living-room lights off. Then she stopped for a second and turned towards Maria. "I don't do this very often, by the way."

Maria felt less intimidated in the absence of light. "Really?"

"Really." Nell said. "I think I just got carried away, maybe I also wanted to be naughty, sorry."

"Why?" Maria felt intrigued, and thankful for the honesty.

Nell took a deep breath. "I've just split up with my girlfriend."

"I'm sorry," Maria felt empathic. "I am really sorry."

Nell let a few seconds go by, she stared towards the corner and sighed: "I really don't want you to think that I am like *that*. It's not an excuse at all, I know, but my girlfriend cheated on me."

"I am so sorry." Maria didn't know what to say. "What an idiot."

"I'm better now, things weren't right anyway, so this is all probably for the best."

"Do you know the other woman?"

"She was my best friend, well, now I realise she wasn't, of course."

Poor Council officer. God, these lesbians – what a bitch. This is worse than in the straight world.

"But it's all right. She's not a good person, I don't want to be near her," Nell was looking down. "I'm really tired. Let's just forget it all and get a good night's sleep."

"Yes, let's forget it all," Maria said.

Nell looked at her for a few seconds.

"You must miss your boyfriend when travelling; it must be hard to do business abroad so often."

Maria appreciated the intimacy of Nell's revelations and felt like giving back the trust she had shown her.

"Very tiring, indeed," Maria said. "But I don't miss him at night because we don't sleep together, yet."

"You are getting married in six months and you don't sleep with your boyfriend?" Nell sounded shocked. "Why?"

"We're Catholics."

"Really? I've never heard of anybody doing that. But surely you've slept with other boyfriends, right?"

"Nope," Maria, still tucked in the sofa-bed, lowered her eyes. She felt an idiot.

I know I am a weirdo. And it's not by personal choice, believe me. "I think I need a good night's sleep now," was all she could muster.

Nell was still speechless. "Sure, good-night then," she said, gently closing the bedroom door.

Maria quickly checked her mobile, by now fully charged. Her assistant had sent her all the new details and Jordi had left her at least four messages, he sounded worried. But it was too late and she was too tired to respond. She closed her eyes. *What a night.* She fell asleep right away, holding tightly to a pillow.

88

The smell of tea and the feeling of something very near to her woke Maria the following day, a Saturday. She opened one eye and saw the winter sunshine outside the window, the light drifting in, making the room look more spacious than last night. Nell was sitting on the sofa-bed, with a cup of tea in her hand.

"Good morning, would you like some tea?" Nell said with a smile.

"Tea?" *Oh no. Tea, ugh. My kingdom for a coffee.* "Thank you," Maria held the cup and took a sip, burning her lips.

"Ouch! It's very hot!"

Nell took the cup and placed it on top of one of the books on the table, One Hundred Years of Solitude.

"Good read," Maria said looking at the old, library-borrowed paperback edition.

"I wish I could read it in Spanish, what are you reading?"

Maria let a few seconds go by. "Margaret Thatcher's memoirs."

"Arg!!" Nell shouted. "No way! She's a monster!"

Maria smiled. "Well, she has a lot to say…"

Nell quickly interrupted: "I wouldn't read them, not even if they paid me a million pounds."

"I would read anything for a million pounds, even THE COMMUNIST MANIFESTO," Maria said, giving the tea a second chance.

"Yes, you would do anything for money, wouldn't you?"

"What kind of question is that?"

"Sorry, it's just that you don't understand. Thatcher did some terrible things in this country, I could tell you loads…"

"I would love to, but I'm afraid I have a plane to catch. What time is it?"

"Eight-thirty, when's your flight?"

"At eleven. I should start to get going."

"All right. Would you like to have a bath or a shower? I'll get you a towel."

Nell switched on BBC Radio Four. There was a travel programme on about Cuba.

Maria tried another sip of the tea, now with less hostility.

"Have you been to Cuba?" Nell asked, handing her an old, brown towel.

"No, never, but I may have a grandfather there," Maria said.

"Really? Why in Cuba?"

"I don't know much, it's a sad family story," Maria got up, towel in hand.

"What happened?"

There's nothing wrong in telling her, I guess. "My grandma married a man, a worker employed at the family business. He basically got her pregnant, then abandoned her and stole most of the family money. The rumour is that he went to Cuba. But that's all I know, she never speaks about it. He could be dead."

"Oh no, how terrible!" Nell said. "Did she ever re-marry or find anybody else?"

"Nope, she just brought up my mother, who now wants all of us to marry rich people."

"How awful, is your grandmother happy now?"

"Well, she looks happy to me, with her cooking and her plants. She has Soledad, the teacher you saw on the telly, and my mother, my sister and me," Maria said.

"Do you get along well with her?"

Maria showed the biggest smile that Nell had seen so far in her. "Yes, very well," she said proudly, then looked through the window, still smiling. "My grandmother is the best thing in the world."

"What about your boyfriend?" Nell asked surprised. "I hope you're breaking the family history and marrying him for love?"

"Of course, of course," Maria said quickly. *Really?* A few seconds later she said: "What about you? Have you ever been to Cuba?" Maria didn't want to talk about Jordi – last night's memories were still too fresh.

"No, but some friends just returned a few weeks ago and they loved it, they said La Habana is beautifully derelict, unspoiled, genuine, edgy," Nell said.

"Yes, lovely, seen from the comfort of your own home," Maria said. "I bet you wouldn't like to live there so much, people are just struggling to eat."

"At least they all have access to better education and health services than here," Nell looked at Maria. "In the capitalist world only the rich get the best education and services."

Maria stopped drinking her tea and looked up in surprise. "Are you a socialist?"

"Of course!"

"Of course? Not everybody is a socialist."

"Well, they should be, there are still plenty of things in the world to change and fight for."

"Absolutely, freedom and food, primarily." Maria said. "It's very easy to be a socialist from the comfort and security of a wealthy country. Sitting in your heated home, with electricity and food on the table. You want the rest of the world not to have those things so it feels more exotic when you visit, because you're wealthy enough to do so. But Cubans are too poor to fly and they can't leave the island, anyway. Do you think that's exotic and genuine?"

Nell was just opening her mouth but Maria continued, quickly: "I really, really have to get going now. I can't miss that flight."

"We have to discuss this more, I have a lot to say!" Nell said defeated. "I understand you have to go. I'll cook you some breakfast, do you like scrambled eggs?"

"I love scrambled eggs," Maria smiled and went to have a shower.

They were the best eggs Maria had ever tasted. Nell served them on toast, covered with pepper and a touch of fennel. Maria cleared the plate in two minutes.

She packed her little bag, put on her shoes and left the slippers perfectly aligned, in a corner. *What wonderful slippers. I haven't felt I've been in a home, a proper home, for so long. This has been pleasant.* She took the document rolls under her arm.

91

"Thank you very much for your help and for letting me stay here," Maria said looking away, too shy to look Nell straight in the eye.

"My pleasure, thank you for coming," Nell said, gazing fully into Maria's face. She walked quickly towards the kitchen and came back, handing her a little piece of paper with her mobile phone number on it.

"Here's my number, call me if there's any problem," she said.

"Yes, I must go now," Maria said nervously, moving towards the front door. Nell, still in her slippers, followed her outside and gave her a hug and a short but sweet kiss on the lips.

On the lips.

"Thank you for everything, it has been nice to get to know you in person," Nell said. "I'll speak to you soon, about the warehouse."

God, I'd forgotten about the warehouse. "Yes, of course," Maria responded, avoiding her eyes.

"And about the Civil War!" Nell added. "I want to know more about Belchite!"

Maria smiled, turned and started walking, feeling very light. She turned back before she started down the stairs. Nell was looking at her; they waved.

Maria walked away, her lips closed and tight as if she wanted to keep Nell's kiss.

6

Conchita and Honorato hadn't slept together in years. Each occupied a different room on the second floor of the three-storey house just outside Belchite. Soledad's room, the biggest of all, was in the first floor, by the kitchen, so the ninety-year-old could avoid the stairs.

The house was usually dark and empty and in winter nights such as this one, also cold. Soledad was by far the one with more social life in the household, as she would go for a long, daily walk with grandma Basilisa and some evenings they attended a reading group meeting at the public library.

Conchita spent most of her time at the olive-oil factory, where she kept an office next to Pilar's, while Honorato seemed to live to go to the casino after retiring from the Spanish army a few years ago. He would still go about twice a week to the factory to check the company books, Tuesdays and Fridays, as he had done, without a miss, since he married Conchita, now thirty-seven years ago.

As usual Conchita was by herself, knitting in her armchair in the main room, listening to the ticking of the wall clock. Despite the wealth accumulated over the years, she kept an austere lifestyle, with the same oak furniture and religious paintings that she and Honorato received as wedding presents. The rest was in the bank, accruing good interest.

How superfluous to waste money on luxuries. Better to save for a rainy day. Was there any problem, I wouldn't be caught, like my mother was.

It was almost nine o'clock. She had just come back from feeding Pablito, the pig in the corral at the back of the garden that would be killed in the MATANZA. Soledad and Gran Basilisa were at a city hall meeting debating the opening of the Old Village and Honorato had said he would stay late at the casino's dominoes championships.

He's so useless. I wish he had paid our business the same attention he has paid cards and dominoes. He only cares about the books. Where would this house be without me?

Conchita turned the television on and was startled by a sex scene.

Ave María Purísima, she made the saint cross sign over her forehead, heart and shoulders, but still kept an eye on the images. She couldn't remember the last time she and Honorato had sex, many years ago. She wondered whether he would still be physically capable of it, not that she had any desire to get close to him. Her flame waned years ago.

She continued knitting that little jumper for the grandchild she hoped that Maria would give her after the wedding. Although she hoped they would be better raised than Pilar's children, who were rather noisy and spoiled. *They have everything these days. They should know what scarcity is.*

She looked at the jumper she was knitting. *I wonder why Pilar buys them clothes; they could dress only with what I could make them. What a waste.*

She sighed, and gently touched the white crochet work protecting the arms of her chair.

At least it's peaceful, she thought, focusing on the fast movement of her hands.

It only lasted a couple of minutes more.

"*Buenas noches*," Honorato said walking into the house. His tone sounded livelier than usual.

Conchita changed the television channel immediately, she didn't want him to think that she was watching pornography, although she was sure that's what he did when he was home alone.

Honorato walked into the living room and asked directly, as usual, "What's for dinner? I am so hungry." He never kissed Conchita as a greeting, or at any other time. He took his jacket off and loosened his tie.

"Soledad cooked some rabbit today and she left you some, we had some a short while ago, it may still be warm," Conchita said, barely lifting her eyes from her knitting. She didn't move from her armchair.

"Good, I like rabbit, did Soledad cook it? It must be the first time she has cooked in years," he said.

Honorato and Soledad never got along, one being a former Franco officer and the other a fierce Republican, there was little to do to bring them close. She stopped trying many years ago and came to the conclusion that imposing silence was the best way to keep peace. Nobody was allowed to discuss politics, money or religion at home, at least in front of her. It had already created too many family upsets between Maria, Honorato, Gran Basilisa and Soledad, all of them people of strong opinions.

"Have some respect for Soledad, Honorato, she is good to us," Conchita threatened. *And look who's talking, when's the last time you did anything apart from playing dominoes and crunch a few numbers?*

"Where is she, anyway? Is she already in bed?" Honorato asked, as it was unusual for Soledad not to be at home at that time.

"She went with my mother to a debate in the city hall about the Old Village."

"Ah, that's what she's good at, stirring up trouble, and drawing your mother into it," Honorato said, leaving towards the kitchen for his rabbit. "They shouldn't get into these things, at that age. Plus, Franco already settled all this. I don't know what they're debating. It's all ancient history."

Conchita rolled her eyes and thanked God that Gran Basilisa and Soledad were not there to hear him. *Better not answer.* She sighed and continued knitting.

This family is still together thanks to my endless patience. I am a martyr.

A few minutes later, Honorato was watching the news, eating his meal in silence. He had changed the channel without asking Conchita.

"By the way, I have been thinking about that French machine that Pilar is buying," he said, dropping his fork and knife once he'd eaten his last bite.

Conchita raised an eyebrow.

"I went to the bank and the director said we'd be better off opening a new account to hold the loan, we could save interest," Honorato said. "He said he would talk to you."

The two shared business matters regularly, but surprisingly to Conchita, Honorato's interest had gone beyond finances this time and he had been quite keen on the French equipment over the past few weeks. Pilar had told her that he had helped her choose the model and got involved in the project because she had recently stayed home as her children had been ill.

Maybe he's bored with just doing the books, I don't blame him.

Conchita knew all that there was to know about olive oil and the trees but, since the day they married, she left the accounts and legal matters to Honorato as she found them difficult to deal with, and boring. To her, the company was outside, in the trees, in the olives, not in the books.

"Yes, I popped into the bank this afternoon and he did mention it," Conchita responded. "Are you sure about it? It sounded good to me, but better having a second opinion."

"Yes, it sounds the best thing to do," Honorato said convincingly. "As a matter of fact, since I was there, he gave me the paperwork, so if we get it done here, you won't have to go, queue and go through it all, if you want."

Honorato stood up and brought a little folder from his suitcase, taking some documents from it.

Conchita looked at her husband, slightly surprised at his enthusiasm.

"You've taken quite a bit of interest in this machine, haven't you?" she asked, still knitting.

"Yes, I've been reading about it quite a bit," he said. "You'll see how much quicker we'll be able to pick up the olives, it will be done in days, if not hours."

Honorato left the documents on the telephone table, by Conchita's armchair, with a pen on them.

"There you go," he said calmly. "It's fairly straightforward, I am glad banks are improving all the small print, it used to take so long."

He walked out of the room, he usually put his slippers on and removed his tie after his meal.

Conchita, glad that she didn't have to go to the bank herself to sort it out, took the documents and read them through. They were indeed rather short and straightforward. Everything seemed in place. She thought for a couple of seconds, signed them and left them on the table, by the telephone.

She carried on with her knitting.

I may have just signed the end of an era, Conchita thought, stopping her knitting and staring through the window, to the black night outside. *That French machine will make the stones that my mother used look ancient; I hope they don't change the oil's flavour.*

It was only yesterday when I took that loan, when I begged for it, to buy the German machine. And now look, the loan comes to me.

"Life!" Conchita whispered.

Soledad and Gran Basilisa walked into the house a few minutes later.

"*HOLA!*" They both sounded cheerful.

Thank the Lord Soledad is still with us. Without her, this house would be like a funeral home.

Conchita stood up and kissed her mother and Soledad as they took off their coats in the hall.

"Hello you two, isn't this quite late?" Conchita asked Soledad with a smile. She gave a quick glance at her mother, whom she didn't dare tell off for staying out late.

"We are big girls, don't you worry," Soledad replied, kissing Conchita back.

"It's only nine thirty," Gran Basilisa said, walking towards the living-room. "They were still going on and on by the time we left, who knows what will happen." She sat on the sofa, looking tired.

"Come here, darling," Conchita said walking into the kitchen with Soledad. "Let me prepare your green tea and I'll make one for my mother as well."

Every night, Conchita made Soledad a cup of tea, following the local doctor's instructions. It was life the other way around, as it was Soledad who gave Conchita a hot glass of milk every night, when she was a child. Soledad took care of Conchita while her mother, risking her own life, went to the mill in the middle of the night to exchange olives for bread to feed the three women. It was the time of rationing and Gran Basilisa only got one allocation – Franco's regime didn't recognise her child because she didn't legally have a father, and since Soledad was hiding in the mountains far away, officially, she didn't exist.

When Soledad managed to fool the *Guardia Civil* and make it to Belchite – she even dressed as a priest once – she would tuck little Conchita up in bed, with the milk that she got after stealing a goat in the mountains. She told young Conchita exciting and sweet bedtime stories about a fantasy, wonderful world that never became real. Still, those nights with Soledad sitting next to her in bed, giving her security and comfort, were Conchita's happiest memories, ever.

The three women sat talking about the cold weather when Honorato walked into the living room to say good-night. They all looked him up and down, head to toe.

"I feel tired, too long at those dominoes championships today," he said, standing by the door. Soledad and Gran Basilisa looked at him skeptically. "Believe it or not, but all morning and afternoon in that casino full of people gets my brains a bit." He laughed, nervously.

"Try going and pick olives all day, you'll feel relieved just to be sitting in a casino," Gran Basilisa said, before having another sip of tea.

Mother, let's not have it today, it's too late, Conchita thought. *She's never liked him.*

"Luckily, we have machines for that today," Honorato quickly answered. "Wait to see the new French one that we're buying. We'll pick the olives in no time, you'll see," he said triumphantly.

"Nothing will ever replace the quality of hand picking," Gran Basilisa started saying, when Soledad interrupted.

"You were not in the casino this morning, I saw you parking the car in the garage." She drank some tea.

"I spent all day in the casino," Honorato reiterated. "You must have seen somebody else. Remember you're ninety, Soledad." He turned again and started walking towards his room.

"I am sure it was you, around ten o'clock in the morning," Soledad insisted as Honorato started walking out of the room.

Conchita looked at the two without knowing what to think, although it was not unusual to see them contradict each other.

Honorato turned back. "You are right Soledad; I must be the one who's getting old. I took the car for a quick service this morning, I noticed the other day the wheels needed some air."

Conchita didn't know what she was most astonished by: Soledad's accusation or Honorato's acknowledgement of a mistake.

Her husband looked at the three women and smiled. "Good-night then."

None of them replied. Conchita carried on with her knitting.

Soledad waited to hear Honorato's door being shut to whisper: "Watch him Conchita, watch. Never forget on which side of the War he was."

It was not the first time that Soledad made comments like this.

"Please Soledad, your head is full of stories, the War is over and Franco is long gone," Conchita said.

Gran Basilisa was looking at the two in silence.

"Franco is gone, but his spirit is still alive, through people like him!" Soledad was now getting nervous, her hands shaking slightly; the tea almost spilling from the cup.

"Soledad, please, calm down," Conchita didn't want an argument and the doctor had recommended she keep calm.

"Drink your tea, you know he's harmless. I know he's a bit odd sometimes, but we've been together for almost forty years, I know him like the back of my own hand."

"You know what he's capable of," Soledad said, in a warning tone.

"Soledad, enough!" Conchita hit the armchair with her fists, dropping the knitting basket on the floor. She didn't like being reminded of the time she was cheated.

"Sorry, I just want to protect you," Soledad said.

"I am a big girl, don't worry." Conchita's cheeks started to grow redder by the second.

"What is in the past should be kept there," Gran Basilisa said with solemnity. "Nobody has an immaculate record, this is no time to wake the dead." She looked down.

Nobody indeed, Conchita though, thinking of her mother. She slowly picked up the knitting basket.

Soledad finished her tea. "Maybe I am getting old and have my head full of stories." With effort, she stood up. "Anyway, how's Maria, is she still in London?"

"Yes," Conchita said, relieved at the change of subject. "She should have come back yesterday, she said she would go and see some wedding dresses today, let's see how this goes. Only five months to the wedding and still no dress. My God."

Soledad smiled. "Leave her alone, she'll be fine, I am sure." Soledad walked towards the door. "I am feeling a bit tired, I am going to bed, Basilisa, darling, are you staying for a bit more?"

"Yes, I'll just finish my tea," Gran Basilisa answered, and with a sweet smile to her lifelong friend, she wished her good night.

Soledad left the room, leaving Conchita and her mother in silence, listening to the ticking of the clock. Gran Basilisa excused herself to use the bathroom, leaving Conchita sitting uptight in her armchair. She could still hear Soledad's words in her head. Honorato had indeed been capable of the worst, now many years ago.

He's paid for it now, Conchita thought. *I've made him pay for his cheating during all these years, I shouldn't stir this up.*

However, it still hurt Conchita to think about the youngster with whom Honorato had an affair about fifteen years ago, when her daughters were just into their teens. The idiot left traces all over, different perfume, incoherent alibis, it didn't take her long to find out, and even less for the rest of the village, where news travelled fast.

Ever since, she had become a block of ice to him, and denied him the divorce that he asked for because it would have allowed him access to half of her money. She knew she paid with her happiness for the mistake of having married him.

It's fate, isn't it? One has to be resigned and accept it. Our Lord said we're only here to suffer, happiness is reserved for heaven.

Conchita remembered as if it was yesterday how her classmates, when she was ten and she and her mother had spent two weeks knitting seven lovely dresses for a school function, had looked at the dresses with disdain, and literally thrown them back at her saying they were immodest because they didn't have sleeves. They said she was as much of a whore as her mother.

Conchita swallowed at the memory as Gran Basilisa came back into the room.

"Oh dear, what a long day," she sat down again on the sofa and looked at her daughter. "I just wanted to say that I think Soledad is right, you should keep an eye on Honorato, Conchita. He did it once, he could do it again."

Just what I need. Conchita took a deep breath. "You two are too full of suspicions all the time," she answered. *Old people have the crookedest thoughts. What can she say about being careful after what happened to her?* "Everything's fine, he's too old to cheat on me again, don't worry. And he's taking some responsibilities now, he's quite involved, sorting out a new account for the loan, for the French machine. He's doing everything, I just had to sign the documents."

"What have you signed?" Gran Basilisa asked with interest.

"Just to set a new account to hold the loan for the machine," Conchita said, and quickly tried to change the subject. She didn't want to talk about her husband with Basilisa, perhaps because

101

she knew that her mother could see through her. Conchita put the knitting basket on her knees and carried on with the little jumper.

"Mother, look what I am doing for my new – I hope – grandchild," she said without stopping the knitting. "I can't wait for Maria to bring us a child."

It worked.

Gran Basilisa smiled, with relief. "Ah, let's hope Maria gives us some good news soon after the wedding." She smiled. "Any word about the honeymoon?"

Conchita's smile was now more prolonged. "Yes, well, Maria wants to go on some sort of adventure trail, you know her, somewhere like a safari in Africa, or something like that."

"*Ave María Purísima*," Gran Basilisa said. "I hope they aren't killed by lions or elephants. What does Jordi say?"

Conchita looked up from her knitting. "Well, he wants – you know him – something more classic, like Paris or Rome. Let's see who wins!"

Gran Basilisa stood quiet for a while. "These two don't really have much in common, do they?"

Conchita raised her eyebrow. "What do you mean mother? They are the perfect couple." She continued her knitting. "He's such a handsome young gentleman, and heir to an empire much, much bigger than ours. Well, that is if Maria was to bother about the olive-oil company at all. Still, she has a wonderful career, she's doing so well as a banker. And they both just look good, they have *class*."

"That doesn't make them love each other," Gran said, looking down.

Conchita looked down as well. *And what can you say about love, Mother? Are you saying this to me because of what you just said about Honorato? At least I have kept the family together, and so will Maria. Unlike you.*

"They love each other, I can see it in their eyes. I am sure they will form a lovely, stable family for many years, helping each other," Conchita replied, looking at her mother, distantly. "Don't you think so, *Mother*?"

Conchita looked at her mother's round, wrinkled face, with big blue eyes and soft skin. So unlike her own angular, brown, face and her deep, black eyes. *Maybe I look like my father. If only I knew who he was. Did he really go to Cuba as she once told me? He must be dead by now, I am sure.* Conchita thought of the nuns at school, who made her be a servant of the girls in the class belonging to the wealthiest families, just because she had a single mother. She had to let the others walk in first into the class, and only then was she allowed in, forced to sit in the back row. She was also often asked to clean the room and wash the dishes after meals.

My children have a proper family. Conchita raised her chin and, involuntarily, from the depths of her heart, gave her mother a threatening look.

"Yes, I am sure they will be happy," Gran Basilisa said. She sounded sad, touché.

Oh no, she's noticed it. Now I feel bad for the poor thing.

"Come on Mother, it's getting a bit late for you, isn't it?" Conchita stood up and walked towards her mother to help her get ready.

"Yes, I guess I should be going home," Gran Basilisa said, leaving her tea on the table and standing up.

The two women walked in silence towards the door. They kissed each other good-night, in the air, missing their cheeks. From the kitchen window, Conchita saw her mother walk towards the little cottage she owned by the church, where she moved after Pilar and Maria were born. Conchita understood it now. *I too would love to have my own little home and leave all these problems behind.*

Conchita sat again, with her knitting. Her mother was right, though, Honorato hadn't turned out a tiny piece of the man he promised to be. When they met, the then officer of the Spanish army was tall and strong, looking confident, capable of sorting any problem. It was a good match, they thought, as he brought some money and a couple of mules to help mother and daughter with the olive-oil factory, giving the man a real business for his capital investment.

Life, however, had made him lazy. He had left all the care of the house, the children and the business to his wife, only keeping responsibility for the books, which didn't need more than one or two afternoons per week. He liked to own good cars and spend money in the casino, with his friends, enjoying some comforts that not even Conchita allowed herself.

Mothers are always righ., why?

She had a warning as early as the first day, when he forgot to take the wedding certificate from the church where they married, making them drive back to Belchite on their wedding night as the hotel they had booked – and saved so much for – in Jaca wouldn't let them in without it. They ended up in a cheap pension on the road outside Belchite.

That first night, Honorato, selfishly, turned his back to Conchita after consummating the marriage, without giving her any chance of knowing pleasure for the first time. This scene would be repeated during the following years time after time. Excuses would vary from 'I am tired,' to 'there's something really important on the radio.' Conchita could count on the fingers of two hands how many times she had felt satisfied in thirty-seven years of marriage.

Maybe mothers have a sixth sense. I am sure I am also right now about Pilar and Maria. I was right to make Pilar break up with that MR Nobody that she would have killed herself for when she was a teenager, even if it broke her heart. He is now a butcher – my own daughter with a butcher! She's so much better off now with the pharmacist. Same goes for Maria. Life will teach them sooner or later that I am right.

Maybe it's not strictly happiness what Pilar has with her husband. But at least she's safe. Like Maria, she'll be all right with Jordi, he is of a good breeding, he won't disappoint her. What is happiness if not an illusion? At the end of the day, this is not about being happy, but about avoiding unhappiness, trauma and humiliation. Jordi looks like a good match for Maria. At least he's rich; he won't need to steal her money, like my father did. She will learn.

Conchita continued knitting the little jumper. It was pink.

Maybe this little one will have all the luck that this family has missed during three generations.

7

Phew, my life back.

Maria unbuckled her seatbelt as the Iberia flight 4532 to Barcelona stabilised in the air, a few minutes after taking off from Heathrow. Maria loved flying, it made her see life in perspective, she loved seeing things from above. The big roads, with all the little people furious at traffic jams, just seemed a minor nuisance when seen from the clouds. Like so many things in life, they became pygmies when put in perspective, she thought.

If I could only see things this clearly.

She sighed and opened *¡HOLA!* magazine, flicking through the pages, without managing to concentrate. The Duchess of Alba's second granddaughter celebrates her birthday; another multi-million dollar Hollywood divorce. Bored, Maria looked through the window and Nell's face floated into her mind.

Why did I let her kiss me?

Maria moistened her lips. She could still feel Nell's. She opened them a bit, as if she was going to be kissed again. She also felt Nell's short goodbye kiss. She stayed this way for a few minutes, just listening to the constant run-run of the engines. She felt warm, excited, and mostly confused.

How instinctively we kissed. Too instinctively.

"Ouch!" Maria said when one of the Iberia air hostess threw the lunch tray down on her table, almost dropping it in Maria's knees.

"Be careful!" Maria complained.

"There's not enough space, these days, not even here, in business class," the air hostess complained, without apologising.

Iberia will never change. So rude.

Maria looked back through the window, leaving the unattractively dry chicken breast untouched. She wasn't feeling hungry and preferred to be back in mental limbo, up in her fantasy, unthreatening world. She remembered Nell's scrambled eggs. Who could eat airline food after that?

She looked through the window and sighed again. She was going back to Spain, to Jordi, to her family. Her heart sank.

Maria hated going home, there would always be the classic row with her mother, who would always find something to pick on Maria: 'You have put on weight; you are too thin; you are late; you don't talk enough; you work too much; you work too little.'

There was always something wrong.

Maria usually drove back home on Sundays swearing she wouldn't return to Belchite for a long time. But she always did, mainly to see Gran and Soledad.

She picked up *¡HOLA!* magazine again. The photos of some aristocratic family reminded her of Goya's THE FAMILY OF CHARLES IV. To highlight the decline of the Spanish Empire, the maestro had painted them short, fat and unfocused. Maria loved Goya and his dark realism, sometimes she felt her family had been taken from one of his canvases.

Maria closed her eyes; Nell was all she could see in her mind.

Making an effort to forget about the previous night, Maria picked up a copy of THE GUARDIAN that somebody had left in the seat next to her. She hadn't noticed, but a young, red-haired woman had moved to the aisle seat in her row and was stretching her neck to see their arrival in Barcelona. Maria smiled.

"Is this yours? Can I take it?" Maria asked, pointing at THE GUARDIAN.

"Of course. It's all yours," the woman responded, kindly. She stretched her neck even more to see how the plane turned into the sea, the big loop it always does when flying in from the north to land at Barcelona's El Prat airport.

"It just seems like we're going to land in the sea, doesn't it?" The woman seemed excited.

"Yes. Have you never been here before?"

"No, never. I'm here for a conference, first time," she said. "Look! The *Sagrada Família*!" she pointed at Gaudí's famous building, which could be seen in all its splendour under the big, blue, sunny sky.

"You're right," Maria looked at the woman, whose eyes were wide open. "Would you like the window seat? You'll see it much better from here."

"Oh, no, that's fine, thank you," the woman said, flushing slightly.

They are so polite; Maria thought as she stood up and invited the woman to swap positions. While her neighbour had her nose literally touching the window, looking outside, Maria scanned through the pages of THE GUARDIAN, probably for the first time in her life. She suddenly stopped.

"First Lesbian Wedding in South Dakota," read the headline. "Washington, Nov. 12 (Associated Press) – Caroline A. Adams and Leslie M. Lerude became the first ever female couple to marry in South Dakota, traditionally one of the states more fiercely opposed to same-sex unions. Along with Wyoming and Utah, South Dakota approved gay marriage in Sunday's elections, following a multi-million dollar pro-gay rights campaign led by activist groups throughout the country. About seven percent of the US population is gay and sex between two women has increased six-fold over the past ten years, the latest U.S. census data shows."

Maria looked at the photo: Leslie and Caroline were kissing, just as she and Nell had kissed the day before. Once again, she felt Nell's lips against hers. She gave the photo her full attention.

How do they know? How can they be so sure?

The Boeing 777 touched down in Barcelona. A few minutes later, people started to move but Maria kept her seat, used as she was to the ten-minute wait until the airport staff managed to get the stair to the runway where the jet was parked.

The red-haired woman saw the newspaper opened on the page of the women's wedding.

"That's great, isn't it?" she said with a smile.

Maria didn't want a conversation about the subject as all the people waiting in the aisle could hear them.

"The *Sagrada Família* you mean?" Maria said. "It's lovely."

"Oh that as well, very impressive," the woman said smiling. "I meant those two women, it's about time!"

"I guess so," Maria said. *Why shouldn't they be allowed to marry?* Not that she had ever thought about it, but she couldn't think of any reason to forbid gay unions.

The woman looked at Maria's reflexive posture. "Let them wed! What harm are they doing to anybody?"

"True," Maria said.

The luggage belt Maria had been waiting to move for about ten minutes finally made a noise and started circulating for about two seconds. Then it stopped again, and it wouldn't move for a while because of the baggage handlers' strike. She lit a cigarette, no matter that smoking had been forbidden at the airport for years. A policeman nearby, who was reading *MARCA*, Spain's best-selling sports newspaper, saw her and winked. He put on his sunglasses, leaned against a pillar and continued his reading.

I love Spain.

Maria kept looking at the belt.

Obviously I can't tell Jordi what happened. What am I going to tell Andreu about the warehouse? I have to make another trip and look for more sites. I will have to see Nell again.

The siren went on. The belt started to move, turning for several minutes, but with no suitcases coming out.

Some things never change.

Maria, who always tried to put make-up on and look pretty before seeing Jordi, hadn't done so this time. She felt lost, sad and lonely. And hungover.

I'll just go home to Bombillo.

The suitcases started to appear, Maria stared at them, until she remembered she hadn't checked in anything. It was all supposed to be a one-day trip, although now it seemed ages since she had left Barcelona, just the day before.

Where's my head?

Holding the paper rolls with some difficulty, Maria walked towards the gate; just before crossing the doors to the airport's main hall, she saw Jordi, waiting for her.

There he is. What am I going to say? Always so well dressed, hiding the usual rose behind his back. But that's why I like him so much. He's so safe and reliable. Look at him, like a little soldier, always there waiting. What am I thinking of? How could I ever question somebody as lovely and reliable as him? He will never leave me or have an affair. Maybe this is all just the typical nerves ahead of the wedding. It must be.

Maria smiled and passed through the gate. Jordi immediately saw her and smiled, waved with one arm, hiding the rose behind his back with the other.

"Hello darling," Jordi smiled and handed her the red rose. He gently kissed her lips, which she kept tightly closed. *How different it feels.*

"Hello Jordi," Maria took the rose, without a smile. "I am so tired. How are you?"

"Good, good, so glad to see you! What a shame you couldn't come last night, I missed you so much," he said, from the bottom of his heart. "I am glad you found a good hotel, I was worried until you called me today from the airport."

Maria hated lying – she had told him she had spent the night at a central Hilton hotel. She looked down and started walking towards the parking lot. "You should have seen the weather, it was horrible," she said trying to change the subject. "I don't understand how anybody can live like that, so depressing."

"I know, there's nothing like Barcelona, eh?" Jordi said happily. "It couldn't be a better day, you are here, Barça is playing tonight, who could ask for anything more?" Jordi's face was illuminated. "You are still on time if you want to come along, I got an extra ticket because my father's friend can't make it, can you believe it?" he said, proudly.

"Oh darling, you know it's not really my thing, sorry."

"But a Barça-Madrid match is about so much more than football, you know," Jordi said. "And we could have a lovely evening, we could go for a romantic meal before, and have a chat, I haven't seen you all week."

Maria spotted his begging eyes, but still she couldn't face him. *I need time.*

"I am just very tired darling, sorry." She felt guilty. She knew this hurt him.

Jordi looked disappointed, although he was still making an effort as they reached the car.

"Would you prefer to go to my mom and dad's for lunch or anywhere else darling?" Jordi asked as he started Oscar. "I just have a quick meeting with a supplier in one hour; I'll be done soon. It would be lovely just to spend some time with you, this has been such a long week. And I'd like to hear all about your business in London. I am sure you're doing so well."

No, no, I don't want to spend my youth at my in-laws, talking about business most of the time. In London people looked so cool, so young, doing their own things like Nell's party, with her friends. I just feel like going home. I need to see Bombillo.

"I think I'd rather go home if that's all right with you." Maria was looking down. "I feel exhausted."

"Are you sure you are okay darling?" Jordi looked at her as he drove. "I thought you would be hungry or would like to go for a walk or something, we can do anything you'd like after that meeting, I am sure it won't take more than half an hour. I am all yours."

Oh Jordi please, don't make this more difficult.

"I am all right, I just feel like going home, you know, I think my time of the month is round the corner and I am a bit edgy, sorry darling," Maria lied. That excuse never failed.

"Ah," Jordi said, resigned. "I'll leave you to it then, I understand." He held her hand, then turned the radio up and continued driving. The news was on:

"About half a million people are demonstrating this morning in Salamanca against the move of the Civil War archives to Catalunya. The protestors claim moving the about one thousand boxes of material, including death sentences, may revive a past that's been well buried, without any need of digging up. Another demonstration, expecting double the number of people, is expected tomorrow in Barcelona in favour of the move."

After a pause, the broadcaster announced a commercial break.

Jordi lowered the volume. "This is crazy, isn't it?" he said. "These right-wing people surely have things to hide if they don't want those papers opened up."

Maria had listened to the news with interest.

"They'll start suing each other if they open those boxes," she said. "Many people were not given justice, I guess."

"Our families were lucky, they could keep what they owned," Jordi said.

"Yes, my family kept the land, but who can give me my great-grandparents and my grandfather back?" Maria said. "My mother doesn't even know what happened to her father, or her grandparents."

"Yes, we kept the land as well, but my grandfather will never return," Jordi said. "It's odd, my dad gets all funny when my grandfather is mentioned. You know, the Nationals killed him for teaching Catalan, clandestinely, to Republican children."

"Well, the Reds killed my great grandparents, I've heard," Maria said.

Jordi became curious. "Have they ever told you what happened?"

"Not a word," Maria quickly replied.

"They haven't told me more than what I have told you, either." Jordi let a few seconds go by. "It's funny, our parents generation doesn't want to talk at all, do they?"

"Yeah, and now they're getting upset with all this digging up business in the year of the seventieth anniversary of the start of the War," Maria said.

"They grew up in fear." Jordi spoke as if he had known nothing but a well established democracy.

Not that you and me have exploded into freedom yet, Maria thought staring through the window. She thought of her and Jordi's sexual life, or lack of it.

112

They drove in silence until Jordi parked just outside Maria's flat, in Aribau Street.

"Do you get nervous about the wedding?" Maria asked, with her hand already on the door handle.

Jordi lowered the radio volume. "Do I get nervous? Of course I do! Why are you asking that?" he seemed surprised.

"Oh, no, nothing, I just think it's beginning to get to me. No big deal."

Jordi turned to look at her. "Are you sure you're all right?"

He is on another planet. But that's all men, isn't it?

Maria closed her front door and leaned on it; she felt safe. Bombillo ran towards her and started stroking his little head against her leg. She picked him up and squeezed him so hard he meowed, jumped out of her arms and ran away.

Maria shrugged off her coat and went straight to the fridge to grab some water.

She sat on her terrace, in the early afternoon sun, gazing out across Barcelona.

It must be pre-marital anxiety, or just a plain hangover. I want to be alone. Why am I this sad? Why did I kiss her?

It felt so special, though.

Jesus! I must stop this.

Maria drank some water in one gulp.

When am I going to see her again? I feel so vulnerable. I want my Gran. That's it! Why don't I go tomorrow, Sunday? Today! Why not today? It's all football here today, and I will hate it if they win and all those fans come beeping in the streets and driving like crazy. I hope Real Madrid wins and shuts them all up. Should I call Gran to let her know that I am going?

She picked her mobile phone up, then dropped it, half way through dialling.

No, I'll just surprise her, she'll be so happy. I won't tell Mama. Yes, just what I need.

8

Jordi drove Oscar through the gates of Caves Gratallops, slowly passing the cypresses and well-cut grass on each side. The ash trees still had some leaves; the air was clear under a blue sky. Jordi turned the radio off and opened the window; he loved smelling the crisp winter early afternoons around the *masia*. It made him feel safe, home, near God. He parked Oscar by his brothers' new Porsche. He gave it a quick look over his shoulder. Jordi didn't like his brother's flamboyant lifestyles, so far from the spiritual values he was reminded of every day at mass.

He stayed inside the car for a moment, still feeling a bit disappointed by Maria's cold reception.

Oh well, women. It's a shame she doesn't like football. Maybe a few more years in Catalunya and she'll understand what a Barça-Madrid game means. I also have to be understanding at that time of the month. Birth and death, mysteries of life, our Lord said.

Jordi sighed, then breathed in the clean air, feeling the tranquillity of a relaxed Saturday afternoon. He turned to walk towards the big family house when he saw a still, tall figure standing, looking straight at him, at the other side of the little garden laid in front of the house. The man was leaning on an opulent, silver Mercedes-Benz that Jordi hadn't seen as it was right opposite to where the family usually parked the cars. Jordi glimpsed a driver inside the car.

"Señor Gratallops?" the man said, unsmilingly, giving a step towards him.

Jordi was surprised to see such a big car, and also parked on the grass. As he walked towards him, Jordi saw the chauffeur at the steering wheel, sitting still. *Is this the potential supplier? Coming in such a fashion?* Jordi was surprised.

"Yes, is that Borja Peñaranda?" he asked, now almost next to him.

"Yes, I am Señor Peñaranda," he said, stretching up, lifting his head and shoulders, showing a white-toothed smile under a thin moustache. Standing as erect as a post, he extended his hand. "Nice to meet you."

Jordi looked at his watch, he was ten minutes early.

"I wasn't expecting you until one, sorry if you've had to wait," Jordi said, looking at the man's oiled hair, combed backwards, his thick, bushy eyebrows, almost making one line, and his deep, dark, eyes. He was impeccably dressed, in a black winter coat with leather collar, covering a well-ironed pinstriped suit, the creases sharp, an immaculately white shirt and a light blue tie. The top of a white, ironed handkerchief showed from his jacket pocket.

Who would have said bottle suppliers dressed like that on a Saturday? Jordi, in his usual weekend gear of jeans and a cashmere jumper, felt undressed.

"I am always on time," Peñaranda said with haughtiness, lifting up his eagle nose.

Jordi remained silent for a second, looking around. *Who had opened the gates for him? Why had he parked on the grass? Should I ask the chauffeur to move the car?*

He hesitated and finally decided to move on and get done with it as soon as possible.

"Let's get started then, if you'd like to follow me towards the office, it's just behind the building, this is the family house."

The man looked around over his shoulder as he followed Jordi through a courtyard.

"Lovely home," the man said. "Do you live here?"

Jordi was surprised about the familiarity. "Yes." He sounded blunt, but he didn't want to give too many details to a stranger.

"It seems an ancient *finca*," he said, stretching his neck to see the interior through the windows.

Jordi raised an eyebrow. "You mean *masia*, señor," he immediately said. "I am afraid the *fincas* are in Andalucía, but in Catalunya, we have *masias*. Especially this one, it's more than a century old, built by a modernist architect, successor of Gaudí." Jordi was proud of his family history, the four generations of Caves Gratallops.

"All right, let it be a *masia* then," the man said with petulance. "You Catalans, always so particular." He took a deep breath, lifted his chin and looked away.

Jordi slowed his pace and turned his head towards Peñaranda.

"Very particular," he replied in a serious tone. He continued walking. "It's just over there," he pointed towards a vaulted, stone-made building at the end of a garden.

Who is this man who comes here to my home and dares insult the Catalans? I'll ask my secretary, how come she made this appointment with this madrileño?

Jordi leaned back in his armchair, in the oval office, with the same modernist design as the big family home. The arched ceiling was beautifully tiled and the big French windows let the day's light enter into the room, showing the fields outside. The brick walls were full of shelves and framed pictures, all about the family and its land. The birds could be heard outside.

Jordi looked straight at the man, who was still standing, looking at all the photos and books, rather indiscreetly, Jordi thought. That gave him a couple of minutes to check his email, to see if his secretary had left any special notes about the meeting. There was nothing apart from the memo from earlier that week, indicating Peñaranda wanted to talk to him about some cheap, new bottles.

Jordi, amazed, watched the man snoop around his office.

"When you're ready, *señor*," Jordi said, tapping the table with a pencil. "What can I do for you?"

Peñaranda smiled. Still standing, he looked again at some close shots of grapes, photos of workers labouring on the land; photographs of clear glasses half full of a burgundy-coloured wine. The man pointed at one photo, black and white, of a worker in the fields, very thin, smiling, lifting a bunch of grapes.

"Do you know which year was this photo taken?" Peñaranda asked. "It must be a long time ago, this man looks so famished and poor. Weren't the workers well treated?"

Jordi's eyes widened, his face reddened. "It's my grandfather." He looked the man straight in the eye. "He worked all his life on this land and for his workers until he was killed by Franco."

The man showed a cynical smile. "I am so sorry to hear that." He sat down, without taking his jacket off.

I can't believe this idiot is here. You'd better offer me a really good deal in bottles now, otherwise you're out of here in a split second. "What can I do for you? I don't have much time," he said.

The man took a deep breath. "Neither do I. I must attend a luncheon in central Barcelona with the directors of the football club, we're playing here tonight."

"We?" Jordi felt shocked. *Who are you?*

"I am a board member of Real Madrid," he smiled, looking directly at the little Barça and Catalan flags that Jordi had on his desk. "I am sure you've heard we're playing against Barcelona tonight."

Jordi tried to hide his feeling of disgust.

"Yes, who could miss that one?" He tried to be as diplomatic as he could. "Again, what can I do for you? My secretary said you supply bottles."

Peñaranda stood up, looked around the room again.

"Just because I was coming here today with the club, I thought it would make a good opportunity to drop by and sort out a little business," Peñaranda said, walking back to his seat. "I am very sorry to disappoint you, Jordi, but I am not a supplier." He paused. "But don't worry, I will be brief."

Jordi leaned back and crossed his arms. *I knew this wasn't right.*

The man sat down, crossed his legs. "My name is Borja, second Duke of Peñaranda, grandson of the first Duke of

117

Peñaranda, a Madrid family with ancestors going back to the fifteenth century."

Jordi raised an eyebrow. *Come on.*

The man looked outside, to the fields. "We have owned land in Spain for centuries, we had thousands of hectares, mostly in Extremadura. At one point we owned almost half of the region, along with the Duke of Alba's family. I am sure you know of them."

Jordi swallowed at the thought of that Madrid effete aristocracy, those in *¡HOLA!* magazine every week. He despised them, proud as he was that Catalunya never had that class. In Catalunya, wealth was earned, not inherited, he thought.

"Yes?" Jordi started to get impatient.

Peñaranda smiled. "Ah, the Catalans always want to go straight to business, straight to the point, eh?" He let a few seconds go by. "All right: I am sure you've heard about the Salamanca Civil War archives being transferred here."

Jordi nodded and the man continued. "I was chatting about that a few weeks ago with my good old friend, the Duke of Alba, over dinner at his palace in Madrid, the *Palacio de Liria.*"

The thought of it makes me sick.

Peñaranda continued, sounding proud of his connections. "Chatting about these Salamanca papers and the land that both our families owned before the Civil War, the Duke of Alba showed me some old maps that his very dear mother, who recently died, as I am sure you know, had just given him."

Peñaranda looked Jordi straight in the eye. "And you can guess my surprise when I found that some of that land was here, in Catalunya."

Jordi shifted in his chair. He coughed.

"I was sure it would have belonged to the Albas, of course," Peñaranda said. "They were the wealthiest of all Spanish families, the ones with most land. But the Peñarandas were not far behind when the War started, so it could have been ours, you see." He looked at Jordi intently and leaned forward towards him, looking deep in his eyes, making him feel small.

"I went to Salamanca. I wanted to dig into those papers before they are transferred here – who knows what the regional government will do? Probably bury them, or burn anything that's not in their interest."

Jordi looked at him with disgust, but Peñaranda continued: "And I saw that yes, certainly my family owned that land in Catalunya."

Slowly, he took a paper from his jacket's inner pocket. "Would you like to see it?" He smiled, cynically.

Jordi extended his arm.

He looked at the map and then straight to Peñaranda.

"You are a liar," Jordi said, throwing the map on the table.

Peñaranda picked up the document with care. "I am not: the map, of course this is a copy, shows it very clearly. This land, right here, belonged to my family before the War, but my ancestors had to leave it or they would have been killed by the rebellious communists, socialists and anarchists and all that rabble so abundant in this area. Both my grandfathers were killed by the Reds at the Jarama battle."

Peñaranda paused. "After the War, most of the family documents disappeared, so the fact that we owned this land went unnoticed. Also, my father and his siblings had enough trouble in the forties and fifties claiming back some of the cultivated hectares in Extremadura. Plus, I also found that the land was expropriated during the forties for a few years, as the Government, still aiming for economic autarchy, planned to build a power station in this area, which had continuous blackouts."

A power station here? Who would build a power station in the middle of the Penedès vineyards? Franco, probably.

"In any case, most of our farmers had taken our land over," Peñaranda stared at the terracotta-tiled floor. "They looted our heirlooms; after all we had done to help them. We gave them food and shelter for generations. What for? They just stole the land from us, with all those revolutions; they killed the guards and made horrific changes. They were so uneducated; they knew nothing about the business. It's not easy being the boss; it's

119

something in the blood, something that can't be taught. It's family-bred."

Peñaranda paused, glancing at Jordi, who looked frozen in shock.

He looked at Jordi's grandfather in the photo, and continued: "And that is what your grandfather did: in the Salamanca archives I found that Gratallops was a worker we had here in the twenties, he lived in the hut at the entrance of the *finca,"* Peñaranda said, stressing the word, infuriating Jordi, who bit his lip.

"He clearly took over a land that wasn't his after the War," he said, and added, solemnly. "Now I am here to get what belongs to us."

Jordi put his hands on his oak desk, pushing aside a brochure of Belagua, the Opus church he regularly attended. Peñarada saw the piece of paper move and gave it a quick glance.

"This land has belonged to my family for generations," Jordi said emphatically. "May I ask, who do you think you are, showing up here, saying you're a supplier when you're not, and with a fake photocopy saying this is your land?"

Jordi stood up, fury in his eyes. "An impostor! That's what you are." He leaned towards Peñaranda. "Do you think you can come out of the blue, insult the Catalans and claim a land that's not yours?" He clenched his fist and banged in his desk. "Now go. I have important things to do and can't afford to waste time like this."

He started walking towards the door, but Peñaranda wasn't moving.

"Ah, fiery Mediterraneans," Peñaranda said. "Passion everywhere." He smiled to Jordi. "Well, if you don't want to talk more, I am afraid I will have to start taking legal action."

Jordi looked at him intently from the door.

The man finally stood up. "But if you change your mind, and want to avoid the courts, then please give me a call. I am based in London, but I come *here*, to Spain, every other week."

Jordi took the point that *'here'* was Spain and not Catalunya. He gave him a glance full of hatred. Jordi wasn't a Catalan radical, but this was a provocation. He tried to stay cool.

Peñaranda took a business card from his leather wallet and left it on the table, glancing at a photo of Maria and Jordi, in a silver frame, on Jordi's desk.

"Lovely lady, is she your wife? Girlfriend?" He stared at Jordi's desk, fixing his eyes on the Belagua brochure.

Jordi didn't answer. He was still waiting at the door in silence, frowning.

The Duke finally reached the door and the two men walked towards Peñaranda's car, in silence. As the chauffeur opened the door, before getting into the car, Peñaranda looked once more at the terraced vineyards.

"How little developed this is, what a waste," he stared at them. "I would produce year-round, with more buildings and glass houses. I would exploit it so much more; open it up to tourism, create a shop with gadgets, souvenirs. This must be like it was before the War." He sighed, patronisingly. "Well, in a way I am glad nothing has changed, we can take it then from where we left it."

Before Jordi could get over his shock and reply, Peñaranda closed the door of the Mercedes and the chauffeur started the car. Peñaranda opened the window to say one last thing.

"By the way, good luck tonight," he smiled.

Fuck off! Jordi thought.

"Fuck off!!" he shouted after the car had driven away.

Jordi ran back to his office.

"Montse? Montse? Where are you?" Jordi was desperately looking for his secretary, who rarely worked on Saturdays.

He walked towards the front door of the house, aiming to talk to his father, but he hesitated. Pere Gratallops was seventy-five and had heart problems. Jordi knew that anything related to the Civil War and especially about his own father still made him angry or sad. There was no need to give him a shock just because a *madrileño* had been fantasising about this land. He would fight this one on his own. Also, his father was already battling in Madrid over the Catalan boycott.

He couldn't stop seeing the face of Peñaranda in his mind. Jordi closed his eyes and lifted his head, facing the sky, searching for God's consolation. *Why have you sent me this man, now? What have I done?*

Looking down, he went back into his office, locked the door. He looked at his grandfather in the photo. He was also called Pere Gratallops, like his father.

I will avenge this, Jordi thought, his eyes still fixed on the black and white photo.

His poor grandfather. All his father had told him was that he had fought with the Republicans in the War, on the Aragón front, and survived by a miracle. Back at the Caves, he had been known for teaching Catalan to his workers' children, in secret, at nights, as one of the first things that Franco did was to forbid the language. He had been threatened by the *Guardia Civil,* but that didn't stop him. The *Civiles* finally came one night, in early 1945, and in front of his wife, with guns pointing at his head, took him to a prison in Barcelona. He was shot a few months later. Jordi's father, then fourteen, an only child, took charge of the business and he hadn't stopped since.

Jordi sat down and looked through the windows at the beautiful colour of the vineyards under the autumn sun. The leaves seemed red, yellow, brown and green, all at the same time. He loved the subdued, yellow sun illuminating the terraces. Those terraces built stone by stone by his family, over generations, now being claimed by a *madrileño!*

He shooked his head.

Jordi took the card Peñaranda had left on the table. He had even included the fact that he was a Duke on it.

So grand and flamboyant, it makes me sick.

It was a card from a bank, in London. 'Banque Suisse. Investment banking. Canary Wharf, London.'

Jordi leaned back on his chair, gently touching the edges of the card with a finger.

These offspring of Franco's ministers are now working in London as investment bankers and the like. While the country was famished, those ministers made millions and sent their children to study in England and America. They all know each other, they were the only ones who could afford to learn English, or learn anything at all. The rest of the country just had to fight for food.

Maria had told Jordi a few times about her business trips to Madrid and London, where she met the typical posh *madrileño*, and how they'd all been spending their summers learning English in America, financed by daddy. They usually went for three-hour lunches and solved their business problems, or reached deals, just by making a telephone call, or by attending the same parties. It was a closed circle, Maria had told him.

While here, we sweat for every penny we make.

Jordi sighed and turned the computer on to Google 'Peñaranda.'

There he was, described as Spain's third largest landowner right before the Civil War, after the Albas and the Medinas. He read an account of how the aristocrats owned thousands of hectares, but cultivated less than ten percent, leaving millions of labourers without work, and without food, causing rebellion in the early thirties. Riots exploded during the Second Republic, from 1931, as a planned agrarian reform, which never materialised, promised that the land would belong to those who worked it. Many of the aristocrats, living off the interest of their capital, were uneducated and unable to keep control of their massive estates. Many farmers did indeed take over the land and, in many cases, they assassinated the aristocrats.

Jordi glanced at the telephone. *Should I call Maria?*

No, better leave this lunatic with his tales. He will soon find out he can do nothing here. I'll just get the family lawyer to send me some certificates and then send him a copy and that will be it.

He looked at the Barça flag on his desk. He smiled.

Barça, Barça, I will always have Barça.

Jordi turned the computer off, stood up, looked at the vineyards with immense pride. He felt the tranquillity of God inside him while admiring his land. He walked outside inflating his chest, exposing his face to the sun.

He thought of the match.

We'll fuck the madrileños tonight.

9

Driving her navy blue Volkswagen Polo along Barcelona's Diagonal, Maria left behind the all-illuminated glass building of Banca Catalana, with its Miró-designed logo on top; she drove towards the A7 motorway, heading south. As usual, Bach accompanied her on the trip, the best way of relaxing and calming down before facing her family in Belchite, although this time it would be different, she would only see Gran. Maria sighed and smiled at the thought. She turned the volume up, changed to fifth gear and accelerated towards home.

Maria hadn't even packed. Gran always had her favourite things ready, an old, comfortable, wool jumper, fresh and soft towels, and that lovely pair of fluffy slippers. Maria had brought from home a bottle of Faustino V, Gran's favourite wine, a thirty-euro Rioja that they loved sharing, just the two of them. Maria sighed and relaxed her shoulders as she imagined her grandmother sitting in her rocking-chair, with her little white puppy, Khira, lying by the fire. She liked to tell her stories about the village and its people, now, and thirty years ago. Gran always asked about Jordi, about Bombillo, about her flat. Always smiling, always with an encouraging word.

Just the opposite of Mama.

Her mobile rang. It was Jordi. Maria didn't answer, but put the loudspeaker on to listen to his message.

"Hello darling. Hello! Hello? Maybe you are asleep by now. I was just calling to say that Barça is down 0-1 at half-time, what a drag."

Buff, more football, how boring. He went on.

"The stadium is full, but it's not good, we're losing. I will try you again later at the end of the match, although they play so late now, it'll almost be midnight. Anyway, bye darling."

God, football, business and me; those are the boundaries of his life.

Maria switched her phone off and turned Bach up again. With her hangover practically gone, she couldn't stop thinking about the previous night. She felt happy, she had actually had a fabulous time, it was a long time since she'd got drunk like that. She had a laugh, met new people, and how different from Jordi's Opus friends. What a breath of fresh air. But then, the kiss. Maria wanted to close her eyes and remember every second of it, but she stayed alert on the road. She swallowed.

I can't believe I kissed a woman.

She lit a cigarette, she loved the intimacy of her car, smoking, driving by herself, she felt free and adventurous.

I should do this more often.

She could still feel Nell's lips on hers.

I guess it's normal for somebody like her to kiss other women, she's a lesbian after all. In America, also, they kiss each other on the mouth all the time, family, friends, so I shouldn't make a big deal of it.

Maria continued driving, enjoying every second of it, of her trip to London, of her night visit to Gran. It had been a while since she had felt this alive, she loved the uncertainty, the secrecy. She felt as naughty as when she was a child, climbing trees to hide from her mother, who would usually chase her to tell her off for one reason or another.

About two hours later, Maria left the motorway to take a small road towards Belchite; she'd be there in less than half an hour. She opened the window a bit, she felt the fresh air, she could see the stars above. She felt more relaxed.

The country. So much better than the big city. Peaceful. Quiet.

Maria turned the bend that led to Belchite. The dark night didn't let her see the bell tower, in the Old Town, the village's landmark and a Civil War icon. The impact of the War in the town was so overwhelming that even when driving at night, and without being able to see the ruins, Maria felt their powerful presence. She shivered and sped up.

Maria wound the window all the way down as soon as she drove into the village, she wanted to smell it, the fresh clean air of the Aragón flat land. She slowed down as she drove past her parents' home, and almost stopped when she saw a wheelbarrow just outside that looked exactly like her grandmother's. Curious, she parked and walked back, the only light coming from the moon. It was certainly her grandmother's wheelbarrow; as a child, she had sat on it and enjoyed immensely the rides that her gran gave her around the garden. She could recognise it perfectly, it was old and dented.

What's this doing here?

Maria looked around and heard some noises, as if somebody was digging on the ground, they were coming from the trees at the back of her parents' house. Maria froze. Was it Mama or her father doing strange things in the middle of the night? She felt like moving on towards Gran's, but what if they were thieves?

Maria walked towards the olive trees, trying to follow the noises, which were becoming louder. She could now hear deep breaths, as if somebody was making a great effort. She took her shoes off to walk without being heard, holding her mobile phone in hand, in case she had to call the police.

The sound of a shovel digging on the ground could be clearly heard, along the deep, forced breaths. It was clearly a woman. Astonished, Maria walked further through the trees, she knew where she was as her favourite tree, The Grandfather, the ancient olive tree in the middle of a clearing, was just nearby. There, visible under the moonlight, her grandmother, all wrapped in a heavy coat and with a dark shawl around her head, was covering a hole with a shovel.

What on earth...?

Maria walked silently towards her grandmother, who, a bit deaf, hadn't heard her arrive.

"Gran, what are you doing here?" Maria clutched at Gran's shoulder, making her jump.

"Ah!" Gran shouted and turned towards her granddaughter.

"What are *you* doing here?" Gran Basilisa asked, more irritated than surprised, as if Maria was bothering her or interrupting her task.

Surprised, Maria leaned back and looked at her head to toe. "And you? What are you covering?" She could see the ground had been removed.

Gran Basilisa leaned on the shovel, closed her eyes and said: "Just let me finish this and take me home."

Maria couldn't believe her words, but obeyed. Her grandmother continued.

"Do you need a hand?" Maria asked, bemused. She didn't know whether to laugh or panic.

Gran Basilisa looked at her. "Don't worry, I am not burying anybody."

Maria opened her eyes wide. "Good to know."

Gran Basilisa smiled, making Maria feel calmer, and quickly finished her task.

"All done," she said. She picked up the shovel and with some branches and olives she hid the removed ground.

"Let's go," she said, and started walking back. Gran Basilisa knew those trees better than Maria and Conchita, as she had taken care of them for decades. Maria followed.

With difficulty, the two put the wheelbarrow inside the car and drove home in silence.

In this family, we are all crazy.

"I was just going to tell your mother but it may be just as well that I tell you," Gran Basilisa said, sitting in her rocking chair, by the fire, with a cup of tea in hand. Khira lay nearby.

Maria was comfortably sitting on the sofa, shoes off, her legs crossed, leaning back. She loved the knitted blankets over the sofa, the old, cracking wooden floors.

Gran Basilisa went on. "Maybe it's even better that you know, instead of your mother, she has already too many things to worry about – there's just some money under that tree, just for you to know."

Maria was shocked. "Money under the tree? Were you burying money? Why?"

Gran smiled. "Don't worry, it's safe," she said. "And perfectly normal. I've hidden all sorts of things under that tree all my life. During the War, my father already buried some of the family's possessions there so the Reds couldn't find them. It's the safest place in the world."

Maria didn't know whether to believe her or not.

"But Gran, I work for a bank, why don't you give it to me and we can keep it safely?" Maria still couldn't understand.

"Nothing is safer than that tree," Gran said with solemnity. "I may tell your mother if I get the chance, only if necessary, I don't want to upset her or give her any reason to worry. But if I don't, please promise me that you will tell her, some day, when I am not here any more."

Maria's heart shrank at the thought. "Gran, please don't say these things, I am sure there will be many opportunities to tell her."

"Please promise," Gran said, in a weak voice.

"Of course," Maria said and looked at the fire. She then looked up at her grandmother, who was looking at her. She felt uncomfortably transparent, Gran's big, blue eyes could see through her like nobody else. She looked down, avoiding eye contact.

"No Faustino this time?" Gran asked, making Maria smile.

"Now you're talking!" Maria stood up. "I thought everybody had gone crazy and nobody remembered any of the good things!"

Maria took the bottle from her overnight bag and opened it, bringing one large glass for each of them. *God, I need a drink today: First I wake up in a nightmare area in London, after kissing a woman, then I come home and my boyfriend can only think or talk about football, then I escape to my grandmother, who has gone mad and is burying money under trees.*

Maria had a long sip of the dark, heavy, red wine. *Just what I need.*

Gran looked at her. "What brought you here, so late, anyway? Now, you have some questions to answer, my dear," Gran smiled.

"I just wanted to give you a surprise, I'll leave early tomorrow morning, won't be seeing anybody else," Maria said. "You know, if I go home and see everybody, then it takes all the weekend, and I am a bit tired, I just flew in from London today and felt like making you a little visit."

Gran raised an eyebrow.

Oh, she's spotted there's something going on. Obviously, I show up here in the middle of the night, I don't see anybody else, not even my mother, and then I pretend everything's fine. Who am I fooling?

"You are always so busy," Gran said. "I hope you'll find some time for the wedding dress, we've already seen a few shops and there's no dress yet. You don't have that much time left!"

"I know, I know, it's been manic at work, believe me, time for nothing," Maria said. She wasn't really into wedding dresses, she found them all equally boring, something that just had to be done.

"I am sure you'll find the time, although you know that's not the most important thing, don't let people tell you what to focus on," Gran said. "Just make sure you have time to relax and to make Jordi feel that the love you have for each other is the most important thing, and that the dress and all those wedding details are secondary. These days it feels like people marry for the *fiesta*, for the dress, for the presents."

"True," Maria said.

"Of course I know that's not the case for you, you've been with Jordi now for how many years, darling?"

"Four," Maria said in a tone that sounded more like 'forty'.

"Surely you know each other well enough by now to know what you're doing, and to know that you have so many things in common, you enjoy your time together so much that you want to spend the rest of your life with him, don't you darling?"

Maria felt Gran's penetrating glance and looked away, scared at the thought. *The rest of my life?*

The two reached for their glasses and had a good sip at the same time.

"True love is an opportunity that shouldn't be missed if you're lucky enough to find it," Gran said.

True love? "Why do you say that, Gran?"

"Because it's too precious, or even miraculous, to let it go, you must make the effort and make sure it doesn't fly away – catch it if you can."

Maria looked at her grandmother full of interest. *How does she know if she never married?*

"Letting these things go away is like letting life fly away, and you don't want to see life from the bullring's barrier." She was now serious. "You want to go out there and face the bull."

But that's what you didn't do, right? After Juan Roso left, she's been in this little cottage seeing life pass her by, hasn't she?

"But you never married, Gran," Maria finally said, hoping that Gran would not hold it against her that she dared ask her about Juan. Maria feared asking direct questions. At home, as a child, that would often end up with her being sent up to her room. Questioning the norm, the elderly or the doctrine was rebellious, out of tone.

But Gran was different. She took a breath and cuddled Khira, now sitting on her lap. "Darling, can you get me a cigarette from the kitchen drawer, please?"

"Oh Gran, don't do it, please, you know it's not good for you," Maria said, disappointed.

"Please, I don't have many years left and I want to enjoy them, something has to kill me one day and it'd better be something that at least I've enjoyed." She winked.

"Please," she added, sounding more authoritarian than begging.

Maria brought her the pack and a lighter.

Gran breathed out her first taste of the cigarette and smiled, satisfied.

"I didn't marry but I should have," she finally said.

Maria leaned back and raised her face in surprise. She'd only heard, from Mama, that Juan stole her money, left her pregnant, and that he escaped to Cuba.

"Juan?" Maria asked in a very soft, low tone.

"Yes, Juan Roso. I am sure you've heard something about him."

"Vaguely," Maria said.

"And what have you vaguely heard?" Gran felt distant now.

"Not much really," Maria said. "But in any case, I'd rather hear it from you."

The clock struck midnight.

Gran stood up and took the keys from her apron's pocket to open a cupboard in the living-room shelves, coming back with a pile of letters wrapped in a blue ribbon. "These are from Juan, letters he sent me from Cuba, where he went after the War," Gran said, softly touching their edges. "There are dozens more in the hut, at the end of the garden."

She looked at the window, her face full of sorrow. "In the beginning, at the peak of the Franco's repression, he had to write a cover medical letter, hiding the rest at the back, and send the envelope to Andorra, where the local doctor went once a month for medicines – and to pick up the mail that, like mine, the censors would have intercepted."

Maria saw her grandmother's hands shaking while holding the old, fading letters. "How did you answer back?"

Gran looked down. "I didn't."

"Why?" she asked. Maria felt terribly sorry for her grandmother. She knew that at the bottom of her affable and warm heart, lay a dark, deeply hidden, sad story.

Gran sat down again in her rocking-chair and drank a bit more wine. The bottle was now empty. Maria took another one from the kitchen and came back with two new, full glasses. She sat and listened with full attention. She'd never had a conversation like this with anybody in her family. The De la Vegas only talked about the things that didn't really matter, the rest was kept inside. They asked 'How are you?' but not 'How are *you*?'

and donkeys began to disappear. The lack of money made people start stealing and selling the cattle in regional markets. Vegetable fields became war zones, so the crops also fell by half. Juan was hungry every night when we met at the windmill, I always brought him bread and *jamón*. His anger towards the landowners, including my father, rose, as he saw that we still had plenty of food, but my father wouldn't share it with his workers, some clearly starving. I don't blame him for the hate that rose inside him. His father became ill and my father didn't even send a doctor. His father died shortly afterwards."

What a great-grandfather. How come you're so sweet, Gran?

"One spring night, full of stars, in 1938, the village *fiesta* was still due to be celebrated – Santa Ramona, our patron. The troops insisted that the band play and plenty of wine be served, for free of course. They walked around fully armed, while people formed two clear groups at opposite sides of the *Plaza Mayor*: on one side those helping the troops, almost everybody who had a business, and on the other, the labourers, the teacher and two Catalans who lived here then. Juan and I just went to the windmill and talked to each other for ages, he told me that he thought the Red army would enter town soon, although he didn't say when. We listened to the music from the *Plaza*; after all, it was a relief that music was still being played. We saw the stars through the window; we smelled the cows and donkeys outside. We hugged each other for a long time, finding peace in the midst of such tension."

Gran Basilisa drank a bit more wine. She looked at Maria with complicity. "But then we weren't children any more. It was that night that I got pregnant."

Gran…

Gran had a little sip of the wine; Maria had almost half a glass in one gulp.

Maria swallowed. *If you knew I haven't even been there.*

"Two gunshots woke us up in the middle of the night."

Maria swallowed, again.

"This is what happened dear, somebody needs to know. I probably owe this to your mother, but you're here now, and you've already started me up tonight," Gran said.

She sighed.

"I must have been a bit younger than you, just before the War. My sister Ana and I…"

I didn't know you had a sister.

"…used to play in the fields with the children of my father's workers. Back then we also produced corn – this land used to be a lot more fertile than now. We had at least a hundred donkeys and another hundred mules to do the work; they carried the water from the creek to the windmills."

Gran stared at the fire.

"I grew up playing in those windmills with Juan, the son of my father's foreman, an honest man. Everybody thought that Juan would inherit his father's job, staying at the hut near the windmills where the family lived. Juan helped his father during the weekends, from sunrise to sunset, still making time to do his school homework, even if his father could barely read and write. My father, who never did much for any of his workers, not even give them medical assistance, felt a weakness for Juan, he liked him for his hard work and he let him play with Ana and me. But I always got along better, Ana preferred playing with the pharmacist's son, who was quieter and used to help the priest in the church."

Maria listened, speechless.

"We spent years like this, until we became teenagers. Our bodies changed, but we didn't lose a bit of complicity, we grew together. We stole cigarettes to smoke – we almost burned the farm down once." Gran smiled. "We felt good in each other's company. We didn't stop swimming naked in the creek, as we had done as children."

"The creek behind the fields?" Maria asked.

"Yes, that same one." Gran had a smile.

"Interesting, Mama never let us play that far from the house, let alone swim naked, she would have had a heart attack," Maria said.

"Don't blame her," Gran Basilisa said. "The Franco years were very different. Life was open and liberal before the War; it was Franco who brought this country back to the Middle Ages. After he won, people weren't allowed to be natural anymore."

Maria was shocked by her Gran's words.

"When Juan and I were together, nothing mattered, there was nothing that we feared," continued Gran Basilisa. "We knew that if we got into trouble at school or at home, we would see each other soon afterwards, finding peace and comfort."

She paused to take a breath.

"The night that Father slapped me in the face four times for coming home late – he was still the old sort of man – I ran away to the windmill and he saw me through his window. He jumped out of his bedroom, one floor, and came to my rescue. We spent the night hugging each other, sleeping on the straw, with no more heat than our bodies. It was so warm and peaceful that we did that again and again. Sometimes we would just cuddle up in the middle of the day, or at siesta-time."

I've never done this with anybody. It sounds wonderful.

"Then the War broke out in the South and Franco flew some troops from North Africa. That was so far away that we received the news only days after it had happened, it sounded so far away. We heard they had taken some cities in Andalucía, but we never thought the War would arrive here, in the middle of nowhere, to our peaceful land. We were teenagers and continued to play and spend time in each other's arms at the windmill, telling our little secrets, like whom we liked, what we thought of our parents, the changes in our bodies. It was a world of our own. I helped him at school and he gave me peace and comfort when Father shouted at me, which was almost every day.

Now I see where all Mama's shouting comes from.

Gran drank more wine.

"One year later, in 1937, a group of Franco's soldiers arrived in Belchite, they said they just needed to recover from some injuries sustained at the front. Ana's boyfriend, by then, the son of the pharmacist, helped them, along with his father. Some had broken legs, I remember, another one had a bullet in his arm that

had to be removed. They were middle-aged and very rude. They took over the old farm of the Mateos, just outside town, without asking permission from old Mateo, who was too old to even think of a fight with about a dozen armed Franco soldiers. They went to the shops to get food and assumed they didn't have to pay. Their tall, imposing bodies and their guns made everybody in the village feel threatened. They started entertaining the children at school, playing football and table games, at first, but ultimately ended up in charge of the teaching, making children sing pro-fascist songs every morning. Soledad, the teacher during the Republic, and the priest in charge couldn't do anything to stop them. When Soledad challenged them once for hitting a boy who stood up to them, one of the soldiers slapped her in her face, throwing her on the ground, in front of everybody. The priest couldn't do anything as they threatened to report him to the Church in Madrid, which was on Franco's side from the very beginning."

Poor Soledad. Maria's heart felt smaller and smaller.

"News about the Red army advancing towards Belchite started to arrive. Merchants bringing produce from nearby villages brought horror tales of heads being chopped off, or landowners being assassinated by uncontrollable anarchists and communists. Juan, always on the workers' side, became more and more involved in a local group that secretly planned to help the Red army enter Belchite and overthrow Franco's troops. Belchite had grown increasingly divided between those who either supported or just needed to back the soldiers, and those, like Juan, who opposed them. My family supported the troops, from the start, as they were Catholics and anti-communists, but mostly because they wanted to keep their business. Also, Ana, my sister, was about to marry the pharmacist's son, a family with strong links to the soldiers as they needed medical help.

But Juan saw his food becoming scarcer. Father's business shrank as the War slowed down everything and nobody had any money. Everyone was terrified and no one trusted anyone else. The baker only sold bread for cash; he wouldn't take anybody's word any more, after years of doing so. All of a sudden, cows

"We ran to the *Plaza*, where we thought the screams were coming from. On one corner, under the arches, we saw Soledad lying on the floor, crying, with her skirt torn and her blouse around her neck. One of the soldiers, the tallest, who wasn't wearing any trousers at all, had been shot on the leg. Mateo, the village's official drunk, had shot him as he saw he was trying to rape her, right behind one of the pillars, while the loud music hid her screams.

In front of everybody, the soldier took his gun and shot Mateo back, killing him immediately. Juan ran to Mateo, got his gun and hid behind one of the columns.

The soldier shouted for help because of his bleeding knee. Less than a minute later, the pharmacist and his son, Ana's boyfriend, arrived to help. Ana was also watching, standing next to me. The soldier shouted he wanted water. It was an order. The pharmacist, who needed his son's help with the leg, asked Ana to bring some water. When Ana came back with a bucket and a white cloth, the soldier shouted: "What are you bastards looking at? Go home!"

Juan went to help Soledad, who was still lying on the ground, half naked, terrified. The soldier shouted to leave her alone; she was only a socialist whore. He shot at the sky and shouted, "Go Home." People left, terrified. Juan stood and tried to hold Soledad. The soldier, now surrounded by the pharmacist, his son and Ana, warned: "If you don't leave her here, I'll kill you."

Juan, then young and naïve, disobeyed and held Soledad, he carried her in his arms. The soldier shot twice, fortunately only hitting his leg and his arm, and missed Soledad. Juan shouted for Ana, the pharmacist and his son to run away. The men did, but Ana, petrified at the scene, didn't move. When Juan turned around, he shot her, instead of the soldier, dead. He ran away, with Soledad in his arms. It was a terrible night. I haven't seen him since."

Maria was immobile; she wouldn't have felt a needle on her skin.

"In his first letter, he told me he left Soledad at the priest's house, where the soldiers would never look, and spent the night running away and hiding in the mountains. Despite his injury, and God knows how, he walked for six days, eating whatever people gave him, and made it to Sitges, where he managed to hide in a cargo box on a boat to La Habana."

Gran drank half a glass at once.

"He wrote to me daily for many years, asking me to join him in Cuba to marry him, and apologising from the bottom of his heart for his mistake. He wrote me the tenderest words, offered me the sky, promised to love me to the end of his days."

"Why didn't you go?"

"He shot my sister; he killed her in front of me."

"But it was an accident, it was an act of honour, very brave, he was trying to defend Soledad." Maria's heart was aching at her grandmother's suffering.

"Still, he shot my sister. Things got worse. Two days later, the Red army entered in Belchite, seeding terror everywhere. People had built tunnels under their homes, creating an underground labyrinth. That's where I hid, pushed by my mother, who risked her life to take me to a friend's house in the *Plaza*. They couldn't stay because there wasn't room for all and my father also wanted to guard the house, fight the Reds. They did indeed vandalise the village, they burned the church, killed the priest and assassinated every landowner, or every capitalist, as they called them."

My God, her parents. Maria felt tears coming to her eyes.

"Silence finally arrived after three days of gun shots. Three whole days without food or water, toilets or any other facilities. Then, we came out to find the village in total ruins, as you see the Old Village now. It was silent, it was horrific, bodies lay around the streets, people had to turn them over as they searched for family and friends. I ran home. A woman, who died a few years ago, wanted me to wait to go with her, but I was terrified, I wanted to see my parents."

Oh no.

"I saw them, very well. After hours looking for them, I found them on a pile with others, by the walls of the cemetery. Their faces absolutely destroyed, their heads almost apart from their necks, both lying on top of other bodies."

Tears fell down Gran Basilisa's eyes. "I was eighteen. It took me two days to open my eyes again. With the help of others, we buried the bodies wrapped in blankets, just outside the cemetery – they didn't let us bury them properly, in a box, until Franco's troops regained the city a few months later."

"I went back home to find the place had been trashed and robbed. Fortunately, the Reds didn't know my father kept some of the money under the olive tree – yes, the same one – so I could live on some of that for a while. To this day, I still don't know who gave those assassins my father's name. I sometimes wonder whether it was Juan who put them on the black list."

"Wouldn't the rest of the workers have done so if your father treated them so badly?"

"Perhaps, but Juan was always the most outspoken."

"What did you do?"

"I had no other alternative than to rebuild the business, try to make olive oil out of nothing. The War devastated everything, I didn't even have a mule to push the stones to press the olives. I had to do it with my own feet."

Poor Gran, what a life. And I complain about mine.

"The money under the tree helped me, but there was not as much as I had thought, Juan had taken some. He knew the money was there because I had told him a few months before, we had no secrets."

Maria wanted to ease her grandmother's pain. "Maybe he just took a little bit to survive. In a war…"

"I don't blame him as much for the money as for my sister and my parents' deaths," Gran said. "I had also told him that he could get some of the money, if he was in desperate need, which he was." Gran remained silent for a few seconds. "But I certainly needed every penny afterwards, when I was alone and soon found out I was pregnant. Money became very scarce and thieves were all over the place. People distrusted one another, lived in silence. Getting food was the one and only objective for each and every day. Those were years of misery."

"Why didn't you go to Cuba, it would have been easier for you to live there, right?"

"I couldn't, in those days. I was alone and pregnant and after your mother was born, where would I have gone with a baby? You know in those days, women needed a signature from their husbands just to find a job or open a bank account; you even needed a special permit to go to Zaragoza, thirty miles away. You couldn't even go to the *Plaza* after dark, there were policemen in every corner. How could a single mother ask for a permit to go to abroad to meet an ex-Republican in exile? They would have shot me for that, and what would have happened to your mother?"

"How did you survive?"

"I ate the potatoes and the few vegetables that I grew in the garden. The house, miraculously, had survived because it's just outside the Old Town. I knitted my own clothes, and your mother's. We had nothing."

Maria lit a cigarette. She looked at her grandmother full of compassion.

"And then after the War, when your mother was about two or three years old, by then my heart had died. The struggle to feed the baby and myself was exhausting, the memories became vague, and the resentment at Ana's death increased. I reinforced in my mind that Juan had killed Ana, that he was an assassin, to justify my staying here. I did that for years. Sometimes, when the circumstances are tough, it's just easier to do nothing. It's much harder to fight for happiness. But you should, although you need guts for it."

Gran drank more wine.

"Not everybody wants to be happy," she said. "Being happy is hard, and trying to be is even harder."

A silence followed. *Oh Gran, you should have gone.*

"Do you regret not having gone to Cuba?"

"Of course I do. Even though the circumstances were against it, I should have gone. What I had with Juan was worth that, and much more. It was worth the world. But I wasn't strong enough to fight for it. I had very tough circumstances, but at the end of the day, I succumbed to them. Also, the church dominated much of our daily lives during those years – and they reminded us every day that pleasure and happiness are bad. We're in this world to suffer. My life made sense."

"But you don't even go to mass, Gran," Maria asked, confused.

"Not now, but I had to in those days, everybody did." She paused. "Still, in this country, whether we like it or not, whether you believe in God or not, we all bear the weight of Catholicism on our shoulders. Good things make us feel guilty, no matter what."

Maria looked at the fire, by now dwindling.

"You are such a Red, Gran, I didn't know," Maria smiled. Far from being a socialist herself, she looked with immense pride at her grandmother, who was holding a cigarette with one hand and a glass of wine with the other.

"All the way," Gran Basilisa said, looking satisfied. She sighed, as if she'd just removed a heavy stone from her back. "I have always been with the poor, the handicapped, women, children, the elderly, the Blacks – now, even the gays," she said with a small laugh.

Maria's eyes opened wide. *Gran, you're so cool.*

"The gays as well?" Maria was curious about her grandmother's thoughts on a subject that she'd never discussed with anybody else, until the previous night in London.

"Of course, there've always been gay people around, it's silly to hide and pretend. Life is like a harvest: with great patience, you seed, then work on it, then you lift it and you let the wind and nature separate the grain from the straw. The grain, the substance, always comes back, it will fall on the ground, returning to you, whereas the superficial things, let the wind take those away, and let nature decide what goes where."

Looking exhausted, Gran took a deep breath and stood up, kissed Maria and slowly walked to her room. She turned towards her granddaughter before opening her door.

"At the end of the day, we can't fight nature because it will always win. We can't beat nature." She went into her bedroom and closed the door behind her.

Maria leaned forward and held her head in her hands.

Nature, nature, what nature?

10

The smoke of Jordi's father Habano swirled in front of his face, reducing his view of Barça's stadium, and the one thousand voices cheering the team. Jordi, probably, was the only one not paying attention to the pitch, as he was, through the corner of his eye, covertly watching the Duke of Peñaranda, who was also sitting in the VIP area of FC Barcelona's stadium, one row behind, to the far left.

Father and son had planned to meet a junior minister from the Madrid central government, the same one that Mr Gratallops had briefly met just the day before in Madrid. Inspired by Jordi's father's comments about the atmosphere of the match, the minister decided to go, well aware of the number of television cameras covering the event.

Jordi looked up as the minister arrived in his seat, smiling on every side, ignoring the starting line-ups announced on the speakers at that precise moment.

He just needs a blue ribbon on his jacket, like an American politician.

The night was also a good opportunity to approach Andreu, Maria's boss and a high-ranking director at Banca Catalana. It was now apparent that the Caves needed a loan to make the traditional double-pay bonus that it gave its workers every Christmas. Sales in Madrid and Andalucía had fallen below Jordi and his father's worst forecasts. Cava was the most exposed, publicised and genuine Catalan product, therefore becoming the main target of the national boycott. Negotiations to revise the Catalan statute of autonomy, pushed by a minority of radical nationalists in Barcelona, had created a backlash throughout Spain, making cava sales sink to historic lows.

Jordi hadn't shown his father the latest figures revealing the sharpest decline, as he wanted to protect his health and give him the best possible year before retirement. The seventy-five-year-old, still aware the company was going through one of its worst times, hadn't panicked about the cash shortage and the need for a loan. Sales would recover the following year, he said; the loan was just an emergency measure and would be paid off as soon as sales picked up early in the New Year. He had seen worse during his more than fifty years running the Caves, he had said.

Soon, the central government would need the support of the Catalan nationalists in Parliament to pass the budget, so surely they would be forced to help the region in exchange. The pendulum would swing towards their side in a few weeks, his father told Jordi over lunch that same day.

In the meantime, his networking efforts among the Catalan establishment, over cigars and cognac at the Barça stadium, would get them going, he had said.

"Don't worry, you'll see how after tonight things will improve," he told Jordi as they walked into the Camp Nou. "I'll show you how to treat these people from Madrid. They think they're God, so just treat them like God and they'll be all yours."

Jordi, keeping an eye on Peñaranda, was counting the seconds to the whistle, when Real Madrid scored in added time. They were winning in the Camp Nou stadium for the first time in a decade.

Jordi tapped on the ground with his foot. *Damn. What a day I am having.*

About a hundred men and two or three women, all smartly dressed, walked into Barça's presidential lounge room, where waiters offered cocktails and first-class canapés.

Spain's industry under-secretary, shadowed by the Catalan President and Spain's chancellor, tapped on Pere Gratallops' shoulder and gave him an effusive hug, right when the television cameras were filming him.

They just want to be in the photo, Jordi thought, bemused at seeing his father greet the politician with enthusiasm. The two men had only met once before – the previous day – but it looked as if they'd been friends for life.

"The great, great Gratallops, how are you today? Good to see you!" the junior minister said. "How're the Caves? They've called me from Seville today, this friend of mine said the supermarkets are full of cava. That's good news, right?"

That's precisely the problem: the shelves are full because nobody buys it. If all government officials are like this, God help us.

Jordi's father coughed. "Well, well, I wish it was that easy," he tittered. "What we need is a good government policy to stop this anti-Catalan nonsense, as I mentioned yesterday."

"Yes, yes, excellent, excellent," the official said, looking around the room, smiling at everybody passing by, regardless whether he knew them or not. "I'll see you in a second, wait for me," he told somebody.

A waiter came offering cava, Jordi's father took a glass for the under-secretary and one for himself, making the politician finally turn to him. He took the glass.

"Of course, of course, we must do something," he said, sipping the cava. He smiled. "Mmm, I am sure it's a Gratallops!" he exclaimed, his eyes darting around the room.

Pere Gratallops smiled and bowed. "Oh, your Excellency, you are too well educated in these matters; of course it is a Gratallops. What great knowledge you have."

Jordi rolled his eyes. *Oh father, you know how to play the game.*

"Anyway," the official said, waving at people at the back of the room. "After you left, I finally caught the industry minister and talked to him about a publicity campaign to encourage people to buy Spanish products. He suggested we could market cava as a product of Spain. What a great idea, how does that sound to you?"

Jordi and his father were speechless. Jordi coughed.

"But *señor* minister, cava is quintessentially Catalan," the father said after a tense silence.

145

The minister looked at the old man, blinking his eyes haughtily. He continued: "Yes, it's Catalan, but that means it's Spanish above all." He stopped to look at the Gratallops seriously. "Things would improve if we printed a Spanish flag on the bottles." He patted Mr Gratallops' back and turned, leaving father and son glancing at each other in mutual shock.

We'd better go and secure that loan; we may need it more than we think, Jordi thought as he raised an eyebrow to his father, who, still astonished, was watching the minister walk away.

A Spanish flag on a cava bottle; over my dead body, Jordi thought.

Peñaranda walked across the room, between Jordi and his father, pretending he was looking somewhere else. As he passed, he briefly said to Jordi: "Not a bad match so far, eh?" He smiled grimly and continued walking, saying no more. Jordi didn't reply, but followed him with an intent glance.

"Who's that, son?" his father asked, looking surprised at the scene.

"An idiot, obviously," Jordi replied, turning to walk back to his seat.

The second half got harsh for the locals, with Real Madrid beating the home team 1-4. Jordi and his father, like everybody else except Peñaranda and his group, sat with their shoulders dropping, their heads in their hands, in despair. People started leaving before the final whistle.

Jordi spotted Andreu puffing and walking towards the VIP lounge. He discreetly elbowed his father, glancing over at Andreu. The old man understood and the two immediately followed the banker. They didn't want to see more of the game anyway.

Inside, Andreu was waiting in the cloakroom queue, discreetly joined by the Gratallops.

"Hello Andreu, not a good day I am afraid," Jordi's father muttered.

Andreu, a short, plump man, in his fifties, raised his big, brown eyes, full of disappointment. "A tragedy," he grunted, looking down.

"They got the points, but they're dreaming if they think they can win the league," Jordi said, trying to help his father, who didn't seem to like the interruption.

"Jordi, would you mind getting a coffee for me while I pick up the coats?" he said. "I'd like to avoid the traffic, if possible."

Jordi obeyed, getting the hint that his father preferred to do business on a one-to-one basis. While waiting for the coffee, Jordi suddenly turned at the sound of a now familiar hammering voice.

"Uuhh, problems are piling up, Jordi, aren't they?" Peñaranda cynically said, tightening the knot of his tie, and then adjusting his silver cuffs, with Real Madrid's emblem engraved.

Jordi looked at him, frowning. He said nothing, but felt Peñaranda like a blow to his stomach. First, he intruded in his own home; now, at Barça, two of the places closest to his heart. Jordi, feeling invaded, put his chin up.

Peñaranda gently touched Jordi's arm, making him recoil immediately.

"Don't be afraid, young man," Peñaranda said. "Everything has a solution. Even if the problems are big. Even if you need a loan to survive, your company can't bear more debt and the Chairman is retiring this year, and..." he left a few seconds go by. "And if you're also buying a flat."

Jordi felt aghast. *You son of a bitch – how do you know all this? Get out of my life.*

"I don't know what you're talking about," Jordi said. He turned, paid for the coffee and started to move away without saying a word.

Peñaranda stepped in front of him. "Remember you can always call me if you're in trouble, we can *negotiate*." He paused. "Do you still have my card?"

Jordi gently pushed past Peñaranda and walked away, shaking slightly, so that the coffee spilled over the cup as he walked towards Andreu and his father.

Why does God allow these people on earth? I don't understand.

Pere Gratallops, who had missed the scene as he had his back to the bar, seemed to be finishing his conversation.

"Yes, I'll pop in next week and we'll talk about the details," Jordi's father looked satisfied. "I know this is temporary. Wait until they need us. See how much they'll help us then." He took the coffee and smiled at Jordi.

Andreu nodded. "True," he said. He acknowledged Jordi with a slight bow. "Hello Jordi, how are you?"

"As good as one can be after this," Jordi tried to smile, keeping his composure.

"Better talk about the cava." Andreu was short.

Hum, I don't know if that's a better story.

"We'll always have cava," his father said, putting his heavy, long coat on to leave.

"How did it go?" Jordi asked as they walked towards his father's car.

"It was good, we'll get about one million euros, that'll solve the Christmas bonus problem and it will also help us get going with the warehouse in England," the old man said, proud of his negotiation.

"That's good news, Father," Jordi said, relieved.

"Well, I had already hinted to him here, a couple of weeks ago, that we might need that liquidity," his father said with resignation. "I don't think it came as a surprise to him."

Jordi was looking at the air, calculating. "It is indeed good news, but that amount leaves us quite leveraged."

With his car keys in hand, his father turned in surprise. "Son, I've managed this business all my life and I didn't go to University. I don't know about debt ratios, I just know it'll be fine. This Catalan phobia will be over soon, I know. Hate, and love, don't last long, both are temporary in nature."

"Just what I need to hear five months before my wedding," Jordi said, disappointed.

He immediately felt the penetrating look of his father. "You know I would never lie to you," Pere Gratallops said, looking at his son sternly.

"I know, Father," Jordi kept it short. It was not the time or the place to have an in-depth conversation. Not that they ever had any. Jordi couldn't remember the last time they spoke about anything other than work, in a relevant manner. His father was always so busy, at work, at the golf club, or at Barça. He barely was at home for dinner; he always seemed to have arrangements somewhere else.

"Should I drive you home?" his father offered.

"No, thank you, I am going to see Maria, I haven't seen her much this week," Jordi lied.

"Give her my love." The old man, now visibly tired, got into his Audi and left for home.

Jordi still kept his Opus Dei membership a secret from his parents and siblings as, he told himself, they wouldn't understand. For a start, they didn't believe in any God at all. Watching his father's opulent car disappear in the distance, Jordi felt relieved about the thought of sitting at Belagua within minutes. Belonging to Opus was, precisely, the best way of avoiding ending up like him: a life where only work, football and the golf club seemed to matter. His attention was only on the here and now. He didn't seem to believe in love or in any form of spirituality. He seemed only to enjoy his time outside the house. Jordi wanted the opposite, he longed for a big family, with as many children as God gave them, sitting around a cracking fire on a Sunday afternoon. And he would be happy to keep Oscar all his life. He didn't need more cars; the Cherokee had been an unsolicited present from his father that he barely used.

Jordi reached his car and looked up, at the parking roof; he closed his eyes, apologising to God for lying to his father about his destination. He had indeed planned to call Maria after the match, but just before he arrived at the stadium she had said she was still feeling a bit ill.

Women.

Kneeling down, Jordi sat and prayed, finally finding some moments of peace. Even if he had been there the previous evening, so much seemed to have happened since then.

"*HOLA* Jordi, how come you are here on a Saturday night?" Father Juan Antonio walked towards him a few minutes later. He was the only person in the church. "I though you would be at Barça. I am sorry they lost."

Jordi looked down. "Oh well."

Father Juan Antonio looked surprised. "Oh dear, dear, I am sure there're worse things in life, though." He smiled, then looked at Jordi's pale face with interest.

"What's up, boy? You look tired," Father Juan Antonio asked, putting his hand on Jordi's shoulder.

Jordi turned back and saw some tables at the end of the church, with the remains of a party, some empty cava bottles and glasses and empty canapés trays. Jordi walked towards them.

"What have you been celebrating here today, Father?" Jordi was surprised, as he always participated in Church activities, or at least that's what he thought. "What have I missed?"

"Ah, nothing, don't worry, just a little gathering." Father Juan Antonio was vague. "But tell me son, is there anything I can do for you? Have you sinned? Do you need a confession?"

"What gathering? Who was here?" Jordi insisted.

Father Juan Antonio seemed to doubt for a second. He finally said: "We had a businessmen get-together."

"I always come to those," Jordi said surprised. "How come I didn't know about this one? You didn't remind me last night. Was it during the match? I wonder who came then."

"It was in the mid-afternoon, and yes, they all left for the match." Father Juan Antonio looked down.

"How come nobody told me? I would have loved to come. I always come for the praying and I don't want to miss the fun." Jordi looked inquisitively to the priest.

What's wrong with everybody today?

"Jordi, son, you know that I love you dearly and you're an example to us all, but I still need to run Belagua," Father Juan Antonio said.

"To the point, Father, I am a businessman – what's going on?"

"Well, you know this estate here is very expensive, and so are some of our activities," he rubbed his hands. "It is my duty to keep a little bit of exclusivity among the members to encourage donations, if you know what I mean."

Father Juan Antonio touched his golden ring. "I do it for the good of our community, so we can reach hundreds more people with our apostolate, make the world a better place."

Jordi didn't understand. "But I have always been part of that community. I am one of the biggest donors, right?"

Father Juan Antonio looked away. "I am afraid not anymore, after you cut your monthly assignment."

Jordi's eyes opened wide. "I cut my payment for two months and I am already out?"

"It's not like that son, you know God will always love you."

"What is this? This is not very Christian," Jordi dared to say, regretting it right afterwards.

Father Juan Antonio lifted his chin and looked at Jordi imposingly. "I am sure, Jordi, you behave like a Christian, showing respect and obedience to the organisation." The priest paused for a second. "I am also sure you don't want to spoil your reputation in Belagua, either."

I can't believe this.

Father Juan Antonio put his hand on his shoulder. "I am here for you. Would you like to go to confession? Is there anything else worrying you? You know I am here to help."

Jordi thought for a couple of seconds.

"No, thank you, maybe tomorrow," he said. "I am just very tired, it's been a long day, but it's all fine. Thanks."

He took his jacket and left.

What's wrong? Is God sending me a message? What am I being punished for?

Jordi tried to pray inside Oscar, still outside Belagua, but he couldn't concentrate.

All I can do, I guess, is to stick to God. He'll take me the right way. I have to obey.

He called Maria; she was still on voicemail.

Two nights in a row that I can't get hold of her. Maybe something's wrong with her mobile. Maybe she doesn't want to talk to me. No, it must be her mobile.

Jordi looked on both sides of Belagua's parking lot. There was nobody. He felt sad and lonely. His land was being claimed by a stranger who had dared to walk into his own home; his girlfriend felt distant; his father seemed to solve everything with debt and his team had lost against the archrival. He shuddered. Jordi closed his eyes tight and moved his head up. He could feel tears about to come to his eyes. He fretted his hands and held them tight against his face, trying to stop them.

Don't cry, don't cry. I have to be strong. A man.

After a few seconds, he clenched his teeth and put his chin up. The image of Peñaranda came to his mind. He raised his fists and banged them against the steering wheel.

Then he sighed.

God is testing my faith. I have to respond well, and I will. I have to stay calm.

He started the car and slowly drove to the Diagonal. The big road that crosses Barcelona side to side was dark and empty. Nobody was celebrating any victory. The lights were off in the office buildings. Jordi accelerated and drove towards the Penedès in complete silence.

Less than forty-five minutes later, Jordi was sitting at the desk in his room, in the *masia*. It was a big, oval space, overlooking the back garden and the vineyards behind. On clear nights, he could see the stars. Not that he looked at them very often.

Jordi had his nose almost on a little book on his desk, THE WAY, the main prayer book written by the Opus Dei's founder.

"Don't say: 'That person gets on my nerves.' Think: 'That person sanctifies me.'"

Jordi thought of Peñaranda and tried to make a Christian sense out of today's encounter. It was hard.

"The world admires only spectacular sacrifice, because it does not realise the value of sacrifice that is hidden and silent."

He then thought of Maria, how pretty she looked this morning, despite the fact that she wasn't feeling well. He thought of her now, peacefully sleeping in bed. How much he wished he could be near her body. He sighed and carried on reading.

"Where there is no self-denial, there is no virtue. Let us bless pain. Love pain. Sanctify pain... Glorify pain!"

Jordi shifted in his chair, dabbed his left leg. After a few seconds, he stood up and decisively pulled his trousers down. He undid the celice's lock, to tighten it more. He could already see little blood marks on his flesh; he had worn the instrument that Father Juan Antonio gave him years ago for about ten minutes, but he felt he needed more strength on it. He needed to suffer. Today had been such a long and hard day; he needed that discipline to feel back on his feet, in control. He sat down again and continued with his readings.

"When you see a poor wooden Cross, alone, uncared-for, and of no value... and without its Crucified, don't forget that that Cross is your Cross: the Cross of each day, the hidden Cross, without splendour or consolation..., the Cross which is awaiting the Crucified it lacks: and that Crucified must be you."

Jordi didn't use the celice often, only when he felt that emotions, such as hate, range or sexual temptation, became too hard to bear. Like in the old Pamplona days, the discipline of the mortification method brought him a sense of control, of victory, of peace. He thought that was a much classier way of dealing with mundane vices, as opposed to his father and siblings, and mostly everybody else, who just fell to temptation. Opus people were of a purer cast, stronger, he thought. They didn't let themselves fall into emotional traps.

A knock on the door made him close the book in a second, hiding it underneath some finance manuals on his desk. His father's head came out from behind the door that Jordi had forgotten to lock.

"Hi there," his father said. "I thought you were going to stay at Maria's," he said.

You know I never stay there father, what is this all about?

"No, I have things to do here tomorrow," Jordi's reply was short. He tried to minimise the conversation; if he had to stand or walk, his father would suspect there was something wrong with his leg. "I was just going to go to bed this minute."

Jordi's father remained thoughtful. "Son, sometimes I think you should go out and have more fun, enjoy yourself more, go to discos, have a dance, have a drink, a laugh," he said. "Those opportunities become less and less with time, an old man is telling you!"

"Yes Father," Jordi replied, again, purposefully short.

The old man seemed to get the hint. "All right, I'll leave you to it, good night then."

"Good night, Father."

Still at his desk, Jordi looked absent-mindedly through the air, leaning his head on his arm.

Oh Father, you could never understand me, or the meaning of what I do. But it's all right; you're only my biological family. My natural family is Belagua. Sometime, very soon, I'll have my own family, in my own way. I won't have to regret the passing of time because my happiness won't be based on vulgar, material things, such as discos, women and drinks. You worry about age because your happiness is based on wealth, cars, football; and because you don't believe that the best comes after this world. The pleasures the earth gives us are shallow, they can go in the

154

blink of an eye. Instead, I want my life to be based on spiritual matters. I despise the material traps of this world. But you will never understand.

Jordi turned to his book again, rescuing it from under the pile.

"Anything that does not lead you to God is a hindrance. Root it out and throw it far from you."

Jordi read for another hour. Then, with a red circle around his left leg and some spots of blood, he limped towards his bed and fell asleep shortly afterwards. He felt relieved, *clean.*

11

Gran Basilisa could chop onions with her old, round, red hands at a speed that Conchita had never seen any where else. She held the onion with one hand while, with the other, and with no trembling whatsoever, she cut perfect circles using the long, sharp, old knife. Then she cut in the opposite direction, and finally, upside down, transforming the onion into small pieces in less than thirty seconds. Then another one, and another one, for more than half an hour. Without a single tear.

Conchita, however, had plenty of tears; her eyes turned red after just glancing at the dozens of onions the two women had already chopped. She could feel the strain in her arm.

"Mother, isn't it time we bought a kitchen robot?" Conchita looked at her mother, almost cutting herself with the knife.

Gran Basilisa didn't look back, she finished the onion she had in her hand. "Never," she said, taking another one from the straw basket in the middle of the big wooden table in Conchita's kitchen. "Machines will never replace the quality of hand labour." She continued with her task.

Conchita shrugged and carried on, unable to contain the tears.

"I can't understand why you don't cry like everyone else," she said.

Gran Basilisa stopped and took a deep breath. "I've cried enough in my life, already."

Conchita was surprised by the comment. She had only seen her mother cry once or twice, when she was a little girl, and always out of anger, not sadness. Conchita didn't think her mother had cried much, although she definitely had reasons for it. No husband, only one child, and the shame of being a single mother in a small village full of gossip.

The two remained silent until Soledad walked in with a couple of logs to revive the kitchen's fire. It was a cold, cloudy first Friday in December.

"Just fed Pablito," Soledad said proudly. "I bet he must be at least one hundred and fifty kilos now."

Conchita smiled and turned towards her. "Splendid, what *jamones* we're going to have this year, I can't wait. The little piggy we had last year wasn't that good, this year we've fed him much better, we'll have *chorizo* and *jamón* for months, and weeks of fresh meat, wonderful." Conchita wiped her hands and started preparing some coffee, leaving the percolator on the stove.

She sat by the fire and looked around, the onions now more than half done in the huge clay casserole, Soledad inspecting the rice, her mother in extreme chopping mode, the light coming through the big windows. The three women were busy and happy preparing for one of Conchita's favourite days of the year, the *matanza*.

I love this atmosphere, I love the life it brings, this is life in a pure state. Kill to eat, and not all this sophisticated nonsense, all those packaged products at supermarkets. This is the real thing.

"Ah, there he is," Conchita said after seeing through the window a middle-aged man walking towards the house. She stood up and quickly walked to the front door to welcome Pepe, the local specialist who killed the pig each year.

"*HOLA* Pepe!" Conchita said happily, drying her hands on her old apron, kissing him on the cheek. "Would you like to come in for some coffee?"

The tall man, dressed in old corduroy trousers, an old wool jumper and a beret, smiled at her. "No, thank you, I need to run a few errands."

Conchita looked at his strong body, his blue eyes and dark face, always as if he hadn't shaved in a few days. She smiled. *That's a man.* "No worries, let's go and see Pablito, I want to

157

show you how fat we've made him." She raised her head and started walking towards the little corral at the back of the garden.

"Are you all ready for the big day tomorrow?" Pepe asked, rubbing his hands together to warm them up.

"Yes, we have the onions for the *morcillas* and I went to the market early this morning for the rice and peppers," Conchita sounded decisive.

"Good, I can't wait for your *morcillas*, although I hope they're better than last year, some of them broke while cooking," Pepe said, half jokingly.

"Don't remind me of last year, that daughter of mine, Maria, can't really do a thing right with her hands," Conchita said. "She's more of a financier, you see, she's turned out like her father, not me."

"She's a lovely girl, don't be too hard on her," Pepe said. "Is she coming tomorrow, with her boyfriend?"

"Yes, both her and Jordi are coming, although I don't think either of them is too much into the *matanza*, unfortunately," Conchita looked down. "City kids! These youth, they eat *jamón* and *chorizo* but they don't even know where it comes from."

The two reached the corral and saw the big, fat pig eating cereal out of a huge load, specifically prepared to fatten him as much as possible.

"What a boy this Pablito is," Pepe said; he looked impressed. "Good job Conchita, look at the *jamones*, what a boy!"

Conchita smiled, modestly.

Pepe walked nearer the animal, which had moved to a corner. He came closer to the now frightened pig and tried to hold his snout in order see inside his mouth, which Pablito resisted. After a few attempts, Pepe finally accomplished his task.

"Good canines, I'll be able to put the rope behind them tomorrow, excellent." He came back towards Conchita.

"Will you join us for lunch as usual, tomorrow?" she said as they started walking back.

"Well, I am afraid I can't tomorrow, I will go to the opening of the Old Village, I'd like to be there," he said, taking his beret off, looking down.

Conchita glanced at him in surprise. *I didn't know you were a Red, or that you were into politics.* As far as she knew, Pepe was an old peasant who had a way with animals, who lived off his lettuces and other vegetables, selling them in the daily markets nearby. He and his wife shared a small flat in the village, with no entertainment other than their little allotment and daily walks down to the park or playing dominoes in the bar – not the casino that Honorato and other Belchite *señores* frequented, but a bigger social club, mostly for workers.

"I am sure you know, of course, about the opening," Pepe said, still with his beret in his hand.

"Yes, of course," Conchita said. "We're lucky about the coincidence, happy to keep my mother and Soledad out of it. You know, they are getting old and I am not sure if reviving these memories is good for them."

"Your mother has not been as vocal, but Soledad has certainly been an advocate of the opening up," he said.

Conchita sighed. "Tell me about it," she took a deep breath. "I suspect she plans to go in the afternoon, let's see what happens."

Conchita walked in silence until they arrived at the front of the house.

"I will see you in the morning, nine sharp for a good breakfast," Conchita said as Pepe started walking away, putting his beret back on his head.

I hope this opening of the village doesn't ruin my matanza.

She rolled up her sleeves and walked into the kitchen, full of energy, ready to take on the last few onions.

The sun was half-way up in a beautiful, crisp winter's sky when Conchita saw Jordi parking Oscar just outside her house.

Late, as usual, she thought looking at the kitchen clock which said ten o'clock. By now, about twenty people, including neighbours and some of the family's workers, were already sitting around a big, long table, set outside for the occasion. They were eating baguette sandwiches and drinking brandy – enough to give them strength for the task to come.

"Good morning everybody," Conchita heard Maria say from the half-open window in the kitchen. Jordi, shyly, stood behind her. Conchita carried on watching the rice, now almost boiling in a twenty-litre casserole. Many kilos of *morcillas* had to be prepared today.

The young couple walked into the kitchen a few seconds later, both of them kissing Conchita on the cheeks, both of them missing and making contact with the air instead. Conchita raised her head and looked at the pair head to toe.

These expensive clothes and cashmere jumpers. They don't understand the spirit of the matanza. Who would kill a pig in a cashmere jumper. Jesus.

"There are some old clothes upstairs if you'd like to change," she said.

Maria looked at Jordi. "We're fine, I think."

Conchita shrugged. "Well, we have already started," she said in a hard tone. "See if you can get some sandwiches, although they may be cold by now."

Maria looked at her distantly. "Barcelona is three hours from here, mother, remember. We left very early."

Conchita turned to stir the rice. She looked at her youngest daughter again.

"Do you remember your task for today, right?"

"Yes, Mother," Maria said and started to walk away. "God, I can't wait for the blood," she said. Her sarcasm provoked a quick disapproving look from her mother.

The couple left their small bags in the hall and went outside.

They don't understand, they don't understand this land.

Ignacio and Inma, Pilar's children, stormed into the kitchen a few moments later.

"Gran, Gran, when are we going to get Pablito?" Ignacio asked with his eyes full of excitement. Pilar was standing behind her five-year-old son, bringing some of the breakfast left-overs inside.

Conchita smiled. *Finally somebody in this family has my genes. Maybe they skipped one generation.* Conchita took her apron off, straightened her bun, and looked straight into her grandson's innocent eyes.

"Are you ready Ignacio?" she asked.

"Yes!" the boy nodded excitedly.

"Let's go, then."

Conchita and Pepe led the party towards the corral. The group circled the small, fenced area, full of straw, where Pablito slept peacefully. Finally rousing and noticing everybody, the pig moved to the opposite corner, looking around suspiciously.

Once everybody was standing still and after about a minute of complete silence, Pepe raised his hand and a man tried to get hold of Pablito's curly little tail, making the animal grunt and run back to the other corner, where he started banging his head against the fence. Another man tried to hold him from the back legs, unsuccessfully. Showing his strength, the hundred-and-fifty-kilo Pablito moved towards the centre and gazed around, his triangular ears well raised, paying absolute attention. Pepe ordered a few men to walk inside the fence and after he raised his arm, a man jumped to get Pablito's tail, two more people caught one ear each, and a fourth person snapped the snout, opened it and made room for Pepe to insert a cord behind the canines. Pablito, looking terrified, growled and kicked one of his short, back legs, pushing one of his captors to the ground.

Ignacio laughed.

"Strong boy," Conchita smiled at his grandson, holding his hand. "When you're a man, you'll be able to do this."

Ignacio's eyes shone, his eyes fixed on Pablito.

Conchita gazed around, Jordi and Maria, standing next to Gran Basilisa, were looking away.

"Now!" Pepe shouted, prompting the four men try to hold more tightly Pablito's ears, tail and front again, while the pig grumbled and shook violently. Joined by more men, Pepe tied one of Pablito's front legs to one at the back. Pablito raised his head suddenly, forcing some of the group to step back.

161

"Come back!" Pepe ordered, still holding the rope around Pablito's canines, his tight muscles showing his effort.

Everybody, except Gran Basilisa, Jordi and Maria, joined in and the group managed to lift the animal, now growling in desperation, his eyes wide with terror. They moved him onto a wooden bench.

Quickly, Pepe got his knife out and stuck it right into Pablito's jugular, prompting a swift struggle and one last, long, desperate growl. Pablito slowly dropped his head onto the bench, his eyes looking now almost white, still pleading for mercy. Saliva started dripping from his half-open mouth.

Conchita turned to check her daughters. Pilar was coming with the big bucket to hold the blood, while Maria, pale, had a hand on her mouth and looked as if she was about to burst into tears.

Wimp. "Come on Maria, help your sister!" she ordered.

Maria walked slowly towards Pilar, who had already placed the bucket by Pablito's neck to catch the approximately fifty litres of blood that would be used to make the *morcillas*. Every few seconds, Pablito's nerves twitched in his back legs – the future *jamones* – as if he were still trying to escape.

At last, Pablito fell into his final silence, his soft, pink body lay totally still as the flow of blood slowed to an irregular drip. His eyes were still wide open, with desperation written on them. Pepe closed them and put his knife back in his belt.

The crowd cheered, Pepe receiving many slaps on his back.

Pepe, you're a star.

As she did every year, Maria got the long wooden spoon and then looked away as she started to stir the blood. She needed strength to move the heavy, dark liquid that gave off a strong, sour odour.

The group then moved Pablito outside the corral. They placed him in the middle of some logs and straw and started the fire – used to clean the skin and remove the hair. While the children ran around, the crowd gathered around the fire to watch Pablito's body disappear under the flames.

The fire was soon extinguished. Conchita, as she did every year, used an old, rough, terracotta tile to scrape the body, removing the few hairs left.

With the help of five or six men, Pepe turned Pablito with his belly up and cut him in half. Pepe and Conchita took the intestines out while one of the workers cut a bit off the tongue to take it to the local vet for inspection. Afterwards, a few men hung Pablito from a specially prepared hook to ventilate his insides.

The group applauded and sat around the big table. The women started preparing the *tortillas* and soups for lunch, while the men cleaned Pablito's blood from the ground and started another fire to keep themselves warm.

What a lovely day, Conchita thought as she walked into the kitchen.

"Mother, you're not eating much today," Conchita said to Gran Basilisa, sitting next to Maria at the corner of the big table outside where the group sat for lunch. *These two always side against me, they're always together*. At the other side of the table, Jordi sat next to Honorato, who hadn't done anything in the *matanza*, as usual.

"I am all right," Gran Basilisa replied, in a delicate voice.

"This *tortilla* is wonderful, Gran," Maria said in a sweet voice.

"I made that one," Conchita quickly added.

The group laughed. Conchita looked around the table, satisfied, to see the big group, including all her family, sitting close to each other. *This is what life is all about, all together here and now.* She tightened her bun and smiled.

This is my masterpiece, all this happens because of me. I've had and raised these children; I've worked this land with my own hands, even during the worst times. I've made this happen.

But her smile waned as she noticed the front of the local demonstration, going towards the Old Town to celebrate its opening. She could hear a street band playing old Republican songs. The group turned and they could all see the three-coloured Republican flags, Pepe at the front.

"There's Pepe, I wondered where he was," Soledad said. "Good old man that Pepe. He has some guts." She took her glass of red wine and exclaimed: "*Viva la República!*"

Half of the table, including Gran Basilisa, cheered: "*Viva!*"

The other half, Conchita among them, stayed serious, quiet.

A silence followed, lasting a tense few seconds.

"What's *República?*" Ignacio asked.

People gave a nervous laugh, thankful that somebody had innocently broken the silence.

Gran Basilisa looked at the little boy and smiled: "It was a political system a long time ago, before Franco killed hundreds of thousands after a coup against democracy," she said. "Now, happily, we have a democracy again."

Nobody said anything. Conchita saw Honorato placing his fork and knife on the table, as if he was going to speak.

I knew this would happen. Oh please God, let's have a peaceful day.

Conchita could see Honorato looking around the table and rushed to change the subject.

"I put extra bacon in *the tortilla*, that's why it's tastier," she said quickly, serving herself another piece. "Does anybody want a bit more?"

People remained silent. The band now passing nearby played protest songs, old songs that had been forbidden for decades, like *Bella Ciao*. These songs were now being sung aloud in Belchite, which still had streets named after Franco and his principal generals.

As the music faded, Honorato looked at his grandson.

"Not only Franco killed people," the former army officer said solemnly. "The Republic had some Red barbarians who killed landowners like us, like my family, because they didn't want to work, they just wanted to steal our fields, and that's why Franco came along. He brought peace and order."

Everybody turned to look at Honorato.

"Honorato, not today," Conchita ordered, in a tone that could have come from Franco himself.

"Who do you think you are to teach this to your grandson?" Soledad asked furiously.

Honorato leaned back.

Idiot, idiot, you just like to stir things up.

Ignacio looked at both ends of the table, looking lost. "Who is right?" he asked, innocently.

Pilar immediately put her arm over her son's shoulder and whispered: "Enough Ignacio, don't ask more, I'll tell you later, just stay here with Mummy."

Ignacio looked down and continued eating his soup.

Gran Basilisa looked at Ignacio and spoke. "It's all right Ignacio, don't worry, you can ask as much as you want, it's always good to ask. They certainly killed each other, but it was Franco who started it, he killed more, and won. The worst is that he continued killing after that."

Honorato smiled, cynically. "Sometimes, Franco didn't have to worry because the Reds would kill each other," he said. "You don't have to go very far to see examples of that, of Reds killing the families of those close to them."

Conchita saw everybody look at Honorato in shock. She immediately glanced at her mother, who went pale. She had to lean back. *You're the Devil, Honorato, the Devil. Everybody knows you're talking about Juan Roso, and how it is understood that he killed, or made others kill, Gran Basilisa's parents, and then left with the family's money. You can't say this in front of my mother, in front of everybody. You simply can't.*

Soledad stood up, pointing her shaky finger towards Honorato: "What the fuck do you know?" She stared at him for a few seconds. "Gossip, that's the only thing you know."

I knew, I knew. Damn it.

"Enough everybody!" Conchita violently hit the table with her fists. "This is the *matanza*. Let's have the day in peace."

Conchita looked at her mother, being held by Maria and Soledad. She looked weak, tired, pale, unable to speak. Conchita felt like going towards her to give her a hug. But this wasn't the time for sentimentalism. She had to stay in charge of the situation. Perhaps she'd talk to her later, and certainly to Honorato. Better just to carry on.

This is my day, my family and my land. It's taken me a life-long effort to create and sustain this. Nobody is going to destroy it. Nobody and nothing.

She raised her chin and took more tortilla. "The War ended a long, long time ago. This is the present and thank God we're celebrating that we have enough to eat. Let's just carry on." She ate a piece of tortilla.

They all followed suit, in silence.

Gran Basilisa, Soledad, Pilar, Conchita and Maria were in the kitchen preparing the meat and other ingredients for the *morcillas*, while the other women washed Pablito's intestines in the fountain. Outside, the men smoked cigars, played cards or chess. After the vet came back with a positive check, a few men took Pablito off the hook and placed him on the big table outside to start the butchering, taking the fat, the ribs and the *jamones*.

"I am sorry about Honorato's comments, Mother," Conchita said while mixing Pablito's blood with the rice and the onions.

"Father's an idiot," said Maria, who was sitting next to Gran Basilisa, holding her hand, by the fire.

"Watch your words, Maria," Conchita replied. "Gran has reason to be angry, but not you. And you could also come and help, you haven't done much today, as usual."

Maria grumbled. "I have helped; I have stirred the blood, which makes me almost sick."

"I wonder why because this is what you eat almost every day. You are just not used to it but how do you think they kill the pigs then?"

Maria shifted in her chair. "I am sure they don't slaughter them like we do, there are better ways, without so much suffering."

Conchita looked at her daughter. "What do you know about suffering?" She continued working on the mixture, now adding some of Pablito's fat. "You don't know anything about suffering."

Maria looked at her mother. "I don't need to have lived through a war to know about suffering. I have some *empathy*."

Conchita thought for a second and replied. "Of course I feel for the poor little animal, but there's nothing to do, he's a pig, we use him for food, to survive. Why be sentimental about it?"

"It's not being sentimental; it's just some sympathy!" Maria sounded irritated. "And in any case, what's wrong about being sentimental?"

No Maria, you're wrong. If there's nothing to do, better keep those feelings inside. Otherwise you're exposed, vulnerable.

Conchita looked at her mother, who was making eye contact with Maria. She was pale and looked tired and sad. "I am really sorry about Honorato, Mother. I'll talk to him and this won't happen again."

That husband of mine, useless. Maybe I could talk about that, they'll definitely be on my side for once. See that empathy they were talking about, whether it's real or not. Hum.

Conchita put water in a big casserole, ready to pour the mixture to start boiling the *morcillas*. Pilar, who never said much, was standing next to her.

"Honorato doesn't do much in the *matanza*, to be true," Conchita finally said. "I have to do everything, and then it's Pepe and the other men who do all the hard work. He doesn't really contribute much."

Conchita saw her two daughters and mother looked surprised.

"True," Gran Basilisa said.

Jordi walked into the kitchen at that precise moment, looking shy. "Ah, hello all, sorry to interrupt, but I got my shirt a bit stained with all this blood, I wonder if you could perhaps wash it and I could borrow some old clothes?" He gave a nervous laugh. "I am not used to this in Barcelona, it's quite a different tradition."

The women stared at him in silence.

"Jordi!" Honorato shouted from the outside. "Come back! I've moved the bishop, it's your turn, come back."

Jordi looked at the women and said, still shyly. "I may come back later, when the game is over." He left.

Soledad finally broke the silence. "Who needs a man?"

"True," Gran said, raising an eyebrow to Maria.

"I agree," Conchita said, seeing her younger daughter open her eyes in astonishment, more so than Pilar.

"Why do you look so surprised, Maria?" Conchita asked.

Maria looked at the air for a few seconds and took a deep breath. "Well, it's not what a bride wants to hear just four months before her wedding." She looked absent again. "I am sure some men, like Jordi, are fine. Look at Pilar, with her children, looking happy, aren't you Pilar?"

Pilar, holding the *morcillas* as she was about to put them in the boiling water, didn't seem to disagree. "My marriage is as good as everybody else's, which I guess is good enough, or as good as it gets."

"And you have a good deal, believe me," Conchita said, and then sighed. "At least your husband is a good bread-winner and bears the reins of the house. Here, I have to do everything – everything!" She shook her head several times, her eyes fixed on the boiling water.

Maria stayed quiet for a few seconds staring at the kitchen fire, her shoulders down. She then stood up and walked towards her mother and Pilar. Slowly, as if she feared the closeness, Maria's hand gently touched her mother's lower back, just for a second. Conchita shivered, she wasn't used to affection. Maria stepped back.

"Thank you everybody for your honesty," she said. She got a metal fork and started moving the *morcillas* inside the boiling casserole, although her mind seemed far away.

She has realised being Mama is hard.

Conchita wanted to smile at her daughter, thankful for the touch and the willingness to help. But she didn't turn, or look at Maria at all. *I can't do it. I have no guts. I hate feelings.*

Conchita closed her eyes for a few seconds; hiding was always the best way out.

"Shit!" she shouted when she opened them and looked inside the casserole. "The *morcillas*! The *morcillas*! You've ruined them again, for a second year in a row!" Conchita's anger started to show on her red cheeks. She looked inside the pot again and saw the delicate, long, round cylinders full of a mixture that had taken two days to prepare, bursting in the middle of the water, spreading the hundreds of tiny pieces of onions, peppers, rice and pig fat all around. There was no way they could be re-packed, the delicate skin that held them was totally gone, dissolved in the water. Conchita looked at Maria in fury, tears of wrath about to come out of her eyes.

"I can't believe you've ruined them again!" she said astonished. "You are the ruin of this family, you're useless." She closed her eyes again. "Get out of this kitchen. Now," she snapped imperiously.

Maria stayed immobile.

"*Fuera!*" Conchita shouted as loud as she could.

Grabbing her small bag at the door, Maria left the house, without saying goodbye.

Conchita, Soledad and Gran Basilisa stayed in silence.

"It's not her fault," Gran said.

"I know she didn't mean to, but can't she just pay a bit more attention?" Conchita was covering her face with both hands, reclining on the kitchen counter. She then realised Maria had stirred the *morcillas* with a fork, instead of a spoon. She knew the slightest pinch would make them burst. She had told Maria so many times before.

What a disastrous day. Everything's gone wrong, as usual. Why can't we just sit in peace? What's wrong with this family? All year looking forward to this and see what I get. I do all the work, and nobody responds.

Conchita opened her eyes and asked her mother and Soledad to go. They obeyed, saying they would be at the Old Village, at the opening.

Once alone, Conchita poured herself a glass of red wine and sat by the fire, in the kitchen, the room where she felt most comfortable.

Honorato walked into the kitchen briefly to say he was going to the casino. He didn't ask her anything, not even where everybody was, or how the *morcillas* were. He left.

Nobody is close to me, I am not close to anybody. Nobody understands it; they're all selfish, they just look out for themselves, while I sit here and work for everybody, making things happen. But then, they don't happen.

She took another, long, silent sip.

***

"Can I listen to some music please? How long will the football last?" Maria said, feeling bored in the car. They'd driven already for half an hour, but there were more than two hundred kilometres to go.

I hate football. Always football. On television, on the radio, on his Blackberry. There's no escape. Football, football and more football.

Jordi lowered the volume. "Darling, aren't you into it? It's nerve-wracking. If they don't score, we'll go into extra time," he said, excited.

Maria rolled her eyes and yawned. A few minutes later, during a commercial break, Jordi briefly held her hand. "Extra time, great!" he smiled. "Plus, this is my little prize for being here in this medieval day. Good God the poor little animal. No offence, but this is the closest to jungle-behaviour that I've ever seen."

Maria looked at him admonishingly. "You know I agree, but it's my family and you have to respect that. My grandmother and Soledad are there and it's important for them, so it's important for me as well and it should matter to you."

Jordi smiled. "I hope when we marry you don't slaughter piglets for dinner and hang their parts around the house, darling." He laughed again.

Maria didn't think he was funny.

"Jordi, don't give me shit, I've had enough already today, please." Maria looked through the window, the black night now settling, nothing could be really seen from the car, only the boring, straight lanes ahead with very little lighting. "I can't believe I burst those *morcillas* again. Do you know how many hours of chopping and preparing my mother and grandmother put in?"

"Sshhhh," Jordi quickly said, without responding or looking at her. "The extra time is starting. Damn, I should be watching this on television and I can't because I've just been to a medieval feast. Damn it." He continued driving.

That's as much as he said for the rest of the journey.

Who needs a man? Maria couldn't keep her mother and grandmother's comments out of her mind. *Even Pilar, whom I thought was happy, now seems to have accepted mediocrity. Is that what people do?*

She looked at Jordi, concentrated on the football and the driving. *Am I doing that as well? Gran said I should love him so much that I would just feel like spending all the time in the world with him.*

She looked at Jordi again. *This doesn't feel like that at all. But Gran only experienced that when she was young. Maybe things naturally evolve into that zombie state that everybody seems to accept. Should I believe them?*

She looked through the window again. *Poor Gran, how much father's comments must have hurt her. I'll write to her as soon as I get back. She looked so delicate and tired, so fragile.*

Maria stared through the air, it had started raining. She closed her eyes, wishing she was next to her grandma, at her home. She would tell her of her adventures in Barcelona to cheer her up. She would sit in her rocking-chair, as usual, drinking a glass of wine, smoking cigarettes. Those were the times she enjoyed the most. She loved Grandm's delicious soup, she could feel the warmth of her cottage with her eyes closed. Like the warmth of Nell's flat, the same smell of soup, the same comfortable, welcoming slippers, similar ambiance of peace.

171

Just the opposite of her own family's home. Maria so wished she was at one of the two places now.

She looked at Jordi who, concentrating on his football, didn't notice her look.

Maria gazed out through the window again. Tears fell from her eyes.

12

Maria was relaxing to the sound of *Jingle Bells* being played on the harp. She was holding a large glass of Pinot grigio, with her long, tanned fingers sensually following the glass's contours, up and down, as if she was trying to seduce it. Not that she felt she could ever seduce anybody, starting with her own boyfriend.

Maria sighed and gazed around the lobby of Islington's Hilton hotel, just off Upper Street, observing a tall, tacky Christmas tree and a Santa Claus greeting hotel guests. It was a cold, early-December Tuesday night and she had just arrived in London.

Maria looked at the harpist, who was taking a break, although nobody else seemed to notice – the hotel catered to business clientele, men in suits walking purposefully from one place to another. They could be part of an army, Maria thought, they all looked the same.

Sitting on a comfortable armchair at the bar, waiting for a quick sandwich, Maria's head was full of scattered thoughts about the wedding, the warehouse, Gran's confessions and, mostly, the kiss, Nell's kiss. Three weeks on, she hadn't been able to put it out of her mind.

Hungry, Maria ate her *panini* while watching people coming in and out of the hotel with multiple shopping bags. She observed the business executives carrying numerous luxuriously wrapped parcels, probably containing unnecessary items. Maria's family didn't give presents like these, packed in beautiful boxes, with a lovely card attached. For Christmas, and for about fifteen years, her parents had given her and her sister an envelope with some money, a modest amount. Maria corresponded with a little present, a book or a scarf.

Maria hadn't enjoyed Christmas since she was a child, when she spent the holidays building little houses for her dolls on top of the trees at the back of the garden. She wrote to the Three Wise Men, asking for exotic fabric to make dresses for her dolls. Gran Basilisa always gave her some shiny, silk material that was the envy of all her friends. Sitting with Gran to make those dresses was Maria's best Christmas memory. Everything had gone downhill afterwards, especially after her father's affair with another woman, when Maria was a teenager. She remembered the slow, depressing carols being played on the old tape recorder at home, although she barely heard them as she spent most of the time locked in her room. Sadly, on the long-awaited day, on January the sixth when the Three Wise Men bring in the presents, she never received the bicycle she kept wishing for year after year. "Bicycles are for boys," her mother always said when she asked why the Magic Three ignored her wishes. Instead, she got little clay images of baby Jesus and the Virgin Mary, or a princess costume that she never wore.

I hate Christmas, Maria thought as the hotel's Santa smiled at her.

Maria was looking forward to seeing Nell the following day. Since they kissed that night at the party, when she had got so drunk, Maria had felt warm when remembering Nell's apartment, her cat, Pepa, her comfortable slippers and the wonderful scrambled eggs. She secretly loved her London adventure.

I am just a fool. I am sure Nell won't even remember that kiss.

The two had spoken a few times on the phone since, without mentioning the party at all. They had discussed some sites that Patrick, Maria's agent in London, had seen after the one on Brewery Road had been discarded. Patrick and Nell had spent time studying new locations and both had briefed Maria about them. She was now here to check a couple and to negotiate the Council's requirements before submitting an outline for planning consent.

Her Blackberry beeped; it was Jordi, wishing her good-night as he was going into his club for mass. During December, on the build up for Christmas, he went to Belagua almost every day.

If he spent less time at church and more time talking to people, he would understand human nature better and we'd be a normal couple.

Maria had tried to convince Jordi to come to London, to spend the weekend with her, but he had declined in order to avoid the temptation of sleeping with her. Booking separate hotel rooms didn't quite make sense just four months before the wedding.

What's wrong with temptation? Gran's words came to her mind: *"We can't beat nature."*

Maria remembered the lascivious kiss of the two women at Nell's party. *When will it be my time?*

Maria finished her food and went upstairs to her spacious room with its big double bed. Slowly, she opened her leather wallet and took the piece of paper on which Nell had written her mobile phone number. She walked towards the window, then towards the telephone on the bedside table. It wasn't too late.

A few seconds went by.

I am sure she is not that bothered about the kiss, and here I am, nervous about a business call.

She finally dialled the number, her hands trembling slightly, her breath gaining pace. The two still had to arrange an exact time to meet as Nell needed to confirm another arrangement.

Maria hung up after the first ring tone; she felt shy. It was easier to call her from Barcelona, protected by the distance.

She walked again towards the big window, looking out over the busy Upper Street.

What if she's cold and distant and the deal falls through? What if she thinks that I am a wimp who collapsed after just a few drinks? After everything I told her about Jordi, she now knows my intimate secrets. I shouldn't have spoken. I am a fool. But I still have to do this – let's just be professional.

She redialed the number and, after a few rings, Nell's voicemail came on. It sounded sweet and polite. Maria left a quick, clumsy message.

I am an idiot. She's lovely, nothing to fear, everything's all right.

Relieved, Maria prepared herself a hot, foamy bath. Reading her copy of *The Celestine Prophecy,* a self-help best seller tipped in *LA VANGUARDIA*, she started to feel horny as she flicked through the pages where one character describes a woman's naked body in detail. Maria slightly raised her stomach from underneath the foam; it was lean, shiny and dark. She slowly caressed it.

All this bloody effort to keep fit and slim and nobody puts a hand on me.

When Jordi, when?

Relaxed, but feeling a bit lonely, Maria got ready to go to bed, she fell asleep shortly afterwards.

The ring of her mobile woke her up about half an hour later. After a second, she remembered she was in London and her heart gave a little jump with the thought that it might be Nell.

"Hello?" she mumbled.

"Hello Maria, it's Nell here, I am so sorry, I hope it's not too late to call and that you weren't sleeping," Nell said slowly.

"No, not at all." It was ten thirty-four p.m., Maria saw on the television set. She tucked herself under the goosedown duvet, smiling.

Nell.

"How are you? Thank you for ringing back," Maria said as softly as she could. The thought of Nell seemed to put her into slow motion.

"I'm sorry I missed your call earlier, I was out, at the pub." She sounded happy. "Where are you?"

"I'm in a hotel, in Islington. I arrived a couple of hours ago." She didn't know what else to say. "I walked a bit along the streets, very entertaining, with all the Christmas lights and the shops, but I went to the hotel early, I was a bit tired."

Nell laughed. "Tired of the shops? A banker like you? I don't believe that," she teased, her tone warm.

"Right, thank you," Maria was disappointed. It was not the sort of thought she wanted to inspire, a lonely banker shopping around. It was a cold night, she was in a hotel room away from home, and she'd just been fantisising in the bath because her boyfriend wouldn't go anywhere near her. *Give me a break.*

Nell let a few seconds go by. "Right, we're meeting up tomorrow to have a look at the Post Office site, aren't we?"

"Yes." Maria had turned monosyllabic.

"Let's see, that meeting I was waiting to hear about has been scheduled for nine in the morning, so I could do eleven o'clock, before another meeting that I have in the afternoon. Is that good for you?"

"Yes, eleven is fine," Maria said. "At the council's offices on Upper Street?"

"All right," Nell left a couple of seconds go by. "Have a good night's sleep and I'll see you tomorrow."

"Yes." Maria sounded blunt, although she didn't mean to. "See you tomorrow."

Maria hung up and pulled the duvet over her head. She hugged the pillow. *How cold she is. She could have asked if I had a good trip or something. But this is straight business, she probably doesn't even remember the kiss. They are English, they are rational. Better to complete the deal and go home.*

Maria picked up *The Celestine Prophecy* again. She read on about how nothing happens by chance, that every single detail in people's lives has a meaning, everything is a little step that builds up each person's path.

Did that kiss mean anything? What has it brought to my life? Being more open-minded? Am I becoming as close-minded as Jordi's Opus friends?

Although this book could be a pile of crap. If I had to believe everything that's in print, where would I be?

Maria had never listened to Melissa Etheridge before, she didn't know who she was.

"Really?" Nell said surprised, sitting in the car. "She's a lesbian icon!"

"Why should I know about lesbian icons?" Maria smiled. "I am not a lesbian – may I remind you that I am actually getting married in April, and I couldn't be happier about it."

Maria pronounced the last words so unconvincingly that she could not look Nell in the eye. But Nell watched her sideways said nothing and continued driving. After a tense, nervous encounter at the Council's building on Upper Street – how many kisses, one or two? – and the usual, random, 'how are you's?', the two walked towards Liverpool Road, where Nell's little, blue Ford Fiesta, which looked quite old, was parked. It could have been taken out of one of those old English comedies that made Maria laugh so much from an early age, like *The Young Ones*, or *Robin's Nest*. Inspired by Soledad, who also loved them, Maria had always had an ear for English humour.

Maria watched Nell start the car; she seemed different this time. Her hair was shorter and a bit spikier, giving her a sexier look, Maria thought. Her skin was just as white and her eyes as blue. Maria looked at them again, their big, round shape and their clear, light colour reminded her of her grandmother's. They brought her peace.

"Thank you for showing me the Post Office site," Maria said while they waited at a traffic light. "I know you have reservations, but I still would like to have a look, I could explain a bit better what we're trying to do."

"All right." Nell continued driving, slowly. "The site is only down the road, but I'd like to show you the area so you can see that I am not lying when I say that Barnsbury is full of period houses. You'll see the contrast that a new building, like the one that you're proposing, would make. I know it's only an artists' impression of it, not the detailed plan, but residents will have a big problem with it. But since you insisted, here we are."

Maria looked at Nell. "Thanks," she said. Then looked through the window. "This is a lovely square."

"It's Londsdale Square, one of the best addresses in Islington," Nell said. "It also has a great pub."

Maria started feeling more relaxed. "That I should definitely check as well."

"It's lovely in the winter, they have some fireplaces; you can eat as well, it's one of those organic pubs," Nell said. "Coming here, sitting with a friend by the fire with a good bottle of wine is one of my favourite things."

It'd be one of mine as well if only I could drag my boyfriend away from his office, his church and his football.

Maria opened the window slightly to feel the fresh air. It was a cold, cloudy morning, but at least it wasn't raining. She loved the peace of the streets, the smell of chimneys, the clarity of the air. She loved the black iron fences, the Victorian street lamps. She thought how much better it seemed to live here, rather than in the noisy Aribau Street in Barcelona. People seemed calmer and cars weren't beeping all the time. She could see Nell blending into those streets, her manners quiet and polite, her tone warm and confident at the same time; her colours soft and tame, in tune with the surroundings. It felt like the opposite of Belchite, Maria thought. *That's why I love it.*

Nell looked at Maria, absorbed in her thoughts, noticing she wasn't wearing her seatbelt.

"The seatbelt is just here, sorry it may be a bit hidden," Nell said, moving her left arm in search of the belt, slightly touching Maria's trousers.

Maria quickly found the seatbelt and tried to buckle up. Nell's hand met Maria's as they both tried to fix it and the contact sent a quick current through Maria's body. Maria looked at Nell's hand in contact with hers, it was so white, she could even see the veins. Hers, instead, was dark and strong. It was such a contrast to see them together, they seemed out of two different worlds.

Nell pulled her hand away to change gears.

Maria stared through the window, seeing the white rows of houses, perfectly aligned on Gibson Square, where they finally parked.

"Lovely homes," Maria said, getting out of the car.

"They're worth more than one million each, or more," Nell quickly responded.

"We're just behind the Post Office." Nell continued as she started walking. "As I said, I am sure the homeowners with gardens backing onto the Post Office will do everything they can to avoid an industrial tenant."

"They wouldn't have more noise than they do now with Post Office vans coming in and out all day."

"Yes, true," Nell said. "But the point is to improve the area, to reduce the traffic. It has to be an exceptional project to convince the Council and the residents to let you build a warehouse here, even if you're not using all the space." Nell walked a bit further. "Let me show you from one of the sides, there're more houses like this on Moon Street. The residents there have fought other developments, they're a group of highly determined middle-class activists, believe me."

"I am sure they will be open to negotiation," Maria said confidently.

"There may be little to negotiate with all these millionaires. I've tried many times, they're used to getting their way," Nell said as they reached Moon Street. "Anyway, let me show you the area inside."

As they walked along, Nell looked at Maria's strong and comfortable shoes and her sporty, but elegant, navy blue coat. This time, Maria had left her suit, the high heels and the handbag at home.

"You look more comfortable today," Nell said. "It's good to be well protected in this cold." She smiled.

Maria didn't like people commenting on her clothes, it just reminded her of her mother, which was never a good thing.

"I wear different things all the time," she said defensively. "Sometimes I have to wear high heels for work, but that doesn't mean I don't love wearing my Campers."

"Ah Campers, they're fashionable here, and very expensive," Nell said.

"I've been wearing Campers since I climbed trees at home and at school, they've only become a fashion item recently,"

Maria said, observing Nell's surprised look. *You just think I am a posh banker, don't you?*

The two passed the Post Office security gate and walked into the courtyard, surrounded by three main buildings. Maria looked around.

"This is fantastic." She observed the loading gates, clearly visible as vans were being loaded and unloaded. She counted them. "You see? Eight loading points, and this is a much bigger area for the vans, I think we'll have about ten or twelve. That'd make the process so much quicker and organised."

"I see," Nell said. "But the design you propose is too functional, it will definitely raise concerns from the Conservation Officer; remember almost half of Islington is a conservation area."

"Well, not that this Post Office is prime architecture." Maria gazed around the site.

"As I said, we want to improve it," Nell responded. "And let's not forget that the Islington Master Plan says that all industrial licences should be in the Brewery Road area, *only*."

What a bureaucrat. Maria remembered how she almost fell asleep a few months ago reading the borough's official Urban Guidelines, when she started her search for a site.

"I am sure we could negotiate the design, especially on Upper Street, where our shopfront would be," Maria said. "Plus, we would only use one of the three buildings."

"Wait for the neighbours' reaction." Nell didn't sound convinced. "Also, the Council desperately needs more space for new homes and this would be ideal."

The two walked inside one of the old buildings.

"It's great that the Council wants to offer housing to those in need, but what if there're no jobs around?" Maria said. "The Council could build flats in the other two buildings and some of those people could work for us; we'd create a community."

"You're not interested in developing communities." Nell looked defiant.

Maria felt disappointed. "You're wrong," she said. "We want our workers to be involved in the plant. We want hands that are well-trained and that care, as we do in our main site in Vilafranca. We handle cava bottles as if they were delicate wine glasses. We make a high-quality product, we have an image to maintain. Can you imagine some under-paid, unprepared workers crunching boxes of Don Perignon all the time? We want the same care."

Nell nodded. The two walked out again to the patio.

"What cava do you produce, *sec, semi* or *brut*?"

"We do it all." Maria was impressed by Nell's cava knowledge. "But our specialty is *Brut Nature*, the high-end, which you can't find on the shelves of Tescos."

Nell smiled. "Let me show you the front, on Upper Street, although you must have seen it yesterday, right?"

"Yes, I walked by, but it was dark. I definitely need to see it again," Maria said.

A couple of minutes later, after inspecting the front door, the two crossed to the other side of Upper Street to get another perspective. They sat on a bench outside St Mary's church, right in front of the building. The sun had come out.

"Are you too cold here?" Nell asked.

"No, this is lovely." Maria, happy to feel the sun on her face, looked around, at the park behind, the church, the flower shop, and the little trolley selling coffee and bagels next to them. "I could do with some of that," she said, pointing at the seller.

Wrapped in their coats, the two drank coffee and ate cheese bagels under a crisp winter sun.

"This would be perfect for us," Maria was excited. "A shop-front here would help us build the brand name, selling some selected cava and gourmet foods. We need to change the image of cava as a cheap, second-class product that you buy in supermarkets. It's a proper, high-quality drink."

"I wonder why it's different here?" Nell said, taking a bite of her bagel.

"It was a mistake from the beginning, I know this from Jordi, my boyfriend," Maria said. "When the two largest cava companies started exporting to England, about ten years ago, they got into a price war and pushed prices lower and lower. In

Spain it's different, the cheap bottles barely give us any profit, it's the higher end that makes it for us. We really need to step up a level here."

"Not to be a party pooper," Nell said after a short while, "but do you think that a little shop in Islington is going to change the country's perception of cava?"

Maria looked at her intently. "Of course not," she said. "We need plenty of small actions such as this one. But we need them."

"What else would you sell in the shop?" Nell asked after taking another bite of her bagel.

"Almonds, nuts, olive oil, *morcillas*, you name it," Maria loved talking about Spanish food, she loved it and missed it when she was abroad.

"What's a *morcilla*?" Nell asked.

"It's a black sausage, made with the blood of a pig, mixed with onion and rice," Maria said.

Nell almost dropped her bagel. "Ugh," she said, looking as if she was about to be sick.

Maria thought for a few seconds. "Sorry, I forgot you are a vegetarian."

"It's all right," Nell said, delicately. "As long as you don't mention it again."

Maria looked bemused. "I don't know what you'd do at the *matanza*," she said.

"Where?"

"The *matanza*, we…" Maria paused. "I don't think you want to hear this."

"No, it's all right, I am curious now, what's a *matanza*?"

"In my family, we get together once a year to kill a pig and make *jamones, chorizo,* meat and other products, like *morcillas*, for the rest of the winter," Maria said. "Families have done this in Spain for centuries."

"How do you kill the pig?" asked Nell, dropping her bagel disgusted.

"Somebody does it for us, in front of the entire family." Maria paused, realising more than ever the brutality of what she was describing. She could understand it back home, but it sounded extremely out of place in London.

Nell looked astonished. "Is this in Belchite?"

Maria was surprised that Nell remembered her hometown. "Yes, it was actually last week."

"Do you enjoy that?"

Maria's face turned sad as she remembered the *morcillas* bursting in the water. "No."

Nell looked at her with curiosity, so Maria continued: "My mother always complains about my cooking, and I always seem to do something wrong. This year I broke the *morcillas* again. I ruined them, my grandmother and my mother had worked on them for two days and I just went and ruined them." Maria held her lips tight.

Nell laughed. "Sorry," she said as she saw Maria's serious face.

"You don't know my mother, it's not funny," she said.

"Banking is better than killing pigs, eh?" Nell seemed amused.

"Definitely."

The two smiled at each other, leaned back on the bench, watching people walk by.

"What do your parents do in Belchite?"

"They have a small olive oil firm." Maria didn't like to talk much about the family business, she always played it down. "It's mostly local, or maybe a bit national, but we don't export. My parents don't speak a word of English. They grew up in another time, you know, under Franco nobody learned foreign languages, there were few international ties, so they stayed mostly local."

"Olive oil, how delicious, I love it," Nell said. "And you don't want to work there?"

Maria sighed. "No, it's too local and I would have to live in Belchite, which I don't want to do. It's too small, and some people still live in the War, they haven't moved on. It's a sombre place."

"I understand," Nell said, looking at Maria full of interest. "I checked a few books after you told me about Belchite and after I saw that programme on the BBC. I read one by Paul Preston and he mentions Belchite. It's barbaric what happened."

Maria felt touched by Nell's interest. "How come you're so interested in this?" She looked at her.

"I love history and I love Spain," Nell said. "That programme really caught my interest, especially because they said the problem is still alive and well."

Maria looked away. "Very alive indeed," she said, staring into the distance. "But in Belchite nobody talks about it. It's hidden, there are many deep waters, still. And it's worse in other places. In Belchite, all the Reds were either killed or escaped, so there are very few left-wing people, barely any. It's all very conservative."

Maria remembered her last visit to Gran Basilisa. Nell looked at her as if she understood Maria was deep in thought. She carried on.

"As a matter of fact, my grandmother recently told me a few things," she said. "She'd never talked to me before about what had happened to her."

"Was she injured?" Nell was full of interest.

"No, she was all right – but both her parents, my great grandparents, were killed. She found them dead. It's a horrible tale."

Nell took a deep breath and briefly put her hand on Maria's. "Is this the grandmother whose lover went to Cuba?"

Maria raised an eyebrow and remembered how she told her about Juan Roso over breakfast that morning in November, after the party. "You have a good memory," she said.

"Not really." Nell looked down, her hand still in contact with Maria's. "I just got the impression you had a very good relationship with her."

Maria nodded, gazing ahead of herself at a fixed point. "She's a magnificent person," she said. "She has the biggest heart in the world."

Maria put her hands in her pockets, holding her fists tight, as if she wanted to keep the warmth of Nell's hand on hers.

Nell gave Maria a long look. "Belchite seems such an interesting place," she finally said. "I'd love to visit it some day, do you get many visitors?"

"No, nobody goes," Maria smiled. "Believe me, it's a sombre place. It is indeed incredible to see, but there're no explanations, no tours, no talks, nothing. The place is shut because it's dangerous to walk around the ruins, but now the mayor wants to open it up."

"Yes, that's what the BBC was saying," Nell said.

"It will take years before they can show it properly. There's no historic perspective yet – still too soon, and it will be like this for as long as there're survivors."

"You must talk to them now, urgently, otherwise they'll take their stories with them, forever," Nell said. "I'd certainly do it if it was my history, my family."

"I should." Maria thought for a few seconds. "And more so now that I've already started."

The two women sat quietly on the bench for a few minutes. Both seemed absorbed in their thoughts, without worrying about the silence. They looked comfortable. They could hear the wind, the cars, people's conversations. Three Santas walked past, ringing bells, making Nell and Maria turn to each other and smile.

"Just not like Belchite, eh?" Nell winked, then looked at her watch.

"Damn it! I have to fly!" she immediately said. "It's gone so quickly. I have to be in Camden in ten minutes. Damn it, I'll be late."

She stood up, followed by Maria. "No time to go and get the car – I'll have to take a cab."

Maria walked to the street and quickly got one.

"Good call, thanks," Nell said. "Sorry I must fly. I'll call you later about tomorrow, we'll meet in the afternoon to have a look at the other site, right?"

"Yes, don't worry, go."

Nell jumped in the car and left, waving Maria goodbye from the window.

Maria looked back at the bench where they'd been sitting.

What a wonderful morning, I wish all my business deals were like this. Sitting on a street bench watching people go by is much more interesting, and fun, than eating in a luxurious restaurant with boring men in ties. I wish I could also do this with Jordi. We don't really do many things together, only restaurants, family gatherings and a few cinema trips. But we don't sit on a bench, or in the park, or on the beach, just being together.

Maria walked back to the hotel. She felt excited, alive.

13

Conchita left the shopping bags on Gran's big wooden table, drew the curtains and opened the windows to let the air and the sun fill the kitchen. It stank of cigarettes. She looked around and immediately saw a full ashtray on the table. *I am going to throw away all her cigarettes, as soon as I find them.*

"Hello Mother, I am here, how are you?" Conchita shouted while taking her coat off and putting some vegetables and milk in the fridge. "How are you feeling? You didn't sound too well on the phone." With a parsnip in her hand and still holding the fridge door open, Conchita turned her head towards the silent living-room, waiting for a reply. There was none.

She put the parsnip on the wooden kitchen counter and walked towards the living-room to check if Gran Basilisa had fallen asleep in her armchair. She wasn't there.

"Mother?" Conchita accelerated her pace towards Gran's bedroom.

"Hello?" she said while opening the door abruptly, as she usually did, always in a rush.

Gran was quietly lying on her big, feather pillows, half asleep, with dark, baggy eyes. Her little body was wrapped under the duvet, she looked small and delicate. Khira, her terrier, was patiently lying on the carpet by the bedside. She raised her ears and growled sadly as Conchita walked in.

Oh Mother, you look so weak, Conchita thought, used as she was to seeing Gran Basilisa energetically moving around, cooking, feeding her chickens. She had never seen her mother look this vulnerable before.

"What happened? Are you ill?" Conchita sat on a chair by the big, double bed that Gran had kept for decades. Conchita looked at her mother's face, exposed without her big glasses. Her eyes, half open, showed exhaustion. She looked thinner and alarmingly pale. Her chest moved slowly with every breath, whistling as if she was an old, hard-core, heavy smoker.

I will burn those cigarettes.

"Mother," Conchita whispered, bending towards her.

Gran slowly opened her eyes and gave Conchita a glance without much focus. She then opened her eyes a bit more, showing their clear blue light.

"Hello!" she muttered with effort.

"What is it Mother?" Conchita asked.

"It's all right, Conchita, I am just a bit tired, I didn't sleep very well last night," Gran Basilisa said, slowly. She then coughed. "But I'm fine. Where's Honorato? You should go for a walk with him, it's a beautiful day."

Conchita rolled her eyes. "Mother, where are those cigarettes? I've told you a million times, and so has the doctor, you can't smoke, it makes you feel worse."

"I'll die with or without smoking, what does it matter?" Gran raised an eyebrow. "Anyway, I wasn't expecting you today."

Conchita leaned back. "I just brought you the milk and vegetables that you asked for," Conchita said. "The lettuces are fresh, one of the workers just picked them. This has been such a warm winter."

It felt bizarre to talk about the weather with Gran while she seemed so ill, but that was the depth of their relationship. Years filled with work and official gatherings had left inner thoughts and feelings hidden behind the daily routine. Even in her mother's bedroom, Conchita couldn't relate to much: there were no photographs of her, only of Maria and Pilar, and the children. The white walls were almost bare; there was only one painting – of the bleak, flat Aragón land – above the bed. The rest was polished, almost too clean to feel human. Such a contrast with the rest of the house, which was warm and full of memories, cosy cushions, handmade blankets and dry flowers in old copper pots. Conchita thought of the people she knew of her mother's generation; they had mostly thrown out letters, books, or anything personal related to their youth, the turbulent years before the War.

This generation just wants to erase its past. I don't blame them.

Trying to avoid the tense silence, Conchita turned on her chair to arrange the water jar and a glass on the bedside table.

"Right, where are your medicines?" Conchita asked, pouring some water in the glass. She expected the usual 'I don't need any medicine.'

"In the top drawer in the kitchen," Gran said.

Conchita turned towards her mother, surprised that she recognised the need of some help this time. She could count the times her mother had shown her any vulnerability. Gran never needed anything, she always played down any problem; any issue was 'nothing' and would undoubtedly resolve 'in time.'

"I'll bring them right now," Conchita said, walking towards the kitchen.

She's as strong as a rock, but nobody can escape the effects of those nasty cigarettes. I won't let up until she quits.

On her way, Conchita picked up another full ashtray from the coffee table, emptying it in the bin. *Ugh*, she thought with disgust.

Back in the bedroom, Conchita watched her mother take two pills with some water. It was quiet, they could only hear the noise of the chickens outside. Conchita slightly opened the window and a little black bird flew onto the sill, staying still, singing, as if it was a spring day instead of a cold morning in December. Gran smiled and, showing a little bit more energy, sat herself up, leaning back on the pillow.

"I've felt a bit tired over the past few days," she said.

Apart from delivering the usual food, drinks and olive oil, Conchita and her mother met two or three times a week to discuss the weather, the state of the crops, Maria and Pilar, the grandchildren, and not much else. When Soledad was around, the conversation opened up and became funnier and more entertaining, but between mother and daughter, the years of distance could still be felt.

Both of them had worked all their lives and found it hard to relax, making their contact with other people most often tense and hurried. They were always on the run, despite threats from Soledad, who kept warning them about their health. Basilisa and Conchita only stopped when their bodies said 'enough', forcing them to bed, exhausted, as Gran was now. Mother and daughter only had two speeds: on and off.

"I can't believe you're still smoking," Conchita scolded her mother. "I will go around the house to get all the cigarettes that I can find. I will also ask the shopkeeper to stop selling you any. You won't smoke ever again, is that clear?"

Gran Basilisa was already looking away, sad. She inched down in the bed, took a deep breath and closed her eyes.

Conchita heard her breathing almost from the door as she went on her cigarette hunt.

"Don't touch anything," Gran warned, but her voice was so low that Conchita was already opening the living-room cupboards and couldn't hear her. She found a pack there, more by the little table next to Gran's armchair and more hidden behind the geraniums on the kitchen counter. In total, seven packs of *Ducados*, the heavy, black tobacco, the cheapest of all, smoked mostly by truck drivers, labourers and punks.

Good God, at least she could smoke something with a bit more quality. These cigarettes are what I smoked in the toilet at the convent, hiding from the nuns, fifty years ago, when Marlboros were only for Hollywood stars. Ugh, this would kill a bull, Conchita thought.

After a thorough search, Conchita was about to return to her mother's room, when she noticed she hadn't checked the guest room, where she immediately saw another full ashtray and a bottle of wine on the bedside table.

Intrigued, Conchita walked inside the little room and opened the window to ventilate. She looked around, not quite able to imagine her mother there, smoking and drinking by herself. Gran Basilisa barely drank and she never used that room. Conchita looked at the ashtray and the bottle, which was still half full. She then moved towards the table, on which she saw a plane ticket. British Airways, it said. When she picked it up, she read 'Maria de la Vega' printed on it and the date: Saturday Nov. 7. It was just about a month ago and some three weeks before the *matanza*. She remembered Maria had told her then that she had been to London, but had she been to Belchite before she saw her at the *matanza*, without telling her?

Conchita let her arms fall, still holding the ticket, and raised her head, glancing through the window. *What am I missing? What's going on between my daughter and my mother? Surely it must be Maria bringing her all those cigarettes and drinking with her. What trouble that girl is. She is so irresponsible. She will now hear me. Both of them are like children. They're laughing behind my back.*

Conchita's anger was rising and her face went pink, almost red.

The little black bird came to the window and started singing again. Conchita tried to hit him with the plane ticket, but the creature flew away a split second before.

I spend my life working twelve hours a day. I have to take care of my husband, who doesn't help me a bit. Then I have to manage my two hundred workers, who only want more money, more holidays and less work, because my two daughters are hopeless at running the business. Maria I don't even see, plus I end up doing everything for her wedding. Does she care about the colour of the flowers? She doesn't! What sort of flowers would she have at the wedding if I didn't bother? Eh? And Pilar, she is slow and not very bright. God help us if she has to inherit the business. I wish I had had a son. Not that I didn't want any, but with that husband I have, who's always ill, complaining or tired, how was I going to get pregnant again? And what do I get? Nothing! What help do I get? Nada. And what do my mother and my daughter do? Sit and conspire together, drink wine and smoke cigarettes behind my back. After all I worry about them, and the million times that I've asked them not to smoke, do they care? Who do they think they are? I am going to impose order very soon. I am getting the doctor now and afterwards I will call Maria, she will have a few things to explain.

Conchita threw the plane ticket into the bin by the bedside table, she was all ready to storm out of the room and start her action plan, when she suddenly took two steps backwards and looked into the bin again. There was a letter.

She stretched her neck and saw a handwritten page. It looked like her mother's old, big, round handwriting. She had never seen Gran writing a letter, only Christmas cards to friends and family. But this looked more personal.

She couldn't stop herself and picked it up.

She felt awkward about taking it, it was wrong to nose into other people's business. She hesitated for a second. Quickly, she glanced at the page just to see a couple of words: 'Dear Juan.'

Conchita's heart gave a quick jump. Her eyes opened wide and her body felt cold and tense. Her hands started shaking.

Juan! That's my father! Juan Roso? Is he alive?

Stunned, without even thinking whether her mother could just wake up and see her through the door that she had left open, Conchita let all the cigarette packs that she was holding fall on the bed. She sat down heavily.

Juan Roso
Paseo Maragall, 81
La Habana
Isla de Cuba

Belchite, Nov. 15, 2006:

Dear Juan,

After so many years we don't need many words. Thank you for your letters, sorry I didn't reply. As you can imagine, life wasn't easy here after you left. My parents were killed and I had to take care of everything.

I am writing to you now to let you know that, after all these years, I have finally broken my silence and told my family about you – our family. We have a daughter, Juan, her name is Conchita, and she was born nine months after the night that you left. She's been a good daughter, she's never caused me any problems and always helped in the house and the fields, which she has been running entirely by herself over the past few years. I am too old to do anything now.

She married Honorato, an army officer. As you might expect, he's quite serious and distant, I am not sure how happy they are, but our daughter is strong, she holds out well. She is like you, keeps herself to herself.

They have two daughters, Pilar, the eldest, and Maria, whom I love with all my heart. She came to see me the other day, a bit distressed. She's about to get married and seemed to need some help, so I told her our story, about what we had together. I am not sure she shares quite the same with this boy she's going to marry, so I thought it's about time that somebody knows about us. Maybe it can help her. I hope she has, some day, what you and I had, and that she can make it last. I missed it, I think our daughter missed it as well. I don't want a third generation making the same mistake.

Now I am in bed, old and tired. I just wanted to let you know that over all those years, there hasn't been a day that I haven't thought of you, your loving eyes, your protective arms, the warmth of your body against mine. That's what made my life move forward, all these hard, long and lonely years.

I deeply hope you've been and still are well.

Yours forever,

Basilisa."

Conchita held her breath for a few seconds, one hand over her mouth. Without noticing, she dropped the paper on the floor.

She stayed immobile, with her eyes closed. Her face became paler as the seconds ticked by.

Is my father alive? He is living in Cuba. Why hasn't he come to find us? What is he like?

Poor mother, a life of silent suffering. Bless her.

She re-read the letter.

A good daughter? Not sure how happy I am?

Missed? What have I missed? What have we missed?

Conchita started sweating, her eyes fixed on the letter.

What about Soledad? She must know all this – have they both hidden this from me, all these years? Why?

Speechless, she gazed around the room, without knowing what to do, until she saw the wine. Without thinking twice, she grabbed it and took a long gulp, straight from the bottle, for the first time in her life. She sat down and read the letter again, and once more.

What's wrong with Maria's wedding? The same mistake over generations? Have I also made the same mistake as my mother? Keep myself to myself? Maria not in love? But they look so good. My mother is getting too old.

A loud cough from Gran Basilisa reminded Conchita that she was nearby.

"Mother!" she said, standing up, remembering Gran's fragile state. As she was about to leave the little room, she thought for a few seconds. If Gran's health was delicate, better to leave the letter where she had found it, don't let her find out she'd seen anything. Conchita put the paper back in the bin, rubbed her eyes with the little handkerchief that she always kept in her sleeve, and walked towards her mother's room.

Better leave this for the moment. I must think about it first, then find the right time to bring it up. Maybe I should talk to Maria first, I can't believe she hasn't told me anything. That girl, she doesn't trust her mother – how little she knows about life. She'll learn one day, the hard way.

Without saying a word, Conchita walked into her mother's bedroom, where Khira was still loyally lying next to Gran. She

195

sat on the bed, next to her mother, who didn't notice the shock in her daughter's face.

"What were you doing?" Gran Basilisa asked, in a weak tone.

Conchita could not look at her mother in the same way, but tried to simulate normality. "Just picking around your smoking mess, Mother."

Conchita got a little white linen towel from the bedside table, put some water on it and placed it on Gran's forehead, holding it for a few seconds. "This will relieve you."

Conchita's own sweet tone surprised her. Her mother seemed a new, different person now. Taking care of her didn't feel like a duty suddenly. For the first time in many years, Conchita felt loving towards her mother. She hadn't been this close to anybody or felt needed like this since her daughters were children.

They don't know how much I care about them.

Conchita gently stroked her mother's head.

Why have you hidden this all those years? We could have been so close.

As Gran fell asleep, Conchita observed the tiredness in her mother's face, the years of suffering.

She's kept her heart hidden all her life, but it's there, now I can see the woman behind my mother. We could have given each other support, instead of fighting the world by ourselves like Don Quixotes. Had she only opened up to me, her only daughter, her only direct family member, we could have shared so much. She could have helped me as I try to help my daughters, arranging their weddings, all those details that nobody has time for – only mothers do.

Conchita looked at Gran's arms, now outside the duvet. They were tanned and ragged, they'd worked the land for years, under the sun. *She is such a strong woman. Where did she find support from? I am as alone as her, but at least I have religion, God, but she doesn't rely on him, as far as I know, although we've never really discussed it. She comes to Sunday mass, but more as a social habit, I think. Where does she get her courage from? Maybe I could help her, perhaps we have some wonderful years ahead, now that I am beginning to understand her. But she should have told me a long time ago. So many years wasted now.*

Conchita felt tears coming to her eyes.

Still sleeping, Gran started coughing again. Conchita sat up and made an effort to think straight.

"I'm calling the doctor now," she said, sounding efficient again.

She made the sign of the Cross and left the room.

14

The jog was twice as long as usual and the abdominal exercises twice as hard. It was also wonderful, for somebody used to working twelve-hour days, non-stop, to be at a hotel gym at two in the afternoon, with all the American businessmen's wives. For once, Maria had decided to take things easy and enjoy herself. She had already met Patrick, her agent in London, early in the morning and, after a client had cancelled their lunch meeting, she had gone to the antique market off Upper Street, the big bookstore at the Angel, and visited the little shops along Chapel Market that sold the typical junk that she never had time for. Looking around, she had found a little fish-cane toy for Bombillo, and happily imagined him having the time of his life chasing it around the flat. She couldn't wait to see him. After hesitating for a couple of minutes, she had also got one for Nell's cat.

It started to rain, Maria noticed through the big window in her room, wrapped in a rope after a hot shower. But she didn't mind. She was in such a good mood she even caught herself whistling while putting on her creams, make-up, doing her hair. She also painted her toenails while watching daytime TV.

It is a sign of maturity when one has time for toe nails.
There is a life outside the office.

Nell also had some make-up on, Maria noticed as soon as she got in her car at four in the afternoon on the dot. *Nice touch*, she thought.

Nell looked more relaxed than on the previous day. She was wearing a pair of trendy jeans, with big patches on her knees, and a light blue polo-neck jumper that matched her eyes, perfectly shaped by the mascara. This was the most feminine that Maria had seen her.

She is actually quite pretty when she makes a bit of an effort.

"What have you got there?" Nell asked, seeing Maria get into the car with the little, orange, woolly fish hanging from her coat. She smiled.

"It's a fishy, for Pepa." She showed her catch with pride. "I saw it in a shop this morning. I also got one for my cat, aren't they great?"

Nell looked at Maria warmly and took the fish, examined it in detail. "What a cute toy!" She seemed surprised. "Pepa will love it, thank you."

"Oh, it's nothing, but I couldn't resist buying it." Maria leaned back. Dressed in jeans and an anorak, she felt comfortable.

The two drove to Vale Royal, a wide, unevenly surfaced, grim street not far from Brewery Road. After passing a plumbing supplies business, they parked across from a corner pub that didn't look very inviting. Two men in woolly hats and thick anoraks were smoking outside. A gang of hoodies loitered further down the road.

"This is usually busier but now, just before Christmas, the place slows down," Nell said, aware of Maria's concerned look. "Come on, you'll like the site."

Maria followed Nell looking cautiously around. She observed a number of cranes and some buildings under construction nearby.

They walked a few metres, avoiding plastic bags and broken glass, and entered a business area designed for small and medium companies. Nell walked towards the corner.

"The units on the sides are much bigger, they are for industrial use and have quite a few loading gates at the back," Nell said. "Let me show you."

The two walked around the three-storey modern brick building, spacious and with good facilities. As Patrick had told her that morning, it had enough gates for loading and unloading the vans and trucks. Maria noticed a sign saying 'New Channel Tunnel Rail Link. King's Cross.'

Nell noticed. "We're very close to the new Rail Link – the Eurostar now goes from Kings Cross to Europe, very near here."

"I didn't know, that wasn't on the maps that Patrick gave me," Maria said, surprised.

"Well, this is very new, I'm not surprised it's not on the maps yet," Nell said. "Why? Is that relevant?"

Maria looked around. "There's also quite a bit of construction just next door."

"Yes, this area is becoming very busy, partially because of the rail link, although it's the East Coast rail line that comes really close to here. I thought good communications would be an advantage to you."

"Well, all this movement isn't good for the underground cellar that we would need here, because this building is quite low-rise." Maria sounded worried.

Nell thought for a few seconds. "But your buildings in Vilafranca don't have underground storage systems, right?"

Maria was surprised at Nell's research. "True, but most of the cellars that are being planned now, with the latest technology, are underground. Wine and cava must be kept in a dark place, without vibrations or sudden changes. All these train lines and this construction would definitely bring too much disruption. Are they freight trains?"

"Yes," Nell said. "Does that make a difference?"

"Of course, they're heavier," Maria said. "Wine and cava are so delicate. They need to be kept quiet and at thirteen degrees, always. If that changes, which it does all the time because of the weather, an underground cellar lets us bring the conditions back into place in just twenty-nine seconds." Maria paused, looked at Nell. "It's all about consistency; if it's too dry, corks shrink and wine levels reduce, and if it's too moist, then the label and the cases deteriorate. It's not easy."

Nell remained silent for a few seconds.

"Well, you should have specified in your plans that it had to be a quiet area," she said.

"I know, sorry." Maria saw Nell's look of disappointment. "I knew there were train lines, but not this concentration of freight transport and building work so nearby. I thought Patrick would have picked up on that, but they are agents, not wine experts. Sorry about this."

Maria remained thoughtful, then carried on. "We would only be interested in an overground cellar in the case of Upper Street, because obviously what we gain in terms of PR with the shop-front is fantastic, but not in a site like this."

Nell looked defeated. "Does this mean that this site is out?"

Maria felt a slight vibration under her feet as a train passed through a tunnel nearby. She looked at the multitude of cranes around.

"I am afraid so, sorry." Maria looked down. "This is certainly too much; wine and cava need a quiet place. I hope you don't think that I am wasting your time."

"Well, I am also sorry about this," Nell said looking down. "But of course we will make an effort to keep looking for sites. The Council needs local jobs."

Nell started walking back towards the car. "Oh well, good things never come easy."

"That's the way to look at it," Maria liked her attitude. "Another solution would be to redesign the Post Office site, negotiate the Council's requirements."

"You'll definitely have to if you want any chance there at all," Nell said. "I must warn you about English Heritage, which has to be consulted. I am sure they will say your design shows 'undistinguished architecture.' That's what they always say. They've blocked so many projects."

"You'll have to give me more details about what the Council wants exactly," Maria said.

Nell sighed. "You really like that place, don't you?"

"That shop would really help us."

"Should we go and talk about it in the office?" Nell asked calmly, getting into her car.

"That sounds good." Maria lowered her shoulders.

This is starting to go well. She's now opened up to the idea.

"Actually, I'm a bit hungry – I didn't have any lunch at all," Nell said as the two drove back to Islington. "Fancy going for some food? Discussing urban guidelines may take some time and you're leaving tomorrow, right?"

"Yes, in the afternoon, but I have back to back meetings in the morning – some investors that my boss wants me to meet for something else," Maria said. She looked at her watch. "But food now? It's only five o'clock. In Spain, we don't eat until nine or ten."

Nell smiled. "I know, but it's bad to eat that late, I usually eat between six and seven," she said. "But in any case, I have to check a couple of things in the office, if you don't mind giving me a few minutes there, it'll be almost six by the time we eat, how does that sound?"

"All right." Maria felt happy. She enjoyed Nell's company.

Does Nell enjoy mine? She wouldn't offer if she didn't. Maybe she's just being polite, or just interested in the local jobs – most probably.

Maria looked at Nell as they drove slowly down Offord Road, listening to her Melissa Etheridge music, reclining well back in her seat, moving her head slowly, in time with the music. She'd read somewhere that people drive the way they are. Nell seemed confident, relaxed, open.

"Do you have anywhere in mind?" Maria asked.

"Mmm, let me think," Nell pressed her lips, touched her chin. "There're some places along Upper Street, right by your hotel, but they're all chains, unfortunately, it's pretty sad."

"I don't like chains either," Maria said.

"Don't you?" Nell asked surprised. "I thought that international business people liked chains because they know what to expect."

"Yes, some people think like that," Maria replied. "But I don't like boring, uniform restaurants." Maria held her glance at Nell. "Not all bankers are the same."

"Ah." Nell looked a bit embarrassed.

"Sometimes I feel that people misunderstand the banking profession." Maria continued. "Without banks, there would be no factories, no supermarkets, nothing, and who would pay taxes? People would keep coins and notes under the mattress or buried under the trees, believe me, I have seen that with my own eyes."

"Under the trees?" Nell seemed amused. "Where?"

"I can't say."

Nell looked at Maria, intrigued.

She'd think I am mad if I told her about Gran hiding the money. "Sorry, I don't mean to be secretive, but I really can't, not this time."

"I understand, don't worry," Nell said in a warm tone.

She has good empathy. Maria felt chatty and relaxed.

"Coming back to the bankers," she said, "It seems that these days, you need a suit to be a businessman, or that to be a hippie, or a poet, you have to dress as such. That's a very materialistic idea, isn't it?"

Nell listened with attention.

"I know what you mean," she said. "I know some people at work, or at other councils, who speak of ideas, and are manifest socialists, but then they wouldn't hesitate for a second to let those property developers sprawl more apartments throughout Islington if that gave them more status or money."

"What's wrong with apartments?" Maria asked as Nell parked in front of the council offices on Upper Street.

"We want a balance between homes and jobs," Nell said, turning the engine off, but without moving from her seat. "Islington is becoming just like Chelsea, or Chiswick, a residential area for the middle classes. If we don't create more jobs, all those living in council housing will eventually go where the jobs are. We want to keep them, have a mixed community, for everybody."

She's so thoughtful. And true.

"Spain seems more mixed than England," Maria said. She thought of her Eixample neighbourhood in Barcelona, home to some wealthy people, as well as to some who barely made it to the end of the month. The Eixample also had a substantial immigrant and elderly community. Maria liked the mix. "Ghettos can't be good for anybody," she said.

Nell nodded and quickly grabbed Maria's hand. "I'd love to talk more about this, but I really need to finish something," she said, then looked out of the window. "Why don't we go to that pub that we drove past yesterday, near the square that you liked? It's called the Drapers' Arms. They do organic food and I have a friend who works there."

Maria remembered Nell's comments about the place. "Sure, let's go."

"I'll be right back," Nell said, stepping out of the car.

I wish all my deals were like this – in the pub!

"Shit!" Nell whispered, grabbing Maria's arm as they walked down Liverpool Road some twenty minutes later. "It's my ex, right there."

Maria couldn't reply because the woman was now too close. But she managed to press her arm back showing complicity and support. She also felt curious to see who this woman was, wearing an old, ugly green trenchcoat with very short red hair.

"Hello you," the woman said.

"Hi Fiona," Nell replied, taking her arm off Maria's.

"What a coincidence to bump into you *two* here," Fiona said, looking at Maria head to toe. Maria felt the check-out immediately. *What are you looking at?* Not even the oldest gossipers in Belchite would have been as rude as that.

"How are you doing?" the woman said, speaking loud and slowly.

"I'm well, and you?" Nell was short.

"Not too bad," the woman replied, now looking both Maria and Nell straight in the eyes.

Nell started to move her feet as if she was ready to go, but Fiona wanted more.

"Where are you girls going?" she asked.

"Just out and about," Nell replied, again starting to move. "All right Fiona, it's good to see you, bye." And she started walking, quickly followed by Maria.

The two laughed as soon as Fiona was far enough away.

They laughed more as they sat at the table by the fireplace at the pub, which was indeed a lovely, local, intimate place. *The sort of place I like*, Maria thought. She wished she went out to these places more often with Jordi, but he always preferred to stay at home, watching football or a movie. And then, when out with his Opus friends, all they talked about was the Pope's latest encyclical texts, and of course they all agreed with each other. They mostly met in each others' homes, in the upmarket Pedralbes area, and rarely went out. Maria missed the nights out in Pamplona, spontaneously hopping from bar to bar.

She loved this pub's dark wooden floors, the candles, the cracking fire, the old bucket with dry flowers, and the low guitar music that gave it a homely and welcoming air. It also started raining outside, making her feel even happier to be inside.

"Good choice," Maria said.

Nell smiled as a waitress arrived with the menus and two glasses of champagne.

"Hello Nell! Compliments of the house for the regulars, but only for Christmas," the waitress said, gently caressing Nell's hair. Nell stood up and kissed her briefly on the lips.

"Emma, this is Maria," Nell said.

Maria smiled at Nell's friend, she felt comfortable.

After they picked their food and wine and Emma left, Maria smiled at Nell, in complicity.

"Thank you for introducing me to your friend, although you didn't introduce me to Fiona." Maria felt curious about Nell's ex. *Had they lived together? Was Nell still heartbroken? Was Fiona Nell's type?*

"Well, it's still awkward," Nell said and drank a bit of her champagne. "But it's all right now, it's fine."

Nell paused and looked at Maria's dark, olive-skinned fingers in contrast with the pristine, white tablecloth. "To be true, the relationship was never that deep or good," Nell said. "You know she went off with my best mate, from football. I don't know if they are still together, I don't have a clue. I don't want to know, either. I still miss my friend, but not Fiona, definitely not Fiona."

Maria put her long hair behind her ear and looked into Nell's face in the candlelight. It was white and clear, almost like a porcelain doll. Her big nose and short hair gave her the look of someone with strong character, she thought. Maria couldn't stop looking at Nell's big blue eyes, just like Gran Basilisa's; they had the same intelligent, penetrating and compassionate air. They were eyes that observed. Being looked at by them made her feel special.

As they waited for the food to arrive, Maria told Nell about Barcelona – about the sea, the architecture, the secret courtyards, her favourite cafés.

"I can't believe I haven't been there," Nell said. "Is that where you'll get married?"

"No, I wish!" Maria said. "I have to get married in Belchite, my mother would cut me out of the will if I didn't." Maria gave a nervous laugh. "In Spain, brides have to marry in the place they grew up, or where their parents live. You can't just pick your favourite place and marry there. Shame!"

"It sounds very traditional," Nell said. "What about the details, are they all sorted?" She sat back on her chair, as the waitress put their plates in front of them.

Ai, ai, ai. The wedding. Maria started feeling the cold from the door as people came in and out, which she hadn't noticed before. She looked down, then swallowed.

"Yes, it's all getting there," she said without a pinch of excitement in her words. "I can't wait."

Nell lifted her head and looked at Maria with interest. "Good. What about the honeymoon, where are you going?"

"Well, we're still deciding," Maria said, taking a bite of food and looking at the fire. "Jordi, my fiancé, wants to go to Paris, he's quite traditional, but I would love to go on a safari, in Africa, it's once in a lifetime. They are very expensive, so this is the opportunity."

"A safari, how exciting," Nell said. "You should convince him, you're the bride, you're supposed to get your way." She smiled, although the comment didn't seem to cheer Maria up.

"Well, it's not quite like that," Maria said. "Jordi is lovely and open, but there're some things that are non-negotiable, and I am afraid this is one. He's not a traveller, so I think we'll end up in Paris." Maria looked down.

"Oh dear, are you a traveller?" Nell asked.

"Yes, as much as I can be."

"Well, then Paris is lovely as well," Nell said. "Have you been?"

"About a hundred times, I had to go there for work, for a deal last year, almost every other week." Maria sounded down.

Nell had another bite of her food. There was silence. "I am sure you'll get to decide other things," she said.

"Oh yes, sure," Maria said. She had stopped eating.

Nell gave her a penetrating look that Maria felt straight in her heart. "Have you chosen the house?" she asked. "If he's so traditional, that must be your area."

Maria's face was becoming more serious by the second. She looked away.

"Well, that's again something that he sort of rules," Maria explained as her food grew cold on her plate. "He comes from a conservative family and he's quite conservative himself. He feels he has to provide for his wife, so he has bought a flat in a lovely neighbourhood, but I haven't seen it yet – well, first, I don't think it's finished, and also, it's supposed to be a surprise."

Nell raised an eyebrow. "You haven't seen where you'll live? But if you're paying…"

Maria quickly responded. "It's his present, to me."

"Ah," Nell said.

She's noticed something's wrong. Because it is actually wrong that he's so conservative and gets to decide all these things, as if I was a bimbo girl who wanted to be taken over.

Maria remembered Gran Basilisa's words about seeing life from the bullring's barrier – was she doing that? Was she taking the bull by the horns, or was she watching it all from a safe, comfortable distance?

Maria sat back on her chair, she wasn't hungry any more. This, all of a sudden, wasn't fun. She felt like crying.

Maybe it's the wine.

"Weddings aren't easy," she struggled to say. "Everybody focuses on the dress, the flowers and the like. Nobody talks about the true meaning of a wedding."

What rubbish am I going on about? Maria thought, hoping she sounded credible enough.

"Of course, I understand, most of my straight friends say the same." Nell put her hand on Maria's, on the table, making her feel calmer; it felt so soft and delicate. But scared, Maria hid both her hands under the table, moving her fingers nervously against each other.

Nell continued. "I'm sure you would just like to marry him in secret and live with him on a desert island, away from all the fuss."

I would die if I was left alone with Jordi on a desert island. He'd be lost without Opus, without his cava and his football.

Maria felt scared at her thought. Her grandmother's words came back into her mind: "True love is too precious, or even miraculous, to let it go, you must make the effort and make sure it doesn't fly away." *Is this true love? Is this 'miraculous'?*

Maria felt her body temperature rise, she was hot and cold at the same time. She felt uncomfortable and shifted in her chair. She just wanted to go home and hide. *Bombillo...*

Nell had already finished her food.

"Sorry I'm feeling a bit tired," Maria finally said. "Would you mind if we asked for the bill and got going?"

"Sure," Nell said looking at Maria, surprised. "Are you all right?"

"Yes, yes, don't worry about me. You know, every bride gets a bit paranoid before the wedding, that's all."

Nell made a gesture to Emma to bring the bill. "Let's split it, eh?"

Maria nodded.

After a silence, Emma came back saying Nell's card had been rejected. It made her blush. Maria asked to add it all to hers.

"Don't worry," Maria said. That was the least of her problems.

"I am so sorry, I think I've gone over my overdraft," Nell admitted, looking down.

"Overdraft?" Maria looked at her, surprised.

Nell looked to the fire place. "I'm just not very good with numbers or budgets."

Maria looked at her. *She is honest and isn't scared of admitting things.* "I can help you create an easy programme for your accounts if you'd like. That's what I spend my life doing."

Still embarrassed, Nell said: "That would be kind."

Maria felt useful. "Come on, let's go," she said, standing up.

15

Jordi felt the Christmas spirit rise up in him as he drove into Barcelona, seeing all the decorated shops on the Diagonal, the Christmas trees outside, the red and green lights in the buildings. Closely shaven and smartly dressed in a tweed suit, Jordi whistled along to the songs on the radio on this beautiful, sunny, winter morning, as he approached Belagua, his club.

He had spent the week working on the company accounts to include the million-euro loan that his father had arranged with Banca Catalana, and which would soon be in the bank. Jordi had budgeted for the staff salaries, the Christmas bonuses and also left some margin for the ever-present unexpected items. After all the tension over the sales – still falling because of the boycott against Catalan products – the year would end up well. He felt as if he'd saved a match ball. Another company would not have received the loan on similar conditions, but that was the advantage of being an old business, one could build long-term relationships with lenders who trusted the firm.

Jordi turned the volume up as the radio played his favourite song, REM's Happy People. He sighed, he felt God and Christmas inside. Such a shame Maria was still in London, he thought, otherwise he would have loved to go out tonight, walk down the Rambla Catalunya, listen to the Christmas carols in the streets, stroll towards the Cathedral, pray for their future together.

Oh well, soon enough she'll be my wife and I'll see her every day. I can't believe my luck.

Jordi parked Oscar and went into Belagua with no more distraction. Father Juan Antonio had called him the previous night asking if he had time for a chat.

Perhaps he wants to improve things a bit, Jordi thought. His relationship with his spiritual director had tensed since November, when Jordi hadn't been invited to a gathering for the club's biggest donors. The costs at the flat that he was refurbishing were still rising, although he felt more secure now, with the company's problems solved with the loan.

"Good morning, Jordi," Father Juan Antonio said as soon as he walked in. Dressed in his usual cassock, he was sitting on a chair in the church's lateral aisle, as if he'd been waiting for his arrival. "Would you like a confession or have you already been to mass today?"

Jordi was momentarily unsure. "Maybe I'll go tonight," he said. "Maria is in London, so I will probably go then. Also, I have to be back at the Caves soon."

Father Juan Antonio nodded and the two walked towards his room, behind the church, in the same building. The priest sat on his usual big, leather armchair, leaving Jordi on a lower chair in front of him.

"*Ave María Purísima,*" Father Juan Antonio said, blessing Jordi.

The two bent their heads and sat in silence for a few moments – it was a regular Opus practice to bless conversations.

"How have you been, son?" Father Juan Antonio asked. "Looking forward to Christmas?"

Jordi smiled. "Very much so, Father," he said. "My last Christmas as a single man," he said with enthusiasm.

"Next year will be your year, I am sure of that," the priest said and looked down. "I am not so sure I have such good news on my side, though."

Jordi was surprised. "What do you mean, Father?"

Father Juan Antonio rubbed his big hands together, touched his golden ring, the symbol of his marriage to Opus Dei. He sighed. "You know Belagua is in one of the most expensive locations in Barcelona, of course," he said.

Jordi nodded, with pride. *Of course.*

"Well, I don't know if you were aware of it, but we don't actually own this site, we're renting it," he said, passing his hand through his ample, bald head.

Jordi raised an eyebrow. *I didn't know that. Why would you then pay top rates, just to be here? We're a Christian organisation, not a luxury shop.*

Father Juan Antonio continued. "I know, it was also a surprise to me," he said. "I thought we owned everything we use, but that's not the case. The finances are handled from Madrid directly, so I was never aware of it."

Jordi looked at his spiritual director with incredulity. He went on.

"It turns out they've doubled our rent here – what we paid was fixed since the eighties, but the new owners who took over last year have been trying to change it," the priest said, letting a few seconds go by. Jordi raised his eyebrows as Father Juan Antonio continued, "The finance department went to court and lost, so now, not only do we have to pay double rent from now on, but also back-rent for the previous year." Father Juan Antonio swallowed.

"That's bad news," Jordi said, still not understanding how this affected him. "Are you looking for other locations, then?" *Surely nobody would pay these exorbitant prices just to be here.*

The priest shook his head. "Never, Jordi, never. We can't."

"Why not?" Jordi was surprised. *We can't be that focused on appearances, on seeming rich if we are not.*

Father Juan Antonio crossed his legs and whispered. "It's at the heart of Opus Dei to attract the best members. Remember we want first-class, top quality people. That's why our organisation is so successful and why we draw such top people into it. We can't go into a poorer area because we would find mediocre people there, and that's against our spirit."

Jordi frowned. "I am sure we can find quality people anywhere, Father."

"No, Jordi, the orders come from high above, we have to stay here, find a way to pay."

This is a bit silly, if we can't afford it, why don't we go somewhere else? Jordi remembered Father Juan Antonio didn't like to be contradicted and, if the orders came from above, there was nothing to do about it. Obedience was highly regarded in Opus. Still, it was hard for him to agree with such an idea.

Jesus picked his twelve apostles from among the humble fishermen of Galilee. They had few possessions, only big hearts, and that's all he needed. Opus Dei seems different, though, I wonder why? Founder Escrivá de Balaguer didn't pick a handful of people according to their morals, but a group of high-brow, rich and conservative 'señoritos', all men. Maybe these days it's different and the organisation needs better prepared people to spread the message, but it seems odd. Sometimes I understand when they accuse us of elitism.

Jordi noticed father Juan Antonio was looking at him, intently. He coughed and tried to fill the silence. "How are you going to pay, does the club have enough funds with the donations and the fees?" Jordi asked.

"I am asking the members." Father Juan Antonio fixed his glance on Jordi's eyes.

I see. He wants money. This is not a good time for me.

"Right," Jordi sounded hesitant. "Is there any range per member that you are recommending? Any indication? What are the others saying?"

"Of course I am talking to everybody, obviously I can't say who, but everybody in your group is being extremely understanding and generous," he said.

Jordi started to feel hot in his jacket and loosened his tie. He wasn't enjoying this. He had increased his contributions after being excluded from the last gathering, hoping that his mentor would welcome the gesture instead of asking for more.

I know the Catholic church is not a model of democratic habits. But asking for money like this isn't fair. Shouldn't we all sit and talk, openly?

Jordi shifted in his chair as Father Juan Antonio continued.

"In appreciation of such a Christian response from the members who participate, I am creating some sort of top-tier group," the priest said. "For those chosen few, I am planning a visit to the Pope in Rome, and a tour around our Torreciudad sanctuary. We will also go to Madrid to meet some high-ranking people – Opus Dei members in the Government, academia and the press. It will be interesting and educational, top level, an excellent opportunity."

Jordi remained silent. "But what about the people who can't afford large donations, will they be left out?" he dared to ask.

"They won't Jordi, of course they won't." Father Juan Antonio said. "You have such a good heart, son, always thinking about the other people, but remember, fairness means that everyone gets what they deserve."

Yes, I know the world is like that, but isn't this precisely what the Church is expected to help with? Try to make things as equal as possible, in a naturally unequal world? What about Christian charity? I know Opus Dei helps those in need and organises campaigns, but are we doing enough? Is this the right thing? Should we pay so much to keep our privileged location instead of helping those in real need?

Jordi stayed silent for a few seconds. "Is there a specific amount that you're seeking?"

Father Juan Antonio coughed. "About fifty thousand euros each," he said, looking away.

Good God. "That's a lot of money," Jordi said, trying to hide his shock and unhappiness. "How much is the rent for this place, if I may ask?"

Father Juan Antonio looked at him as if he was a naughty child. "You know we can't reveal those figures, Jordi. I am sure you understand."

This can't be right. We shouldn't spend this amount just to keep up appearances.

Jordi felt hotter and hotter, he felt like taking his jacket off but didn't want to look vulnerable in his spiritual director's eyes. He had to stay firm. He tried to quell his negative thoughts, stay positive.

I shouldn't have these rebel thoughts, sorry God. I hope I won't be punished for thinking along those lines. Maybe the organisation is like this because the numeraries running it aren't married or don't have families, they're not used to saving or cutting costs. They are just trying their best and I should help them. Of course I should, of course I'll be part of it.

Jordi coughed and finally spoke. "As much as I would love to give all I have, you know Father that I am getting married soon and I am preparing a home," he paused. "Also, you know the embargo against Catalan products is hurting the Caves, we've actually had to ask for a loan, as a short-term measure, but still a loan." Jordi, embarrassed, saw the impassive look of Father Juan Antonio. He coughed. "Is there a way, would it be possible –" he cut his sentence short, nervously "– are you accepting smaller donations?"

Father Juan Antonio nodded his head up and down. "Of course it would be possible, Jordi, and I am deeply thankful for your generosity," he said. His smile froze, his face became tense, tight. "However, I am afraid I would be obliged to invite you to join another group, at another church in central Barcelona. If you contribute less than the others, it's only understandable that they would want some exclusivity. It would also be odd when we went to see the Pope, or when we prepared for the other trips, to have you here since, as a smaller donor, you would not be allowed to go." Father Juan Antonio looked straight at Jordi, as if he was waiting for an immediate response.

The comment felt like a needle in Jordi's heart. He looked down. *I hope we don't have to go down that route, Father. I am sure you'll help me.*

Father Juan Antonio looked away. "I know it's hard Jordi," he said. "I know I am asking you for a lot, but it's for a good cause. We must help this organisation. Opus Dei is our life, it has given us everything meaningful, what's this amount of money compared to the lifelong happiness and wealth of spirit that the club has given us, and will continue to do so for as long as we live? How much is your life worth?"

I see. Jordi closed his eyes, covered his face with his hands. *I have no escape. I have to give them the benefit of the doubt, surely they must be acting with their best intentions. I can't see my life outside Opus Dei, I would end up superficial and vain like my brothers, or insensitive like my father. I don't want to be like them, I want to be a good Christian. But this is such bad timing.*

Jordi lifted his glance towards Father Juan Antonio. "Is it urgent? Do you need an answer?"

"Sorry, but yes." The priest tapped his armchair with his long, thick fingers. "We need to plan. I am sure you understand."

I can't lose this, I can't lose my club, it's my entire support, more now with the problems at the Caves, and I'll be a married man soon. Where would I go if I had any problem, if anything happened to Maria, God help me, but where else would I find any consolation or support in times of trouble? They've stuck with me since I was a lost teenager, they've taught me the right values, I am the man I wanted to be because of them. I don't want to go to another club in central Barcelona. These are the people that I know, I went to school with them, it wouldn't be the same somewhere else, I would be unprotected, out of my natural world. But if I give this money I won't have a penny left for the flat if anything goes wrong. Although that's unlikely, my builder said yesterday that everything is on schedule. I have to take the risk, be confident, behave like a man. Nothing ventured, nothing gained. I've stuck to this group in the good times, I guess now I have to do the same in the bad times. I can't run away like a coward as soon as the tide changes.

"All right, Father, I will send you a cheque as soon as possible," Jordi finally said.

God help me, God help me.

Father Juan Antonio stood up and smiled. "What a great man you are, Jordi, I knew I could count on you." He walked towards Jordi, tapped his shoulder. "God will be with you, we'll bring this forward together, you'll see. God will reward us for this. Sacrifice is good."

Jordi said nothing and walked away, his legs shaking slightly.

16

Conchita was looking at her mother's tired, pale face and her weak body, connected by several tubes to machines beside the bed, when doctor Jaime tried to remove from her neck the silver cross that she always wore.

"Is it totally necessary?" Conchita whispered, trying not to wake her mother up. "She's worn it all her life, I am sure she'd want to keep it."

Conchita looked at the doctor with begging eyes, then looked outside the window, seeing the high-rise buildings of Zaragoza, the city with the nearest hospital to Belchite. After seeing Gran at home the previous day, Jaime had recommended bringing her here, where he visited patients twice a week.

"That's fine," he said after a few seconds, making Conchita sigh in relief.

"The tests are good, she'll be fine," continued the doctor, who had seen Gran Basilisa for more than a decade. Putting his pencil in the pocket of his white gown, Doctor Jaime continued his explanation in his usual low, unclear voice. "She's still under the effect of the drugs but she'll wake up soon. She will be all right, but absolutely no smoking at all, under no circumstances whatsoever, from now on. Her heart is just about fine for her age, but cigarettes can seriously damage it. She will be at high risk if she continues smoking."

Conchita quickly thanked God for giving her mother another chance.

Gran Basilisa made a low sound, slightly moving her thin lips and half opening her eyes.

Conchita grabbed her mother's hand and spoke to her in the softest tone she could. She hadn't stopped thinking about the letter she had found the day before, about her absent father, about her mother's broken heart.

"Mother, it's me, Conchita, I am here with you. Can you hear me?"

"Um," Gran Basilisa grunted. She then looked around the room, her eyes still not fully open.

"We're in Zaragoza, mother," Conchita said softly. "You were ill and Doctor Jaime suggested you take some tests here; we're at the Descalzas Hospital, you know it well, we've been here before. We arrived yesterday." Conchita remembered the week they spent here ten years ago, when she was given a heart bypass, following a diagnosis of arteriosclerosis. After the initial alarm, it all went as smoothly and quietly as now, with the staff being equally confident and reassuring.

Gran Basilisa raised an eyebrow. "I see," she said. "I'm fine." She smiled, making the others smile as well.

"You'll survive," Doctor Jaime said with a raised brow. "A tough woman like you still has many years ahead, but not if you continue smoking. You must stop it now. This is not advice, it's an order."

Gran Basilisa rolled her eyes – she had obviously heard this many times before.

"All right, ladies, I have to see other patients now, but a nurse will come in a short while." Doctor Jaime walked to the door. "By the way, you can keep that cross, I wondered whether it would interfere with the machines, but you'll be fine." He winked an eye at Gran Basilisa, who smiled in complicity.

The two women sighed as soon as he left.

"Where have you slept?" Gran asked. "I hope you went home."

Conchita smiled. "The sofa-bed is perfectly comfortable."

Gran shook her head. "I don't understand all this fuss, I am perfectly well," she said. She then raised her arm, slowly, to hold her *lingus cruces* – the silver cross with one diamond on each edge – tight in her hand. "I am glad they didn't take it from me."

Conchita looked at her. She'd never been this close to her mother, just the two of them, in such circumstances, away from

218

home. When they'd been to hospital before, Gran had looked more in control and usually there would have been more people around, like Pilar, Maria, Doctor Jaime's father and some neighbours. But now it was only the two of them and Gran looked more depleted, older.

Gran Basilisa was still holding her cross.

"Yes, I asked him not to take it from you," Conchita said. "You always wear it, it's beautiful."

Conchita's words were intentional. She had promised herself not to push her mother into telling her anything about Juan Roso, or about the letter. At her age, and with a bypass, doctors had warned that emotional shocks were better avoided, although she had wondered for a long time where the cross came from. She was now sure that it had some connection with her past.

"It's the one thing that I'd like to keep, if anything," Gran Basilisa said, holding her cross tight.

It must be related to my father. Conchita's heart pounded.

Gran Basilisa took a deep breath. "You should know how important it is, maybe it's about time," she said and turned her head, staring through the window. "I already told Maria a few things some time ago. Sorry, I should have told you before, but Maria seemed in such distress, as if she needed some guidance."

Gran Basilisa let a few seconds go by. "Although I should never think of myself as an example to anybody, to be honest," she said.

Conchita remained silent, her fingers nervously tapping her chair.

Finally.

"I owe you so many explanations, darling, so many," Gran Basilisa said.

Conchita held her breath, looked at her mother with wide eyes.

Slowly, and with effort, Gran Basilisa told her daughter the story of Juan Roso and their passionate love. While speaking, Gran didn't stop looking out of the window, avoiding eye contact; her look was lost, far away. Stunned and without making a single sound and barely blinking, Conchita listened to her mother's memories of what happened in the Plaza, of Ana's death, and of Juan Roso stealing the silver cross from the local church in 1937, giving it to Soledad so she could pass it onto her, the night he left.

A long silence filled the room after Gran Basilisa finished her story. Conchita held her breath for as long as she could.

"*Ave María Purísima*." Conchita finally said, making the sign of the St Cross on her forehead, face and shoulders. *Mother*.

Gran Basilisa took her cross from her neck and opened it with extreme care, using her nails. From the inside she took an old photograph, small and sepia-tinted, delicately rolled in one of the axes.

"This is Juan, your father." Her hands were shaking. She looked deep into Conchita's eyes.

Conchita swallowed three times before taking the small photograph, old and ragged. Her hands were trembling. The photograph was tiny, but she could see, with fierce intensity, a young man with dark skin and a long nose, so similar to hers. His eyes were deep and black, as hers, and as Maria's. They were almost the opposite of Gran Basilisa's pure, crystal-clear ones.

"*Santa María Madre de Dios*." Conchita could only resort to religious thoughts to express her shock. She returned the photograph to her mother and made the sign of the St Cross again. Nervously, she did the last top button of her blouse up, as if she needed protection. She looked down, staring at the tiles on the floor.

She was too confused to think. She couldn't get her father's face out of her mind. It felt as if she had just discovered a new side of herself; as if a stranger had invaded her body. The air in the room felt cold. Conchita shivered.

Gran Basilisa looked at her. "There's nothing to pray so much about, Conchita, this is life, this is what happened."

"Why be silent, all these years?" Conchita finally muttered, still looking down.

Gran Basilisa took a deep breath. "Those days, Conchita... it's not like now. It was better to stay quiet, I could have been killed if they'd found out my link to a Red activist, and what would you have done? We had absolutely nobody. Soledad was hiding in the mountains and I was all by myself, what would have happened to you if I had been taken to prison or killed?"

Conchita looked at her mother, she had to make an effort to contain the tears. *My father, my own father, the one I've never met, and now, when I'm sixty-seven, there he is. Good Lord.*

"Why didn't he come back afterwards? Why didn't you go?" Conchita didn't understand.

"It was still dangerous, especially for somebody who had been actively involved in politics as much as he had. And then, years later, Cuba turned into a communist country, making things even worse." Gran sighed, looked at Conchita. "Also, time erases many things. You can't just carry on with your life as if no time had passed… so many years later."

Raised at a time of deep respect for parents, when direct questions were barely allowed, Conchita felt intimidated about interrogating her mother. She had a long history of having constantly bowed to her, of 'yes' answers to almost everything. But now, this conversation was becoming the most direct and sincere one that mother and daughter had ever had. For once, Conchita didn't fear opening her heart in search of answers.

"Didn't you stay in contact?" she asked, still not daring to look her mother in the eye.

"He wrote to me every day, for years."

"Did you reply?" Conchita was trying to make sense of the letter she had found.

Gran Basilisa closed her eyes. "It wasn't easy, Conchita, you must understand," she said with effort. "I wrote to him the other day, after telling Maria about him, I thought he should be aware that the family knows about him now. It took me many drafts, but I finally wrote to him."

I see, it was a draft that I found, but I can't tell her, yet.

Conchita bit her lips and took a deep breath. "Is he alive?"

Gran Basilisa looked through the window. "I don't know," she said. "I doubt it. He stopped writing a few months ago."

221

Conchita remained pensive for a while. "How could he send you letters from Cuba? Weren't they censored? Wasn't that a threat for you?"

"Yes, but people in those days found a remedy for everything. A friend of his, Jaime, the father of Doctor Jaime, and a long-time Belchite doctor himself, escaped to Barcelona with him. From there, your father took a boat to Cuba, while Jaime went into exile in France, settling in Toulouse. They stayed in touch, so Juan wrote the letters to Toulouse and Jaime managed to smuggle them in via some contacts who regularly walked into the country, through the Pyrenees – sometimes they would pick up more letters in Andorra, where Jaime knew another doctor he could trust. A handful of people, mostly members of clandestine communist cells, must have read those letters before I did."

Conchita remained pensive. "Then Jaime returned, I remember that." Conchita frowned as she remembered the numerous changes that Franco's death brought into the village, including the slow return of the exiled.

"Yes, in 1977," Gran said. "He returned with his son, already a doctor in France. He carried on delivering the letters, but that stopped some months ago."

"Why didn't he write to you directly?"

"I asked Jaime never to give him my address," Gran responded. "I guess I feared the direct contact. You just can't continue a life that you abandoned so long ago. Things aren't that easy."

Conchita thought for a few seconds. "Jaime's father died a few months ago, do you think that his son, Doctor Jaime, knows anything about this?"

"I don't know, Conchita, I don't know," Gran said. "But Juan must be dead by now. In one of his last letters he said he was ill."

Conchita thought for a few moments. "Would you like me to try and help you find out? Perhaps we could…"

Her mother interrupted. "Not now, it's too late."

Jesus. And I thought all she did and cared for in life was work. She's sacrificed her life to keep me afloat, and Soledad as well, and the house, the land. She's missed her life for us. What a woman. And I thought I was the strongest one. How stupid of me.

"And you stayed faithful to him, all your life?" Conchita said, after a long silence.

"I did have another man, once – or rather, he had me," Gran Basilisa said. She blushed for a few seconds and looked away. "A local general fell for me, a brutal inspector for the Falange. I had to be his mistress on condition that he wouldn't try and capture Soledad, who was under a death sentence."

Gran Basilisa turned towards Conchita. "It worked, she survived – but this is not something that I am too keen on remembering."

Oh Mother. Conchita felt like holding her mother's hand, but they weren't used to any closeness, or physical expression of affection. She looked down and held her head with both her hands, covering her face.

"You've done so much, and kept the business afloat, we should build you a monument."

Gran Basilisa smiled. "You would have done the same, and actually have done exactly the same: you have made our local business national, it's a big company now. You've done very well, Conchita, your hard work, consistency and determination have impressed me."

Conchita felt lighter with every one of those words, her heart expanded.

Finally somebody appreciates what I do.

"You did a lot more, Mother," Conchita said, modestly.

"But you did what you had to do. You added trucks and crops, bought fields, the same way that I had to buy and replace chickens and sheep. My first mule felt like a space rocket!"

The two laughed, relieving some of the tension. This was more familiar territory. Emotions had been kept inside for decades, mother and daughter could only handle them for a limited amount of time.

Gran went on: "I felt rich when I could grow onions, tomatoes, beans – it was a luxury when I got a goat to make cheese, you were actually one of the first children in Belchite to eat cheese after the War," she said proudly, making her daughter smile.

"Maybe that's why I love it so much, still when I wake up in the middle of the night and I go to the fridge, I am not tempted by biscuits or chocolate, it's cheese that I reach for."

Conchita felt her heart grow bigger, warmer.

"You also had lovely jumpers," her mother said. "I stole a sheep myself, one night, to get some wool; you don't know how precious that was."

"You stole a sheep?" Conchita laughed.

"And so would you, if you'd had a baby to keep warm in the middle of the Belchite winter."

Conchita breathed and undid the top button of her thick, grey blouse; she was feeling a bit hot. "True."

"I hid the sheep in my bedroom, your bedroom as well, for months, so the inspectors wouldn't see it, it was all rationed in those days." Gran was now smiling, had more colour in her cheeks. "But of course, being a single mother, I got less rations of rice, bread, olive oil, chick peas and beans than the others, so I had to fight for it myself. And we also had to share it with Soledad, who came from the mountains in the middle of the night, every now and again."

"She used to read me stories when you were in the fields," Conchita remembered, feeling Soledad's tender words on her ears, as if it was yesterday. "Didn't anybody help you?"

"Not really," Gran said with resignation. "The new regime condemned single mothers. Women moved to the other side of the street when I went to the open-air laundry rooms. The butchers always gave me the worst cuts. The neighbours looked me up and down when I walked along the street, and of course I was never invited to anything. But to be honest, between you and me, the fields, organising the workers and Soledad coming unexpectedly, risking her life, as well as ours, that kept me busy enough."

Conchita watched Gran Basilisa's peaceful face, now with her eyes tired, half closed. She was full of admiration for her mother, and for the first time in many, many years, she felt the cord that had once united them. Her cheeks coloured as she recalled things she thought were deeply buried in the past.

"I remember we hid sacks of flour in the middle of the night!" Conchita exclaimed with the enthusiasm of a little girl. "You made me hide some bottles of olive oil, and we had to be completely silent, until a man would knock on the corral and we traded the olive oil for rice or flour, right?"

"Those were the days," Gran Basilisa said. She closed her eyes and yawned.

Oh maybe this is getting too much, shouldn't get her excited. But Conchita couldn't stop the torrent of memories that all of a sudden invaded her heart.

"But then I left for boarding school, in Zaragoza, and the fun stopped." Conchita's face became sad.

Gran Basilisa, visibly tired, looked at her daughter and reached out her hand towards her. Conchita moved slightly, leaving a very short distance between her hand and her mother's.

"Yes, I know," Gran admitted, in a sad tone. "But I didn't have any alternative. What future or education would you have had in Belchite, being raised by a mother who was completely ostracised? Nobody would have taught you anything. Also, that was the time that I had to start seeing that inspector, it wouldn't have been good for you, as he wanted me to cook for him, give him almost my entire attention. It's sad, but that's also how we survived, Soledad as well."

Conchita's heart shrank. *Oh Mother, you gave your life for us.*

Trembling, she took her mother's hand, holding it gently. Conchita couldn't remember having seen the two hands together before. They had held hands in the past, but they hadn't been *together*, like this.

Gran Basilisa closed her eyes, breathed deeply, under the blanket.

"I know, Conchita, I haven't been a good mother to you," she said, very slowly, still with her eyes closed. "But please believe me when I say that I tried my best, always trying to do everything in your best interest. I wanted you to have your own life, unlike me. I didn't want you to miss the boat, like I did."

Conchita couldn't stop looking at her mother's face. She now saw her differently, as a person in her own right. She didn't look like her mother anymore, she'd turned into a heroine with a deep, noble past. "You did what you could, and that's all that matters," she said.

Gran Basilisa opened her eyes again and smiled at her daughter, who looked away, fearful and unaccustomed to the emotional tension. Gran Basilisa took the cross from her neck and handed it to her daughter.

"You keep it, now that you know, it's part of you, you deserve it," she said. "You've been a good child, you've never given any trouble, have always done as you were told and have built a lovely family – something I failed to do."

Conchita felt appreciated for the first time in many years. With shaking hands, she took the cross, holding it as if it was the most delicate object in the world.

"I'll keep it forever, Mother."

"Some day you can pass it to Maria – she seems as if she needs it."

Conchita was going to ask her about Maria, but on second thoughts, she refrained from it as it could be too much for her mother's delicate heart. *Another time. When she comes back home.*

A gentle knock on the door alerted Conchita to the arrival of the nurse, who walked in silently.

After looking at the two women, she said: "Maybe it's time for a rest." She looked at Conchita and said: "It's getting quite late and your mother needs to sleep."

Conchita nodded and kissed her mother on her forehead as gently as she could.

"I'll come back in a few minutes," Conchita said, putting her coat on.

She closed the door behind her, holding the cross tightly. Standing by herself in the middle of the hospital aisle, she didn't know where to go, what to do.

I love my mother. I've seen my father. I've been a good daughter. After all these years, it turns out I've been a good daughter and I've built the family she always dreamed of.

Conchita quickly covered with her hands the tears she could no longer stop, and rushed towards the hospital's chapel.

17

Jordi took a long, deep breath, feeling the cold air travel down into his lungs. He fixed his glance on the blue horizon of the Mediterranean sea, flat and sparkling under the late afternoon sun – his favourite time of the day. He preferred the Barcelona beaches in the winter, quiet and silent, such a contrast to when they are packed with tourists in the summer. Shoes in hand, Jordi rolled up his trousers, took his tie off and walked along the shore, feeling the icy water on his feet.

What a relief that work on the flat is going well, he thought.

After his meeting with Father Juan Antonio earlier on that day, Jordi had rushed to Sarrià to check on the apartment. The builders looked busy; the construction was going according to plan. He'd had second thoughts about his agreement with Father Juan Antonio to give him a fifty thousand-euro donation; it was an amount that would leave him with no margin of error. He needed to think and, after cancelling a meeting in the afternoon at the Caves, he went for an early afternoon mass in Santa Maria del Mar, his favourite Barcelona church. While admiring the Gothic style, Jordi listened to the priest's sermon about charities, about giving to those in need, a typical topic just ahead of Christmas. He prayed on his knees for half an hour after the mass, finally deciding to write the cheque to Belagua, his club. He posted it just outside the church.

In need of fresh air, Jordi walked to the beach, a stone's throw away from Santa Maria del Mar, in the old part of Barcelona.

I don't know what I'll do if anything goes wrong, but I'll keep my fingers crossed. I have to help Opus: they help me, I care for them, as simple as that.

Jordi stretched his arms out to the sea and breathed in the wind. He was walking along the shore when his mobile rang.

Maria, maybe it's Maria calling from London. Finally.

He searched hurriedly for his phone in his jacket's inner pockets, but frowned when he saw it was Robert, the company's lawyer. He let the phone ring three times to recover from his initial disappointment – he'd been trying to get hold of Maria for a couple of days, she seemed so busy in London.

He answered, wondering what his lawyer had to say about Peñaranda, the duke who visited him in the Caves last month, claiming the land.

Jordi barely spoke during the short conversation. He kept looking at the horizon, his eyes wide open; then he shut them tight. When the call had finished, Jordi dropped his arms, still holding the phone, frowning. He looked at the sea, then at his phone, then closed his eyes again. He shook his head several times.

It's not true.

Jordi put his hand over his mouth, then over his head.

Why is everything going wrong? What have I done?

He looked at the sky, imploring God for calm and patience. He could still hear the words from his lawyer in his head. Yes, Peñaranda was right. The Duke's family owned the Gratallops' land in the Penedès.

Calling from Salamanca, his lawyer had found evidence of the Peñarandas' ownership in the Civil War archives, as well as in the Barcelona and Madrid land registry offices. Indeed, Pere Gratallops, Jordi's grandfather, the foreman of the Caves before the War, took over the land after the War ended in 1939. As Peñaranda said, most of his family had been assassinated and it wasn't uncommon for the surviving foremen to gain control of the land they had worked.

There was no way around it, the lawyer had stated, confessing his shock. He would now explore ways to fight the case in court.

Jordi sighed again and walked, randomly, a few steps to one side, then to the other, still holding his mobile phone tight.

I have to think clearly. God is testing me. And I just sent that big cheque, what an idiot, maybe I will need that money now. This may be an expensive process. Damn, damn.

He almost pressed the key to call his father but thought that his fragile heart wouldn't welcome this shock. He would talk to him face to face. He had to. *What about all the times he's told us the land has belonged to four generations of Gratallops?*

Jordi wanted to call Maria, how much he needed her now; how distant she had been recently, with all the trips to London. He called her, but all he got was her voicemail.

He pressed the mobile phone hard with his hands. He almost threw it into the sea.

The image of Peñaranda came to his mind. *These madrileños, always the same. Bastards.*

Jordi watched the waves come and go for a few minutes, listening to their peaceful sound, smelling the salty air. He looked at the sky, trying to feel calm, the support from God, the calm of the red Mediterranean sunset.

I am yours, I am in your hands, he prayed. *If this is a test, I'll take it. If this is a step to settle this issue for the generations to come, I'll accept the challenge. But please, stay with me at all times.* Jordi bowed his head to the horizon, although he couldn't keep the questions out of his mind.

Why didn't Dad tell me? He must not know, otherwise he would have told me. I have to give him the benefit of the doubt. He could not have lied to me, or to the entire family.

Jordi looked at the waves, breaking on the shore, covering his bare feet.

I have to talk to Dad, now.

He walked back to Oscar, leaving the peaceful beach behind. He looked at the buildings nearby, the buzz of people and cars. He felt distant from the world, detached.

The good things are reserved for heaven, this world is for suffering. Now I understand.

About an hour later, Pere Gratallops leaned back on his wide leather armchair and lit one of his favourite Habano cigars. He had listened to Jordi without a single interruption, looking straight into his eyes. He took his glasses off and left them on his wide oak desk.

"Yes, what you say is true," he said, with a serenity that pushed Jordi to the edge of his chair.

"What?" he shouted at his father, probably for the first time in his life. "Why didn't you tell me? What is this? Why did you lie to us, saying that this land has been ours for four generations?"

Jordi felt betrayed. In one day, Opus Dei, his lifeline, had threatened to demote him if he didn't pay an amount that he didn't have – although he'd paid it, using some of the funds for the wedding and the flat. And now he had learned his father had let him, and the entire family, down. Jordi felt alone.

Pere Gratallops stood up and walked towards the big windows overlooking the vineyards; it was almost dark. He inhaled his cigar a few times while Jordi, biting his nails, stared at him.

"I didn't lie to you, Jordi," the old man finally said. "It is true that four generations of Gratallops have worked this land and have produced wine from these vineyards."

"But not as owners, they were labourers, the foremen!" Jordi quickly said, biting his lips.

Pere Gratallops walked to his desk and took an old, battered folder from one of the drawers. He took some old photographs from it, spreading them over his desk. Jordi looked at them keenly. He recognised his grandfather, also called Pere Gratallops. He had died when his father was fourteen, or that was what he'd been told. Other photos were almost too old to recognise anything.

"This is a long story, Jordi, maybe I should have shared it with you and your brothers, but one never knows what's best,"

Pere Gratallops said with sad eyes. "I owe the truth to you, but I always tried to look more at the future than at the past, as a father, as head of this family. Sometimes it's better to ignore things and move on, son, I am sure you'll learn that some day, if you haven't learned it by now."

"I want to know the truth," Jordi said in an unusually commanding tone.

Pere Gratallops swallowed and looked at his photographs.

"This is in the late nineteenth century," he said, pointing at a round photo showing a man with a large moustache and a woman covered by a black mantilla. "They are my grandparents, whom I never met. They lived in a village in Extremadura, very poor land now, imagine what it was like back then. Their ancestors were Catalan, which explains our last name."

Pere Gratallops took the photograph and looked at it in detail. He smoked more of his cigar and continued. "My grandfather was a labourer who worked himself to death in the fields, but he saved enough to buy my father a train ticket to Barcelona, the only place in Spain where there was some industrial development. Like hundreds of others in the south, my father came to seek opportunity in the beginning of the century, following the boom after the Universal Exhibition in 1898. He was fourteen when he arrived in Barcelona in 1907."

Jordi looked at his father in amazement, he had never heard him tell a story like this. He was used to seeing him running around, working hard, but not sitting like an old man, sharing his thoughts. The change made him nervous. Jordi hadn't smoked in years, but he took a cigarette from the pack his father had on the table. He coughed after inhaling, but kept the cigarette in his fingers, playing with it, almost dropping it a few times. Ignoring his son's clumsiness, Pere Gratallops stood up again, walked slowly towards the window, fixing his glance on the vineyards.

"Your grandfather found a job in a factory in Barcelona, but they paid less than nothing and his dreams of owning a little business were killed within days," he said. "The old-time Catalan industrial families shut themselves off from the new immigrants, isolating them in the new working-class areas that were being built, the same ones that you see now." Pere Gratallops swallowed.

And I thought that I came from an old, established, Catalan bourgeois family; now it turns out my grandfather lived in those horrible, high-rise suburbs, Jordi thought in shock. *Not that I have anything against them, but...*

"Your grandfather was a man of the land," his father said, returning to his armchair. "He'd grown up in the fields of Extremadura, he knew about mules, oil and grain. He felt trapped in the smoke of the big city as soon as he set foot in it."

"So he came here," Jordi interrupted.

Pere Gratallops nodded. "He was a hot-blooded man, strong and hard working, and soon found a job, under the Peñarandas, but the working conditions were even worse than in the city: only one rest day a week, no annual holiday, no medical treatment and little food. In those days, Spain could have been in the Middle Ages."

Jordi nodded. "But it was already the early twentieth century."

"This country had been in lethargy since the Inquisition, never forget that," Pere Gratallops said.

Jordi was surprised to hear his father talk like this. Jordi felt it was him who always pushed to give decent pay rises to the Caves's workers, and usually had to fight to get his father's approval. It was odd to hear him talk now as if he cared about workers, odd to see his human side. Odd to talk to him man to man.

"But your grandfather was too proud and soon organised a workers' union, there was a strong anarchist and communist movement in Barcelona in those days," Pere Gratallops said, surprising Jordi even more: his only relationship with this past was through history books. Little did he know his family had been part of it. His father continued.

"Your grandfather was sixteen during the so-called Tragic Week that devastated Barcelona, with the anarchist bombs killing dozens at the Opera House," he said. "He battled all his youth to help those in need, always against the masters, the

233

Peñarandas in his case. Not until his late thirties, when he saw the Republic would eventually triumph, did he settle down with a woman from Vilafranca, very Catalan herself. She taught him Catalan grammar during the years of the Republic, showed him the country, the folklore, helped him read the classics, learn the traditional songs. He fell in love with the Catalan land and became a devotee of the Virgin of Montserrat. They married a year before the Republic was proclaimed and had me in 1931, and a little girl two years later."

Jordi raised his eyebrows. "Did you have a sister? I didn't know." He lit another cigarette.

"You see?" his father said. "I am not sure if you need to know this. The past sometimes is better kept where it belongs, in the past."

Jordi smoked his cigarette, looked at his father intently. "If she was my aunt, I'd like to know, I think I have the right to know."

His father gave him a look of understanding and carried on. "She was killed in the War, during an anarchist attack on the Caves," Pere Gratallops said. "I was only six; all I remember is that my father and some other anarchists wanted to gain control of the Caves. They killed some of the Peñarandas; they got the master, but other family members survived and retaliated, firing against the rebellious workers and their families. They shot the little girl as we all ran to the refuge, she was in my mother's arms, they could have shot her as well. But they got little Montserrat; she was four."

Pere Gratallops put down his cigar in the ashtray. Jordi's blood froze at the thought of his father running away while his little sister was shot dead.

"I loved her very much," the old man said. "I used to take care of her all the time. I remember teaching her how to clap her hands, how to say her first words."

Jordi remained silent, looked at his father's sad, broken face.

Father you've suffered so much in this life, and you've kept it all to yourself.

Jordi felt admiration for his father for the first time in years.

"The rest is history," Pere Gratallops said. "My father escaped the fighting and walked to France, returning incognito in 1940, wearing a wig to avoid being recognised. This house was in ruins, all the Peñarandas had disappeared. My mother had been waiting with me at her parents', in Vilafranca, so we moved to this house, taking control. He worked the land by himself, and with my mother, until he could hire two workers. He built it all from scratch. He offered his workers good conditions and taught them Catalan and played Catalan songs, they danced *sardanes*, even when they were prohibited. You know what happened afterwards. The *Guardia Civil* warned him but he was too stubborn to change. They finally took him and shot him in Montjuïc. I am sure he preferred to die than kneel down to them. He was too strong-minded, one has to be a bit more flexible in this life, it's not healthy to be so strong-headed. I was fourteen and had to take care of the business and my mother, who died a year later of a broken heart."

Jordi lit another cigarette, looking at his father with respect. *That's why you are so fickle, Father, that's why you can flirt with all those Madrid ministers. You don't think that ideals are worth a broken family, you lost your parents so early on, you had to do it all by yourself and now you just want to protect those around you. I see.*

"Why didn't you tell me all this before?" *I could have understood you so much better earlier on.*

Pere Gratallops took the photographs, put them back into the old folder and looked at his son. "Some things are better buried in the past. No need to revive them," he said in a solemn tone.

He let a few seconds go by. "I would appreciate it if you kept this between ourselves. Please promise."

Jordi tightened his lips, shut his eyes. He hadn't told his father about Peñaranda's claims, he had only said he'd found out about the land by chance, digging into old archives. *I can't tell him about Peñaranda. It is too sensitive. I can't tell him – at least not now, not with his delicate heart.*

"Promise," Jordi finally said, and inhaled his cigarette. His father observed him smoking, he didn't seem to have noticed before.

"I didn't know you smoked," Pere Gratallops said.

"I don't, sorry Father," Jordi said, putting down his cigarette and lowering his head.

"You don't have to be sorry for smoking, son. Sometimes I wish you had more vices, sometimes they're good for you," he said, and took a long pull on his cigar. "Life isn't perfect, you may as well admit it and give yourself some breaks."

Jordi didn't dare respond. *I spend my life trying to avoid vice. I can now see that you fall into vice to keep sane – I am even suspicious that sometimes you've seen other women. Sometimes you arrive home so late, when I know nothing really relevant is happening at the Caves.*

"I now have work to do," Pere Gratallops said, turning his head towards some folders by the side of his table.

Time to go.

Jordi left his father's office in silence.

Maybe I should fall into vice as well.

18

Maria and Nell came out of the Drapers' Arms both looking down, feeling the cold and the wind. The streets were almost empty, except for the random groups of drunken office workers, already out for one of their many Christmas dos. The evening had started well for Nell and Maria, both feeling excited about negotiating some guidelines for the Post Office site, as well as spending time in front of a warm fire in a comfortable pub. But Nell's questions about the wedding had put Maria in a sad mood. Deep in her heart, Maria knew there was something wrong with the wedding. It all became clearer away from Barcelona, with the sense of perspective that London gave her. Maria walked after Nell, looking down at the cobblestones.

"When are you going to see your cat again and play with the fish cane?" Nell asked, grabbing Maria's arm and walking beside her.

She's trying to cheer me up. The thought of Bombillo chasing the cane around her flat in Barcelona brought warmth back to Maria's heart.

"I am going back tomorrow afternoon, after the morning meetings," Maria said with a sigh.

The two walked across Gibson Square towards Maria's hotel.

"We're just behind the Post Office again. Funny, we haven't talked about the guidelines at all," Nell said.

"Yeah." Maria didn't sound that interested. *The Post Office site, the wedding. Problems piling up.*

"If you don't have time tomorrow, I could show you the guidelines now, online, if you have a laptop," Nell said. "Our website is a bit tricky, you have to know how to use it."

Maria looked at her watch, and at Nell. It was late, but she needed to see it before going back if she wanted to have any chance with the site. She appreciated Nell's company as well, especially as thoughts about the wedding were lying heavy on her heart.

"Yes, I have a laptop in the hotel, it has fast Internet connection," she said. "I could also build a little model for your budget, it will only take a few minutes. You don't need to tell me the exact figures, we can do it in principle if you want."

Nell looked down. "I certainly need that." She still felt embarrassed about her card being declined at the pub.

As they turned into Upper Street, the wind became stronger and Maria had to put her hair back as it was being blown all over her face. Nell moved closer to her and put her arms on her back, searching for the hood on her anorak. She then lifted it and put it on Maria's head. Nell looked into Maria's black eyes and tied up the lace, then tapped her shoulder and smiled.

Maria looked down, feeling both uncomfortable and excited about the closeness. She pressed her lips together and didn't know what to say. The two walked towards the hotel in silence, arm in arm, listening to their own steps on the ground, hearing their own breath above the wind.

With only one chair available at the desk, the two women sat on the bed, their backs leaning up on the pillows against the wall, both looking at the screen. They ordered hot chocolate to warm them up from the cold outside. Their cheeks were still rosy from the freezing weather.

"This building was just approved and it took them two years," Nell pointed out a social housing development near Percy Circus that had had to be redesigned as many as three times. "You see, you need windows bringing in masses of light, only three stories, bricks, and never aluminium, never."

"I see," Maria said, leaning a bit towards Nell, trying to have a better view.

Nell went through the Council's website, explaining where the urban guidelines were, while Maria took notes on her comments about what mattered most to the Council.

Tired, Maria placed her notebook on the bedside table and took a deep breath.

"It's going to be difficult, isn't it?" she said. "Do you honestly think we have any chance at all with the Post Office site?"

Nell moved her hands from the laptop and turned to face Maria. "Very little, to be honest. It would cost you a fortune to build something that the Council would accept."

Maria looked towards the window. "My future father-in-law, who owns the company, has already said that he won't put one euro more into the project. I don't know, it's going to be very hard to negotiate with him, he's tough."

"I see," Nell seemed interested. "It must be difficult to do business with family."

Maria looked into her eyes. "That's precisely why I am not at home, in Belchite." She let a few seconds go by. "Plus, I don't really get on phenomenally well with my parents, which would only make things worse."

"Don't you?" Nell asked. "What a shame. I thought Spanish families spent time together, that they were very close to each other."

"That's the idea from the outside," Maria said. "But it's not always true, especially in a place like Belchite, where some family fights are as old as the Civil War and still haven't been solved. We have some of that in my family."

Nell slowly turned round to face Maria, still with the laptop on her lap. "Still? Haven't they managed to move on yet?"

"No, it's all buried in their hearts," Maria said. "My grandmother's best friend, who's always lived with us, Soledad, she can barely talk to my father, a Franco supporter – would you believe it?"

"Still?" Nell asked, surprised.

"Still." Maria turned slightly towards Nell. "My father isn't a good man. Apart from his ideas, he also cheated on my mother, a few years ago."

Maria stopped for a few seconds. She felt comfortable talking to Nell, she was a good listener, she was easy to talk to, understanding. She hadn't talked to anybody like this, with such an open heart, lying on a bed, for years. Not since her friend at school, when they shared teenage secrets and slept in the same bed, sometimes holding hands. Maria closed her eyes and felt a sparkle in her heart. She loved Nell's company, the friendship, the closeness.

"I have never seen any affection between my mother and my father, you see," she continued.

Nell touched her hand briefly. Maria felt the link between the two.

"But you have to understand it," Maria continued. "It's not a drama, it's just unfortunate. They grew up in the Franco years, with all the repression, the hunger. It was the same for everybody, no matter which side you were on during the War."

"There're no winners in a war," Nell said.

"Everybody loses," Maria agreed. "My parents' generation only learned how to survive, and the only way of prospering was by cheating or stealing. Nobody got any education, really. Everything was imposed."

And that's what I was taught as well. When I tried to raise a point to my parents, all I got was a slap, that was the only language they knew. Maria remembered her father's usual response: "There is no dialogue." But she kept these thoughts to herself.

She looked at Nell. "In my generation we were a bit luckier, but at school, still, we were only asked to memorise lists of facts, kings and queens, but never to understand ideas, least of all challenge them."

"Well, you look as if you have your own ideas," Nell said, taking Maria's hand. "I liked what you said before about having to dress as a poet to be one. I agree with that, I try to see through people, whatever the outside."

240

Maria smiled. "Well, you thought I liked restaurant chains just because I am a banker."

"I was teasing." Nell hit Maria's arm gently with her fist. "You are a smart person, and it's easy to talk to you."

Maria blushed. "Of course I can listen, but I am sure most of the people that you deal with do as well."

"You would be surprised at the characters that I come across," Nell rolled her eyes. "But you are open-minded. You even came to a lesbian party!"

Maria quickly looked away. *The party. I hope we're not going to talk about the kiss. Maybe she wants to. Oh no, please, not now. I was feeling so comfortable.*

She tried to change the subject.

"Well, I try to stay open-minded," she said. "Open is good. I'd like my home to be bright and cheerful, with people coming in and out all the time – quite the opposite of my parents', which was full of closed doors and shouts." She paused. "I love it here, in England, the fact that that people are polite, they don't shout."

Nell laughed. "They do, believe me – but maybe not so much."

Maria looked at Nell's eyes, now darker in the absence of daylight, but still blue. She felt at peace.

"I love coming to England, for work, or for a holiday. I love that people are so quiet and respectful." Maria stopped, while Nell put the laptop on the bedside table on her side, then turned and curled her body towards Maria.

"Sometimes I wish we were more natural, a bit less stiff," Nell said. "I've always loved the Mediterranean countries, much more open to nature, and not only because of the weather, it's also in the personality, isn't it? Less rational, more instinctive, more natural."

"Sometimes too instinctive and too natural!" Maria smiled. "It's funny you say that, my grandmother recently told me about nature, she said it will always win."

Nell nodded. "I believe that."

Maria turned her body, facing Nell. She felt like having a good, open chat in the anonymity of a London hotel. She loved the freedom to do that.

"I guess that being a lesbian, this is something that you've obviously thought about."

Nell thought for a few seconds. "Yes, nature tells you you're gay, and there's not much that you can do about it," she said. "But it doesn't say which woman you should go for – that's the difficult one!"

The two laughed.

"Fancy a drink?" Maria asked. The conversation had cheered her up, the intimacy had made her feel special, alive, accompanied.

I love my London adventure. Love it.

"I can make you a *mojito* if you like them, there is some rum in the minibar and I could ask room service to bring the other ingredients. Fancy one?"

"I love *mojitos*," Nell said, excited.

A few minutes later, she was watching with admiration as Maria made the cocktails, diligently crushing the ice, chopping the mint, adding the soda to make two tasty, fresh *mojitos*.

"You have all these hidden talents," Nell said.

"Hidden?"

They toasted each other and took a sip; Nell smiled immediately. "Mmmm," she mumbled.

"I can do other things apart from spreadsheets," Maria said, sitting on the bed again. "Talking of which, I haven't done your little budget yet." She stood up to take the laptop, lying back on the bed again. She built a spreadsheet within minutes, colour-coding the spending categories to make it more user-friendly.

"You're so quick," Nell looked at Maria in admiration, making her blush. She reclined her head on her own arm, lying on the bed.

Maria said nothing, Nell continued. "You must be very excited now, you're about to start your own family, you will be able to create the atmosphere that you want at home," she said. "That must be very liberating."

242

Maria had a sip of the *mojito* and looked at Nell. She felt like opening her heart, finally, to somebody willing to listen. Nell could be trusted. What did she know about Spain, Opus, her family? Nobody would ever know that she'd spoken to her. She would go back to Barcelona tomorrow, and that would be it. It was a one-off, and she was enjoying it more than she could have ever thought. She hadn't expected a girly, friendly chat like this. She now realised how good it was. How much she'd missed it over the past few years. She liked Nell as much as she liked her friend, back at school. It was the same innocent friendship. She needed this closeness. Her heart needed it, badly. She'd spent too many years shut in on herself.

"Well," Maria sighed. "I am sure you've gathered by now that things aren't perfect with my boyfriend."

Nell nodded.

Maria continued: "Although they're never perfect, are they?" She gave a nervous laugh. "Maybe I am just having a pre-marital crisis."

Maybe not.

"Sometimes I feel a bit out of the picture with Jordi," Maria said. "I saw you with your friends, you seem to blend, to be natural with them, even physical, you kiss each other, you touch each other. That doesn't really happen with Jordi. But maybe I am only being impatient. Maybe it will all work out once we add that element to our relationship – I already told you he's very religious, so he can't really do anything before we get married. It's a pain, believe me."

"I can understand," Nell said, touching Maria's hand.

Maria looked at both hands together, again, the difference in colour was striking, and so attractive to observe.

"I miss this type of affection, the lack of it makes the relationship too clinical, as if we were children, or robots. But I want somebody to touch me, to desire me, to treat me as a woman. Do you know what I mean?" Maria looked at Nell intently with her big, black eyes.

"Yes," Nell said. "I can't understand how he can avoid the temptation, you're beautiful, you have gorgeous hair, doesn't he want to caress it?" She put her head down on the pillow.

Gorgeous hair. Gorgeous hair.

"Do I?" Maria blushed. "Well, not really, he tries to avoid as much contact as he can." Maria now had a cheeky look. "Sometimes I've worn short skirts, or sexy underwear that he could see under a clear blouse, but there's no response, he's made of cast iron."

Nell smiled. "I wouldn't be able to do that. I'd spend all day playing with your hair."

"It's only because I am dark and in England there're not that many people with black hair, otherwise, there's nothing special about it."

Maria looked away and didn't see Nell's hand coming towards her head until she felt an extremely gentle touch on the side, just behind her ear. Her heart pounded fast. Neither of them moved an inch. The silence was sepulchral. Maria, still looking away, couldn't look at Nell, she didn't want to feel too exposed. For a few seconds, she held her breath as Nell's delicate, long hand touched and slightly curled her hair.

"It's very special," Nell said, taking her hand back. Maria breathed. "It's long and black, thick and strong. Shinier than I've ever seen before." Nell smiled.

"Um." Maria didn't know what to say.

"Let me give you a little head massage to relax, I like doing that," Nell said softly.

Maria said nothing but turned, lying on her stomach, a few seconds later. She felt like she used to when she was a child, playing in the tree houses she built at the back of the garden in Belchite. She would spend hours, unaware of the time or the risk. Those were the days when time didn't matter, when nothing mattered.

Oh yes. Maria sighed.

With her eyes closed, she remembered her teenage friend. That's what they used to do in her Belchite bedroom, stay close and gently touch their heads, their hands, during the long summer nights, with only the light of the moon. That's when she'd been the happiest in her life. That's when she didn't need anything else, as she felt now, something she had never experienced with Jordi.

Nell slowly stopped what she was doing, went to the bathroom and came back with a little hot towel. Slightly pushing her jumper upwards, Nell placed the towel on Maria's lower back, making her feel like she was in heaven.

I could stay like this forever.

"What about yourself?" Maria said, still facing down, her head buried in her own arms – it was less embarrassing. "What sort of women are you interested in? They are lucky if you give them massages like this."

Nell stopped moving her hands for a few seconds, then continued, now moving towards Maria's neck. The touch of Nell's hands gave Maria goose-pimples all over. It was so delicate, so different from Jordi's tough, masculine touch.

Don't stop, don't stop.

"I guess it's the people that I most enjoy spending time with, and that I can't stop looking at," Nell said. "But above all, it just feels right. I believe in fate. I think we all know, deep down in our hearts, what's going to happen to us. We know if something is right or not."

Again, nature.

Nell's caresses, now extending to the top of Maria's back and her shoulders, felt as tranquil as she'd ever experienced. They were so slow she hadn't even noticed when Nell's hand moved from her shoulder to the centre of her back, and up to her neck again. Maria felt like sleeping, peacefully, although she was wide awake. Nell lay next to her, her body very close to Maria's, who welcomed the heat, the closeness, the intimacy. The two, instinctively, gently moved their bodies towards each other, Maria's head still buried in her own arms. She then turned and leaned it against Nell's shoulder.

Nell's hand moved to Maria's forehead and, with a finger, she drew the lines of her eyebrows, her eyes, her cheeks, then around her nose, behind her ears, and her lips. Maria felt her lips getting warmer and warmer as Nell's long finger drew a circle around them. She closed her eyes. Nobody had treated her with this delicacy before. She opened her mouth, slightly, and without knowing why, she touched Nell's finger with her lips, without kissing it. The two stayed in silence for a few seconds. Maria felt Nell's hand now being placed, almost like a feather, on her stomach, and staying there. Maria held her breath.

She felt Nell closer and closer, then her mobile phone rang, loudly, insistently. The two lay without moving, their lips so close to each other that it was a miracle they didn't touch.

Confused, Maria looked at the clock on the bedside table. It was past midnight. Who would call now?

The phone didn't stop ringing. Maria, now back with her feet on the ground, moved quickly towards the desk and saw it was her mother. *Weird. How weird. Now? Why now Mama? You always ruin everything!*

"Hello, what's up?" Maria said, short, angry.

"Maria, it's your mother," Conchita said. "You have to come home immediately. Gran has died."

19

The veil of the mantilla covered Conchita's face as she walked, feet dragging, towards the Santa Fátima de los Dolores church in Belchite. Dressed impeccably in black, along with Honorato, Maria and Pilar, Conchita slowly climbed the few steps to the church. Soledad, Jordi and Pilar's children and her husband followed, silent. Behind them came about one hundred villagers, most of them praying aloud, rosaries in hands. The two human-sized white angels guarding each side of the church entrance looked down the retinue as it reached the steps. Gran Basilisa was going to be buried on this dark, cloudy December afternoon.

With an effort, Conchita reached the top of the stone steps and sighed. Everybody stopped and looked at her sombre figure, covered in black from head to ankle. The group ended its fourth consecutive rosary as the church bells announced the funeral. Belchite, with most of its shops closed, had stopped its life to say farewell to one of its daughters, a moral example and a generous employer, who fought isolation with care and love, the local priest had said around the village. He had also asked for support for Basilisa's daughter, the immaculate Conchita, a call that the locals had responded to en masse.

Conchita's sobs, and those of Pilar and Maria, were drowned out by the sound of the bells. Such a contrast with the absolute silence inside the church, once everybody had entered. Impossibly packed, all those attending kneeled.

After a few minutes of silence, the bishop of Zaragoza entered the church, golden staff in hand, dressed in a black cassock and a white palio band, his head covered by a mitre. He bowed in front of the altar, kissed it, and turned to face the crowd. Summoned by the local priest, he had come from Zaragoza to make the first service by a bishop in Belchite, ever.

"In nomine Patris, et Filii, et Spiritus Sancti," the bishop said, signalling the holy cross with the stick.

"Amen," everybody replied.

"Gratia Domini nostri Iesu Christi, et caritas Dei, et communicatio Sancti Spiritus sit cum omnibus vobis." The bishop had his eyes closed, his hands lifted together.

"Et cum spiritu tuo," the congregation responded as one.

After the first prayer, the bishop welcomed the deceased's family and the other members of the congregation. Within seconds, Conchita started to feel hot, almost dizzy and heavy, standing up in the packed church and with the heating turned up full. The bishop hadn't given the order to sit down yet, but Conchita couldn't hold out anymore, she hadn't slept in two nights, she hadn't stopped thinking for hours and hours. Soledad had forced her to eat the very little she had taken in since Gran died two days ago. On the verge of fainting, Conchita sat down, immediately feeling Pilar's hand on her shoulder. She was sitting between her two daughters and near Soledad, the four of them in the front row. The rest of the family was behind. Jordi, as usual in mass, was concentrating deeply on his prayers, eyes closed.

Conchita, holding her mother's cross tight, continued praying – she had already prayed more than she ever imagined, trying to compensate for the thoughts of culpability she'd been bearing like a cross for two days.

Had I not brought those issues up she would still be alive, she kept tormenting herself, despite Soledad's words of consolation. Conchita had told her mother's best friend about their conversation in hospital because she was unable to keep it to herself. She had to share her mother's legacy. It hurt so much that she was gone. They could have had years ahead without secrets.

Maria sat next to her mother, equally unable to stand. Covered by the mantilla, Conchita couldn't see her face. They had barely spoken as Maria had been practically silent since her arrival from London, shocked by the terrible news.

Isolation isn't the best way, but I have to respect her reaction, accept it. Maria is the way she is.

Pilar sat down with the rest of the mourners and immediately crossed her arm through her mother's, holding her tight. Conchita welcomed the touch.

As the bishop referred to Gran Basilisa, and her honourable life in Belchite, Conchita could only remember her mother's words about the ostracism she'd suffered. Looking out from the corner of her eye, Conchita observed some women of her mother's age, sitting two rows behind, and opposite, in mourning dress; they were sobbing loudly. She couldn't stop thinking those could have been the same ones who moved aside when they saw Gran Basilisa at the public laundry, those who didn't invite her to their parties.

I shall be strong, I shall be a rock to defend my mother's memory, Conchita thought. She saw other faces, like Doctor Jaime and Pepe, the man who came year after year to kill the pig at the *matanza,* and others who also looked deeply affected. Conchita didn't dare to turn around. The imposing silence of more than a hundred people, all showing respect to her mother, simply overwhelmed her.

The bishop began the absolution of Gran, with the usual Latin prayer:

Qui missus es sanare contritos corde: Kyrie elèison.
Qui peccatores vocare venisti: Christe, elèison.
Misereatur nostri omnipotens Deus et, dimissis peccatis nostris, perducat nos ad vitam aeternam."

The crowd answered: "Amen," although, of course, nobody understood a word.

The bishop told the congregation how Gran Basilisa's life had been full of sin, like any human being, and how she'd find redemption and ultimate happiness in heaven. Patronisingly, he referred to everybody's 'mistakes' in the past, those moments to regret, the products of a human being's weak flesh, which would now be forgiven in the doors of heaven, thanks to strong penitence.

To Conchita's surprise, the bishop made clear allusions to Gran's sinful life, about the fact that it was fair that somebody without a Christian family, somebody unable to give a father and a mother to a child, had already suffered the consequences of an act outside the holy sacrament of marriage. That earthly suffering would also now help her go through the gates of glory. As he carried on preaching about the mistake of choosing political sides that were against Catholicism, Conchita heard a snort from Soledad and, to her shock, she saw that Maria, sitting on the corner of the bench, suddenly stood up and walked away. Conchita turned her head and looked at Maria's back as her youngest daughter walked down the lateral aisle. She expected her to turn, expressing some urgent feeling of illness, but she didn't. She was just leaving her grandmother's funeral, Conchita understood, unable to believe it. She tried to make eye contact with Soledad and Pilar, who just gave her a complacent and sympathetic look. They held her hands and looked down. She turned to look at Jordi who, kneeling down, head between his hands, had missed everything.

What is it now, Maria, what is it? Maybe he's going too far, but he's the bishop. You can't leave like this. This is the ultimate lack of respect to your grandmother. What will people say?

Conchita felt her anger rising, but was able to control it. *This is my farewell to my mother, not even Maria can spoil it this time – but she's going to hear from me afterwards. Poor Jordi, he'll need all the patience in the world.*

The bishop, whose stare also stayed fixed on Maria's back, was silent while she walked down the aisle, diverting everybody's attention – except Jordi's – towards her. As soon as she was gone and the sound of her shoes could no longer be heard, he continued:

Gloria in excelsis Deo.
Et in terra pax hominibus bonae voluntatis.
Laudamus te, benedicimus te, adoramus te, glorificamus te,

gratias agimus tibi propter magnam gloriam tuam.
Quoniam tu solus Sanctus,
tu solus Dominus, tu solus Altissimus, Iesu Christe,
cum Sancto Spiritu: in gloria Dei Patris.

"Amen."

Some two hours later, Conchita and Soledad found Maria sitting by herself on the ground, by *El Abuelo*, still in her mourning clothes, but without her mantilla.

There she is, sulking like a teenager. Maria, I don't have time for this today.

Holding the small, polished, wooden box with her mother's ashes, Conchita walked past Maria, without glancing at her. Soledad and Pilar stopped and helped Maria stand up. The three joined Conchita by the ancient tree. The four black figures, arm in arm, stood in silence, looking down, for a few long minutes. The sun was setting, giving the old, green leaves a mystical air. Soledad, looking paler than Conchita had ever seen, took the box from Conchita's trembling hands, opened it and took some of the ashes. Maria and Pilar started crying. Conchita put her chin up, looked straight to the tree.

"Symbol of peace for centuries, please take these ashes to heaven," Conchita said with a catch in her voice.

Slowly, Soledad walked a few steps forward, opened her hand, and let the small breeze take the ashes towards the eternal tree. In a very deep voice, she said: "Thank you for a lifetime of companionship and joy." Soledad could barely speak, but she continued. "You shall be in my heart, forever, as well as in the hearts of the many people who loved you." Looking down, she put one foot forward, but it was apparent that she couldn't walk. Pilar was first to react and walked towards her, helping her back.

Maria, in a stream of silent tears, took some ashes from the box and without looking at anybody, repeated Soledad's move, although she didn't say anything. She couldn't.

Pilar followed. "I love you Gran," she said. "You'll always be with us."

Conchita took the rest of the ashes and held them tight in her hand. She looked around the olive trees, the hills around her fields. She took a deep, long breath and closed her eyes, seeing her mother young, sickle in hand, her blouse wet with sweat from the hard work under the sun. She saw herself, as a child, playing with her favourite doll, among the trees. *You have been a good daughter, Conchita* – she couldn't stop remembering her mother's last words. She frowned with intensity, she couldn't bear the frustration of not being with her mother now that the truth was known. Her anger turned into tears, into more pressure in her hands.

A few instants later, she lifted her veil and looked up to the tree. With a lump in her throat, she said: "Lord, please welcome these ashes into heaven as nobody else deserves more so," she spoke it clearly, despite her tears. Slowly, she opened her hand and let the wind take the ashes away. "I shall join you some day, I hope, for an eternal life together."

The four women stayed in silence for a few minutes, until they heard the church bells strike another hour. Conchita raised her head and looked at Soledad and her daughters, they were all looking at the ground, their shoulders hunched. It was getting cold and dark.

I have to pull myself together, I have to be the strong one. Someone has to do it, and it's my duty.

"Come on, let's go home," Conchita said, and started walking. The others followed her, without saying a word.

They had been walking for about a minute when a football burst out from between the trees, with Ignacio running behind.

"Ignacio," Pilar said gently. "Not today, you can't play football today, son."

The boy picked the ball up and put it under his arm. "Sorry Mother." He looked down.

"It's all right," his mother said. "You will understand someday."

Soledad took Ignacio's hand. "Don't worry, we used to play football all the time, right here," she said.

Ignacio looked surprised. "You played football, Soledad?"

"I was a midfielder," she said, provoking the group's first laugh in three days. It released some of the tension.

"I will test you," Ignacio said. "Do you also play, Gran?" the boy asked Conchita, who didn't even look back at him.

Soledad carried on, Conchita appreciated it: "We played just as you do, boys and girls, although we didn't have these fancy, colourful balls. Then we made them ourselves, sewing some cloth: it worked. We didn't have a pitch, either, we played in the fields when they cleared the land before the sowing. Because it was round, we couldn't kick corners, so the rule was that three corners became one penalty," Soledad explained with pride. "You see? All you need is a bit of imagination."

The group, relieved by the change of subject, walked back home through the trees, listening to the sound of their shoes on the ground, the dry land of Belchite.

Holding back her tears, Conchita held the last eggs that her mother had given her from her hens; they were still fresh. She was about to cook some fried eggs and omelets for Soledad and her two daughters. The four were sitting in silence around the open chimney in the kitchen, warmed by the fire. Jordi had driven back to Barcelona soon after the church service, Honorato had gone to bed and the children were with their father. Khira was also with the women, lying in a corner, looking around with melancholy eyes, her ears down. She had paid no attention to eating all day long.

Pets understand everything, Conchita thought, looking at the sad animal.

She hadn't decided what to do with her yet but, although she'd never been too fond of dogs, she was warming to the idea of keeping her, especially because Gran had loved her so much.

Holding the eggs in her big hands, as if she wanted to protect them, Conchita stared at the garlic lines hanging from the ceiling and at the multitude of ceramic and clay pots, plates and jars, pinned on the white walls. She looked up at the wooden beams, rebuilt by her mother decades ago. She glanced at Soledad, remembering how she cooked eggs exactly like this, with her mother and herself, when she was a child and Gran came tired from the fields. Conchita would have been outside all day as well, playing, although not football – during the Franco years that was only for boys. Instead, Conchita played with her mother's gun. She emptied the bullets and, with some friends, they hid in the depths of the olive groves to play cowboys, inspired by the new, fashionable Hollywood movies. Sometimes they hid behind the workers' stone homes, in the middle of the fields, as Conchita usually brought them some extra sacks of bread, meat and rice, prepared by her mother.

I laugh about the children today and those ridiculous machine-toys. We played real games in my time.

"Conchita, the oil is about to burn," Soledad said, softly.

Conchita reacted immediately and, as if she was going to break a porcelain statue, she cracked the first egg and poured it over the pan, seeing the beautiful yolk and white expand.

"She took such good care of her hens," Conchita said, her eyes turning watery. "I have yet to see eggs as good as this in a supermarket."

Soledad took the wooden spoon from her hands and continued with the cooking herself.

"Do you remember we used to sit here, the three of us, and do exactly the same?" Soledad asked.

"Very much so," Conchita smiled. "But it was four of us – there was Mariquita Pérez, as well, my doll."

Soledad smiled. "Of course, how could I forget? Your mother gave you that doll the night you went to Zaragoza, to the boarding school. You loved that doll so much, you always brought her back with you in the school holidays; the nuns said that you slept with her at night. You must have been heart-broken when you lost her."

I never lost her, Soledad, she's in my wardrobe, still in perfect condition. I would never lose her. She was my one and only friend, all those years in Zaragoza.

"You didn't like that school much," Soledad continued. "You were so happy to come home to us."

Conchita looked at her, a glance full of meaning and memories. "Indeed. I loved the land here, the space, jumping on the coal train to steal some logs, throwing them out, then jumping off – to sell them around the village."

"You learned business early, mother," Pilar said, sarcastically.

Conchita gave her a condescending look. "It was fun," she said. "Much better than the courses at school; see if I can remember them: Cooking, Family, Practical Knowledge, National-unionism, Sewing, Floriculture, Domestic Science, Singing and Domestic Economics."

Pilar and Maria laughed. "What an intellectual," Maria said – the first words she'd spoken, practically, since she arrived from London.

"Don't make fun of your mother," Conchita said, in a tone that sounded more harsh than she had wanted it to.

After only a couple of bites of her omelet, Maria stood up and left her plate by the sink. "Goodnight, I am a bit tired," she said bluntly.

"Maria, don't take it the wrong way, stay with us a bit longer, try to finish your food," Soledad said.

"No thank you, Soledad, I want to go to bed now." She started walking away. "Goodnight."

Pilar leaned back and sighed after Maria closed the door behind her. "I'll go and talk to her," she said standing up. "She has to get it out of her system. It's not good to keep it in."

"Thank you, Pilar," Conchita said. "I am quite tired myself as well."

"Let's go," Soledad said. "Tomorrow will be another day."

The three women stood up and quickly cleaned the kitchen in silence.

Alone, under the clear sky full of stars that she could see from the patio inside the house, Conchita turned the lights on to see the old agricultural tools that her mother had hung on the walls. Wrapped in a woollen poncho, Conchita gently touched an ancient sickle, a plough from the 1920s, and even some mule's ropes that her mother used on her own head.

She worked so hard. Harder than all of us put together.

She jumped and quickly turned when she heard a noise at the top of the stairs. Maria had shut the door to the upstairs balcony and was coming down.

"I thought you were asleep," Conchita said.

"I just came to make myself some hot milk," Maria said, walking past her mother, straight towards the kitchen without stopping.

Conchita sighed. "I'll do it," she said, following her daughter. *I have to be so patient with you, Maria.*

"I'm fine, I'll do it," Maria said, curtly.

Mean, Maria, we're all sad, it's not only you.

Conchita walked into the kitchen and pottered around, pretending to be busy, she wished she had something to do. Maria was opening the sugar pot, with disdain, while the milk warmed slowly on the stove. She had left her mobile phone on the counter, nearby.

"Are you calling Jordi this late at night?" Conchita loved her future son-in-law. "He's so good to you." *And I am not sure if you appreciate it enough.*

Maria didn't respond. "Who was that man with long, white hair at the back of the church, standing by the doors?" she asked, her glance fixed on the milk. "I've never seen him around Belchite before."

Conchita leaned on the counter and looked at her daughter, surprised. She still hadn't forgiven her for leaving the funeral. "Who?" she asked, still too overwhelmed by the death, the funeral, the attention, to remember a single person at the back of the church.

"As I said, I don't know who he is, that's why I am asking you." Maria sounded irritated.

Conchita gave her a look of disapproval. *I don't have time for your trifles, Maria.*

"I don't know," Conchita said, although she felt curious. "What did he look like?"

Maria poured the hot milk into her mug, an old clay pot that she had crafted at school. "I don't know, old, tall, with white hair," she said, turning towards the door.

Conchita shrugged. "Maybe somebody from Zaragoza, one of the accountants, perhaps?"

Maria looked sceptical. "Perhaps." She said nothing else and left the kitchen, climbing the stairs from the patio towards her room.

Conchita took a deep breath. She looked up to the sky and felt the tears coming down her eyes.

Mother, I just wish I was with you in heaven. How much I wish that.

20

It was an unusually crisp, sunny morning in London, in the middle of January. People were coming in and out of the busy shops on Upper Street, children were on their way to school, adults rushed to work, coffees in hands.

This is not that grim, Jordi thought as he walked from the Islington Hilton hotel towards the Council offices on Upper Street where he was supposed to meet Patrick, his agent in London, at nine o'clock. Less than a month after Gran Basilisa's funeral, Maria said she still didn't feel like travelling, and she had taken the week off to rest in Belchite. Jordi had barely seen her over Christmas. His duties at Belagua during the busiest time of the year hadn't allowed him to visit her in Belchite as much as he had wanted. Although the sad truth, he knew, was that Maria had shut down to the world since the funeral. She rarely picked up the phone and, according to Conchita, all she did was sit in limbo, walking in the fields and watching old black and white movies with Soledad.

I have to be patient, give her the time and the space she needs.

Jordi had practically spent his entire Christmas praying for her and for their future together. Thankfully, the work on the apartment was going well, something that relieved him because he would not be able to afford to fix any adversity after his donation to Belagua.

Looking the wrong way when crossing the road and just missing being hit by a car, Jordi greeted politely Patrick at the front door of the Council offices. They shook hands.

"You must be Mr Gratallops," Patrick said, looking at Jordi's elegant navy-blue suit.

"Hello Patrick, glad to meet you," Jordi answered in English with a heavy Spanish accent. "Thanks for your help on the telephone. It's much appreciated as it's Maria who knows the ins and outs of the project. But of course I have to lend a hand now."

"I hope she's feeling better," the agent said.

"Yes, thanks." Jordi looked around. "Let's go in, we have lots to talk through and I must catch a plane in the early afternoon."

Jordi and Patrick sat impatiently in the functional, sparsely decorated Council office when Nell appeared with her black boots, black cotton trousers and a tight black jumper. She wore a long, orange scarf around her neck. Jordi glanced at her head to toe. Her short hair gave her a rebellious air that he wasn't used to.

"Nice to meet you Mrs Easton," he said, standing up.

"Ms Easton," Nell replied quickly.

Jordi felt Nell's straight look; he felt intimidated.

Both men adjusted their ties nervously.

"How's Maria doing?" Nell asked, sitting down, fiddling with some papers without looking up.

"She's all right, thanks," Jordi said. "She told me how much you helped her last month, with the urgent return flight, the lift to the airport, the company. I can only show my appreciation for your help."

"It's fine," Nell said. "She seemed quite upset."

"She loved her grandmother very much," Jordi said, looking down. "But now that she's in heaven, I am sure she'll be praying for all of us."

Nell opened her eyes wide and glanced at Patrick, who coughed nervously and suggested getting started.

"Thank you for being here Mr Gratallops," Nell began. "The Council is delighted about your interest in our area, but there have been some misunderstandings that we need to address to make sure we all know what we're looking for."

"We'd like the Post Office site," Jordi said without hesitation.

Nell sighed. "You obviously know what you want."

Jordi moved forward. "Yes, we do," he said. "England is an excellent market for us. The people here like our products, but they only know the cheaper ones. We're thinking of a big PR campaign to position the more up-market *cava*. Apart from the ads, a shop-front in a neighborhood like Islington would help us spread the brand name."

Nell looked him straight in the eye. "I see," she said. "But as I am sure Maria and Patrick have briefed you, the Post Office site is in a conservation area with plenty of restrictions. Unfortunately, your preliminary drawing doesn't even come close to what the Council would accept."

Jordi leaned back. "That's all right," he said. "That's why we are here, so Patrick and I understand perfectly what those requirements are."

While Nell unfolded some large plans on her desk, Jordi looked at the walls, noticing a calendar showing a photo of two women looking at each other with a strange intensity. Jordi observed the picture for a few seconds, it seemed as if the two women were about to kiss each other. He tried to imagine whether they were sisters. He looked at it again but no, it seemed certain there was something more. Surprised, he leaned backwards a bit and quickly looked at Nell, who had spotted his discomfort.

Nell gave Jordi a defiant look that made him feel a bit small, then extended the maps over the table and talked the two men through several points.

"First of all, that building needs to keep its façade," she said, firmly. "It's a period, historic building that the Council isn't prepared to let go. Second, no extra buildings can be added; if more space is needed, there's an adjacent building that could be leased as well. However, if the inside of the building isn't suitable, a refurbishment could be approved by the Council, provided of course it doesn't alter the external appearance."

Jordi stared at Nell, still with the image of the two women in his head. He'd never seen anything like that before. He looked at Nell's unmanicured nails.

With such short hair, this look – is she a lesbian? And nobody says anything about her having a photo like that in her office? Open to the public? Just like that? What if children see it?

Not that Jordi was particularly anti-gay, since he had never even met anybody who was actually homosexual, but like any Opus Dei member, he thought same-sex relationships were a sin and therefore had to be treated, if possible; if not, then suppressed and condemned.

Jordi made an effort to concentrate as Nell continued.

"And of course, traffic restrictions would apply as neighbours would complain if there was a significant increase in traffic," she said, dropping her pencil on the map decisively.

"We would only use the vans during normal business hours," Jordi replied.

"That's great," Nell said. "But how do you feel about the façade? The materials that Patrick and Maria have shown in the plans so far are rather out of place in an area such as this one. Aluminium isn't welcomed in conservation areas."

Both Patrick and Jordi coughed. "Well, it was only a preliminary plan, just to give you, and us, an idea," Jordi said. "I am sure it will be better developed when we submit the proper application."

"Of course now we have to study the costs of keeping the façade," Patrick said.

Jordi nodded. "Is it an absolute necessity to keep it?"

"Yes, it is," Nell said. She looked at the wall clock. "I have also some questions about the finances of your company," she said. "Given the site, the Council requires some proof of the financial well-being of the company. I am sure you understand."

The two nodded. Nell continued, looking straight at Jordi. "We have already searched some of the official records in Spain, but I'd also like you to take the time to read these forms, they are quite short and simple, just to make sure that as a representative of the company you can confirm the official accounts represent, in all material respects, the state of the firm. We need to

261

guarantee that, as far as you know, there are no more debts or payments due other than what's stated at the moment."

Damn. Damn.

"Of course." Jordi raised his head and took the papers. They obviously didn't include the loan from Banca Catalana, which completed on Jan 2nd, so it wasn't in last year's accounts. *That's so much debt, this Council wouldn't take us seriously if they knew. What to do? I can't turn back. We need this site here. Things in Spain are only getting worse and we don't have time to look for another site and start all over again.*

Jordi turned towards the calendar, again. Nell saw his look.

"Is everything all right?" she asked.

Jordi gave her a distant look, as if his thoughts were miles away. *I guess I could always say that my father had arranged the loan without my consent, that I didn't know about it at the time. They may never find out that it even existed. Once national sales pick up, we'll return the loan, so no need for anybody to know, it's only a short-term measure. If things go wrong I could always ask Dad to protect me. I kept his secret about the family, he can keep this one for me.*

He took a Montblanc pen from his inside pocket.

Please God I do this for the sake of my father and my workers – what would happen to them if we didn't have enough funds to pay them? And for Maria, so we can have a future and a happy family together. I will accept penitence. I promise I will.

Jordi signed the documents.

"Thank you," Nell said, putting the document inside a folder. "I look forward to hearing more about your plans, gentlemen, and to see how they develop from now onwards."

Nell glanced at the clock. "Sorry, I don't mean to rush you but Islington is so busy now, I have somebody else waiting for me."

The two men stood up immediately. "Of course," Jordi said. "And once again, thank you for helping Maria, it's much appreciated."

Nell said nothing. The two men left.

Jordi took a deep breath as the plane landed in Barcelona a few hours later. He shrugged his shoulders as he passed the police control, feeling relieved about the London project being on the go again. It was now in Patrick and the architects' hands to come up with a design as cheap as possible that would still meet the Council's criteria.

His mobile phone started ringing as soon as he switched it on while waiting for his little suitcase inside the terminal. It was a message from the builder at the flat in Sarrià saying he didn't have good news, he wanted him to go over there as soon as possible.

Not the flat, I can't afford a single thing going wrong in the flat, Jordi thought. He tried to call him back, but his mobile was engaged. He also tried to call Maria but, again, she had her phone switched off.

Jordi, usually patient, started to feel irritated about other people not being immediately accessible. He felt like slamming the door as soon as he got into Oscar, parked overnight at the airport. *I must control myself, God is testing me. Be patient. Good things happen to those who wait.* He shut the door gently and drove towards the flat.

His heart sank when the head builder told him that a supporting wall had collapsed most likely because the concrete contained some sort of aluminium, weakening it over time. Replacing the affected structure would cost about thirty thousand euros and delay the work for as much as eight months.

Bye-bye love nest for the newlyweds.

Jordi took his tie off and unbuttoned the top of his shirt. He was sweating.

"I am sorry, there was no way we could have foreseen this," the builder said.

Jordi looked away. "I know, it's not your fault."

He looked around the flat, still unpainted, with the stairway of the duplex half-way built, the three bedrooms upstairs, the integrated kitchen behind him, full of daylight. The windows, still with some tape on them, showed huge views across Barcelona. This was the surprise home that he expected to share with his wife and children in the years to come. The intimate space that he had dreamed of for months, far from the *masia's* grandeur, which he wanted to avoid at all costs. Jordi longed for his family to stay close together, not spread across multiple wings like at home.

Maybe the insurance would pay for some of the damage, but he had read about similar cases in the newspapers and it was always the owners who ended up paying for it, or simply moving somewhere else. There was no way he could borrow thirty thousand euros now. He had given all his savings to Opus and he couldn't ask his father for more – Pere Gratallops had already injected large sums into the company to offset dwindling sales. Jordi couldn't borrow from any financial institution either, especially as his company was about to take on this new loan.

Jordi placed his hands on the windows, looked out over Barcelona; the builder tapped him on the shoulder.

"Everything in this life has a solution," the big man said.

Are you sure?

"Please carry on with the work," Jordi said. *I will find the money, somehow.*

He took his mobile phone out of his jacket. *Maria, Maria, where are you? I need you so much.* He called her and again, his call went straight to voicemail.

Jordi only had one place to go.

Biting his nails, his stomach empty, tapping his foot against the ground, Jordi waited for Father Juan Antonio's answer. The priest looked at him intently, sat back comfortably in his chair. He had not moved for several minutes, since Jordi finished telling his story.

Father Juan Antonio looked over his shoulder and brushed a bit of dust from the sleeve of his impeccably ironed cassock. He sighed, leaned back even further.

"I am a bit worried about you, Jordi," he said finally. "Are you sure you're all right?"

"I am as all right as the situation allows me to be, Father," Jordi said, bending forward. "If I could have some of that money back – which I would of course return as soon as it's feasible – then at least I could start trying to sort things out, move on."

Jordi felt the weight of the priest's eyes and looked down.

"It's not the money that worries me, Jordi, it's the thought." The Father raised his voice. "The thought that you can think of yourself ahead of the institution. The thought that you've degenerated into a state where your own interests come ahead of those of Opus Dei. What has happened to you, to your generous, giving self, Jordi? You don't even look as if you're taking that much care of yourself."

Father Juan Antonio looked at Jordi's wrinkled suit and sweaty shirt, still without his tie. "Have you sinned my son? Remember it's never too late to confess."

Jordi gave Father Juan Antonio an angry look. *I don't need more shit, not today.* "I haven't sinned, Father," he said. "I am just exhausted by this stream of bad luck and I need some help. I am not asking for anything, I am only calling for what's mine, I'd like some of it back because I am desperate, I really need it."

Jordi looked up at Father Juan Antonio with begging eyes.

"Being desperate is never good, my son," Father Juan Antonio said and shook his head. "And may I remind you that when something has been given, with a Christian heart, as you did, it's gone. It's not very Christian to claim it back."

"But I need it, Father," Jordi pleaded.

"I can't Jordi, you know I can't, the organisation needs it more and I am here to take care of the Club, not the individual, selfish interests of its members."

Jordi put his hands over his face.

I can't believe it, I can't.

"Father, you've always been with me, always helped me, now I need you more than ever."

"What you need is serious spiritual guidance Jordi, you seem lost," Father Juan Antonio said. "Of course I will help you. I will give you time to help you reconsider your thoughts. We could meet daily after the morning mass, that's what you need."

Jordi felt almost sick and immensely hungry. To Father Juan Antonio's surprise, he simply left the room and walked away, without saying goodbye.

Images of the two women in the calendar at Nell's office, the builder and Father Juan Antonio blurred in his mind.

I can't lose it, please God help me.

A cheap, packaged sandwich eaten in the car at a petrol station between Barcelona and Vilafranca helped Jordi feel a little better. Just as he'd found some peace, his phone rang again and, to Jordi's surprise and infinite joy, it was Maria.

"Darling! Darling!" he said desperately, almost dropping the phone with excitement. "Where have you been? Oh so much has happened!"

"I am in Belchite. What's up? You sound nervous," Maria said on the line.

"Thank God you've finally called," he said. "When are you coming home? Can I see you? Can I drive to you? Now?"

"No Jordi, sorry, I am not feeling very well yet, I am sorry," she said. "But tell me, what's going on?"

"They've found that awful type of aluminium in the concrete of our flat darling, the flat I was building for us," he said. "Sorry I know it was meant to be a surprise, but it's all gone wrong. I am so sorry, I am such a loser."

A few seconds went by. "Of course you're not a loser, Jordi, but I told you a long time ago, we should have shared this, done it all together."

"Well, that's not the problem." Jordi coughed. "The thing is that it won't be ready for April, or May, or June, maybe towards the end of the year. They have to rebuild some walls." He paused, took a deep breath. "I'm afraid we'll have to rent somewhere, I am so sorry darling, I know this is not what you deserve."

Maria stayed silent.

"Are you there darling?" Jordi felt impatient.

"Yes, yes," Maria said. "Jordi, maybe we should see each other, but I just don't have the strength, I swear. It seems that problems are piling up, with my family falling apart, the warehouse in London, and now the flat."

"What do you mean, Maria?" Jordi frowned.

"Well, Jordi, maybe we need to talk." She sounded hesitant.

"Talk about what?" He became aggressive. *I don't want to postpone the wedding. I can't wait any longer.*

"Let's not discuss this over the telephone, Jordi, please," Maria said.

Jordi was becoming upset. What else could go wrong? "Please don't leave me in suspense," he said.

Maria sighed. "I am not leaving you in suspense, Jordi," she said. "It's only that I am feeling particularly weak. It just seems that it's a horrible time for both of us. But as I say, let's wait, let's not talk about this over the phone."

Jordi dropped his head onto to his chest and clenched his fist in agony.

"Are you thinking of postponing the wedding, is that what you want?" he asked, almost in tears.

"I am not going to decide anything without you, Jordi," Maria said. "All I am saying is that we need to talk."

A silence followed.

"Jordi, darling, are you there?" Maria said.

"Yes," he said. "It feels like it's all a nightmare."

"Same here," Maria said. "Let's talk, though. I will let you know when I am ready. I am sorry about this, but please understand. I know it's hard, let's be patient with each other, please."

Be strong, be strong. God help me be a man.

Jordi sighed and raised his chin up. "All right. Let me know. I will be here waiting for you as long as you need. You know how much I love you. You're my life."

Maria hung up.

Please God help me. Now you're really the only one I have. The only one.

Jordi's mobile rang yet again as he walked into his room at home, finally within the shelter of the *masia*.

Who's this now?

"Hello?" Jordi picked up his phone as if it weighed a tone.

"Hi Jordi, how are you? It's Borja Peñaranda here," the man said.

Fuck. Fuck. Jordi wanted to hang up, but stayed on the line.

"What do you want?" Jordi was surprised by his own rudeness. He'd never spoken to anybody like that before.

He deserves it.

"Just wanted to let you know that since I haven't heard back from you in a while, I've started to do a little bit of work – what is mine is mine, and if it doesn't come through a gentlemen's agreement, then it will come in a rather less pleasant way," he said. "Just wanted to let you know, as a friend, that along with some hedge funds, we've bought part of the Caves loan from Banca Catalana. We will continue buying unless we reach an agreement over the land; I am saying this as a friend. I want to save you trouble."

"Fuck you," Jordi shouted at him over the phone. "Fuck you!"

Peñaranda laughed and hung up.

21

Conchita walked alone in the backyard thinking it was exactly a month since she had come back from the hospital chapel to find her mother dead. The shock had been hard to accept, especially since the doctors had stated that Gran Basilisa would recover well. But her weak heart and the memories revived during her last days of life had been too much for her. She had died because she didn't want to live, Doctor Jaime had said, arguing that she was physically strong enough to continue fighting. He had asked if Gran Basilisa had suffered any recent shocks, or emotional upsets. "Yes" Conchita had to respond. Doctor Jaime failed to give her any reassurance, leaving Conchita with a sense of guilt that she still couldn't shake off. Gran had died minutes after their last conversation.

Slowly, wrapped in her thick woollen coat and with a black scarf covering her head, Conchita walked through the trees into the fields, listening to the sound of her old, rugged boots against the red land of Belchite. Still in her mourning dress, Conchita, wearing no gloves despite the freezing weather, touched her rosary and recited the customary 'Our Fathers' and 'Hail Marys'.

It was also nearly a month since Honorato had left, Conchita thought as she reached *El Abuelo*, now bare of leaves, standing apart from the other trees. She felt like that now – lonely, fruitless, old and tired. She looked up at the cloudy sky and around the bleak land and naked branches. She misplaced her fingers on the rosary, losing count of her prayers. It didn't matter, all she'd done since Gran Basilisa died was pray, looking downwards, covered by her black scarf and a veil, alone or with her neighbours. She had no more tears, her eyes were dry. She closed them tight. At least she could smell the land, feel it as she continued her walk.

This land is all I have, they can never take it away from me. My own mother can go, as well as the father and the grandparents I never met, but nobody can ever take away this land and these olive trees from me.

That would be a bigger loss than Honorato, to be true, she thought as she opened her eyes again, sighed and put the rosary back in her pocket. Her long, strong hands were so white from the cold that she could see her blue veins through her skin. She took a pair of black leather gloves from her coat pocket and slipped them on.

I knew, I knew at the bottom of my heart that my marriage wasn't right. But whose marriage is? We're all the same, which couple is still in love after so many years? At this age, it's not about loving, it's about commitment to an idea, to marriage, to the holy sacrament, to this land – not that he did much for it, though.

Conchita was hardly even surprised when Honorato appeared with a suitcase, dressed in a suit and a hat, while she was cooking him breakfast, just a week after Gran Basilisa's funeral. Maria had already returned to Barcelona and the villagers weren't visiting as often as in the first few days. "There's no need to continue pretending," was all he said, and then left. She would have felt humiliated, hurt by the public embarrassment, but after Gran's death she hadn't found time to worry about local gossip. At the end of the day, her husband's departure wasn't such a big loss.

He must have thought that leaving right after Gran's funeral would be easier because I'd be more vulnerable. Ha. I should have packed him away decades ago.

Conchita walked back towards *El Abuelo* and taking off a glove, gently touched its branches, its wide, twisted trunk, its ancient surface, still so full of life. She leaned against it, looking around the fields she'd spent a lifetime taking care of, the same as her mother.

He did nothing. Nothing.

I was the silly one. The nuns brought me up to marry well, to take care of a man, smile at him, be patient, have his meal and slippers ready for when he came back from work, be understanding – what for?

Conchita swallowed and looked at the sky. She put her hand inside her blouse and, holding her mother's cross to her chest, she looked at *El Abuelo* intently.

My mother, my husband have gone, but I still have this, she thought as Ignacio suddenly appeared on his bicycle between the trees.

"Look, Gran," he shouted. "I can ride with no hands." He took both his hands off the handlebar, and immediately crashed into a tree.

Conchita ran to him, checking he had only suffered a few scratches. Normally, she would have shouted at him for cycling in the fields, but now she felt too tired.

"Let's go home," she said. "It's almost lunchtime."

The two walked together in silence back to the house. Conchita looked at her grandson, happy with the bike that the Three Wise Men had brought him for the Epiphany.

The bike I never had, she thought. One year, a girl at the convent in Zaragoza came back after Christmas with the first bicycle Conchita had ever seen for a girl her age: it was beautiful. It had big wheels and a basket at the front to carry bread or flowers. She shared it with all her classmates except Conchita, who either hid or was working. Since then, Conchita had hated bicycles and refused to buy one for Maria, who as a child asked for one repeatedly.

They're for boys, in any case.

Having recited two rosaries after lunch, Conchita sat in her armchair, knitting. She was making a scarf for Soledad, the winter would be cold and long, the weather woman on the television had said.

Next to her, on the sofa, Maria and Soledad were watching *Rebecca*, the old black and white movie, although they wouldn't shut up, Conchita thought, concentrating on her knitting.

"Do you know that cardigans in Spain are called 'rebeccas' because of this movie?" Soledad asked Maria, who looked surprised by the fact.

"Really?" Maria said, looking at Soledad only, as if her mother wasn't even in the room.

I still have to tell her off for walking away at the funeral, and she's not even in her black mourning dress, either. She has no respect.

Conchita had a sip of coffee, still fresh from the percolator. Despite the despair caused by the recent family events, she loved the tranquil moments after lunch, after cleaning the kitchen, when she sat to enjoy her coffee, the newspaper, or sewing. But however content in her isolation she was, Conchita still needed to talk, which she could do easily with Soledad, but not with Maria around.

She shifted in her armchair, lifted her glance over her glasses and, with a look of superiority, glanced at the screen, catching site of the old Manderley mansion.

"All the girls in my school wanted a man like Lawrence Olivier," she said, causing Maria and Soledad to turn and look at her in surprise.

They're not used to hearing me talk about female desire like that, it would seem – what can I do?

Conchita carried on knitting.

"But you know *he* is not the point of the movie, don't you?" Soledad said, with a cheeky smile.

"What do you mean?" Conchita asked, without lifting her eyes from the knitting.

"Mrs Danvers doesn't give a damn about Lawrence Olivier, it is his first wife that she's in love with," Soledad said with excitement.

"Don't be silly," Conchita said. From the corner of her eye, she saw Maria looking up at Soledad with a raised eyebrow.

"Did you know that, Maria?" Soledad asked her.

"I would never have guessed," Maria answered.

"It's because Franco's translators hid all the clues and made it sound more like a 'normal' relationship, as they did with so many other movies," Soledad said. "In *The African Queen*, Humphrey Bogart's extramarital affair with Ava Gardner was dubbed to make us believe that Grace Kelly was Bogart's sister, instead of his wife. They swapped infidelity for incest, a lower crime, can you believe?"

"Noo." Maria said with raised eyebrows and an open mouth. "That's monstrous."

Conchita looked at her daughter. "Maria, everybody has a different opinion on this. Spain's morals had fallen so low, they had to be raised." She lifted her glasses up, wrinkled her nose and carried on with her knitting.

Soledad went on. "Well, in Rebecca's case, since you speak good English, you can read a copy of Daphne du Maurier's novel, and you'll see it for yourself, she was such a lesbian."

Conchita dropped her needles and looked up at once. "Soledad! Please!" she said. "Don't be blasphemous in this house."

"It is a reality, whether one likes it or not," Soledad said, turning to Maria, who looked bemused. "What do you think, Maria?"

Conchita saw her youngest daughter cross her arms and legs and begin to tap her fingers on one knee.

"Oh, it's totally normal these days," Maria said. "I have a friend like *that* in London, she works for the Council that I am doing business with, she's perfectly okay."

Soledad leaned back in the sofa, smiling, while Conchita took her glasses off and stared at her daughter. She stopped knitting.

"I see," Conchita said. "Is that the friend you keep talking to? I hear you on your telephone speaking in English quite often these days."

Maria changed her position, leaned towards Soledad.

"Well, she's a good friend, but I have other people that I talk to in London all the time, for work." Maria sounded defensive.

And it's costing me a fortune. The phone bill has skyrocketed this month, all from calls to London, Conchita thought. *What have you lost in London, why can't you call people in your own country?*

"In any case, we don't have to worry about that," Conchita said, finishing her coffee. "There're no lesbians in Spain, I've never even seen or heard of any." She stood up. "Would you like more coffee?"

Conchita returned a few minutes later with a percolator of steaming fresh, black coffee. She served cups for Soledad and Maria.

"All we have to do now is to think about positive things in this family after everything that's happened," Conchita said, leaning back in her armchair. "Like the wedding." She looked up as she heard Maria cough slightly. Her daughter was leaning forward, holding her head with her hands.

"What's wrong?" Conchita asked immediately, lifting her chin, looking alert.

"Mother, Soledad," Maria said, without facing them. "I have been thinking, and maybe it's wrong, but after everything that's happened..." She swallowed and blinked a few times, then continued. "Jordi told me last week that there are some delays with the flat, it will not be finished on time, so maybe it would just make sense to postpone the wedding, just for a short while."

Soledad looked at Maria. Conchita dropped the knitting needles in her lap, took her glasses off and gave her daughter a long look.

That's the last thing I need in the world. No, not this. Not now.

"Don't even think of it," Conchita said. "You can't bow to circumstances. You have to be strong, row your boat, without letting anything or anybody turn you. This is what you want, it's good for you. It will be all right."

"But Mother..." Maria began, when Conchita suddenly stood up.

"I've given you everything I had, I worked my whole life so you would have the best opportunities, go to the best schools, gain a good position in life," she said. "And now that you have

274

it, now that you have somebody decent who's not going to walk away like your father did, are you going to throw it all away?"

Both Maria and Soledad looked down at the reference to Honorato. The three hadn't discussed his departure at length.

Conchita raised her head and shoulders and walked towards the door, then turned back, looking directly Maria. "You think you can do anything you want, that the world will follow you? You're wrong, you have to go with the world, the world won't come to you." She paused for a second, then continued. "You think you can leave a funeral just because you don't like what you hear? You have to learn to be strong, persistent, otherwise any storm will blow you away. I've tried to teach you this all my life. Now I can see it's all been wasted, after all the effort."

She shook her head and went on. "The wedding will be on April twenty-first and I won't discuss it again," Conchita said, and walked away, leaving the door open.

I don't even have strength to slam the door. It's all gone wrong, a lifetime of effort.

Turning to see her house from a distance, under the weak winter afternoon sun, Conchita felt the weight of years of work. She shrugged her shoulders and looked down, took a deep breath. The years it had taken her to rebuild the derelict house that her mother could only just keep afloat, and the hours spent in the fields, all to see the family falling apart: her husband gone, her mother dead, her daughters… if only they could have been as steady and responsible as she had been to her own mother, Conchita thought as she walked into the olive groves. She needed to be alone, she needed the silence. She couldn't take any more.

All my life working for my children, to give them everything I missed, and Pilar doesn't seem to genuinely care about many things, while Maria isn't interested in the business at all. That girl hasn't learned yet that, in life, you have to take the opportunities that come to you, they won't knock on your door twice. The wedding was the only thing that I was looking forward to, in this horrible little village. If I had been able to go to Madrid or Barcelona to study, have all the opportunities they have enjoyed, I wouldn't have been trapped here all my life, with the husband that I've been carrying all these years like a cross. I've given them everything and that's how they repay me. This youngest daughter of mine, she'll end up with a hippie or a truck driver who will ruin all the work. Now she's even hanging out with lesbians in London. Ave María Purísima.

Conchita stopped and looked at the sky, feeling the tears come to her eyes. *What have I done? At least when my mother was around I could talk to her, not that we shared any intimacies, but she offered the support, in her way. But now, Soledad and María have made a united front, they're allies, and Pilar doesn't have time for anything. Not even Honorato is there to talk about the weather. I am alone.*

Conchita undid the top buttons of her thick, winter coat and took from her chest her mother's silver cross. Holding it tight, she started to walk between the trees, but suddenly stopped when she arrived at *El Abuelo.*

An old man, with long, white hair, an elegant straw hat and smart clothes was leaning against the ancient tree, looking straight at her. Surprised and a bit fearful, Conchita straightened her back; her face tightened over. She looked him from head to toe; he didn't look like a thief or a murderer.

"Good afternoon," Conchita said, with a raised eyebrow, in a neutral tone – not too kind, not too unfriendly.

"Hello," the man said, looking at her intently. His voice was deep and grave, but also a bit hesitant.

"Are you lost?" Conchita asked, walking two steps closer to him. She could now see his dark, wrinkled face, his deep, black eyes and a long, imposing nose.

"No," the man said, sounding more determined.

Conchita remembered María's comment about a man with white hair at the back of the church at Gran's funeral. She looked at him again, he was wearing polished leather shoes, cream corduroy trousers and a well-cut navy blue coat. She took another two steps forward until she saw the man's face in detail, his eagle nose was just like hers, his eyes were deep, black and

276

shiny, like her own, but frighteningly like Maria's too, with the same expression of power and fear, all at the same time. Her heart sank, then started pounding faster and she instinctively stretched her neck forward, her eyes opening wide. She brought one hand to her mouth. She wanted to scream but no sound came out.

"No!" is the only thing she could say, shaking her head and making the sign of the St Cross with a trembling hand. *Ave María Purísima.*

"Yes," the man said, slowly.

Conchita wanted to run away, but she was too shocked to move.

I am a mature person, I am a grandmother for God's sake, I can handle this.

With effort, the man took his hat off and bowed his head forward; he walked towards her, his legs shaking slightly. He looked at the cross that Conchita was still wearing outside her coat.

"If you open that cross," the man said pointing to it, "you will find a photo of me, if it's still there."

Stunned, Conchita looked at her father. His face was exactly like in the little photograph she'd been staring at most nights, for hours, since her mother died. He had kept himself well – he was old, but his eyes still seemed focused, interested. She could see the sparkle now. His eyes were so dark, so mysterious, so intense and so evasive at the same time, so like Maria's, she thought.

"I know who you are," Conchita finally said.

Juan Roso nodded, looked down.

Father, the prohibited word for so many years. And now I have him right here in front of me, at my age. Good God.

The two stood in silence for a few minutes, listened to the wind in the trees. Juan Roso looked up at them.

"I worked these trees until I almost broke my back," he said. "Look at them now, they've grown so well."

Conchita looked at her fields with pride and gave him a half smile.

This is too late. Now it's too late.

277

"Why didn't you come back?" she asked bluntly. "Why are you back now?"

Juan Roso sighed, moved his well-polished shoes against the red land of Belchite, his look fixed up on it. Then he looked at Conchita.

"I did all I could to contact your mother for years, I wrote to her every single day for so long," he said, then looked around the trees. "I couldn't return to Spain until 1976, when they legalised the political parties. I was on all the black lists, they killed so many of my friends, colleagues from the party, in the forties, fifties, even in the sixties." He stopped his sentence, his eyes wet. "And I didn't know of your existence until I received a letter from your mother just days before she died."

Ah! She sent it. The one I saw must have been a draft.

Conchita gave him a hesitant look. *Somebody must have told you about me at some point.*

He seemed to read her thoughts. "Jaime, my good old friend, the doctor, never told me a word about Basilisa's life. His son said your mother made him promise he would not pass any information to me, none at all. Before my friend died a few months ago, he asked his son to tell me if anything happened to him, or to Basilisa, and so he did. When he died, I stopped writing, I imagined, after all those years, that she would have married and have plenty of children."

Juan looked straight at Conchita who, speechless, swallowed. He continued.

"But as soon as I received your mother's letter a few weeks ago I started making plans to return. Then, of course I came immediately when Jaime's son sent me a telegram with the terrible news." His eyes became more watery, his voice almost broke. "If only I could have had one last minute with her."

He suddenly looked older, his body bending forward, as if he'd lived for more than a hundred years.

He is a poor old man, this is so long ago, I am even a grandmother, I can't give him a hard time, he's my father, after all.

278

Conchita's heart felt small and sad. *This is the family I never had, the father who left, although it wasn't his fault.* She felt a sudden anger. *Damn politics. Damn, damn politics. I hate them, I hate them so much. A broken family, two lost lives, or almost three with mine, and all because of having or not having stupid ideas. What a world, good God, what a world.*

Juan raised his chin. "I am sorry I haven't been there for you," he said, his eyes full of pain and sorrow. He had the look she'd recently seen so often in newspapers' specials about the seventieth anniversary of the Civil War. It was a look of fear, of distrust, of hunger. "Had I known, had I known, I would have come and risked my life to take the two of you with me. I am so sorry. I know I will never be able to compensate for the years of absence," he said, fiddling with his hat.

Conchita looked around; so much to say, where to begin? And was here and now the best time? She looked at him, again; he was still looking down, full of shame.

Conchita felt sorry for the old man, and yet this was her chance to ask all those unanswered questions. She had to.

"Did you marry?" She couldn't look him in the eye.

"Never, Conchita, never," he said, making Conchita shiver as she heard her father say her name for the first time in her life. "What your mother and I had was so precious that anything after that would have felt like a loss. She was so wonderful she filled my heart, I never met anybody like her. I had opportunities in Cuba, but I never took them, I never had other children." He stopped to take a breath. "I spent my life in Cuba, working in the fields as well, sharing all the benefits of my business with my workers, building a community, schools for their children." He stopped, looked at Conchita and then continued. "I've worked my whole life to give younger people what I didn't have. My own father didn't even see a doctor when he was ill, and died because nobody brought him any penicillin. But the masters would bring a vet as soon as a mule started limping."

That must have been my grandfather, Conchita thought, with embarrassment. She looked at Juan Roso with empathy.

He is an honest man, he lives as he thinks. That honours him, even if he's a communist, or whatever he is. Working to pass on what one missed, so familiar.

It started to drizzle and Juan Roso put his hat back on. Conchita suddenly remembered one more thing. *I have to know, I have to know.*

"In the village they say that you left with half of the family's money, is that true?" Conchita felt a knot on her throat.

Juan Roso looked surprised. "Is that what they say?" he looked around the trees, shaking his head. He then looked at the ground. "It was right here where they used to hide it, under *El Abuelo*," he said, moving one foot slowly over the ground.

Another one! Why people in this family keep hiding money right under this tree? I must be the only De la Vega to use a bank.

Juan Roso looked at Conchita. "I didn't steal any money – your mother asked me to take some for my trip, had I gone with empty hands I would have surely died just two kilometers outside Belchite after I escaped. And I also thought I was taking the money that would be the foundation of our future home, in France or somewhere else. Little did I know I would end up in Cuba. It took me years to accept that she would not join me."

Of course he doesn't know my mother's side of the story. Or maybe she told him a few things in that only letter that she wrote to him.

"I know my mother loved you until her last breath," Conchita said, watching the tears well in her father's eyes.

Conchita couldn't handle the tension anymore and started to walk away.

"Conchita please wait," her father said in a begging tone. "Please don't go, I know it's difficult." He looked down. "It's also difficult for me."

Conchita turned back, facing him.

"I know," she said. She didn't know where to look.

I have to be strong.

"Please give me a chance," Juan Roso said. "You're the only legacy of Basilisa. I couldn't have her, please at least let me take care of you, as much as I can. I know I can't do much, I am old and I don't have any money or properties of my own, but perhaps I can do other things." He looked around and slowly kneeled down; he took some of the red soil in his palm and closed his fist as if he wanted to protect it.

"I am sure you know this land well, but maybe I could help you," he said humbly. "My father, my grandfather and I worked it for decades. I can see things have changed, but it's still the same smell, the same colour, the same trees."

Juan Roso let the soil drop from his hand, back onto the ground.

Conchita's heart felt warmer seeing the care that her father had for land, the only thing that the two seemed to have left.

Slowly, he stood up. "I see this has been a good winter, good rain, the trees look happy and healthy," he said, making Conchita smile for the first time in a long time.

"That is true," she said. "They've had a better winter than I've had."

"I know," Juan Roso said. "I am sorry."

"If at least my daughters helped," Conchita said. "I have two daughters, Pilar, who's thirty-two, and has two children, and Maria, twenty-six, who is getting married soon."

Conchita sighed. "I also used to have a husband, but he left, just walked away a few weeks ago."

Juan Roso nodded. "I know."

Conchita gave him a quick look. "Local gossip has kept you informed, hasn't it?"

"I am afraid so," he said. "Nobody has recognised me after all these years. There's barely anybody of my time still alive. But there's talk at the pension where I am staying, Pensión Ramón."

"I know of it," Conchita said. "Small talk. Small village. This is where I've been trapped all my life."

Juan Roso stepped closer to her, showing his bright eyes, still full of energy. "Maybe you're seeing everything negatively today, Conchita," he said. "I don't blame you. But look at what you have and what you've done: I've seen your girls, from a distance, they look beautiful and healthy. I understand they're both doing well. And look at these fields, I've never seen them like this; you've expanded them and in my time, we would have gone mad to see all the fruit that you've got now. You should be proud."

He continued. "As far as Honorato is concerned," he coughed slightly. "Nobody seems to miss him much."

Conchita nodded. "True."

The two exchanged a glance of complicity.

"I can stay here for a few weeks, but after that I'll have to return to Cuba," Juan Roso said. "Perhaps I can help you find somebody to take care of the hardest tasks in the fields so you can take a well-deserved rest."

Juan Roso gave Conchita a look that penetrated to her heart. She felt the force of his eyes, the same look that had meant the world to her mother.

"I feel I haven't rested a minute in my life," she said.

"Maybe it's time," Juan Roso replied.

Maybe.

"You must miss your mother."

I do. I would never have thought that I would miss her so much, but I do. At least she was there, she was my mother and she brought peace around her, wherever she went. Whereas now, what do I have? Nothing. Nobody. I am alone. Totally alone.

Conchita made an effort to contain her tears.

Maybe I am not as strong as I thought I was.

"I miss her too," Juan Roso said.

Slowly, he took a step closer and put his arms around Conchita's shoulders. He gave her a little rub, letting her feel his old, soft, strong hands in her tight bones. Her whole body tensed. When was the last time she'd felt close to anybody? She couldn't even remember. With the wind rustling in the tree branches, Conchita heard her father's slow, deep but firm breath very close. She shut her eyes, smelled the land, felt the hands on her back. Juan Roso hugged his daughter who, very slowly and almost trembling, leaned her head on his shoulder. He pulled his arms tight around her, for what seemed to Conchita a long, long time. Nothing else was said. As she let the tears fall, her father held her close, letting her be, with no questions or conditions, like nobody had ever done before. Calm spread through her heart.

As if suddenly awoken from a long, deep sleep, Conchita started yawning.

"Oh, it's almost half six," she quickly looked at her watch. "I promised the priest I would be there before the seven o'clock mass to help him with a few things."

"You help so many people Conchita," Juan Roso said, proudly.

She didn't take the compliment. "It's a duty, really," she said. "You're staying at Pensión Ramón, then?" she asked, wiping the tears from her eyes.

"Yes, yes, and please don't worry, I won't bother you, you don't have to take care of me," Juan Roso said. "The pension is a lovely place, I've been there for some time now, since the funeral, but I thought I would leave you some time."

That's thoughtful. "Thanks," Conchita said. "I really should walk back now. We can, of course, meet again, if you'd like to." She blushed.

"There's nothing in the world I'd love more," Juan Roso said.

"My daughter and Soledad are in the house," she suddenly stopped her sentence. "Of course you know Soledad!"

"Ah, Soledad! I saw her at the funeral," Juan Roso said. "How is she?"

"She's well," Conchita said. "But why didn't you communicate with her or her with you, during all those years?"

"She probably thought I was dead," Juan Roso said. He let a few seconds go by. "I've heard that she never married."

"Yes, that is true," Conchita said. "But she's lived a good life, I think. She's always been positive and energetic, at least it seems so to me. But we'll have to prepare her for this. She's delicate and I know she's very fragile after my mother's death, although she would never admit it."

283

"Of course," Juan Roso said, politely. "Take as long as you need, I'm here to help, not to disrupt you."

The two started walking towards the house.

"It's not all bad news," Conchita said as they walked back. "Maria's wedding will help us all get back into shape. She's marrying in April, a very handsome young man, it's a good match, I am pleased."

I hope Gran Basilisa didn't tell him any of her thoughts about the wedding.

"How wonderful," he said. "Are they very in love?"

Oh no, she did.

"Well, I think they are," Conchita said, nervously. "I know my mother had some doubts about it, but I don't see why. They seem perfectly fine."

They arrived at the gate of the *finca*, where Juan Roso needed to turn off to his pension. But he stopped and slightly looked at Conchita, who looked away.

"Although it doesn't look like anything near the love that you two had," she finally said, spontaneously, without fore-thought. She looked at the sky and continued. "But I know that this kind of love only happens in the movies, or is only for a chosen few, like one in a million."

"Really?" Juan Roso asked. "I think it's for everybody, it's just natural, isn't it?"

"Natural?" Conchita wondered aloud. "I don't know what's natural for my daughter, sometimes it frightens me to imagine what's natural to her."

Juan Roso looked at Conchita with a raised eyebrow.

"She's always been a bit different, a bit odd," Conchita said, voicing her concerns about Maria aloud, or even clearly to herself, for the first time ever.

"Aren't we all a bit different, a bit odd?" Juan Roso asked.

Conchita didn't answer.

The two parted after a quick, embarrassed farewell, with Juan Roso disappearing through the trees that once saved his life from the men with guns.

Conchita walked home.

Natural? Sins, arguments and wars are what happens when people become too natural.

22

Maria could still feel the warmth of Nell's body after the plane took off from Barcelona, bound for Heathrow. It was a cold day in February, almost two months after her mother had called her at the Islington Hilton hotel to tell her about Gran. It felt miraculous that Nell had been with her at the time, otherwise the sadness and loneliness would have been unbearable. It was Nell who had gone online to book her a flight, who had arranged the logistics, driven her to the airport at five in the morning. It was Nell who had taken care of her when she most needed it.

That night, after the initial shock, and after talking to her sister and parents on the phone, Maria and Nell laid side by side on the hotel room's bed, with Nell gently caressing Maria's hair for hours, until she finally fell asleep – when there were no more tears to cry.

Maria shivered as the plane's air-conditioning was turned up. She imagined Nell's long, white hands caressing her dark arms, slowly, giving her warmth, as she had done that long, cold night in December.

The two had spoken often since. Nell had called her the day after she flew to Spain to ask how she was, as well as after the funeral and over Christmas. Maria had appreciated the calls as Nell was sweet and understanding, unlike the atmosphere at home, with her father gone and her mother permanently complaining about her workload.

Belchite was also an old village full of old ladies who, despite the fact that some barely spoke to Gran Basilisa, had still invaded her parents' home, crying over the loss of her, mourning her. They sat in a circle in the family home, all dressed in black, praying one rosary after the other, every afternoon, for hours.

Talking to Nell at night was a relief. Over Christmas and during the cold nights of January, the two had established a habit of calling each other at midnight, when Maria's family was asleep. Little by little, Nell had become Maria's confidante, the person she talked to about the funeral, about her father's departure, about the problems at Jordi's flat, as well as her own doubts about the relationship. Nell listened with patience, without trying to fill the numerous silences that Maria left on the telephone, unused as she was to expressing her intimate feelings.

Maria had also helped Nell, who said that Christmas was her least favourite time of year. Her divorced parents were in Lanzarote and Madeira with their new spouses and she had no siblings. Christmas was usually a lonely day at her neighbour's home. Friends always invited her over, but she preferred to keep it low-key. The best thing about Christmas, she had told Maria, was their daily chats and, like every year, football.

Tucked up in bed under a heavy duvet to protect herself from the cold Belchite winter, Maria had listened to Nell's tales about her friends, the politics of the football team, and even paid attention to the Premiership results on Boxing Day. Little had she suspected that some day she would listen to an account of Manchester City's 'thrilling' goalless draw with Bolton.

For some reason, football was more bearable with Nell. Although Maria still hated it, listening to the ups and downs of Sheffield United seemed at least more exotic than the ever-present talk about FC Barcelona.

Maria of course knew that Jordi had met Nell in London in January, during a trip that it had been too soon for her to take. Once she'd returned to work after Christmas, she had asked for some more time off because it was still hard to concentrate. Gran Basilisa had been almost everything in Maria's life, the only person unconditionally behind her, who always defended her against anything or anybody, including her mother.

Her loss almost meant the end of the world to Maria. She had felt desperately lonely, abandoned, as if half of her heart had been violently removed from her chest, and then broken into a million pieces. She had spent hours walking around the olive trees in Belchite, and while in Barcelona, stroking Bombillo in silence had brought her peace.

London will help bring me out of myself, a break with routine, Maria thought, looking out of the window as the plane began its descent.

It was a Wednesday morning. Maria was returning to England, not on business, but on a personal visit to see Nell – her new best friend after all the confidences they had shared on the phone.

Nell had invited Maria to attend a memorial to Britain's International Brigade Battalion, a group of volunteers who went to Spain to fight against Franco seventy years ago. Maria immediately thought that it would be interesting to see Spanish history from another angle. She hadn't told anybody, not even her mother, or Jordi about the trip. It was her little, secret London adventure.

As soon as she walked into the terminal and switched her phone on, Maria received a voice mail from Jordi, checking how she was. Their relationship had cooled off after Maria told him a few weeks ago that she needed time to think. She didn't want to lie and had barely seen him since. She needed space.

Maria didn't text him or call him back. Switching her mobile off and quickly combing her hair, she walked out of the arrivals gate, where Nell was waiting discreetly to one side.

"*HOLA*," Nell smiled and gave her a friendly kiss on the cheek.

"*HOLA*." Maria felt embarrassed. It was easier to talk on the phone than face to face.

Nell seemed to perceive it and broke the ice, making some quick, general comments about flying. They walked towards the car-park.

"I thought we could go home first, drop your suitcase and get the bikes, what do you think?" Nell asked.

Maria was excited about Nell's cycling plan. She hadn't ridden a bicycle in years, even if as a child she had asked for one birthday after birthday, Christmas after Christmas, but her

"In this matter, everything is still not enough," Maria responded quickly.

Standing on a bench to get a better view, the two listened to the old veterans telling their stories.

"I would still do the same today," said one, barely able to stand. "I was eighteen and read about fascism in Spain, so I went to fight against it. I was young and believed in ideas. I still do. I've been called naïve, at best, other times a plain idiot. But in the end, following my heart has paid off."

Follow nature. Maria remembered her grandmother's words. *Why is this thought chasing me?*

The event finished with a folk singer, guitar in hand, cowboy hat on head, singing his own Spanish Civil War version of RED RIVER VALLEY, which made the crowd shiver and brought Maria to the brink of tears. Nell noticed and squeezed her hand.

"This isn't cheering you up, is it?" Nell asked.

Maria smiled. "It's not a comedy, no."

Nell jumped from the bench to the ground and helped Maria down as well.

"Let me show you a great place where we'll find wonderful food for tonight," Nell said, walking towards the bikes.

Maria couldn't stop looking at the stalls of Borough Market, even if as Nell kept saying the midweek version was much smaller then the weekend's. Maria loved the colours, the life, the smell of the spices, the various types of bread. She looked at the flowers, the delicious juices, the exotic fruit and vegetables.

"Sixteen pounds for a handful of mushrooms?" Maria pulled a face. "You can fill your shopping trolley for that in Spain."

The two bought cheaper ingredients, for a vegetable stew and a tortilla. Bags in hand, they sat at Monmouth Market coffee shop, with its open entrance and fresh air. Well wrapped in their anoraks, they shared a cake and watched the people walking by. Maria loved every second of it. She sat back and took a big breath.

mother always said they were for boys. She eventually got one at University.

"That sounds like a good plan," Maria said. "Have you been able to find a second bike?"

"Yes, my neighbour will lend me his, you can use mine."

They smiled at each other as they got into Nell's car and began the drive to Hackney.

This time, Nell's neighbourhood looked substantially more elegant than when she saw it first, that night in November, when she had felt so scared.

Daylight certainly helps, Maria thought. *I guess the mindset does as well.*

Pepa sniffed at Maria as soon as the two women walked into the flat. Maria loved Nell's lively cat; she kneeled down to stroke her short hair, until the little creature had had enough and left. Like the previous time, Nell handed her a pair of comfortable slippers, making Maria feel warm and welcome. She walked into the living room, looking at the photos on the walls, the books, the plants, the light brightening it all. Everything breathed with life.

"Pepa loves the fishy cane you bought for her," Nell shouted from the kitchen.

Maria blushed. She remembered the night she spent on the sofa-bed. The night they'd kissed in the pub, in November, when she got so drunk. She swallowed as she remembered.

Nell brought her a cup of coffee. "Here, darling," she said.

"Thank you," Maria said with a big smile. *Thank God it's not tea.*

Nell seemed to read her thoughts. "I know tea is not your thing," she said going back to the kitchen, returning shortly afterwards with some tea for herself. "But I love it."

The two sat on the sofa. "You look good," Nell said. "It looks as if the time off has done you well."

Maria took a deep breath. "Well, it hasn't exactly been a holiday."

Nell held her hand, and Maria didn't pull it away. "I am sure things will get better soon."

"They certainly can't get any worse," Maria said. "Anyway, how have you been? How's Sheffield United?"

"Manchester United!" Nell smiled; she seemed to forgive her friend's mistake easily. "We're good, we won on Sunday," she said, sipping her tea. "Work is keeping me busy and football, healthy and sociable. Pepa is well, what else can I ask for?"

I like that simplicity. I wish I could be like that. Not this mess.

Nell looked at her watch. "Come on, we have to go." She stood up. "I hope you'll enjoy the Brigades' gathering, I thought of you as soon as I saw it advertised."

"Thank you," Maria said, taking a present from her bag and handing it to Nell. "I just wanted to thank you for your help."

Nell sat down again. She seemed surprised. "You didn't have to."

Maria blushed.

Nell opened the long, tall pack, unwrapping a transparent bottle of the most extra-virgin olive oil. Nell stared at it for a few seconds, opened the bottle, smelled it and let out a big sigh. She poured some drops onto her finger and tried it.

"Wonderful," she said. "I love it, it's just perfect. Is it your family's?"

"Yes, yes, I took a good one."

Nell gave her a quick kiss on the cheek; Maria looked away, embarrassed.

"We must use this – fancy cooking something tonight?" Nell asked.

"I'd love to."

I knew that coming to London was a good idea. Two months in Belchite and Barcelona and I wasn't looking forward to anything. Two hours in London and I can't wait for my cycle ride and cooking session. She's a good friend.

Maria loved cooking, and loved even more the idea of cooking with somebody else. It was the opposite from home, where her mother ran the kitchen dictatorially, most of the time

shutting herself inside it, doing all the work, com[...] was a martyr bearing a heavy cross. Instead, Maria lo[...] slowly, in a leisurely way, with love and ca[...] grandmother used to.

Just two minutes after the ride started, Maria fe[...] than she had felt in a long time, pedalling across t[...] stretch of London Fields. She loved the breeze in her [...] freedom. It put her in a good mood immediately.

She followed Nell across London, enjoying the Is[...] squares, the little stands in Exmouth Market, the students [...] Bloomsbury, Marylebone's fancy shops and finally, the si[...] the river. Along the ride, Nell told her little stories about her [...] They were not boring history lessons, but human tales a[...] people who had changed the world. She particularly loved [...] tales about the Bloomsbury group and seeing the square wh[...] Virginia Woolf and John Maynard Keynes had lived.

"Keynes gay? Really?" Maria was shocked. "Nobody to[...] me that at university and I read all his books!"

"My University was a bit unusual," Maria added. *To say th[...] least.*

About a hundred people had already gathered at Jubilee Gardens, by the London Eye, when Nell and Maria arrived. Maria had goose-pimples as soon as she saw the Republican flags from a distance, the old purple, red and yellow flag used during the Second Republic.

It should still be the official one.

"This is fantastic." Maria was shocked to see so many people celebrating the Republic miles away from Spain. The two walked round the stands set for the occasion, tasted some of the tortillas and Padrón peppers and picked up every brochure about the group's activities. Maria talked to the organisers at length, interested in their ideas. She finally gave them a substantial donation and promised to send them olive oil from Belchite, which they greatly appreciated.

"You're very generous," Nell said.

This is life. If only I could do this with Jordi, but of course, being a man, he doesn't like going to markets. Maybe it's easier with two women.

Maria felt relaxed, she could trust Nell, talk to her openly.

"I guess being a lesbian is easier in the sense that two women will always have more in common than a man and woman," she said. "Is that true?"

Nell seemed surprised by the sudden question. "Mmm," she muttered. "I am not sure, I guess it's as difficult as any relationship between two people. It's all about the chemistry, isn't it? It's whether it clicks or not, whether you *get* one person just by looking at them."

"I guess you're right," Maria said, gazing out through the window, sipping her coffee, taking time to put her thoughts together. She watched an old couple, in cycling clothes, debating which cheese to buy. "Relationships in Spain are quite formal, official, maybe more so than here," she said, turning to Nell. "In Spain, it's not about connecting or sharing things. It's more about looking good, fitting in socially. As long as you look good on the outside, it's all fine."

Nell shook her head. "What a shame," she said. "I saw Jordi looked quite preppy, very smartly dressed, a clean-cut boy." Nell smiled.

Maria looked at Nell, she had been wondering what she thought of him when they met a few weeks ago. "Yes, he's very proper, isn't he? Your meeting went well, though, as far as I know."

Nell looked at Maria in silence for a few seconds. "It did, yeah," she said. "It was funny, he kept looking at a calendar on my office wall with some photos of women. They could be lesbians, but they may not – it's just a beautiful picture. He looked as if he thought that they were, though."

Maria laughed. "Really? Wow, he must have been shocked."

"He seemed to be," Nell said, with another smile. Then she grew more serious. "But yes, I got the feeling he was somebody used to doing as he is told. He didn't really challenge what I said, and basically agreed to everything I suggested. He didn't have one single observation, to be honest."

Maria briefly closed her eyes, then looked up at Nell. "Yes, he's not one who seeks to challenge. He obeys." *He has spent his life obeying Opus Dei.* "Although he's quite into his job, you know with his family owning the company. He puts in about twelve hours every day there, and works most weekends."

"That's a shame, isn't it?" Nell looked out of the window, her glance fixed on the people shopping. "Work can give us satisfaction, certainly, but not happiness, what do you think?"

Maria remained pensive. "Yep, I'd never thought of it like that, but I guess it's true. It's easy to convince yourself of the contrary, though."

Nell raised an eyebrow. "I am sure those big companies are very good at brainwashing you, making you believe you're crucial to them, and them to you," she said. "But that's not real, is it? That bond loosens as soon as people quit, but they don't realise. Only when it is too late they suddenly wake up and discover they've spent half their lives in the office."

"That's what I want to avoid," Maria said. "I am always shocked when I think of how short life is, when you put it into perspective. We don't have that much time."

Nell nodded and took another bite of cake.

Maria continued. "Sometimes I find people feel they need things, like a job, or a partner, or a big house, to be happy." Maria thought of her mother, who always ran between the fields and her home, both lovely places, but never enough to satisfy her. "They miss the fact that the point of being happy is *being* happy, not this or that."

"Mmm, I am not sure." Nell smiled and bent forward, fork in hand. "This cake is really making me happy." She took another bite.

So did Maria. "If only it was that easy."

"True," Nell said. "But most of the time it helps me to think less and feel more; just trying to spot the natural clicks."

Maria looked out of the window again. "In my family, it seems that more than clicking, we repel," she said, and swallowed the last bite of her cake.

Nell gave her a compassionate look.

"That's not right, actually," Maria quickly withdrew her comment. "I had that chemistry with my grandmother. We *got* each other. She didn't go to University and she barely attended school during the War, but she understood everything I told her about banking, much more than my own mother, who runs a fairly large business. We had such a strong bond, you wouldn't imagine. She's the person that I've loved the most and who's loved me the most."

"More than your parents?" Nell asked.

"By far," Maria replied quickly. She looked at Nell's immense blue eyes, which, again reminded her of Gran Basilisa's. They brought her calm, filled her with a sense of trust. "It's so sad that she's gone now. I will never have anything like it again."

"I am sure you will," Nell said.

There's nobody I can imagine having that connection with. Maria's heart seemed to stop. *Except with you. You're the only person that I talk to as easily as I talked to her.*

Maria's hands suddenly felt cold, she felt paralysed by her own thoughts.

"I will bet you a meal at London's best Spanish restaurant that you will find somebody who will love you as much, if not more," Nell said, bringing Maria back into the conversation.

"Deal done," Maria agreed. "Free meal!"

"The only free meal you're getting is tonight." Nell stood up. "Let's go so I can show you my tortilla skills. I've been practising."

Listening to Edith Piaf, the two women peeled potatoes and chopped vegetables in Nell's kitchen, surrounded by spices, cooking herbs and plants. They chatted and exchanged views over the right amount of eggs, potatoes and salt.

"Proportion and salt are the keys of the tortilla," Maria stated.

"And of life!" Nell said, making Maria smile.

Maria looked at her. "You seem to have a good balance."

Nell looked through the window at the big, dark clouds in the sky. "I may have proportion, but no salt," she said. "It can get all too boring and predictable here."

Maria prepared a delicious *pà amb tomaca*, with the olive and rosemary bread from Borough. She squeezed some garlic on it, then some tomato and finally some of the olive oil she'd brought from home.

"*Voilà*," Maria said. "I bet this is not boring and predictable."

Nell rolled her eyes with pleasure at the first bite. "Phenomenal," she said, stepping close to Maria, very close. Her eyes were impossibly attractive, Maria thought. She was so taken by them that she only reacted two seconds after Nell briefly kissed her on the lips.

What was that?

Maria continued with the chopping, singing along *Non, je ne regrette rien* She loved Edith Piaf; she also wanted to sing out loud that she didn't regret Nell's kiss at the party in November, or the night they spent in each other's arms.

"This is lovely, do you do this often?" Maria moved her head happily to the music's tune.

"I wish!" Nell said. "Some English women don't fancy chopping vegetables for fun; they prefer to look cool and be seen around trendy areas, like Hoxton or Soho."

"How boring," Maria said. "Some people forget that it's not cool to try to be cool – but that's not particular to English women, there's plenty of people like that in Spain, and I guess everywhere."

"True," Nell said.

"Well, except in Belchite, where nobody tries to be cool," Maria added.

Nell laughed. She put the potatoes in the pan with the hot oil. "You certainly don't," she said, giving her a cheeky glance.

"Thank you."

"But it's true," Nell said. "You don't really give a damn about what other people think, do you? Deep down, you really do your own thing, right?"

Maria stirred the potatoes carefully in the pan with a wooden fork, like her grandmother used to do.

"I guess so," Maria said finally. *And you do as well.*

"That's why I like you." Nell gave Maria a smile that she felt at the deepest bottom of her heart.

Bottle of Priorat to hand, the two sat at the table, face to face, with soft jazz playing in the background and only the succulent food and aromas between them.

The feast took more than an hour, with much gentle conversation about the flavours, many looks into each other's eyes, mouths moving slowly, eyes faster, and Maria's mind, skipping far ahead.

This must be "it."

"Best meal in a long, long time," Nell said, sighing, sitting back in her chair.

Maria's heart felt warm. She felt comfortable, easy, light. The wine and the jazz, the food. Nell. She didn't miss anything, anybody.

Nell pressed the remote to start Almodóvar's *All About My Mother* telling her about her passion for the Spanish movie director. As much as she would have liked to, Maria had never seen the film because Jordi, like every other conservative Spaniard, looked down on the extravagant, gay director from La Mancha.

Maria sat straight up on the sofa while Nell lay down, resting her head in Maria's lap. Maria almost jumped when the impressive shots of Barcelona's *Sagrada Família* appeared, and was close to crying at Manuela's tragic story.

As the movie went on, Maria heard the rain drops tick against the window, and glanced around the room; there was a pale yellow floor lamp casting light from the corner. She felt at home; she lay back on the sofa and Nell adjusted her head on her legs.

Shortly afterwards, Nell touched Maria's hand, slowly, sending a current through her body. Without taking her eyes from the screen, Nell continued caressing Maria's fingers, one by one, for several minutes. Then, she left her hand on Maria's, who closed her eyes.

I don't care. Nobody will know, and I am in an official break in my relationship. I am not being unfaithful. This is different. She's my friend, we are close.

The two continued watching the movie, hand in hand. Nell's head was turned towards the television set, while Maria looked at her friend's perfect, tall, proportionate body. Her tight black top revealed small, round breasts. Her short hair was clean and shiny. Almost shaking, Maria placed her hand on it, then started caressing it, shyly, slowly. Nell pressed Maria's other hand, holding it tight. Maria looked at Nell's pretty face; she loved her big nose, always a sign of character. As delicately as she could, she drew lines with her finger along Nell's eyebrows, her eyes, her forehead. Nell's breath became heavier, her chest rising and falling.

Follow nature. Her grandmother's words resounded in her head.

With the movie credits rolling, Nell turned and gave Maria a long look that captivated her; she couldn't stop staring at Nell, who moved closer and kissed her briefly on the lips. Maria closed her eyes, her heart beating fast. Her mind was almost blank as Nell opened her mouth and kissed her, her tongue searching for hers. They kissed and kissed, eyes shut, until Maria finally drew away and looked at Nell, intently. She closed her eyes, she could still feel the kiss.

I love the taste, so different from Jordi's, now I understand when they talk about sweet kisses. Jordi's weren't, but this is. Maria wanted more.

She drew nearer to Nell and kissed her without hesitation. Nell extended her arm and touched Maria's black hair, stroked it.

"I've never seen hair as gorgeous as yours," Nell whispered, kissing it.

Maria loved her hair being stroked, which Jordi rarely did, mostly to avoid temptation. Maria felt a slight jolt at every stroke.

Maria kissed Nell's neck, then her face, her lips. Nell slid her hand under Maria's shirt, lightly caressing her lower back. Maria felt as if her defences had fallen down all at once. She shut her eyes as Nell's hand moved up her spine, then down again, over and over again.

Oh yes. She's doing what I love the most, with no need to tell her or ask for it. I can't believe this is real. This just fits. I can't stop this now.

Maria kissed Nell more and more passionately. Nell gently pushed Maria on the sofa, her black hair spread over the cushions. Nell looked at her body, flat, moving upwards and downwards with every breath; she touched her stomach, her chest, the shirt over her bra.

"Maria," Nell started saying, but stopped as Maria slowly placed one finger on her mouth.

"Shhh," Maria whispered. *Just continue, please don't break this dream. Please don't wake me up from this. I have been waiting for this for years, please don't do what Jordi does and cut things sharp.*

Nell looked at her. "I don't want to do anything you don't want me to," she said in a low voice. She caressed Maria's long hair. "Not that I wouldn't like to, but I don't want to trouble you, or to do anything that might ruin our friendship, what we have together." She kissed her lips, briefly. "I enjoy our time together too much."

"So do I," Maria replied and closed her eyes. She felt more alive than ever; she felt open to Nell, open to life.

How could this ruin our friendship? This is one of the best things in my life, probably the best. Life is too short and my time is finally here. I am not going to let it go.

Maria gently pulled Nell's head towards her face, kissing her, adjusting her body under hers, immediately feeling her heat, her movements searching for her. Maria touched Nell's back, her long neck, smelled her scent. She moved her moist lips along Nell's neck, the back of the ears. Nell's breath became faster and louder.

"You don't know what you do to me," Nell whispered, making Maria hold her breath for a few seconds.

Finally. Finally somebody wants me the way I want to be wanted. The way I want her.

"I feel the same," Maria said in a very low voice, her mouth only half open.

Little by little, Nell started unbuttoning Maria's shirt, caressing and kissing the skin beneath. Her hand moved towards her breast, unveiling her delicate, silk bra, which she kissed and touched, following its pattern. Maria's eyes were wide. This was only natural, what could be wrong with it? Nell gently turned Maria on her side and unhooked her bra. Maria lay back, facing her, with her top half naked; she wasn't shy or scared.

Take me.

Maria extended her arms around Nell's neck, kissing it, giving her small bites. Nell caressed Maria's breasts for a long time, one after another, both at the same time, giving Maria pleasure beyond her imagination.

She seems to be reading my mind. I hope I can do the same for her.

Maria took Nell's jumper off, removed her bra delicately, and admired her sumptuous body. Maria's heart had never beaten so widely. The two women lay on top of each other, feeling their breasts pressed together, pushing their bodies against each other in perfect synchrony. Maria, who was now moving freely and openly, had never felt so turned on before, so ready.

Ah life. I am catching you now.

The impulse of the two was unstoppable. Their bodies blended. Nell's touch was so delicate that Maria barely noticed when her finger slipped inside her, firm, strong, warm.

On fire, Maria couldn't stop kissing Nell, her body shaking against hers. She'd never experienced such desire to touch or be touched. With one finger still inside, Nell used another to caress her just outside, giving Maria pleasure previously unknown to her. Maria panted aloud as she'd never done before, all those lonely fantasies were now behind.

"*Ostia*," Maria could only swear in Spanish, to Nell's surprise, who looked at her with contagious pleasure.

Maria curled her sweaty body against Nell's and kissed her as if it was the last kiss of her life. They lay in silence, only broken by Maria's still loud, but even breathing.

"Not bad, eh?" Nell said, looking at Maria. The understatement made her laugh.

"No, not too bad for a beginner," Maria said. They both laughed.

I could never have enough of this.

Nell hugged Maria gently, caressed her body. As Maria calmed down, she started to touch Nell. She wasn't lost, it felt as if she'd done this many times before. She caressed Nell's entire body. She turned her around and massaged her beautiful, long back. Maria's two hands followed Nell's spine, gently, before she kissed it, barely touching her, as Nell had described to her that night in November.

I would love to please you, give you my best.

Maria followed Nell's bones, shoulders, touched and kissed her neck, before she kissed the length of her body all the way to the bottom of her long, perfectly shaped legs. Maria rubbed her face against Nell's calf and kissed her between the legs. She instinctively knew where to go. She reached inside Nell with her tongue, loving the intimacy, the contact, and every groan she heard from Nell. She wanted to give her more and more. She felt Nell had just given her the world. Maria moved her lips over her stomach, her breasts, her nipples, erect with desire. With her finger, Maria found Nell easily. She never thought she could make anybody glow as much as Nell did, her face shining with pleasure, with happiness.

So many questions answered at once.

The two lay together calmly afterwards, side by side, their legs entwined. They fell asleep, their bodies perfectly adjusted to each other's.

23

Jordi was back on a plane to London sooner than he expected. Barely a month after his visit to the Islington Council, he had now returned to England for a meeting with Peñaranda and some hedge fund managers. Over the past few weeks, they had amassed most of the Caves' one million-euro loan – supposed to be a short-term measure to offset the drop in national sales.

However, the embargo against Catalan products had only worsened. The central government had struck a deal with the Canary Island nationalists to pass the budget, erasing any need of an alliance with the Catalans, leaving them with no allies in Madrid. Caves Gratallops' Spanish sales were in freefall.

The company had failed to make the first interest payment on the loan, causing the hedge funds that bought the debt to start pressuring the business. They demanded, not requested, that Jordi fly to London on the day of their choosing. Jordi had spoken to Andreu, who had said there was no way out: they owned the debt, and if the company struggled to pay interest, it was them, the creditors, that Jordi had to answer to. Banca Catalana no longer held the debt.

It was still a mystery to Jordi how Peñaranda and the hedge fund managers had persuaded Banca Catalana to sell them the loan, but the credit crunch had led certain banks to pass on risk. Even so, as far as Jordi knew, Banca Catalana hadn't sold other loans. All Andreu had told him was that the decision had come "from above."

I am sure I can persuade them to agree new terms of payment, especially after I show them our warehouse plans, Jordi thought as the plane flew over the Royal Albert Hall, towards Heathrow Airport. *Wait until they open the cases of vintage cava that I am bringing them, even Peñaranda will fall for them.*

Half an hour later, Jordi saw some businesswomen getting onto the Heathrow Express. They looked beautiful and sharp. He thought of Maria, that's what she must have looked like on her trips to London. The image of the two stunning women lasciviously looking at each other on the calendar in Nell's office came to his mind.

Maybe it was those trips to London, the exposure to this fast-paced, consumerist, immoral world that distanced Maria from me, Jordi thought as the train started moving towards Paddington.

He had only seen Maria for lunch a couple of times since Christmas, almost two months ago. They talked about the wedding and the unfortunate timing of recent events, although they hadn't reached any conclusions. She had asked him for time to think, without clearly saying whether she wanted to cancel or postpone the wedding, keeping Jordi's hopes alive. As much as it hurt, he made an effort to be strong, to be there for her.

Jordi had tried to pray and read novels to avoid thinking about his disastrous month. His relationship with Father Juan Antonio had deteriorated since he refused to return or lend him part of his donation, while work on the flat moved slowly – he would be lucky if it was finished by the end of the year. With Maria, all he could do was to pray and wait, more or less the same as on the Caves front.

At least Barça is doing well. I will always have Barça.

A bit thinner than at Christmas, and dressed in his smartest suit to meet the bankers, Jordi looked out of the window at the dark, rainy February afternoon as the train approached Paddington Station. He observed the passengers around him. Dressed in suits, with serious faces, they were mostly glued to their Blackberries in the silent carriage.

In the Penedès, at least we talk to each other.

From the waiting room at Premium Capital's offices on Bond Street, Jordi couldn't stop looking at the Bentleys, Rolls Royces, and blonde women carrying luxury Hermes and Armani bags. He didn't know Mayfair at all, he'd only been to the City and Canary Wharf for business meetings and visited central London as a tourist. He didn't know that this exuberant shopping area had turned into a financial centre.

Here?

It was past six o'clock when the shops began to close; he had already been waiting for fifteen minutes.

These people work late, he though, stretching out the sleeve of his suit, adjusting the knot of his light blue tie, trying to present an impeccable image. He sat down to read the magazines on the coffee table. He scanned Square Meal, Harrods' Property, Med Villas and Yacht World – there were no signs of the *FINANCIAL TIMES* or other broadsheets.

About half an hour later, three young men entered the room after throwing open the door without knocking. One of them wore flip-flops and had sunglasses on. The next was in jeans, while Peñaranda came last, dressed in a black-tie suit. Jordi made an effort to keep his face straight.

"Hi Jordi, how are yah doing today?" the man with the sunglasses said in a heavy American accent. He put the glasses on his head. "I am Brian, yeah, from Premium Capital, excuse my appearance, I just flew back from Barbados this morning, I had to come back for a deal and have been stuck here all day. Have a seat."

Jordi sat down at a table in the centre of the room.

"I am Stuart, how do you do?" said the taller man, in jeans, who sounded English. He handed him a card. "I am with Gama Investments, we're based in the Cayman Islands. I work half of the week here and half of the week there."

Good Lord.

"Don't you get tired of so much travelling?" Jordi tried to be natural.

"I am used to it," he said. "My girlfriend lives in San Francisco, which just makes things worse. But I get lots of free air miles." He laughed and sat down.

After this, ironically, Peñaranda felt familiar, Jordi thought.

You're just a madrileño.

"Hello Jordi, how are you?" the Duke said. "I am glad you could make it. I am sorry but I will have to leave in ten minutes, I have a dinner to attend."

Jordi stood up and walked towards the cava bottles, carefully packed in wooden boxes. "Before you go, I've brought you some cava..." He couldn't finish the sentence.

"No time for that," Brian, the American, interrupted. "I don't have much more than ten minutes, either. I have to be in Zagreb tomorrow at eight in the morning and still need to prepare. Let's get started."

"Sure," Jordi said, leaving the cava bottles in the corner, returning to his seat. He looked at the three men in silence. They didn't have notepads or any papers in front of them. Jordi felt like a schoolboy with his little pencil and a notebook ready on the table. He leaned back, adjusted his tie and coughed nervously.

Peñaranda fired first. "Jordi, we're all very excited here about the Caves, what a great business to be in these days."

Come on Peñaranda. Come on.

He continued: "As you know, we have been buying your debt, it's difficult to track I know, this happens privately between traders, there's no public information. But just for you to know, we own about eighty-five percent of the loan, so really, after missing the first interest payment, now we legally have the right to call in the administrators, unless of course we reach an agreement with the company."

Peñaranda smiled. Jordi was shocked, but reacted quickly.

"I am sorry, but under Spanish law, you need quite a few interest payment delays to be able to call in the administrators," he said.

306

"As debtholders in times of trouble we can move the headquarters to the U.K. and under British law, that would be allowed, we've done this in the past," the Englishman said.

Jordi had read in the *FINANCIAL TIMES* about some predator funds doing exactly this to ailing German companies. *But we are a sound business, they can't do this to us.*

"Is this what you're planning to do?" he muttered. "Are you trying to make the Caves go bust?"

"No, not at all," Peñaranda said. "Or not yet."

Yet? Jordi felt sweat on his forehead, put his hand nervously to his mouth.

"We're not a relic German auto-parts maker facing competition from China," Jordi said. "We produce cava that can only be made in the Penedès and there's a huge demand for it."

"We do like the business, don't get us wrong." Peñaranda looked at his nails with arrogance. "But we must improve the management."

Jordi gave him a quick, defensive look. "The company is perfectly well managed."

"Maybe not, Jordi," the American said, playing with the neck of his flowery holiday shirt, still with his sunglasses balanced on his head. "The firm wouldn't be in this situation if the management was sound."

"It is a short-term blip that will be resolved as soon as we have a new project going," Jordi said, leaning his elbows on the table, decisively. This was his time. "And that's, gentlemen, what I wanted to talk to you about."

Jordi pulled out from his suitcase the preliminary drawings of the Islington warehouse that Patrick had designed.

"Look," he said as he extended the map on the table. "This warehouse will give us access to the British market – in less than two years, we're projecting it will double our sales."

Jordi looked at the incredulous faces around the table. Stuart seemed the only one truly focused – on what he was typing under the table, on his Blackberry, Jordi noticed. The other two were rudely looking away, impatient. Jordi thought of God, took a deep breath and carried on: "I could pass you details…"

"Too late," the American interrupted, looking at the wall clock. He smiled, showing his perfect white teeth. "We're men of business here Jordi, we're not your grandfather or a piggy bank. We can't wait two years, I am sure you understand the banking business. In the financial world, two years is a lifetime."

Jordi gave him an unpleasant look. *Fast money, new wealth.* He despised the type.

"Caves Gratallops is a sound business with more than a hundred years of history," Jordi looked them in the eye, one by one. "And that's the way it should continue. It's not a sausage factory to create immediate wealth. This is an artisan business that is managed with care, owned by the same family for generations."

Peñaranda was ready to speak up but Brian was quicker: "I'm afraid Jordi it's us who are in a position to decide the timetable. Remember we can call in the administrators if an agreement isn't reached."

"I will have to check on that," Jordi said.

"You're very welcome," Brian replied. "You will only waste your money and your lawyer's time."

Jordi looked around the room. "What are you suggesting?"

Peñaranda leaned forward. "We want a management change. Your family, apart from not being the legitimate owners of the land, has also messed up with the debt, dragging the business into this situation. It's obvious that you and your father can't do the job – as a matter of fact, I think he will be relieved about this, given his fragile health." He smiled.

I hate you Peñaranda. "Leave my father out of this," Jordi said. "His health is fantastic, thank you very much."

"I am glad to hear that," Peñaranda said, his face serious again. "The point is that we're going to change the management. It is a fact. If you don't agree now in a civilised manner, I am afraid we'll end up in court, and that will only be more expensive for you, Jordi."

"You are mad if you think I came here to dig my own grave," Jordi said, holding onto the chair arms tightly.

The American stepped in: "I wouldn't come to conclusions that quickly Jordi, maybe now you can negotiate and get a better deal than you would later on."

What do you know of cava? Yank, go home.

"We've researched the company thoroughly, Jordi," Stuart, the Englishman, said. "We want to take the company up-market, abandon the cheap stuff, and just produce vintage for the American and the northern European markets, that's where the money is. The aging process, though, would need a large investment, which we will provide, but of course, on our own terms."

"We will also revolutionise the marketing," Brian said. "We'll build a theme park, we've explored some sites near the Caves, some are for sale. We're planning a superstore with gourmet products, the largest food and wine shop in Spain." He extended his arms in the air as he spoke. "Seven floors full of it. Our model is just outside LA, it would be the first of its kind in Europe, isn't that fun?"

Jordi started to feel a cramping in his stomach.

"And I would manage it all – from Madrid," Peñaranda said, smiling.

Jordi now felt his guts turning over. *Over my dead body Peñaranda, over my dead body you will do that.*

"We would go into profit quickly," Peñaranda continued. "Improved technology would help us make everything more efficient, so we wouldn't need so many workers." Peñaranda wrinkled his nose, looking up. "I reckon we could do with half of the workforce, can you imagine how much money that would save us?"

God help me keep my cool. Please help.

Jordi saw how Brian gave a quick look at his watch. Not that Jordi had been looking at him, but the diamonds around the sphere were so large and bright that it immediately attracted his attention.

How disgusting, Jordi thought. He remembered the Bible verse about a camel's passage through the eye of a needle being easier than a rich man entering heaven. He felt his temperature rising.

This makes me sick.

"Is that all, gentlemen?" Jordi asked, with a raised eyebrow.

Peñaranda took some documents from his suitcase. "If you agree with everything, you can sign the papers now," he said. "Otherwise you can take them home, read them through and return them to us as soon as possible. You know we like to act quickly."

Brian took some chewing-gum from his pocket, put the wrapper on the table and started to chew. "If you act quick, fellow, there could be some substantial compensation there for you." He winked.

"Especially as you're about to get married," Peñaranda said.

How do you know this? Who have you talked to, snake?

Stuart and Brian went: "Uuuuuh" at the same time.

Jordi, who hated chewing gum as much as he hated the *nouveau riche*, leaned back, crossed his arms and looked at the three men, frowning.

He thought of his grandfather, the old black and white photo of him labouring on the land – the man who had been shot for caring about his workers and Catalunya. He thought of his father, so many years running the Caves, with his virtues and defects, but always leading from the front, protecting his family and workers. He thought of Maria, of the vines underneath his window, the change of colours in the autumn, the unexploited land nearby, the smell of the fresh earth after rain.

A theme park! A superstore. Good God.

Jordi stood up determined. "You know what you can do with these papers Peñaranda?"

Peñaranda looked at him with interest. "Yes, Jordi?" he said with deflection.

"You can stick them up your arse." Jordi left the room, slamming the door behind him.

Jordi called Robert from the back of the black cab that took him from Mayfair to Islington. The family lawyer had unsuccessfully spent the past few weeks trying to gain the ownership of the Caves' land, refuting Peñaranda's claims.

"Damn it, Jordi, they're circling us," the lawyer said after hearing the latest developments.

"But that can't be true," Jordi was impatient for reassurance. "They can't move the headquarters, what are they going to do, pack the *masia* and ship it to London?"

"I am afraid they can," Robert said. "I've read about similar cases, in Germany mostly. Small business owners are furious about this breed. These vultures buy the debts of struggling firms, most of the time to gain control of the company; it's called loan-to-own. They're specialists."

"We're not a struggling business!" Jordi protested.

"I hate to say this, Jordi, but we are," the lawyer said. "I know the loan was necessary, but perhaps it wasn't such a good idea."

"How could we know that, instead of negotiating with Banca Catalana, like we've done for decades, we would end up facing these soulless sharks?"

"It's a good question," Robert said. "I'd like to know why Banca Catalana sold our debt. Maybe they're in trouble and need to clean their books."

"But why us?" Jordi still couldn't understand. Such manouvers were practically unknown in Spain.

"I don't know, Jordi, I don't know."

"What can we do now?" Jordi was pensive. "I guess finding an investor or some sort of refinancing is the only way out, isn't it?"

"It seems so," Robert said. "But they'll want a high price. They're in here for profit."

Jordi sighed, leaned his head on his hand. "What about your research into the land ownership, anything new?"

"I am afraid not," the lawyer said. "I am really sorry to say, Jordi, but it seems they are in control."

"All right, let's see what I can do," Jordi said, noticing the cab was about to reach the Angel.

I need a drink.

311

Almost half of the first gin and tonic went down in one gulp. Feeling relieved, Jordi loosened his tie and looked around The Green, the first decent bar he'd seen as he stepped out of the cab. It was more modern than some of the pubs around the area and it also seemed to have a decent food menu.

I will have to talk to Dad about this, there's no way out. After all, it's the loan he negotiated, he needs to talk to Andreu again. But these fuckers, how can they think they can control the Caves from Bond Street? They wouldn't know where to start if I gave them a bucket to pick the grapes.

He ran his hand through his hair repeatedly, staring down at the floor. He raised his glance and was surprised to see people ignore the smoking restrictions. He didn't hesitate. A few minutes later, he was sitting with a second gin and tonic, smoking a Marlboro that the bartender had given him – with a wink. Jordi hadn't smoked since he spoke to his father about the land, back in December.

Who says cigarettes are bad for you?

Jordi crossed his legs, leaned back and exhaled the smoke with confidence. He checked his mobile phone, no messages or texts. He tried to call Maria again, without success, and took a long sip of his drink. Distractedly, he looked at the bar, noticing an unusual number of men. He looked for the women, there were few, and those present were with other women.

Where have I ended up?

Jordi, sitting at the back of the bar, noticed a small rainbow flag by the fruit machine. It was a gay bar. Two men were tongue-kissing at a corner table, provoking his immediate revulsion, while a small group of young men sat in tacky sleeveless tops at a table nearby. Some had tattoos, which Jordi openly stared at.

There were another two women at the front of the bar, at a table overlooking Upper Street. Jordi immediately recognised Nell, from the Council.

I knew it, I knew she was a lesbian! Wow.

He ordered a third gin and tonic.

Nell was wearing the long, orange scarf over a black top, the same one she'd had on the day they met a few weeks ago, in January. Her hair was a bit shorter. She was holding somebody's hand. Jordi felt curious and stretched his neck to see who she was with.

Holy Jesus, Christ, God.

Jordi brusquely moved forward, sat on the edge of his chair, placed both hands on the table. His blood froze and heart sank as soon as he saw Maria, his Maria, happily smiling, playing with her long hair with one hand, while holding Nell's with the other one.

Ave María Purísima. Jordi made the sign of the St Cross without being conscious of it.

He rubbed his eyes to make sure he wasn't dreaming or delirious. Stretching his neck further, he saw Nell rub Maria's back with her arm, then caress her face. Then she kissed her on the lips for a few seconds, which felt an eternity to him. Maria responded with a short kiss, also on the lips. The two laughed, held hands, looked at the street.

Jordi didn't blink while his look was fixed on Maria's face. She seemed relaxed, her face glowing, her smile wider than he'd ever seen it, her body twisted and curled towards Nell in a way she'd never been with him. Jordi saw in his mind a picture of Maria back at University, solitary, looking through the windows in the library. She looked as natural now – only happier.

Jordi covered his mouth.

Can this really be true? Can this be happening to me?

Is she playing? Are they only friends? Is this a joke?

Jordi contemplated the possibility that Maria was still in shock after her grandmother's death. But no, she was old enough to know what she was doing, wasn't she?

Somebody kicked his chair, making him turn. A big man in a tight shirt whispered in his ear: "Darling, would you like a drink?"

Jordi jumped out of his seat and gave him a spaced-out look. Then he anxiously ran towards the corner, where Nell and Maria were sitting. He felt like shouting but all he could do was to push in between the people that now filled the bar area. He used his arms to make his way through until he got to the empty table.

Fuck. They're gone! Gone!

After a moment's hesitation – *did I dream this?* – he ran down the stairs into the street and looked around. They had disappeared. Jordi ran up and down the street, like a madman without a destination. He crossed the street, looking the wrong way, causing a car to break suddenly, shocking two pedestrians who yelled at him. He didn't hear them. He ran to the hotel, almost next door; he had picked it because he knew that's where Maria usually stayed in London, but no room had been booked under her name, or Nell's.

He had lost them. He went back to the street, looking around. He couldn't hear anything. He felt dizzy.

Where's my life going? Who's taking my life away from me?

He looked at the sky. *Is that you God? Have you abandoned me? My company may go bust, my flat is wrecked and my future wife is a lesbian. What else do you have for me?*

Standing immobile in the middle of the street, ignored by passersby, Jordi thought of his father – of how he fell into sin to avoid reality. Maybe this made more sense. It was silly to fight and fight, what for?

For nothing.

He looked at the men around: some drunk, some with pretty girls on their arms. He felt like a wimp.

Am I the only one who cares about other people? Everybody seems to think of themselves first. Everybody wants to have fun, who cares about the rest? Even my dad sees prostitutes, I am sure. Does he care about my mother? Maria is keeping me in suspense, never mind that we're supposed to get married in two months; the builders are taking their time – why hurry? Even Father Juan Antonio doesn't hesitate to shut the money tap on me, even if I am desperate, and if the money is actually mine.

Am I the only fool?

I must have been living a lie, only fools believe those tales of integrity and honour. And I did. Stupid me. It's only the here and now that matters, isn't it? Nobody cares about the past or about the future.

My father is a clever man.

With his lost look, Jordi raised his hand and stopped a cab. He asked the driver to take him to a brothel, any brothel. He tipped him well and just under an hour later, somewhere in south London, for a hundred pounds, Jordi penetrated a woman for the first time in his life. It happened in a dark room at the top flat of a derelict building. He didn't say a word, didn't ask her name, he didn't even look her in the eye. No kisses. He just penetrated her once, twice and three times, until it hurt, him and her.

He left just thirty minutes later. For more than two hours, asking for directions to anybody around, he walked the streets back to the hotel in Islington, tears in his eyes. He didn't know whether he had a broken heart, or was just exhausted or, most probably, mad.

24

Under pointed black hoods that covered their faces and dressed in robes that reached their ankles, the Belchite penitents slowly advanced to the solemn beat of a single drum. Every year the procession moved along Belchite's main street, with the clank of the chains that some wore attached to their bare, bleeding feet, the only noise that could be heard. It was Good Friday.

Maria looked at the sky; it was a cold, spring day. Her mother, sister, niece and nephew stood next to her and, like hundreds of other villagers, bowed their heads as the procession advanced.

It was almost sunset. Maria looked at the penitents through the two small holes on their hoods. She saw their sombre eyes, showing fear and suffering – some carried large, wooden crosses, bigger than themselves; others wore crowns made of thorny branches. They had drops of sweat and blood on their faces.

Maria, shivering, listened to their hard, deep breaths as they advanced.

The procession, which had left the church two hours before, still had as many hours to go. No water and no breaks were allowed.

In London, they'd think we were mad.

The local priest walked ahead of the group, holding a golden cross, his arms outstretched ahead of him. He was followed by fully-uniformed members of the military, the mayor, and the county's government representatives, all wearing golden medals, all looking down, all muttering their prayers in low voices. At the sudden sound of a loud drum, everybody stopped, kneeled down and remained quiet.

In the middle of the sepulchral silence, Maria's phone beeped from inside her coat pocket; it was a text message. Conchita raised her head and gave her daughter a look of disgust. Maria swallowed and looked down.

It must be Nell. I wonder what she's doing today. I am sure it's nothing like this.

The two had regularly spoken on the telephone since Maria's last trip to London. Until this moment, always the darkest and most sombre day of the year for her, Maria had been happy and confused. As much as she enjoyed talking to Nell, she was worried about Jordi. During the past couple of weeks, he'd called her with such anxiety and insistence that she had finally agreed to meet him tonight. She had only seen him a few times for lunch since just after Christmas, when she told him she needed more time. She wasn't looking forward to seeing him, but she felt it was her duty; after all, Jordi was still her fiancé. Maria discreetly looked at her watch: he would be arriving soon, having left Barcelona about three hours ago.

A cast-iron platform with a wooden, full-size statue of Jesus on the cross passed in front of her. About ten men held the float on their shoulders, all walking at exactly the same pace, following the persistent drum.

Maria put her hands in her pockets and touched her mobile phone, held it tight. Belchite was not where she wanted to be.

Ten Roman soldiers followed, dressed in impeccable bronze breastplates and red feather hats, holding lances, swords and trumpets. They were Maria's favourite part of the procession, every year. At least they had some colour.

If only they could smile. Maria stared at their serious, tight faces.

Nell would love to see this.

Silence filled the dark streets as the procession continued its way into the outskirts of Belchite. Conchita and Pilar would follow it all the way to the end, kneeling on the cold ground at the stops, praying with the group. Maria had her mother's permission to go home to welcome Jordi, expected any minute now.

I should tell him today, although it's a bit brutal to have him come all the way from Barcelona, on Good Friday, for this. What a mess. I am a horrible person, but there's nothing I can do. God help me.

Sitting in her parents' home, on the sofa, Maria lit a cigarette. She could avoid smoking most of the time, but not when near her mother. Maria's anxieties and stress surfaced at Conchita's constant comments about her life, her clothes or her lack of attention to the wedding, now only a month away.

Maria exhaled the smoke as if it was the last cigarette of her life.

She had changed her mourning clothes into a sweatshirt and a pair of trendy jeans. She gently touched them; she'd bought them in London with Nell.

Nell.

She grasped her mobile from the coffee-table and read her saved texts, all from Nell, wishing her a good day, good night, or showing her things that she found interesting. She opened one that showed Pepa chasing the cane she gave her a few months ago. Maria dropped the phone on the sofa and remembered the day they met, a dark, stormy November afternoon behind King's Cross. How far away it felt. Then, Nell seemed a cold, distant bureaucrat, looking too mannish with short hair and unpainted nails. Maria laughed to herself at the superficial conclusions she had drawn. Now, she couldn't even remember Nell's clothes. When she thought of her, she felt a wave of warm air, as if her mundane problems were meaningless.

Maria took the phone again, opened a photo of Nell that she had taken in London and stared at it. The two had talked about spending a weekend in Barcelona. Maria thought about everything she would show her, especially as she'd never been there before.

I won't take her to the touristy bits; the Ramblas, Ciutat Vella and El Born have almost turned into Disneyland. I'll take her to Gràcia, its literary squares, the good old tapas bars. She'll love that.

Maria sighed, thinking of the two of them together, sitting on the terrace of her flat, drinking wine. She couldn't wait for Nell to meet Bombillo. She couldn't wait to see her calm smile again, to see her intelligent eyes, full of interest, to sit and have coffee with her, reading the papers, discuss her good-hearted but impracticable socialist ideas. *In truth, I love it that she thinks that way. Much more honorable than all those right-wing fascists that Jordi hangs out with.*

Jordi. Maria felt guilty. *How can I be thinking like this when Jordi is about to arrive? But I can't stop it. Follow nature*

Her phone beeped, her face lit up when she saw it was Nell, sending her a photo of the sunset from Primrose Hill. 'Thinking of you' it said. 'London *can* be sunny.'

It made her laugh, after all the dreadful comments about the English weather she'd made.

Does she think I am her new girlfriend? Does that make me a lesbian?

Maria lifted her knees, hugged them with her arms, dropped her head.

I can't be a lesbian. Me? I don't have short hair or tattoos. I am not like that.

She thought of the night they spent together. She shivered as she felt it had probably been the happiest time in her life. In silence, at night, in her Barcelona flat, Maria had revived in her mind almost every second of it.

If this is not being a lesbian, what is it then?

Maria thought of the new Government regulations, legalising gay marriages, the photos and articles that ran recently in the press, making the gay world look less alien to Spaniards.

Ll PAÍS certainly loves gay people, they're always writing about them.

Maybe it's not that bad being a lesbian.

Maria lit another cigarette.

"I thought you weren't smoking any more," Soledad suddenly said, walking into the living room. "How was the procession? As lugubrious as every year?"

Maria smiled at Soledad. *Thank God you're still around, Soledad.* "Worse."

The ninety-year-old smiled and sat down in an armchair, clutching a copy of *¡HOLA!* magazine.

"You're looking a bit gloomy," Soledad said, flicking through the pages. "I am not surprised, those processions are meant to make you cut your veins, aren't they?"

Maria laughed. "If my mother heard you."

"She means well, Maria."

Maria didn't answer, drew deeply on her cigarette.

"Is this what your English friend is teaching you, to smoke?" Soledad asked, still looking at the magazine.

"What English friend?" Maria's heart pounded fast. *What does she know? Is it that evident?*

Soledad raised an eyebrow and looked at Maria. "The one you keep talking to on the phone and have been talking about recently," she said.

"Me?" *Have I? Maybe I've dropped some things here and there about my trips to London, but I haven't talked that much. I never talk that much.*

"Yes, you, young lady," Soledad smiled. "The Devil knows more because he's old rather than because he's the Devil."

Maria looked at Soledad intrigued. She went on. "Don't worry, it's just that I tend to be awake when the phone rings, only once, at about midnight, and I know you pick it up." She smiled. "I may be old, but I can still distinguish English from Spanish."

Maria blushed. *There's no privacy in this house.*

Soledad carried on. "There's nothing wrong with having a friend in London, it's wonderful to have somebody to share your interests, your concerns; and if they're outside this medieval country, all the better."

Maria smiled, then nervously tapped the sofa with her fingers. *What else has she noticed?*

"Friends are good for the heart," Soledad continued, sighing. She smiled at Maria, making her feel warm. With Gran gone, Soledad was the only sparkle of light in Maria's world at home.

"I've also seen you're reading *Rebecca*," Soledad continued. "Good choice! I remember I recommended it to you. Did you buy it in London?"

"Yes, last time I was there," Maria said. "My friend also recommended it to me."

"Good. I like your friend," Soledad said, giving her a cheeky look and carrying on with her magazine.

You can't possibly know what's going on, Soledad. You're smart, but this is so ahead of your time. As much as I love you and admire you, you can't possibly have worked it out.

"Can I have a cigarette, please?" Soledad asked in an innocent voice, still with her eyes focused on the pages of *¡HOLA!*

"Not you, no, you can't," Maria straightened her back. "I am still feeling awful for the cigarettes that I gave Gran. I am not giving you any."

"Maria, it wasn't anybody's fault," Soledad replied quickly. "But if you're worried about it, then you shouldn't smoke, either."

Maria grumbled. "All right," she stubbed her cigarette out, half smoked, and frowned.

"Are you sure you're all right?" Soledad asked. "Why are you here, why didn't you stay with the others?"

Maria crossed her arms. "I hate Easter, for a start," she said. "And Jordi is about to arrive. He's driving from Barcelona."

Soledad dropped the magazine and looked at Maria. "On Good Friday? This late? Why?"

"He misses me, or so he says."

Soledad rolled her eyes and looked back at her magazine. "I haven't heard much of him lately, your mother was saying the other day that she didn't know how things stood between you two."

Maria put her chin up. "Is this what my mother goes around saying? I see."

"Maria, she only said this to me, and it's only because she is worried about you, you know it," Soledad's tone was serious.

"Please don't give her a hard time; at the moment, it's as difficult for her as it is for us."

Maria looked down.

"Not to intrude, but is Jordi all right to be driving here now? You don't seem desperate to see him." Soledad looked at Maria's face, with no make-up and her messy hair quickly tied in a pony tail.

Maria sighed. "Oh come on, Soledad, please let me have a cigarette, I am a bit nervous."

Soledad raised an eyebrow and nodded. She remained silent.

A few seconds went by, marked by the ticking of the wall clock. Maria stared at her cigarette, slowly consumed by the ash. She could even hear it. Soledad looked at her expectantly.

"You know you can talk to me, if you need, Maria," Soledad said. "Nothing is so bad, there's only one thing that doesn't have a solution, and when that happens, we can't do anything about it because we're gone. *Finito.*"

"That's true," Maria said. "But this isn't easy."

The two women turned immediately at the sudden knock on the window glass, which made them both jump. "Maria! Maria! I am here!" Jordi shouted from the cold outside, putting his face so close to the glass, he almost crashed against it.

Maria felt a tremble through her body. She exchanged a look of complicity with Soledad.

"Do you need anything?" Soledad asked, standing up.

"No, Soledad, thank you, I will be all right," Maria said, helping the old woman sit down again.

Maria grabbed her keys and anorak and walked towards the front door.

"Maria," Soledad said. Maria turned and looked at her. "Remember one thing: do as you feel, do what's best for you, and nobody else. You know what price this family has paid for happiness – or the lack of it."

Maria looked at Soledad with the eyes of a child, full of trust, then she walked out the door.

Jordi said little for the ten minutes it took the couple to reach the olive groves at the back of the house. Maria asked him about his trip, his club and football, but she only received monosyllabic answers. When they reached the clearing around *El Abuelo*, under the generous moonlight and looking out over some distant lights, Maria observed Jordi's face. He seemed to have aged since the last time she saw him, more than a month ago. He looked as if he hadn't shaved in days and had dark circles under his eyes. He was thinner, with his jaws shaping a serious, angular face, far from the youthful, round, clean-cut image he used to have.

"Jordi, I've been worried about you," Maria said finally.

Jordi laughed loudly, surprising Maria. "Don't worry, I am fine," he said. With his hands in his pockets, staring at the ground.

Maria took one step closer to him, looked at him with compassion. "Are you all right, darling?"

He suddenly took his hands out and extended his arms in the air, shocking Maria, accustomed as she was to his usual delicate manners. "*Darling?*" his tone was loud. "What do you mean *darling?* You don't really care about me any more, do you?"

Maria took a step back. "Of course I do, Jordi." She felt defensive. "It's been hard with my grandmother, and my father, my mother."

Jordi smiled. "Yeah... I see, very hard, I am sure," he said with a cynical smile. Maria had never seen such cynicism in Jordi before.

"But we have to move on from our problems, don't we?" he said, pacing around, randomly. "Things are also a bit weird for me these days."

Maria followed him, he had leaned against an olive tree. "I am so sorry about the flat Jordi, I know how much you put into it."

He looked away. Maria felt he was trying to avoid eye contact. She stared at his eyes, trying to spot that spark of innocence that made her trust him before. But she couldn't see it.

Maybe it's too dark, I am sure it's still there. My God I've hurt him so much.

Maria's heart almost broke as Jordi looked at her, like a begging dog. *I should have been more honest with him, instead of leaving him in suspense. Poor Jordi.*

She gave him a compassionate hug. He didn't respond. He stayed immobile.

Then he drew away, looking at her intently. "Adversity has made me grow, it has turned me into a man, I am sure that's what you wanted."

Maria took a step backwards. "What do you mean?"

He grabbed her arms with his hands, holding her tight, too tight.

"You're hurting me, Jordi," Maria said, still in a gentle voice. "You've become so vehement. I almost don't recognise you."

He smiled. Again, the cynical smile. Maria felt uncomfortable.

"Jordi, I think we should talk, although maybe now is not the best time, what do you think?" she said.

"Oh, I think now would be perfect," he said. Gently, he caressed Maria's head. He gave her his usual innocent smile.

Maria sighed. *Thank God he's back.*

Maria leaned her head against his shoulder and couldn't contain her tears any longer.

"I am so sorry Jordi, I know I've hurt you, please forgive me," she begged.

Maria felt Jordi's breath come closer, he kissed her hair, then her forehead.

"It's all right, darling, it's all right, let's forget this nightmare and start all over again, I feel like a new man." His voice sounded tender.

Maria drew back.

Now, I have to. I have to. I can't bear this. This hurts too much. This is not what I am looking for. This is not making me happy. Who am I trying to fool? I don't want to end up like my mother or my grandmother. I have to be strong.

324

Soledad's words came back to her. *The price of happiness.*

Maria raised her glance to him. "Jordi, we must talk, I know you're not going to like it." She felt a knot in her throat, but took a deep breath and continued. "I am not sure this is the best thing for us."

Her heart was pounding fast. She was expecting an immediate angry, shocked reaction. But again, he showed the cynical smile.

"This is very good for us, darling," he said and kissed her head again.

Maria took another step backwards. "Please Jordi, don't."

He came closer to her, held her arms, holding them down next to her body.

"Please, Jordi," she begged again.

"You'll see it'll be all much better from now on," he said. "I've turned into a man. I *know* you will like it." He tried to unzip Maria's anorak.

"What are you doing?" she said, pulling back.

Jordi moved closer to her, put his arms around her, even as she pulled away. "I know you're into experimenting, aren't you?" He smiled again.

Maria started to feel a bit scared. She looked to the left and right, nobody was around. "What experimenting? What are you talking about?"

Jordi put both hands on Maria's breasts, over the anorak, with the urgency and clumsiness of an inexperienced teenager.

"What on earth are you doing?" Maria shouted, pushing his arms away. "Jordi you've gone mad, what's wrong with you?"

Stronger and taller as he was, he held her arms and moved his body against hers, pushing his groin against Maria's, again and again. Maria tried to force him away.

"Leave me alone!" she shouted.

"Isn't that what you do with that dyke from the Council in London, eh?" He spat at her.

Maria froze as Jordi continued pushing against her body. "Do you want to fuck? I can give you a good fuck if that's all you need, do you understand? You don't need to go with a lesbian, I can give you the real thing. Here!" he shouted, pushing his now erect penis against Maria. He shouted even more. "Feel it!"

Terrified, Maria quickly reacted and with all her strength, managed to push Jordi away. *How on earth do you know?*

Jordi fell to the ground. He sank his head between his knees and started crying. "I saw you," he said. "I saw you when I went to London for a business meeting. I saw you in a bar on Upper Street."

Maria remembered the bar, the only one she'd been in with Nell on Upper Street, the day after they'd slept together. She remembered them being especially touchy that afternoon, in public.

This can't be true.

She brought her hand to her mouth. She held her breath, her eyes wide open.

"Don't look like an idiot, Maria, I saw it!" Jordi was now looking at her.

Maria felt cold throughout her body, her legs shaking slightly.

Hold it, hold it, be strong.

"This is not about that," Maria finally said. "This was over before, I have to be honest with you Jordi, I am really sorry."

"You make me sick," Jordi said, still sitting on the ground. "You don't know what you're getting yourself into. We could have had a great life together. You're only going downhill now. You'll putrefy in sin."

Jordi, we all need to give happiness a chance. I am doing what's right for me. That's what everybody is advising me to do. That's what feels right.

Maria offered Jordi a hand to help him stand up. "Come on," she said.

Jordi remained on the ground, holding his head with his hands, he had no more tears. He took a deep breath. "Is this for real or am I dreaming?"

Maria bent down, passed her arm around his shoulders. "I am so sorry, Jordi, but I can't carry on like this anymore. You deserve somebody who will give you her heart, and I am not ready."

Jordi let a couple of seconds go by. "You *were* ready."

Maria sat on the ground, next to him, in silence. She could hear the light breeze, smell the trees, see the stars, feel nature. After all, this was probably the most intimate moment she'd shared with Jordi, much more different – and better – than all those official family gatherings they always had to attend.

If only we'd done more things like this, just the two of us. But now it's too late. It would never have worked.

"I was never ready, Jordi," she said. "I've also grown up. Much has happened in this family, as you know. I talked to my Gran before she died, she told me I had to be more honest, starting with myself. I would be lying to you if I carried on, pretending everything's fine." Maria lowered her head. "The truth is that what should be there, is not."

Jordi shook his head.

Maria felt relieved.

"Do you love her?" he asked, without looking at Maria, who closed her eyes.

"Please, Jordi," Maria said. "I don't want to talk about it, please respect it. This is hurtful and I am confused. I just need time to myself."

He grabbed a small tree branch from the ground. "Should we just postpone the wedding, try to continue as friends, and see if we can try again?"

Maria pressed her lips tight. She felt such warmth towards Jordi, her most loyal friend for years. He'd taken care of her when she'd been a solitary person, every time she had driven back from Belchite, feeling distant, remote, isolated. He had always been there for her, waiting with a rose. She felt immensely guilty.

"I am really sorry," Maria said, and hugged him as she'd never done before. She held him tight, until he pulled away.

He was drawing on the ground with the little branch, then he threw it away with disdain. He sighed.

"Are you sure?" he said. "Maybe I could forgive you if it's just a one-off, or a phase."

I have to be strong. I can't lie to myself, or to him. She looked at him.

"Yes, I am sure." She held his hand and pressed it. He was cold.

"Time will erase this, you'll see," she said.

"Fuck time."

Maria let his hand go.

I can't do this to anybody again. It's all my bloody fault.

"Please forgive me."

"Fuck forgive."

Silence followed.

"Is there anything I can do for you?" Maria's voice was delicate, low. She put a hand on his back. Jordi stood up. She followed.

He looked around the trees. He did indeed look different, taller, stronger. *Would it have been different if he'd been more determined from the start?* Maria looked at his now masculine face, his big hands. The delicate image of Nell's face crossed her mind, their talk in Borough market, their cycle ride, the food they cooked together, the warmth and gentleness of her body.

No.

Maria looked down. She had nothing more to say and Jordi seemed to understand this.

"I guess all I can do is cut my losses and go," he said, raising his chin.

Always a gentleman. "I will call you to make sure you're all right."

"Don't bother." He started walking away, Maria followed him.

They walked for a couple of minutes in silence.

Maria coughed. "Are you driving to Barcelona now? Are you sure that's a good idea? Would you like to stay?"

"I'll go back, that's the best thing I can do."

They arrived at the front of the house, where Jordi had parked Oscar. He looked at the car, then at Maria, who remembered the trips to San Sebastián, from Pamplona. The happy days. Her heart ached as she looked at Jordi's broken face.

"I will call you," she said.

Jordi turned and walked to the car, dragging his feet. He opened the door. "Goodbye," he said, getting in.

Maria shivered. The few seconds before he started the car and drove away seemed an eternity. Maria held her breath as if she could feel Jordi's pain. She knew she meant the world to him. She thought of the flat he was preparing for the two of them. She could see her own family drama ahead as soon as she announced the wedding was off; she could even hear her mother's shouts. She closed her eyes tight, trying to avoid the tears.

I have to be strong. This is what Gran taught me. I bloody hope it's the right thing. What if it's not?

Maria remained in limbo for a few seconds. She felt scared, lonely.

"What's going on?" Conchita asked as she took the bin out, surprising Maria so that she gave a little jump.

Mother, always so inopportune.

"What are you doing there by yourself and why is Jordi leaving in the middle of the night?" She was now close to her daughter. "Did you have an argument?"

Maria put her hands on her face, hiding it. "Sort of." *Not now. I need to prepare her for this.*

"Men," Conchita muttered. "I know it's hard, Maria, I know."

The two remained silent for a few seconds.

"Come on," Conchita finally said. "Let's go inside, it's late and it's getting cold."

The two started walking towards the house when Maria's mobile phone rang.

"Your English friend seems to be missing you a lot," Conchita said and accelerated her pace towards the house, leaving Maria behind.

25

Conchita and Maria left the house through the back, kitchen door the following morning, Easter Saturday, bucket in hand, apron on, sleeves rolled. For once, they enjoyed doing something together: every year, the two hid chocolate eggs for Pilar's children and picked the olive-tree branches that would be blessed the following day, Ash Sunday.

"The trees look beautiful this year with so much rain," Maria said.

She does appreciate this land, at the bottom of her heart.

"They do, it's actually one of the best years we've had," Conchita said. *Just the year my mother dies and my husband leaves, I am blessed with this. It must be a small present from God.*

Conchita wanted to say that the garden would look impeccable for Maria's wedding, but refrained, given the previous night's argument between the couple. She looked at Maria; she seemed sad and tired, her eyes red and swollen. She had been especially silent over breakfast.

I have to be gentle with her; the fight must have been bad.

Maria stopped to take a few small olive-tree branches and made a little bunch. "I love the smell," she said, eyes closed, bringing the bundle towards her face.

"We'll have the best oil this year, I am sure," Conchita said while leaving an egg inside a hole of one of the most ancient trees.

"If it's really better, you should raise the prices, you haven't done that for a few years," Maria said, following her mother.

Conchita turned and gave her a quick look. "You bankers only think of money – its quality that counts."

"Of course, mother, but the business has to run as well."

Conchita slowly placed another egg behind a tree near *El Abuelo*. "There's nothing wrong with the business."

Maria was comparing the length of a few branches. "It could always be better."

Conchita gave her an intrigued look. *What do you know, if you've never expressed any interest in it?*

"Like exporting," Maria looked at her mother. "You should start exporting. In London, for example, people love olive oil. I brought a bottle for a friend," Maria started saying.

The friend, again.

"She loved it," Maria continued. "They're used to much more expensive oil, which the Italians buy in Jaén for nothing, repackage it in flamboyant Italian style and sell in London for a fortune: *Olio d'oliva d'Italia*," Maria exclaimed with an Italian accent and in an exaggerated tone, raising her arms up in the air. She took a brief pause. "Believe me, there's a market there."

Conchita considered the idea for a few seconds. "Nah, the English cook with butter, if they cook at all," she said.

Maria dropped her bouquet in the bucket. "You're wrong, mother, they've changed, now it's fashionable," she said. "Organic markets and cooking programmes on television are ever so popular."

"Really?" Conchita was surprised. "God, the world has changed. Your father and I went to England in the seventies and my stomach still turns over at the thought of meat with marmalade."

Maria smiled. "Mother, that was thirty years ago, they have adapted to the times better than you have."

Conchita walked towards *El Abuelo* and placed an egg inside, extending her arm through a hole. "Does your friend, what's her name? Does she cook with olive oil?"

"Yes," Maria said. "Nell loves it. As a matter of fact, I brought her a bit of our own, she's the Council officer dealing with the warehouse, so I have to treat her well. She couldn't have enough. She just dipped bread on it and ate it, with nothing else."

"Not even a bit of *jamón*?" Conchita was surprised.

Maria smiled. "She's a vegetarian."

Conchita raised an eyebrow. "Oh, no, one of those people who don't eat meat?"

"It's normal there, they just want to protect the animals."

"Jesus," Conchita said. "Doesn't she look pale and ill? I would take her to hospital if she was my daughter. How can you survive without a good steak? I bet her mother isn't happy about that."

"She's quite all right," Maria said. "Mother, you should market the olive oil for vegetarians, they'd love it."

"There are no vegetarians in Spain."

"Abroad! Go abroad!" Maria exclaimed.

Conchita laughed. "I am too old to go abroad!"

Little I knew you had all those ideas for the business, Maria. Good, this is the first bit of good news in a long, long, time.

Conchita left her bucket next to *El Abuelo*. Holding a couple of eggs in her hand, she gazed around looking for good hiding places.

Maria, almost finished cutting the tree branches, walked towards her. She looked tense.

"If you dig the eggs there, those children may strike lucky," she said. "They may find quite a bit of money."

Here we go. It had to come.

Maria looked down, then straight at Conchita. "Sorry mother, I should have told you a while ago, but I didn't find the right moment." She had a slight cough. "I know it's just a bit weird as well but, believe it or not, just before she died, I saw Gran hiding some money right under this tree. She asked me to tell you if anything happened to her."

Conchita took a deep breath and sighed. *Everything is weird in this family.*

"Yes, I already knew." Conchita saw Maria's face of disappointment and walked towards her daughter. "She told me soon after she told you."

Maria looked down. "Maybe she didn't trust me enough."

Conchita touched her daughter's arm, slightly, quickly. "Of course she did, you know how much Gran adored you, but it's quite a bit of money." She looked at the ground. "We'd better take it out soon, probably better at night, I don't want the locals to talk. Can you give me a hand tonight, perhaps now that people are away for Easter?"

Maria smiled. "Yes, let's come as thieves to our own backyard and steal our own money."

"I know it's ridiculous, old people sometimes are just like children," Conchita said. "Anyway, she told me the money is basically for Pilar and you. I am sure it will come in very handy for you and Jordi, you'll be able to enjoy it while you're young, you're lucky. For most people, by the time they get the general's pay, they don't have teeth any more – as Gran used to say."

Conchita saw Maria's suddenly serious face. *It must be the thought of Gran.*

"I know Maria, I know, I also think of her every minute." Conchita reached for her mother's cross on her chest and held it tight.

"It's not that, Mother."

Conchita looked up to her daughter, surprised.

"What is it then?" She felt her guards coming up, defensively.

Maria swallowed twice.

"Come on, Maria, talk to me." *I try to do as my father told me, take care of her, love my children. But with Maria, there's always something wrong. Always. What now?*

"I am not getting married, Mother." Maria looked down.

Conchita remained immobile, her eyes opened wide. "What?"

Maria lowered her head more.

"What did you say?" *No, no, no and no. I shall not allow this, by any means.*

"I am sorry Mother, but I am not getting married," Maria said, with shame.

Conchita gave a step towards her daughter. "Look at me!"

Slowly, Maria raised her head. Conchita's anger stopped when she saw her daughter's face, confused, defenseless.

"What's going on?" she spat.

Maria bowed her head, again.

"Look at me!" Conchita shouted.

Maria couldn't hold her tears. "Mother, you're not going to like this."

"Straight the point, Maria."

"I don't want to get married."

"Why not?"

"I don't love him."

Conchita sighed. *What a child.*

"Couldn't you have thought of this before? Now it's too late."

Maria looked at her, with begging eyes. "It's not too late, it's still a month away."

"Everybody has been invited! Everything's ready!" She let a few seconds go by. "All couples fight before the wedding, they're nervous, it's a responsibility. You'll get back into it, just put in a bit of effort. Believe me, I know. You will learn how to love him over the years. Or at least to stand him."

Maria raised an eyebrow. Conchita felt the skeptical look of her daughter. *I know I am nobody's example.* "Think of everything you're losing, a life of stability and comfort. Jordi is a good man, he'll always be gentle to you. Do you know how many women would kill for that?"

"But it's not what I want."

"Want?" Conchita shouted. "Do you think you can always get what you want? Who do you think you are? Do you think you can throw away an opportunity as good as this, just like that? What about the poor Jordi? He must be heartbroken."

Maria remained silent.

"And what is it that you want, if I may ask?"

Maria looked up. "Nell."

Conchita dropped at once the chocolate eggs she was still holding. Mother and daughter heard them crash to the ground. Conchita, perplexed, looked at her daughter as if she was an alien. Maria, still facing her, looked straight into her mother's eyes in a way that made Conchita feel penetrated, invaded.

"I want Nell, I am happy with her."

Conchita looked away. "The carrot? From England? She's a woman!"

"I know."

Ave María Purísima.

Ave María Purísima.

Ave María Purísima.

Conchita made the sign of the St Cross three times. She looked at the sky and felt her anger rise through her body, her cheeks turning red by the second.

Not in this family. The Devil has settled in this family.

She raised her hand and slapped Maria's face, quickly and hard.

Maria did not move, didn't cry. Conchita felt ashamed of her act immediately. Maria's look of hatred at her mother intensified, it scared Conchita.

"It's my life and I'll live it the way I want," Maria said and walked away.

Conchita stayed immobile.

It's all my fault.

"Here, have some of this, it'll do you good."

"Soledad, please," Conchita said. "At your age and still drinking, you know the doctor says it's bad for you."

Sitting on a deckchair on the patio, by the kitchen, under the early afternoon sun, Soledad was savouring a glass of a Rioja Crianza. "Come sit with me Conchita, seems as if you need it."

"I have to do the kitchen, we have the entire family for lunch tomorrow and nothing is ready. As usual, I have to do everything."

"Conchita, come and sit down at once."

Conchita turned, she wasn't used to Soledad's commanding tone.

335

"If you don't sit here, you may not have a family to feed tomorrow." Soledad said. "There's too much hot blood in this family."

She's already on Maria's side, Conchita thought as she sat next to Soledad.

"Maria only said a few words to me, she was very upset," Soledad said. "At least I've stopped her from driving away to Barcelona. She's upstairs in her room."

"As usual."

Soledad shook her head. "You two are like the cat and the dog," she said. "If only you knew how much you need each other."

Soledad, please don't preach.

"I know I am not a direct part of the family," Soledad continued. Conchita interrupted her.

"Don't be silly, of course you are."

Soledad poured Conchita a glass of wine. "Have this."

Conchita drank half the glass at once. "It's good, actually."

"I told you, if people only listened to what I say."

"I listen to you Soledad."

"Now you will have to – I know I am nobody to talk, but you two have to stop this nonsense. I care for both of you and I am not going to let you eat each other. Do you understand? This is also my house and I want peace."

"Sorry Soledad, I know you don't deserve this."

"*You* deserve it even less, and neither does Maria."

"Hum."

"Let the child be. Why can't you let her live her life?"

Conchita took a deep breath. "You still don't know the latest one."

"I do."

"Has she told you?" Conchita was surprised. *Am I the last monkey to know?*

"She hasn't told me a thing, but I can tell."

"What can you tell?"

"She likes her English friend – am I wrong?"

"No." Conchita looked at Soledad and sighed. "Don't you think it's the worst thing in the world? Jordi is such a good opportunity for her. She's throwing her life away."

"Why can't she decide what's best for her?"

"How can a *woman* from *England* be better than a proper man with a family, a business and stability behind him?"

"If it makes her happy, let her be, and if she doesn't like it, don't worry, she'll come back." Soledad leaned back on her chair. "She's young, let her experiment if she wants to."

"Jordi won't wait for her."

"She'd be with him now *if* that was what she wanted. But the point is that she doesn't."

"But why not? I don't understand." Conchita's heart ached at the thought of the wedding being cancelled.

Soledad turned towards Conchita, looked her straight in the eye. "Because she doesn't want to end up in an unhappy marriage."

Conchita felt the stitch. "She's seen too many around, hasn't she?"

Soledad nodded. "I am sorry, I know it's hurtful to you, but you must try and understand her, she's your daughter. You have to help her – you are *her* mother."

Maybe what I am doing is not very Christian.

"But it's a sin," Conchita said.

"Don't come to me with that nonsense, Conchita," Soledad had a threatening tone. "You're old enough to make your own mind about things. There's nothing wrong with love."

That's true. They're not hurting anybody. Only me.

Conchita drank more wine. "I'll have to think."

"I am sure that if you reach out to her, you'll gain a daughter, even two."

Conchita gave her a look of distrust. "It's not funny."

"Sorry," Soledad said, with a cheeky smile. She drank some more wine and opened ¡HOLA! magazine.

"Look!" she said, pointing at a photograph of Spain's most glamorous movie director. "Almodóvar is gay and here he is, in the middle of this glossy, full of success."

"Ha, he could come here and make a movie about our lives."
Conchita stood up.

"We're too boring for him," Soledad said. "Gays aren't news anymore." She put her sunglasses on, drank more wine and returned to her magazine.

A few seconds later, she looked up. "Mmm," Soledad muttered. "Well, now that there are lesbians in Belchite, maybe this means that democracy has finally arrived in Spain." She smiled and continued reading her magazine. "Maybe."

Conchita sighed and left.

It took ten minutes for Maria to open the door, a few hours later. It was past dinner-time.

"*¡HOLA!*" Conchita said when her daughter finally faced her. She looked desolate. Conchita offered her the hot plate she had carried up. "I brought you some tortilla; I thought you might be hungry."

"No."

Conchita took a deep breath. "Would you like to come downstairs? Soledad and I have started a fire, in the kitchen; it's a cold night and it feels comfortable."

"No."

"Maybe we could get some fresh air, go together and dig that money, if you like?"

"No."

Conchita sighed. "Maria, please."

"Please what?"

Conchita walked into her daughter's room, still with the decoration that she had as a child. Since she went to University, she hadn't spent many nights here and never made an effort to make the room more comfortable. *Maybe she's never felt this is her home.* She looked around: there was a wooden crucifix above the bed and an old poster of a teenage pop group that she hadn't heard about in more than ten years. *Maybe I haven't given her all the attention that she needed.*

On the table, Conchita saw a photo of Maria and a woman, their two faces together, looking sparklingly happy. Shaking, she took it and looked at it closely.

God she looks so English, so white. Ufff. She looked at Maria in the photo; she'd never seen her so radiant.

She looked at her daughter. "I am sorry I slapped you, I didn't mean to." She had never apologised to Maria before, although she always regretted it afterwards. She felt immensely ashamed, she hadn't hit her daughter in years.

Maria, still standing in the doorway, said nothing.

Conchita took the photo again, looked at it.

There's nothing I can do to stop this, better accept it.

"You look happy in this photo, when was this?"

"A few weeks ago," Maria said. "Yes, we are very happy, thank you."

"That's good Maria, I am glad you're happy." *I hope God will forgive me for this. I am doing this only for my daughter, for this house, for this family, for the land.*

Maria looked at her mother. The anger seemed to have vanished from her. "If there's nothing else, I'd like to get some sleep now."

Conchita walked towards her, put a hand on her shoulder. "I thought a bit of fresh air would do you good, you've been here all afternoon. Are you sure you don't want to come to dig that money? It has to be done, before everybody else arrives from their holiday."

Maria looked out the window.

"I need you to tell me where the exact point is. I can't go all by myself and start digging like a mad woman around an ancient tree."

Maria smiled, warming Conchita's heart. She couldn't lose her daughter. Her family, her land, that's all she had. She couldn't lose more, she'd already lost too much.

"All right." Maria took a bit of the tortilla, wrapped in foil paper, and grabbed her anorak.

339

Shovel, pickaxe and oil lamp in hand, Maria and Conchita advanced through the dark olive groves. The two reached *El Abuelo* within minutes and, with no more distraction, set to work, by the light of the lamp and the sound of the crickets, the wind and their own breaths.

"I can't believe she did this at her age, all by herself," Conchita said, puffing. "It's quite tiring."

Maria stopped and looked at her mother. "Leave it, I'll do it."

Conchita took the offer. The air between the two was tense. *Just try to do more things together; show her kindness, interest, she'll come back.*

"Does your friend come from a good family? What do her parents do?"

Maria continued her work, didn't look at her mother. "I don't know about her family, I am not that bothered about it."

"I see," Conchita said. "Well, just be careful, you never know, London is such a big place."

Conchita felt Maria's look of disapproval. *Better leave it.*

"Are you sure it was right here?"

"I saw it." Maria continued the digging, diligently.

"Here, I've hit it," Maria said a few minutes later. After clearing some ground, Maria extracted a briefcase, which they immediately opened. Indeed, it was full of fifty-euro notes, hundreds of them. Mother and daughter were perplexed. They immediately shut it.

"There may be another one," Maria said, digging a bit more.

She lifted a second briefcase within a minute. Conchita's face paled immediately after she saw, on top of the money, the little doll, made out of fabric and cotton, that she knitted for her mother as a child. She'd spent weeks on it.

Conchita covered her face with her hands. She couldn't hold back the tears.

What a day I am having. Maybe I should dig myself in there.

"Mother, what's up?" Maria asked, leaving the case and the shovel aside. She took the little doll, but her mother grasped it quickly from her hands. Maria looked at her mother in amazement.

Conchita removed her hands, still looking down. *How embarrassing, here, sobbing in front of my own daughter.*

"I am sorry," Conchita said, taking a little handkerchief from her sleeve. "It's just that I didn't know that Gran kept it, I didn't know it had meant anything to her." She paused briefly. "Sorry, I shouldn't be bothering you with my problems, you have a lot going on at the moment."

Her daughter nodded. Conchita felt she had finally established communication with her. "I am sorry about what I said earlier today. You're right, it's your life and you have to live it the way you want. I am happy if you're happy now."

Maria shook her head. "Why couldn't you say this before?"

Conchita remained pensive for a few instants. "It takes time, Maria, I belong to another age, but I'll try." She smiled at her daughter.

The two stood in silence for a short while.

Conchita took the small bottle of wine she'd brought along. She drank briefly from it and offered some to Maria. Maria then unwrapped the tortilla and ate some, with appetite.

"Thanks for this, Mother," Maria said. "Too much onion, as usual."

The comment, which Conchita had heard since her daughters could talk, brought a warm air of familiarity to the tense scene. For the first time in years, Conchita felt a bond with her daughter.

"I wish you more luck than I had," Conchita said, now more relaxed.

"Why?" Maria asked.

Conchita hesitated for a few seconds. She remembered a passage in the Bible: Truth will make you free.

She looked at Maria. She deserved an explanation, she was an adult, not a child anymore.

"Your father had planned to leave us taking some of our money," Conchita finally said. "He made me sign some dodgy documents – your Gran saw it as well – so we both felt

341

suspicious. I went to the bank and stopped a loan being transferred to his personal account. And your Gran wanted to avoid us having to split her inheritance with him, so she buried it here. Your Gran was never too fond of your father."

Conchita felt relieved. *At the end of the day, this is just the plain truth.*

"To be totally honest, I am not missing him that much," Conchita continued, then ate a bit of the tortilla.

"You have so many other things to think about," Maria said.

Conchita wasn't used to encouragement from anybody, least of all from Maria. It was a good feeling to share – at least a bit – the weight of the world.

"Why did you marry him?" Maria asked. She had another sip of the wine.

I guess she's entitled to know this. Conchita's mind had flashbacks of Honorato when he was a young officer, when he looked brave and strong. *Silly me.*

"I was young and succumbed to his constant flowers and chocolates when he courted me," Conchita said. "Soledad warned me early, the best boyfriends don't usually make the best husbands. How right she was."

Maria looked at her mother with empathy. "I'm sorry."

Conchita smiled at her daughter. "You don't have to be sorry, Maria. This is life," she said. "They were different times, and at least I had a husband. Those days, after the War, many men had died, there weren't many available; at least I had you and Pilar."

Conchita sighed, shrugged her shoulders.

"The truth is that I didn't have much to choose from," she continued. She was enjoying her intimacy with Maria. "At school, I wasn't cut and clean as my colleagues, I wasn't blond and feminine, my legs and arms weren't thin and delicate, but strong, rugged and dark from the fields. I wasn't invited to the officers' balls in Zaragoza, like they were. Most of the girls in my school married the handsome, tall officers that I could only dream of. They are now generals and live in the main streets in Zaragoza, near the shops."

342

She paused and looked at Maria, whose eyes under the candlelight had a sparkle she'd never seen before. The thought that she could engage the interest of her ever-difficult youngest daughter encouraged her to continue. It made her feel important, relevant. It gave her a place in the world. She felt as her mother.

"I wished I had attracted the cadets from the Royal Military Academy in Zaragoza," Conchita went on. "Instead, this sub-officer in charge of the local prison was the only one who showed any interest in me, so I fell for him, quite easily, like a little lamb."

Maria had a quick laugh. "You? A little lamb?"

Conchita smiled at her daughter, in complicity. "I was very young," she said. "But I can't complain. I have good health, two daughters, two grandchildren and I have Soledad, who is a treasure." She pointed at the fields. "And I have this, the land, to take care of. The most beautiful land, with ancient olive trees. Do you know how many people would die for all this?"

Conchita observed her daughter's attentive look and continued.

"You never have it all at once in this life," she said, looking nowhere. "Life is like a big garden; sometimes the orange trees give their fruit, then it's the turn of the lemon trees, and later, the almonds. But they don't flourish at once. One has to know – and go – where the fruits are, and leave once they're run out towards those that are due. Sometimes we get ourselves stuck waiting for the fruit that's not meant to come, and we forget that in the meantime, there are many other alternatives flourishing around us. And there's always something flourishing. Always."

Maria had her eyes wide open, she'd never known her mother to speak like this. How much she would have loved to hear her wise words before.

The two women remained silent, feeling the chilly night. Conchita looked at the wine and the tortilla, they were almost finished. She had thoroughly enjoyed the bond between mother and daughter, but she wasn't used to it, comfort made her uncomfortable; it itched.

I need this in small doses.

"Come on, let's go, it's getting cold," Conchita suddenly said.

Maria seemed to agree. The two stood up and walked back home, with the shovel, the pickaxe, the suitcases full of money, and the little doll, tightly held in Conchita's hands.

"There is only one thing that I really can't understand, Maria, even if I think very hard," Conchita said right before they reached the house.

"What is it, mother?"

"That she doesn't eat *jamón*."

26

A few weeks later, and straight from the airport, Maria arrived at Fino, a refined Spanish restaurant off Charlotte Street, almost half an hour before she was supposed to meet Nell for lunch. It was a warm day in April, the couple had just spent a weekend together in Barcelona, of which Maria had mentally relived every second, again and again.

Playing with a fork, Maria closed her eyes and remembered the two of them drinking wine, playing backgammon on her terrace, Bombillo running around. Maria could still see Nell's excitement as she walked down Passeig de Gràcia admiring the modernist architecture, and smiled at the enthusiasm she had put in learning a few Catalan words.

"Salut I força al canut!" she'd said at every toast, always laughing afterwards.

Back in reality, Maria looked at her watch for the third time in as many minutes; only twenty-five to go. She took a little mirror from her handbag, checked her lipstick, her hair. She ordered a glass of Raimat, had a look at the *tapas* menu. They had her favourite food, as well as Nell's – she had loved the *calamares* in the old and scruffy bars in the Barceloneta, sitting in the terraces by the sea, smelling the salty air, lifting her head towards the sun.

Maria thought of the lazy afternoons, after lunch, when the two had gone back to the flat for a siesta. Naked in bed, half covered by the duvet, they had chatted about nothing and everything under the tenuous light that came through the blinds, totally unaware of time.

Maria sighed, took a photo album from her little suitcase and opened it with care; it was a present she'd made for Nell, with images of their long weekend. Maria stared at the photos, one by one, for a long time.

The best time of my life, by far.

She stopped at one of Nell holding a cod by the tail at the stands of La Boqueria market. She laughed at Nell's expression of disgust as she looked at the poor creature's head.

Maria continued turning the pages, which also included tickets to museums, restaurant receipts and little images of the city cut from brochures that she'd collected. Maria had spent days calling the tourism office in search of tales and places connected to the Civil War, she wanted to surprise Nell with a tailor-made tour. Nell had loved it, as well as the rest of the city, she had told her. To Maria's delight, she even said she would like to live there one day. "What am I doing in London?" she had said while strolling at the Plaça del Diamant in Gràcia.

Wouldn't it be wonderful to live together in Barcelona?

Maria arrived at the last page of the album, where she had written, "Not bad for a beginner, eh?" She had added: '*T'estimo*', or 'I love you' in Catalan. She hadn't dared to pronounce such words to Nell, face to face. Writing was always easier.

It's about time that I stop pretending. This is the truth and I know it. There's no point in trying the unattainable, it would have never worked with Jordi. I was a child, I didn't know what love was all about. I thought it was about lives or lifestyles matching; but it's really about hearts, minds and bodies clicking, and then fitting. Really clicking and fitting.

Maria looked around the restaurant, it was beginning to fill. There were a couple of handsome men in a table nearby, they looked immaculate, so into each other.

Everybod'sy gay now.

People looked happy and harmonious. The world was, all of a sudden, a beautiful place. *Wonderful life.*

Maria looked at her watch.

Only fifteen minutes to go.

Maria planned to stay two nights in London, both at Nell's, no need to book a hotel this time. She had come finally to present the warehouse project to Islington Council, tomorrow. Patrick and the Barcelona architects had mastered a plan for a renovation of the Post Office site that preserved its façade, as Nell had suggested. Miraculously, it was within budget.

Tomorrow would be Maria's grand day. Gaining permission for the warehouse was an internal coup at the bank; it had been a long and tedious process, questioned by envious male colleagues who said she'd only got the assignment because she was marrying the owner's son. Maria had worked especially hard, dedicating endless hours to the final presentation. Maybe a promotion would follow, she thought.

The deal could also be a platform for Nell; if it went as planned, the investment of the Caves in Islington would attract positive publicity, for its job creation, popularity and cultural exchange. She needed a boost, she had told Maria; she was a bit bored with her job and this could bring a much-awaited step forward.

Maria looked up the second that Nell walked down the stairs towards her. She immediately stood up, clumsily, without realising how close she was to the table; she hit it with her knee, knocking down an empty glass. Nell walked towards Maria, with a straight face.

Oh please, smile, sorry I am clumsy.

Maria picked up the glass and stretched her neck to kiss Nell, who didn't respond.

Is it because we're in a public place?

Maria kissed her on the lips, only briefly as Nell kept hers tight.

"Hello," Maria said, surprised.

The two sat down, Nell still silent. She didn't look ill. She was wearing her usual black clothes, a silk scarf; she seemed fine, Maria thought.

"How are you?" Maria smiled, tried to break the ice. She tried to catch her hand, but Nell withdrew it, surprising Maria.

Who would have said I'd be the one who wouldn't mind being out at a restaurant? But I don't!

347

Maria was elated, she had been waiting for this moment for two weeks, since she last saw Nell in Barcelona.

"I am so happy you're here, would you like to order some wine?" she asked.

"No, thank you." Nell was short. She looked at Maria intently.

Maria glanced at both sides, observed Nell's hands, under the table. "Darling, I've brought you a little present, look." Maria showed her the photo album on the table.

Nell said nothing.

"Darling, it's the Barcelona photos." Maria turned a few pages, delicately, but soon stopped as Nell didn't show any interest. "Are you all right?" Maria was worried.

"No – we have to talk."

Maria raised her eyebrows, leaned back. "What's wrong?" She then leaned forward again and made a quick little jump as Nell, suddenly, opened her bag, took out a copy of The *FINANCIAL TIMES* and bluntly dropped it on the table.

"What is this?" she asked, pointing to an article with one of her long fingers. "I would like an explanation."

Maria didn't understand. Puzzled, she looked at the newspaper, then at Nell. "What do you mean?" she asked.

"That's exactly what I want to know – what does this mean?"

Maria gave her an incredulous look and grabbed the newspaper.

"BARCELONA/LONDON, April 27 (Bloomberg) – Caves Gratallops, a Barcelona-based family-owned winery, is being circled by London-based hedge funds, who own eighty-five percent of the company's debt. The cava maker, struggling because of sluggish national sales, has recently failed to make interest payments on their debt and is now at the mercy of debtholders, who may push the firm into insolvency as a way of gaining control, people familiar with the situation said."

Maria opened her eyes wide and dropped the paper.

Good God.

"No, this is not true," she said. "I don't know where this is coming from, but there's no such problem at the Caves. Hedge funds have never been anywhere near the Caves."

Nell held her look. She was frowning.

The waiter came by. "Would you like to order, ladies?" he gently asked.

"Not yet," Nell quickly replied.

Maria leaned forward, took Nell's hands, but she removed them again. "Darling, please don't believe that, let's order the food, have some wine, talk through it, this is a huge misunderstanding."

"Why would the FT lie?" Nell asked.

"I can guarantee it's not true."

Nell gave Maria a look full of anguish. "I have a full Council meeting tomorrow," she said. "Highly relevant and powerful people with whom I've spent a long time and effort battling for your project, saying how important it is, for the community, for the Council." She looked at the newspaper. "Everybody has seen this today – what are you going to say tomorrow?"

"Of course I will present the case as planned," Maria said. "I have prepared for days and days, I want this as much as you do, even more."

Nell laughed, cynically. "Do you think you have any chance after this? Really?"

"I hope your Council takes decisions based on the truth, not on speculative newspaper reports." Maria paused and took the paper again, glancing at the story. "What do these journalists know, anyway?"

"It's the *FINANCIAL TIMES*!" Nell authoritatively placed her hands on the table. "Do you honestly think that after this we are not going to want more evidence? Do you think the Council is going to be happy about you lying to them?"

"I haven't lied to anybody!" Maria was now loud. Then she paused and continued in a lower tone. "As far as I understand,

349

Jordi signed some documents certifying the accounts; you have to believe that. He would never sign anything that wasn't true."

"He must have known – sales don't plunge just like that," Nell said, gave Maria a threatening look. "He's a liar."

Maria was in shock. "How can you say this?" she asked. "Please."

"I don't want any shit, Maria." Nell felt very distant. "Don't mess around with me. I hope you haven't thought that just because we've spent some time together, very little as a matter of fact, you can get away with something like this."

"Nell, I don't even know what you're talking about."

"That's even worse, what a banker!"

Maria felt impatient. "Darling, this is ridiculous, let's have some food, talk."

"I want an answer – now."

Maria didn't know what to do. This was not the Nell that she remembered, she was cold, more like the bureaucrat she met on the first day. Where was the sweet, warm, friendly person?

Maria took her Blackberry and dialed Jordi's number. "I am calling Jordi right now."

Nell said nothing.

"Hi," was all Jordi said.

"Hi Jordi." Maria felt awkward about the call – they had only spoken a couple of times since Easter, mainly to discuss the details of the wedding cancellation.

"This is not a good time, Maria," he said.

"It's urgent," Maria sounded desperate.

Jordi left a brief pause. Maria heard him sigh. "What's up?" he said.

"Jordi, I am here in London, it's about the warehouse. There's a newspaper report saying that the Caves is in deep shit and hedge funds are almost pushing it into bankruptcy – what's this all about?"

There was a silence.

"Jordi?" Maria looked at Nell, incredulous.

"Have you made the presentation to the Council yet?" Jordi asked.

"It's tomorrow – I thought you were following it more closely. What's going on? But listen, is it true what the newspaper says?"

"It is," Jordi said, in a low voice.

"What!?" Maria shouted. "Why on earth didn't anybody tell me? Does Andreu know? What's happened?" Maria covered her mouth with a hand, looked at the ceiling.

"The boycott is really hurting us and some idiot at your bank decided to sell our loan to hedge funds." Jordi paused.

I can't believe this.

"I can't talk now," Jordi continued. "Why don't we get that Council permit and talk afterwards? We bloody need that site."

"But Jordi, you know I can't do a presentation ignoring this." Maria was shocked. "Do you think I can carry on as if nothing's happened?"

"I don't care, Maria," Jordi said, his tone was harsh. "All I know is that I have dozens of workers to feed and a delicate situation here that needs sorting out. That warehouse is our only lifeline. Please try to get the permission, that's all I have to say."

He hung up.

Maria looked at Nell.

"Fuck, it's true."

"What a good theatre player you are," Nell said. "I am sure you and your boyfriend had all this planned: let's flirt with the lesbian officer, see what discount we get."

How can she think this of me? Maria thought, horrified.

She tried to take Nell's hand, but again, she immediately rejected it. "Please," Maria said.

"See what you do tomorrow, eh?" Nell continued, angry. "Or is there a plan as well? If you don't tell those officers the truth, I will have to – thank you for giving me the most wonderful moment of ridicule of my career: the company I've been pushing for, that was going to help Islington and its workers, well, it's going bust. 'Good job, Nell' they will say."

"Nell, I swear I didn't know anything about this." Maria stared at Nell.

"A day before the meeting and you don't know your company is on the brink of collapse? What sort of banker are you?"

Nell looked at Maria straight in her eyes. "I don't trust you, Maria," she said. "I should have known better. You're straight trouble, trying to mess around with lesbians. It's always the same. They come, fuck, and go." She paused. "Although you were only a one-night stand, a short-term thing. Nothing more than that."

The comment felt like a sword through Maria's heart. *A one-night stand?*

Maria refused to believe Nell's words. She remembered their time in Barcelona, especially when Nell had told her that it was in her company that she felt connected to life, on, alive. Maria looked up at Nell.

"Please, trust me," she said with begging eyes.

"I've already trusted you enough."

Maria shook her head in despair.

Nell's face was impassive, distant, cold. Maria couldn't see any sparkle in her eyes, any way of clicking with her.

"I can't believe you don't trust me," she said. "Please say it's not true. What's happened to you? Where's the Nell that I know? The patient, loving and understanding Nell?"

The Nell that I love more than anything in the world. The Nell I've changed my life for.

Maria didn't have the courage to pronounce those words aloud.

"I've always trusted people too much, and it's always with the same result," Nell said. "That's it, goodbye."

Maria put her hands on her face, trying to hide the tears that now started to fill her eyes.

After a few seconds, she looked at Nell and, stunned, she saw her stand up and go.

She ran after her but Nell was quicker. When Maria came out in the street, there was no trace of her.

This isn't true, it's only a nightmare.

After multiple attempts to call her, Maria gave up. Nell had switched her phone off.

Maria took a taxi to her usual Islington Hilton hotel, she was lucky they had a room available. Without taking her jacket off, she quickly called Andreu, her boss, on his mobile.

I have to get myself together. I have to be rational, active, sort this out.

"Andreu, we're in trouble – have you seen the *FINANCIAL TIMES* today?" she bluntly asked.

"I've heard about it, yes."

"And? I understand it's true."

"Yes."

"Why didn't I know about this?" Maria was furious at her boss. "I am promoting this company in London, the Council has obviously seen the story – what's going on?"

"Maria, some things need to be kept confidential," Andreu said. "But we're all right with the Council: when Jordi signed those documents, the loan hadn't been completed yet. He didn't lie."

"You must have known about this for a while." Maria spoke loudly. "Companies don't go bust overnight."

"This has developed very fast, Maria."

"What would you like me to do? I have to tell the Council tomorrow how sound this company is and what a good project we have."

Andreu remained silent for a few seconds. "Do as planned, say the loan is a short-term measure that will be soon resolved."

"I can't lie to them!"

"It's not lying, say that we'll work it out – which I am sure we will."

"This company has missed interest payments and has fallen into the hands of vulture funds – I can't go there and pretend everything's all right."

"Maria, we have to care for our clients and the Caves needs this project. Be on their side, that's what you're paid for."

Maria's hand was almost trembling as she held the phone. "I can't do this, Andreu."

"I am asking you to," the banker said. "If you don't, it will be hard for me to justify you keeping your job. There's a lot of money involved, we have to help the Caves, they're our client."

Astonished, Maria hung up.

She walked to the window and lit a cigarette, her hands slightly shaking. She exhaled with relief, her eyes fixed nowhere.

Oh Nell, I am so sorry. What a mess I've put you in.

Maria tried to call her again, but still no answer. She leaned against the window, smoked more.

I knew it, I knew that family and business don't mix well. See where that got me.

Maria took a deep breath. She'd never liked the idea of working for relatives and had felt uncomfortable when her boss assigned her the Caves project. A few months down the line, it had only brought her stress, more work and now it might even cost her the job.

It wouldn't be a tragedy, though.

Maria had landed in investment banking almost by default, it was the safe place to go to. She'd studied economics at University because she liked the combination of science and humanities, and working at a bank afterwards was the most natural option. She also believed – at least until now – in banks as the engines of economic growth, as providers of opportunity for those who wanted to create, grow.

I see now, she thought. *This is not about our clients, or about what's best in a situation per se. Forget all that corporate bullshit abut the client always coming first. This is about making deals so the bank gets its fee, no matter what. The Caves certainly can't sustain more debt to build a warehouse, it's ludicrous, but yet the bank is pushing for it. People here only think of themselves.*

Maria heard her boss's words again in her mind, his threat about firing her. *After all his previous uplifting comments, after telling me I was the best in the world, now it turns that if I don't*

*do as I'm told he'll get me out. There is no loyalty here. I am
your ally as long as you're mine – who cares what you think?*

Do they realise?

*Of course they do. They just want to earn as much as they
can and as quickly as possible so they can go and do something
else.*

I am not like that. My job is my job now – not later.

Maria lit another cigarette.

*I am not like them. I'd never push for this warehouse, it's
crazy my boss is backing it. I don't want to end up like him. He
basically works for himself; fuck the client.*

Maria made herself a gin and tonic, put her pyjamas on and
sat in an armchair, by the window. It was getting dark, she
looked at the people walking by.

*I can't believe I've bought this stupid corporate tale, how
young and naïve.*

Now I see – and I don't like it. I don't want it.

She remembered her book, *The Celestine Prophecy.*

If I lose my job, it may be for a reason.

I could come to live in London. With Nell.

Maria closed her eyes.

Nell. If only I could talk to her. If only she would talk to me.

For the following minutes, repeatedly, almost compulsively,
Maria tried to call Nell, again, but her phone was still off. Maria
needed to speak to her confidante, her best friend. But she
wasn't that any more.

Maria felt lonely. She had felt distant from Belchite, from
her family, since she started thinking of herself as a lesbian.
Barcelona, her second home, was also falling apart – she no
longer had Jordi, and soon, she might not even have a job. She
didn't even believe in banking anymore.

Now Nell, her most loyal ally, the centre of her dreams,
didn't even trust her any more. She had lost all her references.

Maria looked out of the window, she could only see the
black sky; it had started raining, tears ran down her face. She
walked to the bed, falling on it heavy as a corpse. She hid her
head under the pillow, holding the edges with force. Still

sobbing, and with wrath, she kicked the mattress with one foot, fast, repeatedly. Then she stopped, took a deep breath.

Where's my life gone?

What have I done to deserve this?

Maria looked at her mobile, still showing no response from Nell. She tried her number once more, with no better luck.

Holding her phone near her chest, Maria cried and cried, inconsolable, like the day her mother had called to tell her about Gran Basilisa. Her world, again, had tumbled. For a second time, the person she loved most in the world, for one reason or another, had left her.

Maria's heart felt empty. The room was silent, she could only feel the cold sheets, the silent air.

Maria hugged the pillow, leaned her head on it, wishing it was Nell she was holding. She remembered her smell, her soft skin, her warm words, the captivating intensity of her look. Those images made her cry again, uncontrollably, desperately, until she didn't have more tears to drop.

I have nothing. Nada.

She looked at the bare walls of the impersonal hotel room and then out the window. She got up and walked to look at the street. She searched for Nell among the hundreds of people.

Maybe she's changed her mind and she's coming over. She would guess I'm here.

But she couldn't see her.

Maria checked her phone again, still no calls or texts. She tried her again, with the same result. She kept trying, obsessively.

I have to talk to her. Now. I need her so much.

After a few attempts, the lines got busier and it started to take longer to make the connection. Her mobile also beeped, signaling low battery.

Maria frowned and pressed it with her hand, almost crushing it. She was going to throw it out the window but she couldn't find the handle, it was one of those windows that couldn't be opened.

I hate these artificial buildings. It's like a fucking prison.

She threw her phone on the ground, making it beep repeatedly as a key probably got stuck.

Furious about the constant, irritating, metal sound, Maria picked up the phone and rushed to the bathroom where, without hesitation, she threw it down the toilet and then flushed it, seeing the four hundred-euro device going straight into London's sewage system.

Fuck you, phone.

Fuck you, Nell.

Fuck you, world.

Maria sat on the toilet, defeated. She shook her head, looked at herself at the mirror: her face was alarmingly pale, her eyes, intensively red, and her make-up, all over. She looked as if she hadn't combed her hair in a week.

She leaned on the basin and stayed immobile for about fifteen minutes, her mind almost blank. She took deep breaths.

She finally raised her head, stood up, washed her face.

I have to do something, I have to fight. That's what Gran would have said. She would have called me 'tontica' had she seen me crying like this.

Dragging her feet, Maria walked into the room, got into bed, lay with her gaze fixed on the ceiling.

Maybe I should call Mother. She's fought all by herself, all her life. She's a brave woman. Unlike me. I am a disaster.

A few minutes later, when she was feeling calmer, Maria dialled her mother's number from the room's land line. *Who would have said I would ever need my mother?*

I guess one does, after all.

Conchita answered after a few rings, in her usual commanding tone. "Hello?"

"Mother it's me, Maria."

"Maria?" Conchita seemed surprised. Maria never called this late – when she did call at all – it was almost eleven o'clock in Spain. "Is everything all right?"

"I am in London," Maria said. For a second, she reconsidered her decision. *Is she the right person?* Maria imagined her mother as a young woman, in her Zaragoza school, working to pay the school fees, and labouring in the fields in the summer. *She is.*

"Mother, something has happened," Maria finally said.

Conchita waited on the line. "What's up?" she asked briskly.

Maria told her mother about the conversations with Nell, Jordi and Andreu, with as much detail as possible.

"So basically," Maria summarised, "I either lose my job or the person I love. Let alone following Andreu's advice and tell a Council that those hedge funds are little lambs under control."

"It's unbelievable that they've let themselves get into this situation," Conchita said. "If those predators ever come near my olive-oil company I'll make sure I dig them under the tree like your Gran did with the money."

"Mother, please."

"What a world," Conchita went on. "Maria, I've always told you, banking isn't guided by Christian values."

"Mother," Maria rolled her eyes. *This is not the time – but you're right.*

"I guess I have to decide between Nell or the job," Maria reiterated, she was impatient for some advice.

"Are you sure?" Conchita asked. "I don't think it's a matter of choosing what you most like, but what *you* feel is the *right* thing to do, don't you think?"

Maria stayed silent, Conchita went on. "Deep in your heart, what's the right thing to do?"

Maria remained pensive. "Of course it's to tell the truth."

"So?" Conchita asked. "Why doubt?"

"Because of the consequences," Maria immediately replied. "I am paid to help that company. I am not marrying Jordi anymore, but I don't wish them any harm. If they don't get this warehouse maybe the company won't survive at all. Even if the project brings more debt, they are more vulnerable without it."

"So the means justify the ends?" Conchita asked. "Is it right to lie?"

Maria said nothing.

"I also think you're paid to use your head," Conchita added. "Who would solve a debt problem by adding more debt? It's not rocket science, is it?"

Maria didn't like it when her mother preached against bankers, although she was right, she thought.

"Would you then tell the Council? Is that what you'd do?" Maria needed the reassurance of a clear answer.

"I would do what felt right, like in everything in life."

Maria closed her eyes.

"All right," she finally said.

"Let me know how it goes," Conchita said. "And if you lose your job, you know you can always come here, I am too old to take care of all this."

Great, Maria thought. *From international finance to walking around olive groves, bucket in hand. What a step up.*

Maria thanked her mother and hung up.

She knew what was right, but was it also naïve? How could she give up her job for somebody who didn't even trust her?

Maria tried to call Nell, once more, still no answer. She shook her head, lit another cigarette and walked to the window, watching the lights spreading as far as she could see.

Is it silly to lose my job for her? Is she that important? Is she the one?

Maria held her head with her two hands, she felt tired. She grabbed a bottle of water. *I need to think straight.*

She sat in the armchair and looked at the photo album. It had taken her a couple of afternoons to prepare, she had loved sitting at her table at home, listening to the radio, cutting photos out of brochures and making the collage, mixing it with the images. She delicately turned the pages, couldn't get her eyes off Nell.

I wonder if I've ever been happier. She stared at Nell, backpack on, smiling, walking around Barcelona with her open, explorative attitude.

Maria swallowed.

I just want to be near Nell, now, and ever. I want to feel her body against mine, to feel that it's only the two of us in the world, that we don't need anything else.

Maria covered her face with her hands. She remembered Nell's soft, tender skin. She missed her look, the impossible attraction of her eyes.

Nell, where are you? Please come. I miss you so much.

Maria shivered as she remembered the nights they had spent together, in London and Barcelona. The passion, the way their bodies looked for each other and matched, the way they hugged while sleeping. They just fitted.

With Nell, Maria felt complete, balanced, she had squared the circle for her. It broke her heart to see it fly away.

Now that I've touched happiness, I can't lose her. I can't.

If I do, what would I live for?

27

"Holy shit!" Pere Gratallops said dropping *LA VANGUARDIA* on the table. "What the fuck is this?" He looked at Jordi, as father and son were sharing breakfast in the patio of the *masia*, under the early morning spring sun. It was just past seven o'clock. Jordi and his father were always the first in the family to wake up and the first to leave for work.

Surprised, Jordi gently dropped the *pà amb tomaca* that he was going to bite and looked at his father. "What is it?"

Pere Gratallops, with his mobile phone already in hand, nervously picked up the conservative Barcelona daily again. He took a deep breath and read aloud a Spanish version of the Bloomberg story – also published in the *FINANCIAL TIMES* that same day.

Jordi's heart sank as his father finished. He looked down, hid his face behind his hands.

How the fuck do they know? Vulture journalists.

Jordi looked at his father, whose face was turning red by the second; he wanted to hide, if only he had a place to.

"Do you know anything about this, Jordi?" The old man had a threatening tone.

Jordi felt scared. His father's health wasn't good, his heart was weak, he couldn't even imagine what his reaction would be. Should he say he didn't know anything about it? Tell him the truth?

The truth will make you free, Jordi remembered the Bible's passage.

He dared glance at his father for a second; Pere Gratallops' eyes were still fixed on him. Jordi had never been too comfortable under the imposing presence of his father, and even less after he announced the cancellation of the wedding. Pere Gratallops had tried to approach him, but since he had barely given any details, isolating himself, his parents, especially his father, had stopped asking. Their relationship was distant, cold, professional.

"So?" Pere Gratallops asked impatiently.

Jordi nervously coughed.

The truth is always the best way out, Jordi thought.

"Father," he coughed again, looked down. "These funds indeed bought the loan."

Pere Gratallops looked at his son in astonishment. "How do you know?" he asked, taking his glasses off, leaning his elbow on the table, clumsily hitting a plate full of toast, two of which jumped out on the pristine white tablecloth.

Jordi was slowly putting them back when Pere Gratallops, now deliberately, punched strongly on the table, making the toasts fly again. This time, Jordi didn't move, he faced down.

"Talk to me!" Pere Gratallops shouted to his son. "Since your wedding was cancelled you're gone, out of this world, can I once and for all know what the fuck is going on with *my* company?"

Jordi swallowed.

"All right," he said in a low voice.

"Speak up!" his father shouted. "I can't hear you."

Jordi straightened his back and, without looking at him, told his father about his meeting with Peñaranda at the Caves back in November, when he claimed the land, and about their encounter at the football stadium.

"That's how you found out about the land ownership, I see," Pere Gratallops said. He remained pensive.

Jordi looked at his father's absorbing, big eyes. He'd been scared of this gaze all his life, it was a look that saw, he felt too penetrated by it, too exposed. But he had to face it now, there was no escape.

"That's right," Jordi finally said. "I checked with Robert and he looked into it: there's no way around it, they own the land."

Pere Gratallops briefly shut his eyes, frowned. "What else?"

Jordi told his father about his meeting with the funds in London, their demands, about their plans to change management, and about the answer he gave them – to stick the documents up their arse.

"That's the first good thing that I've heard today," Pere Gratallops said. He then frowned. "Why didn't you tell me any of this? This is *my* company!" he said, angry.

Jordi looked away for a few seconds. *How can I say that it's because your health isn't good?*

"Jordi, answer!" his father commanded.

"Because I thought I could sort it out by myself," Jordi said after a pause. "I know you've been a bit ill and I didn't want to upset you, or make it worse. It's a delicate issue."

Pere Gratallops punched the table again, this time even harder, knocking the orange juice over, making the cutlery clash. "Nobody decides for me, do you understand?" he shouted.

"Yes, Father." Jordi looked down.

A silence followed, only broken when Jordi's mother appeared through the kitchen door. "What's all this shouting this early?" she asked.

"Leave us alone, this is for men," Pere Gratallops ordered.

Jordi's mother looked at Jordi in complicity and went back into the kitchen.

One of Jordi's brothers came by a few seconds later.

"What happened to the orange juice?" he asked as he saw the mess on the table.

Pere Gratallops stood up. "Jordi, come to my office, now."

It was now past eight o'clock, the first workers were arriving at the Caves and the first delivery lorries left the warehouse, Jordi and his father watched from the office window. Pere Gratallops had just been on the phone with Robert, his lawyer, and Andreu, his banker. He sat in silence, nervously tapping Peñaranda's business card, which Jordi had given him, on his large, oak desk.

"I am going to call this fucker and offer him money, that's the only language those eagles speak," he said.

363

Jordi felt small, alone. If at least he had Maria. How could he tell his father everything he was going through? Certainly not now.

Pere Gratallops dialed the number on the loud speaker.

"Señor Peñaranda, hello?"

"Hi, I am Pere Gratallops, Chief Executive of Caves Gratallops, are you Borja Peñaranda?"

A silence followed. "Yes, I am." He briefly paused. "I hope you're feeling better."

Pere Gratallops gave Jordi the look of a lynx.

"I'm very well, thank you doctor," he said.

Peñaranda remained silent.

"I am aware of what's going on and I am open to negotiation," Jordi's father continued. "But I need to know first of all who sold you the loan."

"Do you mean which bank?" Peñaranda asked. He sounded surprised.

"Yes."

"The holders of the loan, of course, Banca Catalana, who else could it be?"

The two Gratallops nodded.

"All right, yes, that we knew," Pere Gratallops said. "But how did you know of the existence of such a loan? This information is private and confidential."

Peñaranda laughed cynically. "Of course, Sir, you know I can't reveal that."

Fucker.

Jordi leaned forward, towards the speaker. "Hello, it's Jordi here."

"Hi Jordi, how are you?" Peñaranda cheerfully said. "Have you signed those documents yet?"

Pere Gratallops was quicker than Jordi to respond: "He already told you what to do with those papers and I subscribe to that."

Peñaranda laughed. "Ah, I love the good old Catalan bastions – shame you can't really afford to be such anymore."

Pere Gratallops opened his eyes with wrath, Jordi looked at him. *Do you know what I mean now, Father? This is the type I've been dealing with.*

Jordi, though, thought it was better to carry on with business. "You also knew I was engaged – who told you? You obviously talked to somebody we both know."

"Again," Peñaranda said. "I am not going to say that, we all have our contacts."

"There's no deal if you don't tell us," Pere Gratallops said. "And remember, I also have very good contacts at the banks here. I could get you a very good deal."

Peñaranda stayed silent for a few seconds.

"All right," he finally said. "Jordi, think of your Club."

Jordi raised his eyebrows as his father gave him a surprised look, lifting his shoulders. Jordi placed a finger in front of his mouth, asking his father to remain quiet.

"What club, Peñaranda?"

"You know, Jordi, your Club – I understand Juan Antonio is his name."

No.

No.

No.

This can't be true.

"How did you know I knew him?"

"I saw a Belagua brochure on your desk the day I visited you at the Caves," Peñaranda said. "I know that name, I belonged to a Belagua Club in Madrid for years."

Holy Jesus. Jordi tried to remember the visit. It was true he usually had Belagua brochures and flyers on his desk.

"And Father Juan Antonio told you that I was getting married and that my company had a loan?" Jordi was aghast.

"Yes," Peñaranda answered. "We have a duty to help each other, don't we?"

Bastard. Sons of a bitch. Both of them!

Jordi turned pale, he started feeling dizzy. For a short while, he couldn't see anything around him. Again, his world tumbling down. He sank his head in his chest, covered himself with his arms. His father looked at him astonished.

"So, what about the deal?" Peñaranda insisted on the phone.

Pere Gratallops, still in shock, looked at his son, now hiding under his arms, like a child.

"I'll call you later, Peñaranda," he said.

Pere Gratallops hung the phone, stood up, walked towards Jordi, who, feeling his father's presence nearby, slowly removed his hands from his face and raised his head. He felt like a scared, young lamb.

"What's this club?" Pere Gratallops asked, showing one of his most intimidating looks.

Jordi shrank on his chair.

"What's this club business?" his father asked again, loud, still standing near him.

The truth will make you free. Maybe it's about time that I say so. After all, I haven't been to the Club for a while and I was thinking of withdrawing my membership as well.

Jordi closed his eyes, took a deep breath. "It's an Opus Dei club, in Barcelona."

Pere Gratallops took two steps backwards, stretched his neck towards his son, put both hands on his head.

"What?" He looked as if he was about to explode in anger.

Jordi said nothing, still had his eyes closed.

"What did you say?" his father shouted, walking back towards him.

Jordi finally looked at his father. "I've been an Opus Dei member for a while now, father, although…"

Jordi couldn't continue, his father's slap on his cheek hit him like a thunder before he could finish his sentence.

"You? An Opus Dei member?" Pere Gratallops was red in anger. "My own son in the hands of those child brainwashers? Those mental criminals?"

Jordi, again, covered his face with his hands, protecting his – now – red face.

"I was about to leave the organisation, Father," he said in such a low voice that could barely be heard.

His father seemed to calm down, put a hand on his heart and walked back to his armchair. After a couple of minutes of tense silence, Pere Gratallops spoke again.

"Tell me all about it," he said. "I want to know from beginning to the end. You have to, son, I won't hurt you again. But this is important, I must know. These people are dangerous. I am your father, I am on your side, I will help you."

Jordi felt tears coming off his eyes but made a big effort to contain them.

I can't cry here, he would think I am a girl.

This moment had to come, maybe it's better this way.

Pere Gratallops took one of his Habano cigars and, slowly, lit it, took a first taste. The old man reclined in his armchair; he looked at Jordi, expectantly.

His hands shaking, Jordi took a cigarette from the box on the desk, he nervously played with it and finally lit it. With his look mostly fixed on the groves outside, he started talking. Jordi told his stunned father how he joined Opus Dei as a teenager, how he went to their meetings, how they'd helped him when he needed.

After a pause, Jordi also mentioned the fifty-thousand-euro donation, and his fight with Father Juan Antonio after he refused to return it to him. He said he hadn't been to Belagua since.

Perplexed, Pere Gratallops remained silent for a few minutes; he turned his cigar over and over with his big fingers.

The old man finally sighed, looked out at his vineyards.

"Jordi, this saddens me more than all the money we can lose on the Caves, or even if we lose the entire Caves themselves," he finally said. "I don't mind losing the company, but I do mind losing a son to Opus Dei."

Pere Gratallops' eyes turned watery, Jordi noticed, until he saw a tear run down his father's old, wrinkled face. Jordi froze, he'd never seen his father cry before.

Jordi swallowed. "I am not lost to them," he said. "I am here, I haven't been there since the argument, I was planning to leave."

Pere Gratallops nodded. "You could have come to me, Jordi. I am your father, I would have always helped you."

I can't tell him that he wasn't there for me, I can't tell him that he was always in the office. I can't tell him that he only asked about school, never about me. I can't tell him because he gave me all those responsibilities and treated me as a failure if anything went wrong. I found comfort and understanding at the Club, they put no pressure on me. But I can't tell him, he's old and tired. He doesn't need this now.

"I am sorry Father," Jordi said. "I know I should have. But it's over now."

Pere Gratallops raised an eyebrow. "Not quite over, son, not quite." He put his cigar on the silver ashtray. "Let's sort this out, we have to act quickly."

Father and son arrived at Belagua almost an hour later, both in smart business suits. Pere Gratallops walked in first, with his big, tall, imposing figure. He didn't shake the hand that Father Juan Antonio extended him.

"Lovely to meet you Mr Gratallops," Father Juan Antonio said, today without his cassock as the visit happened without warning. "Jordi, good to see you – *again*."

Father Juan Antonio started walking towards his office, the Gratallops followed.

Jordi looked around the room, how different it seemed now. It was a sad place, with crucifixes on the walls, without any plants or other signs of life; it only stemmed reclusiveness and repression, Jordi thought. Father Juan Antonio also looked older, and smaller, less threatening without the sombre cassock.

All those years wasted. All those years here in the dark, when I should have been out under the sky, letting my senses live, like everybody else does. Jordi felt ashamed, of his past at Opus, and of the way he came out to life in London, the night he paid for pleasure.

What a mess I am. And look, I need Daddy to come and sort me out.

"We don't have much time," Pere Gratallops started. Jordi was looking down. "I will go straight to the point."

Father Juan Antonio reclined in his armchair. "I hope it's good news, maybe you have a donation for us, Mr Gratallops?" he said. "We can be very thankful, and God will reward you for it."

Pere Gratallops knocked the table with his hand, so strongly that he knocked down a little clay figure of the Virgin of Montserrat. Father Juan Antonio rescued her, putting it back up. Before he could start his sentence, Pere Gratallops cut him off.

"Listen, Mr Priest," Jordi's father started. "We know you told somebody from Madrid called Peñaranda that the Caves had a loan, and that Jordi was about to get married. Is that true? I wouldn't expect a priest to lie."

Father Juan Antonio looked out the window.

"Why do you want to know this?" he asked. "You're enquiring about private conversations."

"It's life or death for our company," Pere Gratallops said. Jordi nodded.

"Yes, I did," Father Juan Antonio admitted, apparently unaware of the importance of the matter.

"Why?" Jordi asked in fury.

Father Juan Antonio looked at him, bemused. "Calm down, Jordi," he said. "Peñaranda is a member from Madrid and he was just being polite, showing interest in our community. He gave us a small donation, so we had a little chat about our activities and our people here."

So now you sell information for a fee, I see. This makes me sick.

Pere Gratallops held the arms of his chair with force, trying to contain his anger. "And during that little chat, did you also tell him anything about Banca Catalana?" he asked.

Jordi had a knot on his throat. *How could he? How could he?*

"I happened to say that we have a member who is a director there – yes," Father Juan Antonio said, looking at both father and son.

This member must be the fucker "from above" who gave Andreu the order to sell the loan. And the lucky bastard Peñaranda hit the jackpot as he went straight to Banca Catalana, holders of our loan. One-stop shopping. Bloody hell. Little I knew the tentacles of Opus Dei could stretch that far.

"May I ask what this is all about?" Father Juan Antonio asked.

Pere Gratallops hit the arm of his chair and stood up. He placed his hands on the table, leaned over it, facing Father Juan Antonio close by.

"This fucker that you helped went to the bank, bought the loan and because we've breached covenants, now they bloody control our company, do you understand little midget?" Pere Gratallops shouted, making Father Juan Antonio shake.

You get what you deserve, Jordi thought.

"I don't know what you're talking about," the scared priest said.

"And what about the fifty thousand euros that you stole from my son, you don't know what I am talking about either?" Pere Gratallops shouted, now leaning over the table and taking Father Juan Antonio's shirt, holding it for a few seconds, then releasing it.

The priest leaned back on his chair, breathing heavily. "I am going to call the police," he said, looking horrified. "You can't intrude like this. Jordi, what's wrong with your father?"

Jordi said nothing, his father placed his strong hand on the telephone.

"You're not calling anybody," Pere Gratallops threatened. "You and I are going to sort this out, now, otherwise, the one making phone calls it's going to be me: to the press, to the police and to the Holy Spirit to tell them about how you brainwash innocent children, steal their money, take their time and their lives, without saying a word to their parents. Is that clear?"

Father Juan Antonio withdrew the hand he almost had on the telephone.

"I will make calls and I will create a scandal." Pere Gratallops had hate in his eyes.

"We didn't steal the money, it was a donation."

"But you would not return it when he came back, when he needed it, when he said he was even willing to return it at some point!" Pere Gratallops shouted.

A silence followed.

This is all my fault. Nothing would have happened had I been a bit more clever. I should have done like my brothers, life would be a lot happier, I would probably be with Maria now.

"What do you want?" Father Juan Antonio said.

Pere Gratallops smiled, cynically. "I am glad you're open to negotiation," he said. "I want, now, the entire donation back. And I want you to get out of my son's life and never ever go anywhere near him again. Otherwise I will sue you and I will leave you with nothing. Do you understand?"

Father Juan Antonio swallowed a few times, looked at Jordi, who looked down on him.

"All right," the priest said. "In due course…"

"I want it now!" Pere Gratallops shouted, cut him off.

Father Juan Antonio opened a drawer, took a cheque book and wrote the amount. He handed it to Pere Gratallops, who grabbed it immediately.

Father and son stood up and left without saying a word.

"*Vaya con Dios,*" Jordi heard the priest say, just before he shut the door.

And you go to hell, Jordi though. He felt cleansed as soon as he crossed the Belagua doors for the last time.

It took less than two hours to drive his father's Mercedes to Cala Montjoi, in the Costa Brava. The two arrived on time at the lunch they'd just arranged with the director of Girona Bank at El Bulli.

As the transparent soup of *jamón* was served, Jordi's phone rang. It was Maria.

Good God, if she knew what's going on.

Of course she'd found out. The same article on *LA VANGUARDIA'* had appeared in the *FINANCIAL TIMES* as well, also today. *What a mess.*

After the short conversation – in which HE urged Maria to carry on with the warehouse plans – Jordi returned to the table overlooking the crystal clear Mediterranean Sea.

The three men talked over a deal, with the only sound of the waves crashing against the rocks on the background.

"I can offer you a bridge facility to refinance the loan, certainly," the director of Girona Bank said. "We've stayed out of the property business, so we're doing all right."

"I am glad to hear that," Pere Gratallops said, starting his tortilla foam, barbecued sorbet and hot seaweed jelly. "That would be about thirty percent of the company, which we could buy back in due course."

"We could start paying back as soon as the London warehouse starts functioning," Jordi added. He was confident that the London plans would go ahead, despite Maria, despite Nell.

Pere Gratallops sat back. "But if for whatever reason that doesn't work, we could float a stake in the stock market," he said. "In that case, you could be the lead bank, getting all the fees," he told the smiling banker.

The director rubbed his hands, sticking his fork into the foam tortilla, missing it as the substance was hard to catch. He tried again, until he caught it.

The three men laughed and finished their meal.

A few hours later, Jordi and his father sat at the main terrace of the *masia*, both reclined on the comfortable, cushioned straw armchairs, watching the sun go down behind the vineyards.

"Come on son," Pere Gratallops said. "We have one more job to do."

Jordi looked at his father, he admired his energy, he would have left the final call to Peñaranda for the following day. *He's probably right, big problems need big solutions, why wait?*

"Let's go," Jordi said, without much energy.

Pere Gratallops immediately called Peñaranda from his mobile, the loud speaker switched on.

"Hi Peñaranda, it's Gratallops here," he said.

"Hi."

These two would get on well, as a matter of fact. Neither seems to need many words.

"I've got a deal for you," Pere Gratallops said.

"Come on," Peñaranda quickly answered.

"I will pay you the debt at ninety-five cents to the euro and you drop the legal case. Accept?"

"No," Peñaranda said after a few seconds. "The least we'd take would be a hundred."

"You bought that debt at a significant discount – let's leave it at ninety-eight."

Peñaranda remained silent for a while. "Cash in hand?"

"Absolutely."

"Okay, deal done. My assistant will call you with the details."

"Perfect, I look forward to the completion," Pere Gratallops said, ending the conversation.

All those years studying business at University, all those valuation methods based on high maths, and see where it all comes down to. Life is not that complex after all.

"The vultures have been fed, now we can rest," Pere Gratallops said, making Jordi laugh. He stood up and walked towards a small bar at the end of the terrace, returning with two glasses of fine Scotch malt whisky.

"Here, son," he said, handing Jordi one. "This is good after a long day at the office."

Appreciating his father's humour, Jordi took the glass and raised it for a toast.

"To the future of the Caves," Jordi said.

"To *your* future," Pere Gratallops responded, sitting back in his armchair.

Jordi felt the heat of the whisky going down his throat, he stretched his neck, softened the knot of his tie. Lying back in his armchair, he observed the last rays of sun falling on the earthy, clay soil.

Taking a deep breath, Jordi remembered running around the vineyards, as a child, and walking with his mother, who taught him how to pick the grapes, patiently, one by one. He loved the strolls with his father, year after year, touching the soil, feeling it, just before the seed. He was fascinated to see the vines emerge, grow and finally give their fruit; that was the cycle of their life, of his life.

This is where I belong, and not to Opus. This is my habitat.

It is a miracle we've been able to keep it today.

Jordi looked at his father in admiration. *At his age, and still fighting. Good men stand up for themselves.*

Jordi turned towards his father, now smoking one of his cigars. "Thank you for your help today," Jordi said from the deepest of his heart.

Pere Gratallops looked at his cigar, then at the vineyards, and sighed. "This is what parents are for, Jordi," he said. "This land will now be ours forever, and nobody will ever take it away from us."

Pere Gratallops stood up again, walked to the banister, leaning on it; he took a deep breath. "I was a teenager when I saw my father being taken," he said, pointing out to the shed at the entrance of the vineyards. "Just there."

He paused, had more of his cigar. Jordi held his breath, feeling for his father. "My mother was in the kitchen when the *Guardia Civil* stormed into the *masia* and shouted his name," the old man said. "My father didn't resist. They asked him again to capitulate and stop teaching Catalan to his workers, to dissolve the union he'd allowed them to form, but he refused to. We knew the *Civiles*, they'd been here many times before, always threatening. But that last time there were five of them, instead of the usual two in charge of this area, so I knew it would be different. I stood just inside the door of the shed and saw how they handcuffed him. My mother came out of the kitchen, stayed silent. They didn't let us say goodbye to him."

Pere Gratallops smoked his cigar, his look still fixed on the shed. "Take care of the family and of the land', that's the only thing he told me before they took him. He said the land was mine and that I should always keep it. He said: "Do it for me.""

Pere Gratallops turned towards Jordi, who looked up to him from his armchair.

"And that's what I've done, every single day of my life," he said. "And that's what I'd ask you to do, Jordi, please, look after this land as if it was your own heart."

Jordi looked at his father's eyes, then at the vineyards.

It is already my heart.

"I will Father, I promise I will."

28

Maria checked out from the Islington Hilton hotel the following day and decided to go for a walk on Hampstead Heath – after a brief stop at the phone shop to get a new mobile. She felt tired after being awake practically all night, trying all tricks to fall asleep, which she only accomplished for a couple of hours.

Today was the big day, when she was supposed to get permission for the Caves' report. A few months ago, this was the last big deadline before the wedding, the moment after which it would all unfold: the company's international expansion would bring the end to the Caves' problems, settling Jordi and his family for the wedding. This was the moment after which things would calm down.

Taking a deep breath, Maria thought of the old Spanish song that Gran used to love: *'Life brings you surprises, surprises are brought by life, oh God...'*

In her jeans and Camper shoes, Maria got a black cab to take her to the park as soon as possible, that's where she'd carry out her plan, surrounded by fresh air, peace and quietness.

Before, she'd give Andreu one last chance. From the cab, she called her boss, begging for a conciliatory solution: delaying the warehouse until a debt restructuring was agreed or completed. But Andreu answered an absolute 'No'; the Caves were strained and this had to move on as soon as possible.

Maria looked out the window as the cab raced through the streets of London; the shops and the people seemed to pass as fast as her own life over the past few months.

Maria sat on a bench and lit a cigarette at the top of Parliament Hill – once described by Nell as her favourite spot in town. Looking at the city's skyline through this clear, spring day, Maria thought of Gran, of Jordi, and mostly of Nell. It seemed a long time since she had met her on that dark, rainy afternoon in a dodgy street at the back of King's Cross. It also felt ages since Jordi welcomed her with a rose at the airport, back when she was trying to convince herself that he was *the one*. It was only a few months ago, but to Maria it seemed like years. She felt a heavy baggage of experience on her shoulders; she felt as if she could face anybody, anything now.

For once, she felt in control.

I don't have to be in Spain. I don't have to be a banker. It's all right to be a lesbian. I can do whatever I want, it's my life, regardless of what my mother says, or what the professors in Pamplona would have said – God if they saw me.

She looked at her cigarette, had some of it and expelled the smoke slowly, her eyes fixed on it.

I like this, I like London. If I lose my job, so what? I have enough savings. I could live here, with or without Nell, but free.

I have to do this, not for Nell, not for the Caves, but for me. Because it's the right thing, because I control my future and nobody else does. No one tells me what do. I am fed up with obeying, of saying 'yes' to everything.

Now I rule.

Maria wasn't afraid of her plan, she knew what she had to do and it was time to act.

She called the Council and asked the receptionist for the president of the committee in charge of the Caves' case.

It took her less than two minutes to drop the work of months. Plainly and clearly, she told the officer that the Caves were not in a position to face any new ventures and swore that she didn't know this before. In a cold, professional tone, she apologised for not having realised the magnitude of the Caves' problem and insisted that Nell wasn't aware of anything either – it was all her own fault, she should have known better as a representative of the company. She had no other option than withdrawing the planning permission petition.

In an equally professional tone, the President thanked her for her honesty and said Islington would always be open to listen to offers.

Maria sighed in great relief as she hung up.

Done.

Phew. She felt her shoulders relax, the tension in her face almost disappear.

She looked at the skyscrapers in the City, imagined bankers, lawyers and accountants rushing, stressing, fighting to get better returns. More, better, faster.

It's not worth it. It's not.

Maria lit another cigarette. The most difficult still had to be sorted.

I will try Nell once more. If she doesn't react after this, then it's all lost. But I have to give it one last chance. It's now or never. I don't want to sit and regret not having tried or pushed for what I wanted. Like Gran did.

With slightly shaking hands, Maria texted Nell: "Just dropped case, spoke to President. Insisted you knew nothing. I am top of Parliament Hill now. If you come I'll cook you tortilla forever. M."

It was ten in the morning, she had all day to sit and wait on this bench.

Maybe she's in meetings, maybe she won't read this for a while. It's all right. I will just wait. Nothing good ever came easy. I am sure she'll come, when she said those words in Barcelona, I know she meant them. One doesn't stop loving somebody just like this.

Maria looked around. Elderly people breathed hard after the climb to the top of the hill, their rosy cheeks looking younger with the accomplishment. There was a woman who looked like Miss Marple, Maria thought. Her eyes shone with pleasure as she enjoyed the views after her effort, she smiled at her, a peaceful, calmed smile, like Nell's, like Gran's.

I bet this is Nell in sixty years, Maria thought.

How much I'd love to be doing this with her, then.

Maria observed the leisurely class, those with time to go for a walk in the Heath on a weekday, while everybody else, like she'd done for years, was at work.

How secret they'd kept it, Maria thought, feeling increasingly envious of their lifestyle. She looked at the people walking their beautiful, well-kept dogs, at mothers with prams, young couples in love.

Time went by slowly, Maria hadn't brought anything to read. She looked at her watch, almost one hour had already passed. The day was warm, but sitting down for that long made her feel cold.

She suddenly felt sad. How long could she wait here for somebody who she hadn't even arranged to meet, and who had told her the previous day that she was only a one-night stand?

How many movies have I seen? What I am dreaming, that she'll come with open arms? And I thought I was experienced?

Maybe Barcelona was just a holiday romance.

I am an idiot.

A cold idiot.

After wondering for about ten minutes whether to rush for a coffee, Maria finally decided to do so. Only five minutes out of a few hours' wait, she wouldn't miss her if she came. And if she did, she'd probably call her as well.

To the surprise of Miss Marple and a few dog walkers, Maria suddenly rushed down the hill to the park café, returning a few minutes later, sweaty after the effort. Panting, she sat down again, let a minute go by before she had a sip of the drink.

The clocks beneath the spires that she could see around London struck eleven, and then twelve. Suddenly, her phone rang, making her body give a jump on the bench.

Yes! It's her, it's got to be her. Thank God, it was about time.

Full of enthusiasm, Maria grabbed her phone, showing the call came from an 'unknown' number.

She must be calling from the Council, she must be just out of a meeting.

"Hello?" Maria said, her eyes shining.

"I am ashamed of you." Maria's heart sank as soon as she recognised her boss's voice. It was not the sweet tone she had been waiting for.

"Andreu?" It was all she could say, in a low voice.

"Patrick just called me with the news, he went to the Council to give them the last details and they told him you'd withdrawn the case – are you mad?" He was almost shouting.

Maria took a deep breath.

"It was the right thing to do, Andreu, this company can't bear this now," she said.

Andreu practically didn't let her finish her sentence. "You clearly don't have what this profession needs: the confidence to move on, the trust in our clients, in our resources. I knew a man would be better suited for this job, you clearly haven't had the guts."

Wanker.

Maria interrupted. "Man or woman, Andreu, there's nothing we can do – you know those hedge funds *de facto* own the company now."

"You don't understand a word, Maria," Andreu said. "You are too young and inexperienced, you can't take such decisions. We had other options, we could have syndicated a loan to buy back the debt."

"And end up with a company of less than one million in profits and five million in debt?" Maria said. She knew she had nothing to lose. "That goes against any ethical code that I learned at University."

"You can fuck the ethical codes at University, that's because you went to an Opus one and they brainwashed you," Andreu shouted. "I wish you had less Opus on you and a bit more experience."

If there's one thing that I'd save from Opus, that'd be their ethical training.

"I did as I had to, Andreu," Maria said confidently.

"You know what that means, right?" he threatened.

I surely do. I also know that if I was still engaged to the son of your lovely client you wouldn't be treating me this way.

Andreu carried on. "You are not allowed to take such decisions for yourself and in this case you've taken the wrong one," he said. "It is therefore my duty to inform you that such action is negligent. Your contract will be terminated with immediate effect; you don't need to come back to this office – your things will be packed and sent to your home."

With her hand slightly shaking, still holding the phone, Maria leaned her back on the bench, looked at the London skyline.

I knew, I knew.

But I am not afraid to pay the price. I chose freedom.

"All right," Maria told Andreu and hung up without saying more.

Surprised at her own calmness, Maria looked at a bird fly and sit quietly on a nearby tree branch, singing and looking around.

Life is not that complicated, and birds know it.

She lit another cigarette and thought of her boss, her colleagues at the bank.

Let them eat themselves.

The positive thoughts waned as the sun passed its peak and started his descent into west London.

Why? Why? Why doesn't she call?

Maria's eyes felt watery as the clocks stroke two, and three.

Maybe I should call it a day, cut my losses and go.

It was wonderful while it lasted. I am just a silly dreamer. I am sure my mother would say this is a deserved lesson, for being such an idiot. I am so naïve.

Maria looked at the hands in her watch go second through second; she had looked at them so much and for so long that she could barely distinguish them anymore.

Time, time, that's all we have. Better leave and start it all over again. That's what Gran and Soledad would do. No tears: stand up and go.

Just as she squeezed the plastic coffee cup that had kept her company most of the day, Maria heard a familiar voice.

"Is it here where they give free tortillas?"

Maria's heart turned upside down in the split of a second. Her eyes shone as Nell's tall, thin figure appeared walking towards her on the little pathway.

Too shocked, Maria didn't answer.

"So no tortilla here then?" Nell insisted.

Maria smiled. "I'll see what I can do."

Nell sat next to Maria on the bench. They didn't say a word for at least a couple of minutes. Maria nervously played with her phone in her hands.

"Is it new?" Nell pointed at it.

"Yes."

"Did you lose the other one?"

"No, I flushed it down the toilet."

"I see."

The two spontaneously laughed, looked at each other, again, with the same enthusiasm, as if nothing had happened. They both sighed.

"I tried to call you a million times last night, then I got fed up and threw it away." Maria said.

"Are you serious?"

"Yes – and I recommend it," Maria smiled. "Good release."

Nell looked down, then into Maria's eyes. "I came to apologise for yesterday, I am sorry, I should have given you, at least, the benefit of the doubt. I am really sorry."

She looked down again.

Maria felt relief spread throughout her body. She looked at Nell, she was the sweet, pretty Nell she'd dreamed about, day and night, now for months.

"Why didn't you trust me?"

Nell remained silent.

"Nothing is possible without trust." Maria felt her heart as strong as open.

"I know," Nell said after a pause. "I am sorry again – you know, this is not an excuse, of course, but I've been hurt before for trusting people too much, or too soon. I thought this was my string of bad luck continuing."

Maria put her hand on Nell's, giving it a quick squeeze.

"Your hands are cold," Nell said.

Maria raised an eyebrow. "I've been here for a while."

Nell wrapped Maria's hands in hers. "I am sorry it took me that long, I spent time at the Council, trying to sort out the cancellation, calling the other officers."

"It's all right." *I would have waited for you half my lifetime.*

"I also went to see my ex," Nell said, looking down.

"Your ex?" Maria was surprised. Apart from the time they'd bumped into Fiona on their way to the pub, back in December, she hadn't heard about her. "Why?"

Nell scratched her short hair.

"Well, it's not that we're close friends now, but she knows me well, we spent years together." Nell took a break. Maria waited.

"I felt a bit confused," she started saying, then stopped, looked away. "Well, maybe more afraid than confused."

"Afraid of what?"

Nell left a few seconds go by. "Sometimes it's easy to hide in one's cocoon, old habits, or safety zone, whatever you want to call it." She paused. "It's much more difficult to be brave."

"That's what my grandmother told me." Maria remembered Gran's regrets for not having gone to Cuba.

"Yes, it takes courage," Maria said.

Nell nodded, looked straight ahead, to London's skyline. "Fiona used to tell me all the time that I was quite negative, a pessimist and that I never fought for things, she used to say I always wait for things to come to me or to resolve themselves, and I guess that's true."

Maria looked at Nell full of interest.

"Why do you think that is?"

Nell rebuffed a bit. "You know, the usual family shit," she said. "But I don't want to drag on this."

Maria waited for a few seconds, she wouldn't want to pressure her.

"It's always the same, isn't it?" Maria finally said.

Nell nodded. "But this is not the time to talk about this," she said. "And I don't want any excuses – at the end of the day, we and only we are responsible for ourselves."

"True," Maria said. This was a lesson that she'd learned over the past few months, partly thanks to Nell. She felt proud of her accomplishment, she felt strong. "We don't have the past, nor the future, only the present, and that's entirely ours."

Nell smiled. "You are an optimist."

Maria, by now, knew Nell enough to know this was perhaps a bit too emotional for her. She took her hands, the two remained silent, looking at London.

"I love coming here," Nell said. "I like seeing things from above, gives you some perspective."

Maria nodded. "I love it too – I may stay here for a while as a matter of fact." She paused. "I don't have a job any more."

Nell stretched her back. "Really?"

"Fired!"

"Already?"

"Banks move fast!"

Nell held Maria's hand. "I am so sorry."

Maria took Nell's hands. "No need to be sorry," she said. "I didn't like it that much to be honest. I just did what I had to."

The two remained in silence.

"Are you not afraid of the future?" Nell asked, she looked worried.

"Not at all," Maria said with confidence.

Nell stared into Maria's eyes until she leaned towards her and, very slowly, kissed her for a long time.

Maria closed her eyes as she savoured the sweet kiss once more. She could never have enough of it, but she drew back and looked at Nell. She'd never felt this happy, clean, so full of life. She wasn't hot, or cold, she wasn't hungry, she didn't even know what the time was or what would happen in her life next. It didn't matter, she had everything she needed.

"Why would I be afraid – afraid of what?"

Nell gently caressed Maria's long hair, delicately put it behind her ear. "These are your true colours, aren't they?"

Maria nodded.

"Now that I've seen them, I know that I love you."

Maria held her breath for a few seconds; she felt struck by a ray of complete happiness throughout.

"*T'estimo*," she said, looking at Nell's eyes. She'd never felt this open to anybody before, so ready to be seen through, without hiding any more.

29

Conchita left the house wearing her raincoat and her Wellington boots, despite the fact that it was a sunny Saturday in the middle of May. The hailstorms that had tormented the region's wheat and olive fields for a week had finally ceased, the sun was now out to crudely show the irreparable damage.

Conchita walked into the olive groves, her heart shrinking at every step: hundreds of branches had been torn off, thousands of small olives lay on the ground, some of the youngest trees had been dragged down; the earth seemed to have been removed by an army of tractors, stones had flourished everywhere. Nothing seemed to have survived the strongest winds in fifty years, according to the radio; most of this year's fruit had been blown away.

Conchita's eyes became watery, this was the worst she'd seen her fields, ever. Broken branches, leaves and small rocks lay everywhere. The trees looked naked, as if they were in the middle of a snowy winter, instead of enjoying the warmth and the light of the spring.

It was going to be our best year. Why do things always go wrong?

Conchita sighed, bent her knees, picked up some branches, tried to pile them up. She looked around, there were hundreds, thousands of them. She stopped.

I can't do it all by myself, this is now too much. This has to be cleaned, it's going to take weeks, perhaps months. These trees are going to need a lot of care, one by one. I am too old to rebuild this by myself.

She took some of the soil in her hands, looked at it: instead of the soft, fertile earthy land, she now had dust and stones. *How long will it take to rebuild this?*

Conchita stood up, walked towards *El Abuelo*, increasing her pace. She felt she would die if her most ancient tree had been irreversibly damaged; perhaps it was too old to survive this, like herself, she feared.

I can't face it all by myself, this is too much, I can't turn this around, it's somebody else's time now. I've done enough, I can't do more.

She sighed in relief when the majestic silhouette of *El Abuelo* appeared behind other trees, still showing its strong, twisted branches, its green, shiny leaves. Conchita walked closer and saw some olives had survived the thunderstorm.

You are strong, Abuelo, you are the strongest of all, she thought, proudly. *Once more, you will survive us all.*

Delicately, Conchita caressed the ancient trunk, she loved the gray stripes, its crust, soft on the outside, strong on the inside.

Just the opposite of me, that's what I've done wrong. My life would have been so much better had I been the other way around.

Conchita sighed and turned around when she heard her father's voice.

"Nothing will ever kill *El Abuelo*," Juan Roso said, walking towards her.

He was wearing the same straw hat and the same navy blue coat as when she first saw him, right by *El Abuelo*, in January, five months ago.

"Hello, Father," Conchita said, cheered by his company on this lonely, sad day.

The two had seen each other about twice a week, always in the groves, always in secret. After much thought, Conchita had decided not to share her secret with Soledad, now too old for such a shock – according to Doctor Jaime, who had been consulted on the matter. Juan Roso hadn't insisted, saying that perhaps it was better to keep the past in the past, and memories as memories. He had, however, helped her with the cancellation of Maria's wedding, offering her company and consolation as she faced local gossip following the news. The two had enjoyed their walks at sunset, before dinner, sharing thoughts about the children and the fields. They hadn't discussed politics, money, religion or any controversial topic; Juan Roso had kept their conversations positive and human, making their relationship easier. Little by little, the old man had become Conchita's best friend.

Good things never last, Conchita thought as she looked at her father, suitcase in hand, who was scheduled to go back to Cuba today, at least for a short while, he had told her.

"Are you all ready?" she asked.

"It's such a shame I have to go now, just when I feel needed here," Juan Roso said, looking at the fallen trees. He looked at Conchita, then at *El Abuelo*. "But if he survived, I am sure the others will."

Conchita smiled. "They're not as old, wise and strong, as him."

"That is true," Juan Roso said. "But they will be, in time."

"I won't be here to see it," Conchita said, disheartened. "I am too old for this."

"What about Maria?" Juan Roso asked. "Why don't you call her?"

Conchita remained pensive for a few seconds. "That'd be fantastic if she came, we could do with her business skills, but she's never shown much interest in the firm. Although now, without her job and with her new *partner*, I don't know, she might be interested, who knows?"

"I'm sure she'd like to be asked," Juan Roso said.

"Yes," Conchita agreed. "Although I'm not sure how they would integrate in Belchite."

"It'd be fine, Conchita," her father said. "Times move faster than we think."

Um, I am not sure.

Juan Roso picked up his suitcase. "Please let me know how it goes," he said. "I would love to have news from you. But I

will soon come back – of course if you'd like me to, that is."
Juan Roso looked down, and so did Conchita.

"Of course I would," she said, her eyes fixed on the ground.

"I am old, but as long as I can, I'll keep coming," he said.

Conchita smiled at him. She liked the attention, the interest of her father in her life, her groves, her family. She loved to share it all, she wished she'd done that before. Conchita picked up a small tree branch from *El Abuelo* and handed it to him.

"Here," she said. "Maybe you'd like to keep this. It's the symbol of peace, after all."

Conchita thought of the War, of her mother, of her murdered grandparents; she thought of Honorato, of the many arguments she'd had with Maria.

If we could only have had some peace. She sighed.

Juan Roso put his suitcase on the ground and took the branch, his hands slightly shaking. "There's nothing else that I would like more." He looked at it, touched it delicately. "It will remind me of you; you're just as strong as him, as Basilisa was. Like her, you are at the centre of the groves, governing silently, in peaceful control, surviving anything, from hailstorms to wars, and family upsets."

Conchita had a small laugh. *Ai, ai, ai. I don't know if I am governing anything, any more.*

"Well, I am not sure I'll survive this one," Conchita said. "I am too old now."

"Maria might surprise you," Juan Roso said.

The old man took a step towards Conchita and gave her a long, strong hug. After briefly kissing her on the forehead, he picked up his luggage again, turned and walked away. Conchita looked at her father's figure walk through the groves, until he disappeared among the olive trees. She thought of her mother; she might have seen him disappear though the trees the last time she saw him. Would he come back this time?

Conchita turned towards *El Abuelo*.

It's certainly time for me to give the torch to others; I will call Maria. And I will do like El Abuelo, I will sit back, look – and enjoy. This is now going to be my time.

***

Six thousand kilometers away, Maria and Nell were drinking a *mojito* at the terrace of Hotel Nacional, enjoying the sound of a live salsa band, and looking at the turquoise colour of the Caribbean sea. Maria's severance package had bought them a week at La Habana's most famous hotel.

"For me?" Maria said surprised when a waiter arrived with a little table and a land telephone, with a long cord, saying she had an urgent call. "Yes, your mother."

Maria and Nell looked at each other.

"My mother?" Maria asked surprised.

The waiter left the small, wooden table by her side, with the old, black, rotary phone ready to speak.

"Mother?" Maria immediately said.

"Hi Maria, are you still on holiday?"

"Yes, Mother, Cuba is lovely, and the food is very good," Maria said, hearing some sort of nervous cough at the other side of the line. "Are you well, Mother?"

Conchita remained silent for a few seconds, then asked: "Maria, have you not seen the news?"

Maria stretched her back, left the *mojito* on the table. "What news?" she said, alarmed.

"The worst hailstorms have destroyed hundreds of hectares in Zaragoza, our groves resemble a war field, there are broken branches everywhere, some of the youngest trees have been pulled out." She paused. "It's terrible. I've never seen anything like it."

"When did this happen?" Maria pictured the desolate image in her mind. *Poor trees.* At the bottom of her heart, even if she'd never taken care of them, she still loved those olive trees. They were ever present in her happiest childhood memories; the precious adventures she'd lived among their branches, the hours she'd spent with her schoolfriends hiding behind them, or on them, during the day or, more excitingly, in the middle of the night.

"It was last week, Maria, we're all still shocked," her mother said. "The winds were so strong I thought the roof of the house would blow off, but luckily there's been no human tragedy."

Maria sighed, relieved.

"How terrible mother," she said. "Will it be possible to save this year's harvest?"

"No, no, Maria, it's all lost," she said. "Only *El Abuelo* kept some olives, just because he is old and strong, but the rest is all gone."

Maria didn't remember such a bad year, ever. As far as she knew, there had always been produce to sell, even after the strongest storms that she could think of.

"Dear me," Maria said, wondering if the company had enough money to survive a blank season. "I am sure the insurance will cover us, right?"

"Ai, ai ai," Conchita sighed again. "I assume so, but I don't know. I am not good with numbers, that's what your father did, you know. And remember now we also have that loan for the French machine, I think we might have a bit of debt."

Oh no, not another problem with a loan, please.

"Maria, the reason I am calling you is because I really need you here, I am not saying forever, but at least for a while," Conchita bluntly said.

Maria had learned to appreciate her mother's directness. "As you know," Conchita continued, "I am terrible with the finances and your sister is too busy with the children. I am sure that after this, we will have a lot of expenses to clean up the groves, plus all the organisation that will be needed if we're not going to be producing this year, the contracts that will have to be cancelled, what to do with the workers and God knows what else."

I know what's coming.
Belchite.
No way.
No.
Hum.
Why not?
Nell might love it.

"Maria, I wouldn't ask you if I didn't need to, but I cannot stop thinking what a great help you could be here, at least for a short while." Conchita paused. "I can't do this all by myself, I am old and tired, this has been a long year."

I understand. Maria felt close to her mother; it was infinitely easier now that she didn't try to be a strong, invulnerable figure. She loved seeing through her. She loved her when she was human.

But Maria didn't know what to say.

Conchita carried on. "Of course, you would be very welcome with your friend, Nell," she said. Maria, thrilled, heard her mother's quick breath, she sensed her nervousness. "I've thought that if you two came, this house is too big for me," she said. "I could move to Gran's cottage, leaving you the big house, you have the energy and the years ahead to have it your style, if you wanted to."

Maria's eyes opened wide. She hadn't imagined living in the big house with Nell.

What a wonderful idea. A life away from the banks, away from the men in suits, enjoying the fresh air. Nell would love Spain, I would be delighted to show her around, drive all over the country. And how much potential, we could start exporting, Nell would be fantastic, she could open markets in Britain, maybe America. We could do campaigns for people to eat more healthily, maybe even open a small olive-oil museum with Gran's ancient tools. And that big house, the patio, we could improve it so much, I am sure Nell would make it wonderfully comfortable, like her flat, with wooden floors, candles, all the crucifixes away. It could be our home, the way I've always dreamed about a home, sunny, warm, happy, surrounded by nature. Open.

Maria became more and more excited.

Maybe we could live some months in Belchite, the rest in London. Let's see what Nell says.

"Mother, it sounds interesting," Maria said. "But I need to speak to Nell, can I let you know in a couple of days? Do you mind?"

"Of course Maria, of course, take your time," Conchita said. They hung up.

Maria was still surprised at how patient and understanding her mother had turned.

She's changed so much since Gran died, since Father left. Maybe we have all changed.

Maria looked at the Caribbean Sea, then remembered an old Spanish saying: 'In the end, every goat goes back to its mountain.'

She smiled and looked at Nell, still sitting next to her, expectantly waiting to hear the news.

"We have to talk, my dear," Maria said, taking a sip of her *mojito,* feeling the warm air of the breeze on her chest, through her summery blouse. She felt excited, alive.

"You said we were coming to be marketers and financiers, my love, but what we are is nothing but plain peasants!" Nell said, apron in hand, sleeves rolled, picking dozens of branches and piling them up in the middle of the Belchite groves. "This sun is too hot, it's killing me," she moaned, tightening the scarf she wore around her head.

Maria, wearing a pair of shorts and a T-shirt, no need of a hat, looked at Nell's red face, still full of the strong cream she had put on to defend her white, delicate skin from the intense July, Belchite sun.

Poor thing. Now I understand all those tourists that we call 'prawns' on our beaches.

Hiding a cheeky laugh, Maria thought it was a good time for a break. "It will get better, darling, it will improve, this will be cleared soon and we'll do the fun bits – but let's take a break."

Taking the wrapped tortilla that Conchita had prepared for them, Maria walked Nell towards *El Abuelo*, which she hadn't seen yet. They'd just arrived and settled in Belchite, at the family house, a week ago. In principle, the move was only short term, but Conchita had already taken Gran Basilisa's house, happy about the smaller size, excited to emulate her mother's quiet lifestyle in her last years.

Nell stopped as soon as she saw the imposing figure of the ancient olive tree. She removed her scarf and her sunglasses, opened her eyes wide.

"This is the most beautiful tree I've seen in my life," she said. "I can't believe how gorgeous it is."

I knew she'd love it.

"How old is it?" Nell asked, walking towards *El Abuelo*.

"About one thousand and five hundred years."

Maria saw Nell swallow.

"Come, you can touch it, I used to build doll's houses in its branches, I've spent hours up there reading books," Maria said. "He's stronger than anything, you can touch him as much as you want."

Nell extended her arm and gently followed the crust lines with one of her delicate fingers. She seemed fascinated by it. She looked around. "What a magical place," she said, looking at Maria. "More than a thousand years, I wish he could speak."

Maria nodded, looked at Nell's eyes, once more, reminding her of Gran Basilisa's.

"I wish that too," Maria said. "These groves are full of memories. Some are buried underneath forever, but I know others that are alive. I will tell you one day."